INTO *His* COMMAND

THE CIMARRON SERIES: BOOK TWO

ANGEL PAYNE

For Thomas...for everything. Always.

PROLOGUE

"Happy birthday, Prince Samsyn."

The curvy blonde batted her big brown eyes, curled her full dark lips, and then opened her purple satin robe.

She was naked underneath. As he had expected.

His body responded with cold nothingness. As he had also expected.

It was almost midnight. He had officially been twenty-one years old for four hours.

He felt older.

So much older.

Officially, the world was now supposed to be his—how did they say it in America, those "crazy kids" who would be his peers, if he lived there?—his bitch. Yes. That was it. The world was now his bitch, ready to be molded to his will, commanded at his whim. The Ferrari, McLaren, and Jaguar in the garage downstairs would help him do it faster. When he was done, he could return to this twelve-room suite, on the top floor of a palace, with just as many servants to see to his every desire. He could relax on his own terrace, with a view of the Mediterranean arguably better than that of the king's.

Best aspect of that? He *wasn't* the king. On the island of Arcadia, where the twentieth and twenty-first centuries balanced on an interesting teeter-totter, second in line to the throne meant the best of both worlds. All the fun, none of the responsibility.

Or so they said.

Somebody forgot to let fate in on that joke.

As fate liked reminding him, with floods of glee, during moments like this.

He eyed the nude beauty over the rim of the scotch she'd brought. From the moment she entered, he'd known the expensive liquor was just the beginning of Father's "extra" birthday gift. His gut still roiled because of it. He had nearly taken the bottle and then tossed out the woman, but what if Father's minions were watching, ensuring she performed the assignment? He hated how much that made sense.

The scotch bloomed to a burn throughout his mouth and throat. He yearned for the warmth to seep lower, into the ice between his thighs. By the Creator, how he craved just an hour of turning his mind off for the throes of a good fuck—but tonight, it simply was not to be.

Tonight, he could take the hypocrisy no more. The sham of a birthday party Father and Mother had thrown for him, with that room full of people—his brothers and sister included—gazing at King Ardent and Queen Xaria like they were the couple who damn near walked on the sea outside the windows. Like they adored each other as much as they did their beautiful children. Like they couldn't wait to end the party and be in private chambers with each other—instead of Mother summoning the pool boy between her thighs, and Father...

Well...Father liked to have choices.

A fact Samsyn should have been more peaceful with by now. He certainly had not discovered the sham yesterday, after all. Three years was a long damn time to live with lies.

Yes. He was old.

And angry.

And tired.

And needing to forget.

Praying to forget.

He took a bigger gulp of the scotch. It loosened him enough to speak to the woman.

"What is your name?"

She blushed prettily. "Arista, Your Highness."

"You are lovely, Arista."

"*Merderim*, Highness."

"Did my father say the same thing when he fucked you?"

She confirmed his suspicion as soon as her gaze dove for the floor. She feigned insult. "I...I cannot..."

"Cover yourself, Arista." The patience in his tone only came from clenching his teeth. "You are not to be blamed for wanting to make your king happy."

She softly stepped closer. "I would greatly enjoy the chance to do the same for my prince." Slid between his legs. Guided his touch to her naked hip. Before Samsyn could process a protest, she knelt and pressed her mouth to his groin.

He shoved to his feet. Released a ruthless growl. "I said cover yourself." A deep breath reined his rage back in. "You can stay the night, Arista," he muttered wearily. "The scum who sired me does not have to know we never fucked."

Her tiny sob sliced the air. "You are a good man, Prince Samsyn. Honorable and decent and—"

He interrupted her by hurling his glass against the hearth.

As drops of liquor sprayed, the flames hissed and spat like fuming demons. Perfect. Fucking perfect.

Honorable. Decent.

He was anything but either. Hiding his parents' filthy secrets, even from his siblings, had changed him. Tainted him in ways that would never be clean again.

Aged him.

A shrill ring blared through the room. His cell phone. The ring for his most private number, designated as his *must answer* tone. Tonight, he'd never been more thankful for it.

"What?" He gave no further greeting. It would either be Tryst or Cullen on the line, considering the late hour and the number of pissed-drunk mates he had stepped over when exiting the birthday party an hour ago.

"Highness." The deep timbre was all Tryst. The formality was not. Samsyn's skin pricked, not all in a bad way. "Your father begs your pardon for interrupting your birthday celebration—"

"Debatable," he snarled, knowing Tryst understood. The man only looked like a dumb giant. T had seen and heard enough to deduce the truth about the king and queen on his own. "What is it?"

"He requests your personal attention...to something."

"All right." He gave it too eagerly but didn't care. The hook was out of his mouth. No lies would be necessary about how he had handled the situation with Arista.

"We have...a delicate situation."

He almost laughed. Tryst and the word *delicate* were hardly a logical match. "Creator's fucking toes, T." When no commiserating snicker came from his friend, he paced off his disconcertment—and dread—by walking out to the terrace. "Has the *éslik* gotten some poor thing pregnant?"

"No." Finally, there was a laugh in the man's voice—though the next moment, he went straight back to cryptic. "But you had best get here anyway."

"Good enough." He looked out to the darkness of the sea, ordering it to yield Tryst's nonexistent details. No such luck.

"'Here' being where?"

"The airport."

"The *airport*?"

"Your Highness, with all due respect, just get your ass over here."

★ ★ ★

"Un-fucking-believable."

Sometimes, the raw fury of English profanity was a preferable choice to Arcadian. This was absolutely one of those occasions.

Samsyn was tempted to repeat it, but Tryst's grunt covered the debt. The big soldier, braced against a palm tree just outside the island's small airport terminal, folded his meaty arms across his chest. A night breeze kicked against the man's thick black hair. Technically, it was an early morning wind—though two a.m. qualified as an excusable gray area.

"They *lost* Rune Kavill? One of the world's most despicable terrorists, in one of the world's most high-security prisons—"

"Escaped out the garbage chute. Three days ago." T uttered it like he was merely relaying his dog's latest stupid stunt. Samsyn didn't blame him for the mental disconnect. Tryst's sanity likely hinged on it, instead of admitting that the terrorist who'd blown up his mother and sister had broken free by blending in with prison trash. Irony was too ridiculous a word for this circus—especially when the ringmaster himself had wasted no time rubbing everyone's noses in its stench.

"Let me get this completely right," Samsyn stated. "Now the monster has targeted Senator Chase Valen—and his family."

"To phrase it mildly."

Another wry quip. T's tone contrasted the images on the smart pad in Samsyn's grip. "By the Creator," he spat. Image after image of violent destruction filled the screen, depicting what once had been a two-story home, in an American neighborhood of manicured lawns and sprawling driveways. "Chase Valen is a good man. He championed the worldwide manhunt for that fuck. Went to the Hague to make sure Kavill received full justice."

"And his family nearly paid the ultimate price."

Syn's finger froze over a picture. A close-up of some items in the rubble of the Valen family home. Smashed dishes, charred curtains...

And a jewelry box.

It was clearly from a girl's room. Lockets and baubles spilled from it, though oddly, the mirror in its lid had remained intact—along with the tiny ballerina on a spring, poised to pop up when the box's lid was opened. The dancer turned too. A pirouette set to "Für Elise," if it was like the box Jayd possessed in her room.

What would he do if his sister were ever subjected to a horror like this?

Feelings pushed up through him. Hot. Vicious. Protective. Prompting a question. "How old?"

Tryst frowned. "Who? What?"

"Valen's children. A boy and a girl, yes? Brooke and Dillon? How old are they?"

"Both just turned eighteen."

"Twins?"

"No. They are from separate marriages. Valen's first wife

died in an auto accident when his girl was a baby. He remarried a year later. The children have grown up together. They are close."

"So the king has known them their whole lives." Things were easier saying it that way. *My father* pulled everything in too close. The dirt. The lies. The secrets.

"I do not know," Tryst replied. "King Ardent only told me Senator Valen has been a friend for close to twenty years, and that the moment Kavill was released, Valen called, begging to hide on Arcadia if the situation became dire."

Samsyn dropped his glare to the image of the music box again. "This looks dire."

"Indeed."

"How soon until they arrive?"

"Not long." Tryst raked his gold gaze up to the sky. "Valen didn't feel safe even radioing ahead until they were departing Rome."

"And they have nothing with them but their clothes and travel documents?"

"Correct."

"Fuck."

"Agreed."

It had no sooner left Tryst's lips than a distant engine growled in the sky. Sure enough, the lights of a small plane appeared, twinkling on approach to the runway.

Though everything felt like just another aircraft landing on Arcadia, Samsyn tapped the comm piece at his ear, opening the channel to the ten elite soldiers hiding in the foliage along the landing strip. On paper, nearly all of them still outranked him—a factor rapidly pushed aside since he was here as King Ardent's emissary. All the unknowns of the situation, as well the danger they presented, made Father's absence a necessity. Samsyn resigned himself to accept it, not enjoy it.

"Everyone on alert," he directed calmly. "We have to expect anything."

Well-spoken advice. That he completely neglected to take personally.

Or maybe it would not have mattered, anyway.

Prepared or not, maybe he was destined to walk out on that tarmac, watch the plane's door descend, and then remember nothing except one pair of perfect, petrified eyes.

Literally...nothing.

Had he greeted the senator? He vaguely recalled his lips moving on the words, the assurances to Chase Valen that they would be safe and guarded here.

Had he said anything to Mrs. Valen? Her shoulders had trembled when he pulled her in, briefly bussing her cheeks in formal greeting, had they not?

Had he said anything to the boy? Dillon. They'd clasped hands like men, though the young man clung long and hard, silently conveying his fear.

He *had* remembered. All of it.

And that all of it was just going through the motions...

Until she got off the stairway.

Chin jerked high—beneath wobbling lips. Steps taken proudly—on legs so fatigued, they barely held her up. Shoulders set firm—while shaking from each shellshocked breath.

But most of all, it was her eyes.

Her huge, terrified, mesmerizing, crystal-blue eyes.

Reminding him...

of him.

No. More than that. It only started there, this draw he felt toward her...this pull of raw connection, fueled by fires he'd never experienced before. This...*need*...to get nearer to her, though not in any way that would harm her or frighten her. It wasn't sexual or even emotional. It extended so far beyond those labels, into a realm that was...

What?

Mystical?

Fuck.

No. *No.* He was not fairy dust, magic drops, and "Für Elise." He was *not* "mystical." And he sure as hell was not crashing, cataclysmic connection with a fucking teenager, even if she did walk like a queen despite the hell she had endured and the darkness in which she stepped.

He wanted to be this creature's strength, sword, and shelter. He craved to drop to his knees before her, sweep his head low, pledge his fealty forever, and utter all the other knightly things from the classic books he had never learned in school. He mentally stabbed himself for it all now. For not getting past the cramped desks and stuffy classrooms and listening to a few of those lessons, instead of ticking off the minutes until he could be free and moving and *doing* something.

Now, he prayed for a single perfect line from one of those books. One ideal thing to say when walking up to the only person who had ever affected him like a human super magnet, drawing him like a million helpless metal shavings, able to achieve his true form only because she grew nearer.

"Hi."

That was *not* the perfect thing.

"Hi." She blurted it between one nervous glance and the next. He wished her no blame. If he were standing in her cute little tennis shoes, gawking up at a hulk like him, he would steal nothing but glimpses too. At once, he rounded his shoulders and gave into a small smile. It rendered no good. His adorable, brave little refugee still trembled like a star readying to fall from the heavens.

A star.

Yes. That was it.

"Star light, star bright." Though he did not murmur it with the greatest confidence, it felt right. Even she seemed to sense it, that wide blue gaze softening.

"Wh-What?" The accusation fled her tone. A tiny smile threatened her scared scowl.

"Star light, star bright." He was more confident about the repetition, even scooping up her hand and adding a low bow over her fingers. "Look what beauty the sky has brought me tonight."

Her fingertips shook against his palm. Her lips quaked harder, as if she was unsure what to say or feel. That certainly made two of them. "This is...kind of weird."

"Well...'weird' is all right." He laughed a little, as her vernacular teased his tongue. He remembered himself the next moment, straightening back to noble formality. "As long as safe goes with it." He bent over her as far as he dared. "You *are* safe now, Brooke Valen. Of that you can be assured."

Her gold-tinged brows arched. "That so, big guy?"

He chuckled. "That is so, little *astremé.*"

"Oh, yeah?" Her head tilted, blowing little chunks of her hair across her lightly freckled cheeks. Her hair was also intriguing. It was so different than Arcadian styles, chopped at vastly different lengths. "Says who? Because in case you haven't heard, this evil asshole just blew up our whole house and—"

"Brooke." Her mother whipped a glare over. "Language!"

Samsyn held Brooke back, waiting for the woman to keep going, before he leaned closer over her. "'Evil asshole' is about right." Once regaining the full connection of her gaze—because he knew he would get it—he asserted, "And if he comes anywhere near you, the commander of the Arcadian armed forces, Prince Samsyn Cimarron, personally swears he shall slice the bastard from one ear to the next."

"Only if I can help." Tryst emphasized it with a snort.

"*Prince?*" She seemed unaware of even whispering it. "Well, no shit."

He grimaced. "Still weird?"

"Oh, yeah." Her lips quirked. "But cool. Maybe...more than kind of."

Her awkward honesty tossed all his composure into fresh chaos. The shards of it hit his blood like metal shavings, sharpening his senses and making him even more aware of every move she made now too...

Including the new way she gazed at him.

No more surreptitious glances. No more frightened trembling. Her steps still wobbled a little, no doubt due to the hell she'd just survived, but as Syn helped her into the transport van that would take them up into the Tahreuse Mountains, where they could be best hidden in case Kavill gave chase, she looked up to him once more—with a face full of *brand-new* things.

Relief.

Confidence.

Security.

Hope.

She held back none of it. And in giving all of it, gave him

yet one more, incredible gift. A sensation in his heart and soul he had written off as forever lost.

Clean.

For many minutes after the van departed, he stood on the tarmac, in the darkness, with a hand over his chest...and confusion clouding his brain.

What the hell had just happened?

Who the hell was he now?

He still had no answer, even when a circle of familiar faces appeared around him. Tryst had roused the guys from the bushes, and they razzed each other with the normal filthy humor that accompanied the end of a mission. Samsyn, normally the ringleader of that party, remained pulled back. The space beneath his hand was still pristine as new snow. He yearned to keep it that way as long as possible. If he could get back to his suite at the palais, just to be alone and cherish this longer, maybe a little of it would stick. Even to someone like him...

"All right, all right!" Tryst flung up a hand, silencing everyone. "As charming as you apes are, His Highness still has a birthday to celebrate—and, I believe, a certain someone to celebrate it with." The man gave him a nasty side eye. "Maybe a sweet little blonde, keeping the sheets hot for you?"

Fuck.

Arista. Whom he'd told to stay in the suite as long as she needed.

His hand dropped.

Just like that, his best birthday gift vanished. Wiped out with one reminder of who—of *what*—he really was.

"No." It spewed on a growl, though he forced a wry twist to his lips. "I am much more open to getting back and finishing off the birthday vodka."

"Over getting tight and hot with a willing female?" Olyver Frond, one of the team's more boisterous bastards, voiced it. "Who are you, and what the fuck have you done with Samysn Cimarron?"

He summoned a tighter, faker smile—a complete disguise for how he could not bear thinking of kissing a blonde right now, let alone bedding her. How *any* blonde would only remind him of *one* right now...

Fuck.

No.

"By the Creator's balls. Have I not wrestled enough with young females and their needs this evening?"

As he hoped, the men bought the sarcasm—except for Tryst, who was shrewd enough to see through everything and smart enough to keep it a secret.

The pretense was agonizing but necessary. One day, he would be the true commander of anyone in a uniform on this island. Cracks in *their* armor were barely acceptable. Cracks in *his* had to be impossible.

Which meant Brooke Valen—and everything she had done to him, for him—would be subjects never visited again.

For that reason—and that alone—he prayed like hell that someone put a bullet through Rune Kavill's brain soon, making it possible for the Valens to return home...and for Brooke Valen to become exactly what he needed her to be.

A memory.

CHAPTER ONE

"Damn it, Valen. Stop fighting like a girl."

I let my heavily taped hands frame my glower. I was on fire and ready to go again. A challenging smirk answered back. It had a face attached to it, of course, but right now, I focused only on that grin—and how pissed I was at it.

Because it was the truth.

I *was* a girl.

And God, was I sparring with the pathetic ability of one.

Which always happened when I knew Samsyn Cimarron was on his way up Tahreuse Mountain.

Syn.

There he was again, bursting to life in my mind—as he'd done nearly once an hour for the last six years. Prince Samsyn Obsydian Cimarron, second in line to the throne of Arcadia Island, commander of its entire military force, notable collector of any vehicle that could speed him across the kingdom in faster time—but to me, he was simply my noble Syn. The first person who'd uttered a kind word to me here. The source of my first Arcadian smile. My protecting knight, damn near ordering me to feel safe again, filling all the dashing, gorgeous potential of the twenty-first birthday he'd just celebrated...

And in the doing, made me fall instantly in love with him.

That had been almost six years ago today.

I really didn't like letting go of shit.

Especially Syn Cimarron.

I gulped as the image of him intensified. Dark hair on the wind, blown across his huge shoulders. Powerful legs, eating up the ground with his strides. Arms bulging...everywhere. Effortless grace. Complete power. Practically bending the air around him to his will, as if he'd arrived here through some strange time portal and was only putting up with the twenty-first century for the cool man toys. His mighty body would be just as comfortable in thick chainmail, a massive sword hanging from his belt...

My daydreams always had the shittiest timing.

Jagger spotted the distraction in my eyes. He swept in, scooping his right foot behind my left ankle and instantly sending me ass-over-elbows. I sprawled flat on my back, the fresh spring grass jabbing through my lightweight training wear. The bright Arcadian sun glared into my eyes.

"Oof!" I pushed up, ready to pop back to my feet. "Motherf—" And again hit the barrier of his boot, planted to my sternum.

Jag arched his russet brows. No added smirk this time. Wise move. "Well. You have not forgotten how to *swear* like a man."

"*Bonsun!* Let me up."

"Impressive. Profanity in two languages today."

"Let me *up*, Jag."

"Not until I have your promise of twenty minutes without thoughts of him."

Ass. Sometimes he could read me as well as Dillon, which was a little scary. Really, I didn't need any more guys in my life with the psychic-force connection thing going on. At least Dillon had an excuse. My stepbrother had always been more like a twin, especially with his similar coloring and temperament. I had no choice about *his* hooks into my brain.

What about Samsyn?

Samsyn...was different.

Beyond different.

He was the dream. The Pegasus. The dragon on the mountain. The man who'd never be connected to me like that, in spite of my constant pleas to fate for the miracle.

Impossible.

Which meant Jag was right. I needed to toss the man—every beautiful damn inch of him—out of my mind and focus on what mattered here: being mentally and physically prepped for Syn's arrival. Yesterday, his personal envoy from the palace had arrived, having driven three hours from the palace at Sancti, located on the other side of the island. The man had waited to read the missive aloud to Jag, myself, and the eight other guys who trained regularly at the Tahreuse Valley Fight Skills and Fitness Center.

Arriving on palace business Friday. ETA 14:00. Be at your best and ready to roll.

Naturally, curiosities had been piqued.

Maybe a little more than piqued.

But the ten of us had dealt with it as we always did: by doubling the intensity of our workouts. I'd gone for triple the effort, not one speck blind about the importance of Syn including me on this. It was why I'd taken up self-defense and fight skills three years ago and worked my backside off to excel at them all. It was my only avenue to staying close to Syn. If there was any truth that glared loudest about the man, it was his love of fighting—perhaps, at times, even more than "other" physical pursuits. I had no hope of ever sharing something like the latter with him, but I could really do something about the former. Being included in his important "palace business" meant he'd finally noticed my efforts too.

That I'd finally, if just for a little while, be important to him.

But not if I kept fighting like a girl.

"Let's do this." I ignored the hand Jag extended. Chose to grasshopper it back to my feet instead. I jabbed my stare into his. Reset my fists in front of my face. Lifted my chin. Let all thoughts fly free but one.

You're going down, Jagger Foxx.

Jag chuckled, once more reading me like a ten-foot-high banner. "All right, then. Let us 'do this.'"

We wove and danced around each other for a couple of minutes. He cuffed my shoulder; I socked his stomach. My fist smarted from colliding with the protective band around his middle; my lungs pumped against the similar device wrapped around me.

"*Bonrika plute.*" Jag was a little winded from the blow.

Tiny mouth curl. "Of course it was very good." Shoulder roll now, savoring the flush of adrenaline but knowing better than to let it rule. I held position, studying Jag's stance. During this morning's practice, he'd taken a good punch on the right from Victyr. How much did it still bother him? He was masking it well. Too well. A weakness to be exploited?

"This is *not* the Royal Regatta, princess."

"Now you're just trying to piss me off."

I expected his gloating chortle, but his angular face stayed solemn. "Too much *thinking*, Brooke. Evaluate, do not deliberate. Then commit to the move and—"

"Control my enemy." I practically snarled it. "I know, I *know*. I swear to God, you're like a broken sound chip from one of my old toys."

"Because you would treat this like a child's game?"

Wow. He really wasn't just trying to piss me off. He was out to push every button in my book. *Three years.* For three damn years, I'd worked to earn the respect of him and every other fighter who trained here, honing my skills and my work ethics in order to stand next to them as an equal, not the scared girl who'd first wobbled her way onto Arcadian soil. His dig was as good as offering me a diaper.

Take this *nappy, my friend.*

I lifted my fists and prepared to advance, when something ruthlessly grabbed me from behind. My feet left the ground. Adrenaline jacked my blood. Time-honed instincts took over my muscles. The wall of a bastard wouldn't budge. He felt like the freaking Terminator, steeled strength clad in thick leather, deployed with frightening precision. I was pinned in, twisted around, and then dropped to the grass.

Between one breath and the next, my fury burst into panic.

In two seconds, six years fell away. Day turned to night. The surface beneath my body changed from polished walnut boards into a sea of crazy confetti: bits of glass and flowers, the remains of the dining room windows, as well as the vase of my birthday flowers from last week. Dad had asked me to change out the water. I'd forgotten. It smelled awful, but I clung to its pungency; anything to block the acrid violence of the guns and explosions...

Mom screamed. Soldiers bellowed. The guy shielding me was one of the loudest.

We need that chopper now! Those whack jobs aren't going to stop until this place is dust. Land it in the backyard, man. There's two fucking acres back there!

Then he'd yelled down at me. Told me everything was going to be okay, though I far from believed him. Ordered me to stay completely still, faking my own death to our intruders if necessary, as he ran off to find Dillon. The house—the home I'd grown up in—kept crashing in around me. More tumbled in when the helicopter arrived, its thunder throbbing the air. I'd listened with gratitude and grief. The chopper was here to take us to Burlington, where we'd fly to Rome and then Arcadia, where we'd been offered asylum by King Ardent. The rest of the world would be told the four of us died in the attack.

Terror had kept me glued to that floor. Rage had made me long to burst from it. To leap through the rubble and kill every one of those monsters with my bare hands—except their leader, Rune Kavill. For him, I'd invent a special death. Something really painful...

The anger had never left me.

Often, it'd been the only friend I possessed.

Right now, it was my best and dearest buddy.

Let's go, pal.

I drove an elbow into Terminator's ribs. Again. His grunts were like booster rockets, empowering the buck of my hips. He'd expected that and easily pinned his knees into the backs of mine. I grinned into the grass. The asshole was either kind or stupid, giving me that gift. With his weight pinned there, it was easy to twist up, ramming my elbow into his jaw instead.

"Brooke!" Jagger's shout was unexpected—and urgent. "By the Creator! Do not—"

A growl from my new opponent stomped him into

silence—and gave me the chance I'd been waiting for. The guy's second of distraction was my scoop of opportunity. I used my elbow on his forearm, tilting his weight enough to dislodge one pinned knee. Next, a swift roll to my back. Instant curl-up on both legs, locking them around his broad shoulders. Brutal squeeze in, pushing my knees to his earlobes.

"Cry *rahmié* now, or I'll snap your head off like a Barbie after Christmas."

"For the love of fuck." Jag's mutter completely contradicted the humor rumbling from the man in my grip—and the face between my legs.

The face, with eyes piercing like winter skies. With that proud, high warrior's brow. With the gentle smile that dominated so many of my fantasies.

And now, one catastrophic nightmare.

"Oh, my God."

Mortified gasp. Paralyzed shock—not seeming to disturb Samsyn in the least. The bastard chuckled while running his massive hands down—up?—my tense thighs. His mouth kicked a little higher as our gazes met, exposing a rare glimpse of his gleaming teeth. Had I ever seen more of the man's teeth than that? And why the hell was I thinking of that right *now*?

"Well, hello to you too, starlight."

The nickname, understood by all as his alone to use, rolled off his generous lips as if we'd seen each other two hours, not two months, ago. I normally delighted in that dynamic between us, but right now, it was too close. *He* was too close. Too big. Too warm. Too much of everything I desired...and would never have.

Frustration simmered up. Spilled over. With a snarl, I untangled myself. Scrambled backward. That would've been fine—a few seconds to find the game face he hadn't given me time for—if I didn't glance back up, ensuring I didn't decapitate him during my escape.

What the...?

His teeth weren't visible anymore. But neither was his mirth—nor even the lights in his eyes.

He swallowed hard and then dragged in a ragged breath. Raked a shaky hand through the top of his thick dark mane. And his other hand...

Frantically adjusted things in his crotch.

Sizable things.

Ohhhh...wow.

"Brooke? You okay?" Jag, sounding like he spoke through a hundred layers of gauze—that suddenly caught fire. The heat roared through me, drowning my equilibrium, fanned by the force of one unmistakable concept.

I'd done that to Syn. Instigated that reaction. Made him force a rocky laugh to his lips, trying to cover it up...resealing the rift in his invisible armor. A glimpse into the man behind the wall that I'd never imagined seeing. Well...not outside my dreams.

Damn it.

The reality was so much better.

Damn it.

I couldn't do this. Couldn't even begin to think, or even hope, that he saw me any differently than six minutes ago, much less six years. Besides, he was a guy. Their bodies did shit like that, springing up when they weren't supposed to. And I'd baited the damn dragon, after all. Royally.

And now was paying the royal price for it.

A debt I could, and should, just as easily laugh away.

But couldn't.

Just the preview of Syn...like that...slammed in another recognition. The realization that I'd never have him like that again. Like a beggar brought to the buffet, only to be told I couldn't have another bite.

Problem was...I was still starving.

I had to get out of here. Now.

CHAPTER TWO

I made my way to the old bridge at Temptina Falls. The decision stemmed from habit more than logic, and I immediately regretted it. Syn would look for me here first.

"Star light, star bright."

Bingo.

He tried to tease with it. Well, his version of teasing. During my first year here, I didn't think he comprehended the meaning. It'd only added to his allure, making me fall harder every time I was lucky enough to see him when he came to our side of the island for climbing vacations or training trips with his troops. Every time, there was something physically different—his muscles got bigger, his hair grew longer—but the steadfast warrior I'd first met was always there, so different from the brash boys I'd known back home. Not that Vermont could ever be home, with Rune Kavill living as a free man. Even if the vermin *was* existing in some rat-infested cave, Dad wasn't safe—and neither were Mom, Dillon, or I.

That was enough of that. The waters of my mind were muddy enough as it was.

Because of whatever *that* was.

That look on his face...

What the hell *was that look on his face?*

I didn't dare open my mouth, for fear those exact words would come out. Thank God I managed to school my features before he stepped over and leaned against the bridge rail next to me.

"You're early." I shot it as accusation.

"Despicable habit."

"No shit."

He arched a brow. "Fitting in with the boys in *many* ways now, hmm?"

"Not you too." Was Jag sending him reports about my language now? "And when did you decide to be Stuffy McGoo? Isn't that Evrest's job?"

As always, bringing up the man's brother made him stiffen and glow at once. "Evrest has many roles to fulfill lately." He swiveled his gaze over the falls. They rose nearly twenty feet up, emptying from the Temptina River, cascading over the boulders on the hill like sparkling stair steps. "Things are changing fast for Arcadia."

"And you're worried about keeping him safe through all of it."

He snapped his gaze back. It was on fire again, boring into me in a way he'd never stared before.

Damn.

His intensity returned me to the illicit glimpse I'd stolen on the training lawn. That stomach-tingling flash of his hand... right *there*. Only now he was doing the same thing with his eyes, as if questioning why I'd said that...as if thankful no matter what the reason.

He shifted closer. Tilted his head, continuing to study me. The wind off the falls tugged a chunk of his hair free from its leather tie. Flattened his black Henley against his sculpted shoulders. "I truly *am* sorry, astremé."

I scowled. "About what?"

"Frightening you...with the surprise arrival."

There it was. The calm, formal tone with which I was comfortable. Only nothing felt comfortable with him anymore. At least what I'd gotten away with as comfortable when he was near.

"I wasn't frightened." Liar. "Just a little stunned." I shrugged and *psshhh*ed, attempting to lighten...well, whatever was happening here. "And I'm really sorry about nearly Barbie-snapping your head off."

He frowned. "'Barbie-snapping'?"

"Just another childhood tradition from the exotic land of Vermont."

"Hmm. At yule time, you said?"

"Typically. Though Dillion certainly didn't let that stop him from tormenting me at other times of the year, if the chance arose."

The bold lines of his face quirked, deeply searching mine. He looked truly confused, as if trying to determine if I were serious or not.

Eventually, the sarcasm in my eyes registered. He exhaled back into a mellower stance. "Curious."

That was one way of putting it. Over the years, he'd been fascinated about the life from which I'd come. At first that had shocked me. He was a prince of Arcadia, raised in one of the world's most stunning palaces. While my life as a senator's daughter hadn't been schlubby, it had also contained the same stuff as any normal American kid's—like a perturbing brother and broken Barbies.

"What? You never threatened to flush even one of Jayd's dolls down the toilet?"

One side of his mouth lifted, only for a second, at the mention of his stunning little sister. "Jayd did not enjoy dolls."

My turn to frown. "Not one?" I thought of the youngest Cimarron sibling, resembling a porcelain doll in her own right and always seeming as serious as one. "Then what did she play with?"

His turn to shrug. "Us."

I smiled. The implication of his statement was clear, but I voiced it anyway. "You, Evrest, and Shiraz."

"Yes."

"Awwww." I shoulder-bumped him.

"We bonded." His features crunched, appearing grumpy. "We had no choice."

"Choice or not, she was lucky to have you three. She still is."

"I am fairly certain that, at this moment, Jayd would contradict you to the point of violence."

"Oh, dear."

I studied his profile. He gazed at the waterfall again, his expression tensing—but not just because of the cryptic remarks about Jayd. Unable to stop myself, I curled a hand around his huge forearm.

"Syn."

The new stab of his gaze clutched my breath for a second. His pupils raced over my face. His thick brows hunched. A hundred thoughts clearly assaulted his brain at once—and for one crazy moment, he showed it all to me. Compelled me closer because of it. Made me yearn to keep going, to pull him down around me, to take away even a fraction of the strange pressure he was under.

"Syn? What is it?" Besides what seemed like the weight of the world. "Come on. It's me, big guy. What are friends for?"

He still didn't say anything. Pivoted more fully toward

me, which faced our bodies fully toward each other. The hand I'd wrapped around his arm slipped against his waist...feeling so natural. He curved a hand to me, in the same place.

Ohhhh.

What the hell was happening now?

And did I even want to waste brain cells contemplating the answer?

"Starlight."

The husk beneath his voice unraveled my senses another fifty feet...making me fall for him all over again.

As I fell *into* him.

That part was his fault too. If he hadn't raised his other hand to cup the side of my neck, then graze his thumb along my jaw in those soft, slow strokes, my senses would've remained balanced. *Maybe.*

God, how good he felt this close. How small he made me feel. How many nerves he shook to their ends, so aware of him, so alive for him...

"Wh-What?" I had no idea how I managed the rasp.

His gaze grew hooded, descending over my face. "How the hell have you suddenly grown up?"

I wanted to laugh—but his voice arrested everything in my body. There was a new element in that masculine husk. An ache. No...a need. Like he was in pain.

Like he was...disappointed?

I blinked hard, managing to keep the teary sting at bay. "I'm...sorry."

Samsyn's face changed again. It was yet another new expression to me, formed of tense lines and rigid concentration, but not the look he used in the sparring or riding rings. It twisted my stomach...and places lower than that.

His thumb pushed under my chin. His eyes fixated on my lips.

"I am...not."

CHAPTER THREE

Oh, God.

Ohhhh, God.

He brushed his mouth against mine...for about two seconds. Long enough, I sensed, to test if I'd finally gotten the message about that nuance in his voice and that concentration in his gaze.

Message received, Cimarron. Joyously loud and clear.

I told him so by fisting his shirt in one hand, his hair in the other. By letting myself drown in his nearness and heat, his hardness and lust.

Oh, God. Yeah...lust.

This was happening. Samsyn Cimarron was lusty. For me.

He lifted away. Only far enough to reconfirm my desire with his eyes too—perhaps to ensure I saw it in his gaze too.

Check that box, Syn. Then kiss me, damn it.

He growled.

Hurry.

I sighed.

Please hurry.

Galloping chest. Careening head. Throbbing pulse. The cool mist. His warm breath. Perfect. This was so perfect.

"Your Highness!"

Jagger's shout parted us like a pair of lit firecrackers. Our heads dropped, resulting in their violent collision. I barely felt the pain. It was easily eclipsed by—

What?

What the *hell* was this?

Embarrassment didn't feel like an option. Neither did any of the other "shoulds" rightfully belonging in this situation. Mortification? No way. Regret? Not a drop. I wasn't going to repent for taking what I'd always longed for. He wasn't attached to anyone—the Arcadian gossip mill wouldn't be immune to a juicy goody like *that* for long—and I sure as hell wasn't either. This was what I'd craved from Samsyn since the moment his hand first tucked into mine, six years ago. Had it been just a teenage infatuation at first? Of course. But as I'd grown, so had the awareness of how *he* did...the proud, protecting, principled man he'd become. I wasn't the only woman on this island who'd noticed—but I'd always hoped, in the outermost reaches of my heart, that our connection was a little more special than most...

I'd just been on the verge of finding out.

"Damn it, Jag." I muttered it only for Syn's ears. How would he react? I certainly knew what I hoped for. His lips, twitching with reined-in mirth. His eyes, glowing with barely banked passion. Then his voice, turning low and smoky, murmuring that we'd continue our conversation later...

"What is it?"

My anticipation sank. His bellow was all business, his face even more so. His jaw was fixed and tense. And his eyes were stark with...

Remorse. Perhaps even shame. Looked like that was just the beginning of the list.

"Everyone is here," Jag shouted back. "And waiting in the Center's conference room."

"On our way."

Syn kept his eyes on me while issuing it. Even stalled a

moment before turning to leave. But it sure as hell wasn't to promise more conversation later. It was a goodbye—at least to the path we'd only just started exploring. I didn't hide my feedback about that, letting him have the full brunt of my glower. And what did I think that'd get me? A scrap of apology, silent *or* out loud? *Idiot.* Syn offered nothing but a hard nod, driving in his point like a mallet to a stake. The gate was closed and wouldn't ever be revisited.

Your damn loss, Your Highness.

I made sure he knew it too. Stepped around him and led the way back through the woods to the Center, making sure I turned every stomp into a subtle little sashay. When he started with his tight grunts halfway through the trip, I smiled to myself. Tried to enjoy every single second of his misery.

Tried.

Victories were hollow when a celebration had no heart.

* * *

"Merderim to you all for making the time to be here."

Samsyn stood at the head of the Center's huge conference table, huge and imposing—though he'd have a lock on everyone's attention even if seated. I deliberately positioned myself near the opposite end, like the extra distance was going to be any damn help in eluding the extra pull he had on me.

The extra pull he *always* had on me.

Only now, it was worse. A thousand times more intense. I noticed everything more acutely. The daybreak brilliance of his eyes. The midnight resonance in his voice. The grace in each of his steps. The flow in his hands.

Those hands.

Their power, barely banked, curling against my waist. Their passion, urgent to the point of quivering, as he held back on the kiss. Even the command in his damn thumb, sizzling heat up my whole face through that pressure point beneath my chin...

I shifted in my seat. Forced my attention back up front. The task wasn't difficult, since Jag—the shithead with the worst timing on the planet—had just finished with his version of a pomp-and-circumstance welcome to his prince. Syn officially had the floor again.

"There is much to say, so I will get to the point." He braced his feet and squared his shoulders. "As many of you know, my brother has set his mind on bringing some major changes to our kingdom. Whether it likes it or not, Arcadia is slowly making its way into the twenty-first century."

Murmurs rippled around the table, agreeing with him.

"Bring it." Blayze Hardwell, a hulk with a shock of bright-red hair, emphasized it with a fist to his chest. "My shit flushes properly now. I get hot water in the morning." He raised the hand to smack his cheek. "See that? Feels like a baby's ass because of the water."

As everyone's laughter waned, the guy next to him beamed a new smile. "My little sister is taking biomechanical engineering at the university now."

Blayze gave that a nod of approval. Just one. "So when do we get a Yogurtland?"

"Never." Syn's stare turned the shade of thunder.

I suppressed a groan. A vat of chocolate frozen yogurt topped with gummy bears sounded so perfect right now.

Grahm Riggs, the only man on the island with hair rivaling Syn's, was also known as the most stoic of our bunch. He fought like a demon but said as little as a monk. Even now, the care behind his words was evident. "Whether everyone 'likes' it or not," he reiterated. "So are you here because of the *likes* or the *or nots*?"

Syn's posture tightened, confirming a vote for the latter—but he answered wryly, "Both."

Everyone leaned forward, including me.

He took in a noticeable breath. Steeled his jaw. "As you are all likely aware, not everyone in the kingdom supports leaving the old ways behind." He hitched a grin at Blayze. "Including the plumbing."

Anger burned in the guy's gaze. "*Imbezaks.*"

Syn snorted. "Imbeciles may be accurate, my friend, but those voices are also numerous. And growing."

Nods all around. Many people of the population, young *and* old, were still violently opposed to the changes Evrest proposed for Arcadia. They contended the kingdom's peace and prosperity were because of the island's minimal contact with the modern world, not in spite of it. They called themselves the Pura and had been cautious about vocalizing their views—until lately. They grew louder last summer, when Evrest allowed an American film company onto the island; louder still when their king bucked the law of the Distinct, a preselected group of potential brides, and proposed to Camellia Saxon, a member of that film crew.

"Numerous." Grahm echoed his leader once more. And again, elaborated with care. "Which also means dangerous."

"Getting more to the point...yes." Samsyn growled it before jacking his head back, as if also turning it into a skyward plea. Either that or he really knew how incredible that move was, brushing his hair over his beautiful deltoids and traps, causing my instant fantasy of monkey-climbing all the way up his huge body. "Yet into the middle of this *désorlik*, my brother has insisted on taking his fiancé on an island-wide engagement tour."

Monster record scratch.

Fantasy over.

"An engagement *what*?"

It earned me a brief glance, though Samsyn directed his explanation to the entire group. "Now that His Majesty can be as open as he wishes about his hormone storm for this woman, he wishes to share the 'joy' with everyone. He is convinced that he'll win over many Pura, once they meet Camellia and fall for her as he has."

"And he's taking the campaign to *their* turf for it," I supplied.

Jagger twisted a sardonic smile. "It is a brilliant idea. *Déssonum* for the brutal honesty, my prince...but it is."

"Agreed." Grahm clearly didn't feel his apology was necessary too. "He takes the message to the people. Lets them see Camellia as a real person, the woman worthy of their king's true love. In the doing, she becomes a positive symbol of the economic strides Evrest wants to make as well."

Blayze jiggled his knee and frowned. "Hmph. Brilliant. *If* you are not the one having to arrange logistics for all...of..."

His voice trailed off as realization slammed us all.

Jagger was the first to voice our collective conclusion.

"Fuck."

No wonder Syn had braced his stance.

He fielded the burst of reactions, ranging from *hell no* to *hell yes* and everything in between, with quiet composure. It gave me a moment to study him. Not that I wasn't always doing that...but *this* moment was different than any before. I'd seen Samsyn Cimarron in many forms over the years. Stiff and formal. Charming and reserved. Rugged and competitive. The last trumped the others combined. But I'd never gotten to see him as a leader of men, guiding and motivating without props like swords, cars, fists, or battle cries. Right now, it was just him.

And he was riveting.

Regal.

Patient.

Perfect.

I also wasn't the only one who noticed.

I'd observed, of course, that Orielle Preetsok had quietly entered the room when the meeting was called to order, smart pad in hand. As one of the Center's administrative staff, she'd obviously been called in to take notes. As a preening little thing who'd been on the island's final Distinct selection list, she likely also had an agenda—about the possibility of locking her claim on the next available prince in the Cimarron line. I shouldn't have cared—if she made Syn happy and treated him right, wasn't *that* what mattered?—but who the hell was I kidding? Watching her undress him with her big doe eyes, sitting up straighter to flaunt her va-va-voom curves and milky skin, I fought against knocking back a jealousy shooter. The little brunette certainly seemed more his type. She was a woman groomed to say *Yes sir* no matter what the situation.

I didn't like following rules.

I clearly got it from Dad.

Who'd landed his whole family in exile on a foreign island because of shattering a few "guidelines" himself.

Meeting. Important. Thoughts. Present. Now.

I pushed Orielle to my periphery, despite her continued

mooning at Syn. "So you're expecting big crowds," I stated. "And you need eyes and ears in them, to keep track of any potential trouble. Local faces in plain clothes, so as to not arouse suspicions."

Blayze swung a wide grin. "Clever girl!"

"Nah. I just wanted to be Sidney Bristow when I was in junior high." The *Alias* reference earned me a circle of glassy stares. Nothing new; I had the skill down to an art form.

"An equally brilliant idea," Jagger asserted.

Samsyn didn't waste time restating the point—or acknowledging it'd come from me. I pushed down the resulting disappointment. Hadn't I earned my place at this table by proving I could be like the guys? Until half an hour ago, it was all I'd ever hoped to get in the way of proximity to Syn. One stupid slip of judgment later, and I'd forgotten it all. *Maybe you should join Orielle in the swoony pit.*

As I willed the fist in my lap to relax, Samsyn pulled a remote control stick out of his black cargo pants. At his tap, an image came to life in the air over the table: a holographic map of the Tahreuse Mountain Range, along with the surrounding valleys.

Jag whistled appreciatively.

Even Grahm smiled. "Kicks ass on ten Yogurtlands."

"Evrest and Camellia begin the tour in three days' time, beginning with the central valleys and the pastoral midlands." Syn paced around the table, to the side at which I was seated. With every step closer, my instincts were harder to subdue. My body plugged into foreign circuits. My pores popped open. My nerve endings sizzled. My hand coiled again in my lap, helping me hide every shaking breath I took.

What the hell? Why was I vibrating like an exposed wire

because of one kiss? *No.* Not even that, thanks to Jagger and his timing.

As if my pulse, my skin, and the very air around me knew that difference.

"That gives us six days to prepare for things here, for anyone doing the math." Syn halted right behind me—oh, why the freak not?—and punched the clicker again. On the holograph, a red line snaked its way up the slopes of Tahreuse. "On Friday, they shall depart Faisant Township after a community breakfast hosted by the Stanwycks of Sauvage Ranch. That means they will travel here via the Longitude Road, followed by the South Face Switchbacks. To be precautious, we shall close the Switchbacks to all traffic except the royal convoy."

"Which consists of what?" Grahm inquired.

"Five Arcadian security trucks, to start," Syn replied. "One serving as advance lookout, traveling fifteen to twenty minutes ahead of the main group, to radio back if something feels exceptionally out of place. Another truck shall serve as lead on the main group; one more at sweep."

"And the other two?"

"One behind Evrest and Camellia's vehicle." Even without his tight growl, I would've felt his surge of tension. "My brother, looking at the world through his typical Candide glasses, wants to travel with his future wife in the royal Bentley."

Grahm shrugged. "It *is* an elegant touch."

"In convertible mode."

Blayze howled. "I should have saved the imbezak reference for now."

Jagger lurched to his feet. "You refer to your *king*, mongrel. Leash your words!"

Syn lifted a hand. "Jag."

"*What?*"

"Sit." He walked around, taking up a new position at the foot of the table. Good thing? He was farther away, giving my nervous system a break. Bad thing? I now had to view him in profile, and it was just as mesmerizing as head-on. "Besides," he muttered, "I align with Blayze." His hair brushed his jaw as he shook his head, a stunning contrast of silken sable to hard-hewn angles. "Evrest's is the noblest soul I know—but sometimes, that makes it the most foolish."

"We'll figure it out." I tried not to sound impatient. *Yeeaah, not-so-much.* And men said women got stuck on petty matters? "Let's get through the big picture first. Tell us about the rest of the convoy."

"One car shall be for His Majesty, Ardent, and the Queen Mother, Xaria. And after them, a car for Camellia's parents."

Jolt of attention, straight up the spine. "*Her* parents are coming for this?"

"My brother is very serious about the project."

Grahm traced the wood grain of the table with a finger. "So Shiraz and Jayd will be along as well."

"In their own car," Syn clarified. "Though they will be part of the motorcade only and not taking part in any of the official events."

Jagger chuffed. "And I am certain Jayd loves the hell out of that idea."

Syn's growl was low but firm. "Jayd will accept my decision, rendered for her own safety, whether she likes it or not."

I hid a smile. That explained his comment at the waterfall. Good chance I was the only one in the room who'd seen Syn's real conflict about his sister's hostility—and clearly, he wanted it to stay that way. How many difficult decisions must he make like that, every single day? I wondered if there was anyone who knew...or was there to help him with them.

"So what comes after that?" Blayze inserted, smirking wide. "The clowns and monkeys?"

"If that is how you care to classify the assistants and stylists." Syn didn't relent a note of his determined challenge. The message, this time to Blayze, was there. Traditional sarcasm would have to be checked once this party rolled up the mountain.

"Stylists?" On the other hand, Grahm's query was completely serious. "They need to be...styled?"

Syn braced his stance again. *Uh-oh.* "I am told that 'styling' is usually required for a ball."

"A *ball?*"

We all couldn't have blurted it more in unison if we'd rehearsed. Syn drew in a long breath, as unmoved as a teacher handing out extra homework. "My brother wishes to have a ball for his betrothed," he affirmed, "and he feels Le Blanc Tower would be an ideal place for it."

I pushed back in my chair. "I'd feel the exact same way—with more than six days' notice for the occasion."

Heads nodded around me. None of us could dispute King Evrest's thinking. The Tower—kind of a pointless name, since visitors technically walked down to it instead of up—was like no other venue in the world. The huge cavern, hewn into the mountain by time and the elements, had been wired with lighting and given an extended terrace just a few years ago, turning it into the island's most popular spot for any occasion requiring an extraordinary touch. The word only began to describe the place. The entrance walkway and stairs, all carved into the pure white granite found in so many places on Arcadia, first led a visitor to think they were entering a pristine palace with a killer view of Lake Sagique. But the main room itself was the main surprise. Naturally embedded into every wall, as well as the ceiling, were chunks of labradorite, sapphire, and euclase that turned the space into a sparkling wonderland.

"Well, six days is what we have." Syn didn't try to be nice about it. As he scrubbed his face, I realized the reason why. His eyes were sheened with exhaustion, his mouth bracketed by strain. Damn. He'd likely encountered this same argument when assembling a ground team in Faisant and counted on facing the same when moving on to Colluss on the north coast, where Evrest and Camellia would logically travel after Tahreuse.

Making me a world-class heel.

Who tried making up for it by shoving to my feet, squaring my shoulders, and presenting my strongest game face. "Then we'll make it work in six days."

"Agreed." Grahm rose too.

"Agreed." Blayze was next.

One by one, the others stood and pledged their own commitments for the next week. Samsyn accepted each vow with a solemn nod but little else. I watched the shadows in his eyes, sensed him rationing his dwindling energy over the remaining tasks of the day. And damn it, I didn't like seeing it... nearly *feeling* it with him. I hated fighting off all my protective impulses, burning hotter by the second, telling me to march across the room, drag him to the yoga studio, and force his stubborn ass down on a mat for even an hour of the rest he clearly needed.

I hated still caring.

This much.

And wondered how the hell I was going to get through this entire damn week without looking at Samsyn Cimarron... wondering what it would've been like to complete that kiss at the waterfall. How his lips would've reacted to mine. What his body would've felt like. What sounds would've unfurled from him, as our senses awoke to each other...

Oh, God.

I had to turn it all off. Thinking straight, functioning correctly, depended on it.

It had to be easier than I thought. It *had* to be. One quick search inside. Just find the spigots marked *H* and *S*.

H for heart.

S for spirit.

Then crank them off. Lock them down.

I could do this. I had before. I was just a little rusty. And yeah, there was the difference in both experiences too. The last time, I'd been staring from a helicopter at the smoldering remains of my house. This time, I gazed at the most beautiful warrior prince God had ever put on earth. The bold set of his face, while silently assessing the room. The million thoughts behind his crystalline eyes. The sensual tumble of his hair against his nape and shoulders.

The chaos he caused in me as soon as he looked up again.

Looked at me.

Looked into me.

Curled heat and need and longing into so many secret places me.

Crank them off. Lock them down.

Right. And just tell myself to stop breathing too. To stop feeling more aware, more inspired, more alive...

More a woman.

Damn it.

I was in for six days of some major suckage.

Freaking. Lovely.

CHAPTER FOUR

Ten hours later, and it only felt like two. Or twenty, depending on what part of my sanity was still left to listen to.

After the meeting at the Center, briefing packets were distributed about everyone's roles during the three days of the royal visit. Logistics would be intricate, complicated by the news that select members of the international press had also been invited to attend the engagement ball. That was before we tackled the issue about adequately housing everyone in the royal retinue. In Sancti, the Palais Arcadia could house hundreds in luxury. Faisant had the Sauvage Ranch. In Colluss, there was the impressive Librante Villa. But in Tahreuse, the breathtaking scenery demanded payback in architectural challenges. Sprawling buildings? Utterly impossible. Most structures, literally built into the sides of cliffs, had to be constructed with creative usage of space. *Very* creative.

That truth bore just as much weight inside the mayor's house—though I had to convince my plummeting jaw and popping eyes of it.

"Wow." Lame, lame, lame. But what else fit? As I followed Mayor Trieste's magistrate down each level of the Residence Rigale Tahreuse—all twelve of them—it was the only word that surged to mind then lips, over and over. Okay, so the man and his family had twelve levels as compared to the two of a normal family on the mountain, all furnished in an elegant palette of crimson and gold with astounding views of the lake, but everyone in town knew all that already. My astonishment sprang from something deeper. A sensation at the center of my chest, awing me but warming me at once. I couldn't describe it further, except that for the first time, I thought about the day Rune Kavill would finally be caught and we'd be able to go home to Vermont—and violently fought the pull of sad tears.

"Miss Valen?"

I jerked around. The magistrate waited, impatient scowl on his face. He stood next to the fireplace on what was called the ML level, standing for "main living." It was almost midnight. Right now, Mayor Trieste would likely be sitting at the big desk in the corner or reading documents next to the fire. His wife might be in the opposite chair or saying goodnight to their two teenage boys. They were all out of sight tonight, perhaps preparing for their very VIP visitors.

"Sorry." I blinked and sniffed, wishing the stuffy little man would stop scrutinizing every move I made. "It's been a long day. What was the question?"

The magistrate rolled his doughy eyes. "The staff shall need to know if you will be staying here each night during your duties of watching over Lady Camellia and her retinue or departing for your own residence."

"She shall remain here." Syn stepped over, eyeing the man with undisguised defensiveness. "Was there a question of that?"

The magistrate harrumped. "Of course not, Highness. My intention was merely that—"

"You would have some inside details about our operations to share with your 'friends' at the Heron tonight?"

Syn's reference to the little tavern, purported as the place where many Puras met to exchange information and gossip, turned the magistrate bright purple. I chewed the inside of my cheek to keep from giggling. Syn didn't share my mirth. "Go ahead, magistrate. Share your little tidbits. His Majesty Evrest has nothing to hide about his hopes for the future of Arcadia, instead of desires to keep her mired in the past."

Part of me longed to whoop for him. A bigger part wanted to elbow him in the chin again. I was all for calling an opponent into the open—when the timing was right. *This* timing didn't feel right.

In the end, I refrained. Perhaps Syn had a higher plan. During one of our afternoon briefings, the necessity of a scout inside the Heron had been discussed. Perhaps Syn was goading the magistrate on purpose, hoping the man would spill information in the heat of emotion.

"Prince Samsyn...I assure you—"

"I am sure you do." Syn arched his brows and jerked his head toward the stairs we'd entered from. "But you are still dismissed, magistrate."

"But there are four more levels after this. The private residence and bedrooms—"

"I will make sure Miss Valen sees them."

"But—"

"That is *all*, magistrate. Good night."

The man stormed out, accompanied by his own rapid-fire mutterings in Arcadian. As soon as he was out of earshot, I went ahead and indulged a small snicker. "Sorry." I darted a sheepish glance up at Syn's tight stare. "I couldn't help it. You turned the man into a total Oompa-Loompa."

"A what?"

"Oh, come on. You Cimarron kids at least watched movies on disc, right? *Willy Wonka* is a classic."

"Like the chocolate bars?"

"Like the *movie*. Johnny Depp? Or Gene Wilder, if you're a traditionalist."

"Who?" When I threw up both hands in defeat, he scowled and flung his head back, a masculine version of the girly hair toss.

Very masculine.

And very hot.

"Forget it."

The fight left me as soon as my gaze returned to the view...swiftly rendering me in awe. *Holy...shit.* So this was why everyone raved about floor-to-ceiling windows. The moon rose higher over the lake, a spectral smile casting silver sparkles across the water, rippled by a gentle breeze. The far shores were rimmed by mist resembling angel hair.

I shifted closer to the window, falling into silence.

Samsyn, a few feet behind me, was also quiet. Once more, my chest tightened with that strange pull. I took in the quiet majesty of the valley, the mountains its dark sentinels, and struggled to process a wild cast of feelings inside.

"It...hurts sometimes, doesn't it?" I finally whispered.

"What hurts?" His reply, roughened by lingering wrath, was as strong as those mountains.

"Looking at it," I explained. "At all of it." I gestured out the window but glanced toward him, searching for some kind of validation...knowing I'd find it. Sure enough, there it was, resting in the crystal glow of his eyes. "It reminds me of how small I am but also makes me feel huge."

Stillness. Over him and over me. But only on the outside. Inside, I was whirling. Crashing. Feeling as if I'd become the lake and the surface was a serene façade for the wet, wild tempest underneath.

His lips parted. Closed again. "I thought I was the only one who felt that way."

I fought against reaching for him. Poured my heart into my voice instead. "You're not alone, Samsyn. You know that, right? You're never alone, as long as I'm here." When he grimaced, blustering behind fake confusion, I persisted, "How are you doing with all of this, besides exhausted? And when the hell do you get to rest?"

His shoulders stiffened. "A soldier's work begins at exhaustion. You know that."

"I only know I've read that motivation poster already."

"Excuse me?"

"Don't start with proper and princely on me now, big guy. Stop evading the question." I turned fully toward him, wondering if I should dare a step closer. "How *are* you, Syn?" I refrained from moving—barely. "How are you...really?"

So much for restraint. He pivoted toward me quietly. Advanced by three measured steps, until the space between us consisted of just inches. "How are *you*?"

Time to throw him a side eye. "Uh-uh, mister. I asked first." And busying myself with that meant I didn't think of other temptations. Like fantasizing about pushing forward and pressing my face against his chest. Then fitting my arms around him, maybe sliding them beneath his sweater to the muscled warmth of his skin. To behold this breathtaking view in the arms of a magnificent man, feeling the majesty of this land pulsing through his veins, as much a part of him as the stars were of the sky. To give him all my strength in return... letting him feel what I'd already known for so long.

I loved him.

I always had. I always would.

Safer subject. Now.

I attempted a little laugh. "Well, at least I learned something new about you tonight."

His head cocked a little. His brows arched. "This should be interesting."

"You really don't like Oompa Loompas."

"Not *that* one," he snapped. "Arrogant imbezak. He was treating you like the dust on his boots. How those Pura are winning converts to their cause is a mystery to me."

I had no comeback except to kick at the floor. *Treading water. Sea of awkward.* After so many years of hanging with a boys' club, pretending I didn't have one too many X chromosomes, let alone exposing it, the potency of Syn's protectiveness was like feeling the sun after hiding in a cave. Kind of awesome. But still really weird.

"Wow," I finally muttered. "And I just thought he was doing what everyone else does."

"What everyone else does?" He pivoted, now wearing a full glare. "And what does everyone else do?"

Another laugh. Well...an attempt. Wasn't happening with his crystalline blues drilling me like that. "Writing me off as the scrawny bimbo who can't fight her way out of a pile of kindling."

At last, his mood lightened. "Is *that* so?" He chuckled.

"Yeah," I snickered back. "Gee, what a relief. The man's just Pura, not sexist."

He snorted. "Makes more sense than labeling you as scrawny."

I narrowed a mocking glare. "Is that so?"

His grin broadened. It emphasized the dark scruff along

his jaw, complemented the sexy sway of his hair...and turned him into a jaw-dropping sight as he took a steady, slow step to me.

Another.

He practically blended with his own shadow, black-clad and whisper-smooth...threatening to envelop me as he loomed over me...

Yeah. He loomed.

And ohhhh yeah, did I bask in it.

"Want to prove the point by Barbie-snapping me now?"

Shivers took over my body. My head tilted back, surely exposing the wild pulse beating at the base of my throat. "You'd have to lay me out again for that."

His eyes dilated, pitch black against piercing blue. I felt his quickening heart rate, throbbing nearly audibly, as he pushed in, closer and bigger...and hypnotizing. I shivered before his hand even touched mine, tips to tips then knuckles to knuckles...then finally, fingers meshing with slow, perfect sensuality.

Our palms met.

Our breaths hitched.

Oh God...

I wanted him.

He curved his fingers tighter...until the tips scratched my knuckles. I gasped. He swallowed. Then turned, tugging me with him.

"Wh-Where are we going?"

Syn stopped. Swung another meaningful stare back at me. Had he stepped so deeply into the shadows that his irises now seemed totally black...or was his gaze beneath full eclipse for another reason? And was the answer important?

"I told the man you would get a tour of the bedrooms, did I not?"

CHAPTER FIVE

Six months before we were forced to leave the States, Dad took me to see *Phantom of the Opera* for the sixth time. It was my favorite musical show, highlighted by the scene where the masked stranger pulled Christine through the tunnels under the Paris Opera House, to use her for his mysterious passions. The music swelled, the candles glowed, and I always dreamed of having my own dark lover leading the way down a stairwell into the sensual unknown.

My girlish brain had been an idiot.

As my grown-up senses discovered now.

Oh, there were stairs, all right. And shadows and mystery... and yes, the sexiest, darkest man, masked or not, I could have ever dreamed of.

Nobody told me the music got replaced by silence so thick, it was fog in its own right. Or that the pulsing drum track became the eerie echoes of boots against marble, soon swallowed by the hush of entering more intimate spaces. Or that the soaring notes sung by "Christine," the Phantom's timid protégé, would just turn into my rapid huffs, disgusting reminders of my nervousness with every passing moment.

Samsyn was merciful—or maybe it was just my sweaty palm—in letting me go as soon as we arrived on the next level down. This was clearly decorated for Tahreuse's first lady, with a sitting room defined by soft, rounded furniture in shades of ivory and spring green, with double doors at the far side opening to a suite of bedrooms in the same hues.

I stepped into the room. Tried not to think about Samsyn following right behind but gave up on that impossibility after two steps. He'd always made me a little nervous—aware of myself and my body—simply with a passing glimpse or an indulgent laugh, but this...

Felt very different.

Different to the point of scary.

Scary to the point of excruciating.

Excruciating to the point of...

I throbbed. And ached. And knew that if we didn't make this "tour" quick, *I'd* be the one laying *him* out—and dying of humiliation the second he gently pushed away.

The stillness pushed down on us, more weighted than before, as I hurried across the room. I battled not to watch how he matched my pace, the moonlight dappling his legs, the shadows a perfect match for his dark warrior's grace...

I suddenly stopped short. Who wouldn't, when looking at the newest surprise of this place: a section of the room that opened into a rotunda with a window seat, allowing a more breathtaking view of the lake? As I gazed, a pair of white swans floated onto Sagique's surface, gliding peacefully through the liquid moonlight.

"Wow." I was glad for a chance to embrace something like friendly chit-chat. "This place gets better and better, doesn't—"

I had to go and think of chit-chat.

When every concept of it fled my mind...as Samsyn yanked me around, into his arms—and his hard, consuming kiss.

The noble brushes of his mouth from the falls? Also as gone as the chit-chat. He swept his tongue down, demanding and passionate, raking the seam of my mouth just once before pushing all the way in, commanding me to surrender in full. As if I longed to do anything else. A tiny moan, a sigh of need, and he was all the way in. I gave him all of my tongue, letting him take it, twist it, control it with his wet, unrelenting force. Claimed him in return by delving my hand into his hair, curling fingers into the silken lengths, dragging him harder and deeper down into me.

But I couldn't call it the kiss of my dreams.

Because my dreams had never been this good.

So hot. So jolting. So conquering. *Oh, so good...*

And just as quickly, with a rush of freezing air, it was over.

"Fuck." He threw back his head, limning his bold features in stark moonlight, before dropping back down. With his hair draping our faces and his forehead pressed to mine, he sucked in fast, frantic breaths. "*Fuck.*"

I didn't know how to interpret that. Didn't know if I wanted to. The desperation in his voice was echoed by the rush of my blood, the rise of my arousal. It was torture. It was perfect.

I fought through the chaos of my senses, lifting a hand, tangling it in his silken mane, letting sound spill from my tingling lips. "*Samsyn.*"

"Starlight." His voice was just as ragged. "I...should not have done that."

"Why?" I tightened my grip. "I've wanted you to do that for six damn years."

"I know."

I paused, weighing the wisdom of what I yearned to say next—but was there a way to scramble back up a cliff once one had jumped over? We were already airborne. If the landing hurt, there was nothing to be done.

"And you've wanted it too."

His head jerked against mine. "I have. Creator help me."

"Why?" I strained the anger from my voice only because of the pain in his. "*Why*, Syn?"

He wrapped his hand around mine. Used the tension of the hold to push back by a rough step. He had the balls to keep looking at me, though his stare was still tormented. "I cannot want this. Want *you* like this."

"Damn it. I'm not a girl anymore, Samsyn!"

"I am well aware of that, astremé."

"Then...what? Is it because I'm American? An outsider?" I wanted to bite it back as soon as he glowered harder. The assumption was ridiculous, since few in Arcadia had championed King Evrest's choice of an American bride like Samsyn, but I had little else to grab at. "Then what? Why are you glaring like this is wrong? You want me. And I sure as hell want you. Since the moment you bent over my hand, on the night I arrived—"

"Damn it!" He spun, clawing back his hair again. "Brooke... *please*."

Over the cliff, all right.

My heart hit bottom in the emotional valley below, splintering harder because of the height to which he'd already made it soar. It made me whirl and then stumble, heading the only direction that felt right. But even surrounded by the full beauty of the rotunda, I shuddered as if he'd tossed me into a freezing cave.

What the hell was wrong with him? With *this*? With wanting it?

The air vibrated as he stalked over too. The power of his presence pushed into the rotunda, the massive T of his posture on the threshold reflected in the round glass.

"You are angry."

I tossed my head back on a bitter laugh. "Give the prince extra points."

He growled. "This—us—confounds me. I cannot—"

"Believe you're actually attracted to the silly little refugee?" I snapped my head back down. "The fool who's mooned after you for six damn years? I'll bet you didn't even plan on us being here that long. I'll bet you even hoped it would be a few months, and then I'd be gone."

He muttered another Arcadian oath. *Ding, ding, ding. Way to hit that target, girlfriend.*

But then he lifted his head—with pure accusation in *his* stare. "Yes, damn it. I prayed they would find Kavill swiftly and your family would leave the island." His fingers clenched the archway's edges, tips turning stark white. "But not because I could not bear you here. It was because I did not know what to do *about* you...about what you did to me."

My teeth ground. Shit. Just when I'd made up my mind about being pissed-off at his arrogant ass, he proved his head was nowhere near it. That his heart was in even more alluring places.

"I have never met anyone like you, Brooke Valen. Nobody brighter, bolder, cleverer, smarter...yes, even on that night when you first stepped off the plane, so terrified yet so full of fire. Tossing your bright, choppy hair, calling me 'big guy'—"

"You like it when I call you that."

"I like it when you call me *anything.*"

Well, shit.

My chest twisted. My eyes stung. My chin wobbled, fighting off the heavy burn of emotion—even as he swayed forward, leaning his powerful body in, making me hear *and* feel the sincerity in his words.

"No one has ever made me feel as you do, Brooke. No one has ever looked and seen what you do."

My knees were butted against the window seat. I pushed off, approaching him again. "And what do I see, Syn?"

His lips firmed. Then smiled. "The good."

My own lips pursed. "I don't...understand. How does anyone *not* see that?"

"Oh, starlight." He sighed, indulgent as if explaining playground rules to a child. I visibly prickled. He ignored me and went on. "I do not have a degree on my wall, as my brothers and sister do. I cannot quote classic novels or poetry. I do not know the Table of Elements, or even the damn Dewey decimal system. I do not rely on books to tell me facts. I learn things for myself, through instinct and attention and guts. Because of that, I am often labeled as the Cimarron good at but two things."

I kicked up a brow. "Fighting and fucking?"

He matched the expression. "You *do* catch on."

"I've also lived in your kingdom for six years. And heard the same labels. But that's all they are, Syn. Stupid labels." I waited for his gaze to return to mine—as I knew it would. Needing the connection as much as I did. "You're more than that."

"But maybe...I should not be." That took us right back to the realm of quiet, cryptic, and confusing. "Not now, Brooke," he emphasized. "Not to you."

I didn't mask how that felt like a slap. "Why?"

"Because believing anything else would be..."

"What?" I bit it out and didn't care. Until this afternoon,

I'd always just accepted his purposeful distance, assuming there was nothing I could do about it. I figured he'd mentally frozen me at the age of eighteen, and that was that. Learning that wasn't the case had brought the most exhilarating thrill—and the most maddening perplexity. "Would be *what*, Samsyn?"

He gripped the walls harder. His arms coiled, straining the sleeves of his Henley. He finally broke the tension, baring his teeth—and rasped one word through them.

"Pointless."

Forget words being slaps. This was a gut punch. I staggered back from the force, fighting nausea—and rage. All the years I'd waited for this. Ached for him. Yearned for a time when we'd be able to free our feelings into actions and passion and *connection* that was so right and so good...

Pointless?

I couldn't think straight anymore. Nor did I try to.

Three steps, pounding and furious. One grab of his elbow, hell-bent and hard-gripped. I destroyed his pose in the doorway—*yeah, you big bull, this is me, pissed at you*—before slamming him against the wall, as hard as I could. Didn't give him a chance to process his shock before kissing him with just as much violent need.

"Mmmmph!"

His lusty grunt was finished by a guttural moan, torqueing my drive higher. I was enraged and empowered, and it felt amazing. I clawed into his jaw with one hand, his scalp with the other.

At first, his lips opened, giving into a wave of shocked surrender. Then he started fighting back. Grabbed at my forearms. Finally, seized hard enough to shove me back by a

step.

I didn't wait to reclaim the space. Reached up at him, delving for the passionate kill again—until he bared his teeth once more. "Stop. *Stop*, damn you!"

"Damn *you*." I refused to surrender the lock of our glares. He was going to see me, damn it. He was going to look into the pit of my soul and see every drop of confusion and pain roiling there. "How dare you. How *dare* you do this, Samsyn. And don't you dare glower at me like that. I'm not your fucking baby sister, who's just pulled the dog's tail and blamed you for it. How the *hell* do you get off finally exposing your heart to me—the heart I've honored all these years, cherished all these years—and then call the whole thing *pointless*!" I leaned back over, jabbing a finger into his chest. "You aren't pointless. *We* aren't pointless!"

He let go of me—to drive both his fists down against the wall. The rotunda's windows visibly shook. I welcomed the impact. Even wished he'd do it again. Maybe then my hurt and rage would get their perfect expression.

The corners of his eyes tightened. Again he parted his lips, exposing the feral gnash of his teeth. "My heart," he echoed from between them. "You think this is me showing my pretty little *heart*?" Suddenly he was in motion, pushing past me, pacing in front of the window seat. A terrible sound vibrated through him, a snarl and moan mixed. "You cannot have my damn heart, Brooke. No one can. I am the commander of all the warriors of Arcadia. I am not allowed to have a fucking heart!" He splayed his hands up again, this time stamping their fury into the main window pane over the seat. "You have honored nothing. Cherished...nothing."

It wasn't like another slap. Or a punch. But God, there was

pain. So much of it, in so many torturous new ways, tearing me deeper than ever before. From the midst of it I reached out, grabbing at the only comfort I knew would work.

Him.

It didn't make sense. I didn't want it to. I only knew that imagining a world without him—*my* world without him—was like an alcoholic pondering a life of drinking water. He might be the poison that killed me, but one last minute with him was better than years without him.

I greedily gathered up his shirt, using my crawling fingers to drag him back over. He let out that sound again, though the groan of it took precedence now, as I forced him to face me. I breathed him in, all the leather and cinder and wind of him, and burrowed right into him...

Before I simply climbed him.

Yeah, right up him. I whimpered as I went, becoming his needing, wanting, ninja-bitch in heat, letting him grip me as easily as he would a doll. His breath was hot on top of my head...then the side of my neck, the space over my mouth...

Before he claimed me there again. Openly. Wantonly. Smashing his tongue against mine in time to what his hands did to my ass, sliding the core of my body tighter against the ridge of his...

Oh God, he was big.

And hot.

And perfect.

In less than a minute, my sex was soaked. I knew it with certainty as I writhed my pulsing cleft against his growing length, riding his erection as thoroughly as he'd allow. His strength banded me. Guided me. Controlled me.

I didn't ever want him to stop.

I didn't ever want this to end.

When our mouths broke apart, he growled into my neck. The sound turned my blood to fire. The harsh heat in his stare flared along my skin, once more zapping the sensitive tissues between my thighs...especially as he widened his stance, compelling my gaze downward.

Getting a chance to look at him...

there.

Even in the shadows, he was huge. Perfect, bulging man... perfect, bulging erection. I swore it grew bigger as I watched, pushing at his crotch, speaking his meaning to me with blazing, blatant beauty.

A meaning as undeniable as my own breath.

Or the words in my heart...as I pressed a hand over his.

"If this is nothing, what's the harm in giving it to me for a night?"

CHAPTER SIX

I think he actually considered answering me. As if he had that choice. As if either of us did.

I showed him that truth, deliberately and passionately, slanting my mouth to crush the truth into him with every last inch of my lips. Sometimes, oxen had to be dragged to water.

I was half a breath away—only to be forcibly jerked back. His hand, jammed into the ends of my hair against my nape, stopped me like a pull cord on a doll. I didn't resist. The nip of pain was...exhilarating. The force of his strength, radiating across my scalp...even better.

My breath clutched. My heart pumped to accommodate it, thumping between my breasts, which sharpened, tingled, pulsed...so damn aware of how Syn stared at me now. Like he'd never looked at me before. His eyes were a beast's, sharp and all-seeing, not letting me move or breathe without his alert assessment.

His lips parted again.

To release a burst of warm air down my neck.

Before plunging his lips against it.

Then his tongue, wet and thirsty. Then his teeth, hot and hungry. Then his lips again, sucking in, abrading my skin, gnashing over my carotid, my ear, my jaw...back to my lips, where he took over the kiss I'd begun, turning it completely into his own.

He shoved me open, pushing his mouth into mine and

forcing my legs tighter around him. The extra contact of our bodies was significant—and intense. Feelings, primal but foreign, tore in. My skin sizzled. My body shuddered. I clung to his neck, moaning from the magnificence of him straining... hardening...*everywhere.*

"By the Creator." He rasped it between harsh breaths. His face lifted, revealing the conflict across his beautiful features. "I have forced myself not to think of you like this. Fought it so deeply, over and over again..."

"And I've thought of nothing else."

His groan was so deep, it vibrated his body and mine. I gripped him tighter, a well-timed action with his whoosh of motion, lowering me to the window seat. He followed me down, securing my legs around him as he dropped to his knees. Through every motion, his muscles flexed with sensual economy, as if he'd done this a thousand times before. It made me wonder how many times he *had* done this before—but that right wasn't mine. I'd asked him only for this, only for now. Those were the terms I'd accepted, and I had to live with them...

No matter what impression I got otherwise, once our gazes met again.

Holy hell.

I felt like the Rosetta Stone, the Regent diamond, and a gold double eagle melted in one revered piece. The feeling intensified as he dipped his stare, roaming slowly over me. His gaze was hypnotic blue glass. His nostrils flared slowly. His jaw visibly clenched. His hands, now free, skated over my thighs, glided in at my waist, and then explored up and over my navy nylon workout shirt. Higher. *Higher*...

His palms cupped my breasts, possessive and determined. I gasped from the heat, immediate and hot.

"Fuck." He pinched in, feeling me getting erect even through my sports bra. "They are...as exquisite as I imagined."

I circled my hands back, pushing at the seat cushion, arching higher for him. "More." My throat clutched as he cocked both brows. I wondered if his other lovers had openly demanded things from him. The thought stabbed me with insecurity, making me add a whispered, "Please. More, Samsyn. *Please.*"

Maybe the begging was a good idea. It seemed to unhinge something inside him, turning his growl bright and fierce, his stare raw and feral. And his touch... Ohhh, that was the best part of all. He turned bold—and brutal. I gasped from the stabs of erotic pain, which made the world fall away even more. Gone were all the logistics, lists, action plans, and other stresses from the day. Our world was only the lake's reflected waves, the moon's watchful glow, and the joy of discovering each other in this stolen, perfect bubble.

He pinched my breasts harder.

I cried out louder.

"Yes!" Arousal drenched my bloodstream. My muscles went to liquid. I was on fire...everywhere. How many times had I watched those hands take down a sparring partner, masterfully handle a sword, or even tie his damn shoes, only to imagine them on my body like this? Exactly like this. Huge. Powerful. Arousing. Commanding.

Now...against my skin too.

In seconds, his fingers skated beneath my top and then raked my waist and rib cage. He pushed harder, dragging the material upward, before dictating, "Get this off. Your bra too. I will have you bare for me, woman. Now."

I was grateful for my years of familiarity with workout

clothes. In a minimum of motions, I'd complied with his bidding. He stripped to the same degree too. We tossed aside our shirts together, not caring where they went. Stares cemented to each other. Breaths rasping the air. Chests rising and falling, mine so pale and translucent, his so burnished and broad.

"By the fucking Creator." His fingers scraped up my back—as he tilted my torso up. "You are perfect." He dipped his head, licking along my flesh before closing teeth around the bud atop my right breast. *Agony. Ecstasy. Sinful, beautiful sensation.* My breath escaped on a strangle. My nipple hardened like a diamond, coaxed to a more exquisite point by his damnably talented tongue. I dove a hand into his hair, twisting the thick strands, giving in to more pleas...silent this time.

Don't stop. Oh, please don't stop.

By the time he moved to the other breast, electric ribbons of heat tangled through my body, only to dissolve in the liquid fire between my legs. Air escaped me in irregular shots. My shudders became full shivers, arousal pelting me like raindrops in a growing storm. I splayed my other hand to his back, astounded by the ropes of muscle beneath my fingers. I'd come into contact with a lot of fighters' bodies over the last three years. None of them felt like this. Samsyn Cimarron's body belonged in another time, an era in which men were so stunning, people believed in things like giants and satyrs and demigods. The ripples tautened as he worked his lips over my flesh. He surged over me, pushing back until my head pressed against the glass...and my legs gripped him tighter.

"You...make me perfect," I whispered. "And alive. And"—I shrieked a little as he bit the side of my breast—"hot. Oh...so hot...Sams..."

He took the last of it from me with the new seal of his lips. Raised up in order to plunge his tongue vertically, shifting one of his hands to grab my hair and yank my head back. His other hand stroked up from my breast, stretched across my neck, and then braced my jaw, positioning me to keep taking his raw, carnal possession.

"Sweet starlight." Half his face was now masked by shadow. Only his eyes remained brilliant, irises like the night beams on the lake, telling me how high his own desire had risen. "You make me hot too." He teethed my lips and chin. "You burn everything away. You make it all...clean."

I almost gave in to a laugh. The last thing I wanted to be right now, especially with him, was clean. But the scorched honesty of his voice spoke to something deep within. He wasn't talking about literal cleanliness. It was a stain inside him, visible even the night we first met, and had remained a shadow on his soul to this day. It faded when he was around me, which always eased my ache about it, but the blemish never quite went away.

What would it take to make it go away?

I moved my hands up. Framed the sides of his face. His skin was hot, even through the thick stubble. "But not all of it," I rasped, tracing his lips with a thumb. "Let me in, Syn. Let me burn it *all* away."

He went utterly still. Only for a moment. That was all it took to see straight through to the truth I'd just struck...

Before he shoved it all away.

Jammed it down the same way he brought his hands down over mine. Swept it back, far into his darkness, as he swung my arms over my head. Deeper still, as he pinned my wrists to the window. Weighed it down like the cement block he turned himself into, pushing down on me. I mewled, reveling in his masculine bulk. Wanting it. Spreading wider as he twisted in, fitting his body harder against mine.

My cry exploded louder. I didn't care if the villagers in Noir, on the lake's opposite shore, heard me. His erection pounded against every needy part of me, rousing my hottest desire. Every inch of my intimate channel was soaked. If the dark spot in my workout pants wasn't enough evidence, my pointed nipples and puckered areolas definitely were.

He slanted over me again, shoulders curving in. Claimed my lips once more, twining breath and teeth with lust and heat. His lower body moved with mounting friction. My tunnel clenched even tighter for him. Ached for the ultimate fulfillment I needed from him. I'd never been with anyone else like this—and about half the guys at the Center had tried—knowing now that this was what I'd saved myself for. *Who* I'd saved myself for.

"Astremé." His grate vibrated against my lips.

"*Samsyn.*"

"You want it to burn?"

"Yes. God, *yes.*"

A choppy breath tumbled from him. "But if I burn you... the way I long to..."

"The way you need to." I jerked up my face, spearing him with my stare. "The way *I* need you to." Curled my fingertips against his hold, trying to score him with my nails—what there was of them. I was a child of the gym and the armory, not the salon and spa. "Damn it, Syn. If this night is all we get—all *I* get—"

He cut me off with another kiss...but not before I watched my charge impact him like a mortar shell, detonating his resistance. *Stubborn, beautiful bull.*

Beautiful was just the start.

Watching his desire take over his nobility was like witnessing a wave form on the ocean. The visceral knowledge that deeper forces were at work. The awe of seeing them grow, expand, surge free. The mix of dread and exhilaration, acknowledging their danger—and acquiescing to it.

He pulled up though kept me tethered with his gaze. Whatever he saw in my eyes changed the tone of his, the cyan turning almost violet as his pupils flared. His lips worked against each other, as if he were suddenly starving. He slipped his hand free from my wrists, though his face conveyed the order not to move my hands. As if I'd even contemplate it. Even wanted to cut one moment of this magic short. Every second had to count...

He lowered his hands to my hips. Pushed back far enough to drag away my pants, both legs at once. When they were at my knees, he rose and stepped aside, pulling the fabric down the rest of the way.

He sucked a breath in.

I gasped one out.

He swung my legs over, stretching me along the window seat. Lowered his body the same way, tangling our legs as he twisted my hair and pushed his tongue into my mouth. We sucked at each other, hungry and fervent. We clutched at each other, urgent and lusting. Everywhere I touched, he undulated and coiled. His skin was hot though exploded in shivers wherever my fingers glided. Though I'd just marveled at his power, he made me feel like an equal force, every contact of our skin making him swallow and clench.

"Brooke." He sent tingles down my neck with the feverish

rasp. "By the fucking Creator, Brooke..."

I clawed the back of his head, unwilling to let him up now. His stubble abraded my collarbone. His mouth suckled the dip just above it. "Tell me." It pitched into a whimpering plea; once more I didn't care. Was damn near grateful for the sound, vocalizing how deeply I craved him. "Say it, Samsyn. Tell me... please."

"I want this. I want *you*. Fuck...I shall damn near burst from it."

"Not until you're buried inside me." I was ready with a smile when he yanked his head up, stabbing a stunned stare in reaction. "Yes, that's what I want too. What I'm bursting with too." I caressed my hand along his scalp, tugging his hair in rhythmic little yanks. "I'm on birth control." His widened eyes caused my subtle laugh. "A lot of female athletes are. Lots of exercise messes with hormones."

He grunted, clearly disconcerted about not knowing that. He didn't hang on to the awkwardness for long, though. My nudity was certainly a helpful distraction. I smiled as he braced his weight on one hand and then slid the other down my body. His eyes followed the path of his touch, watchful...worshipful.

It astonished me.

Thrilled me.

Overjoyed me. Yes. *So much joy...*

I'd always thought if this moment ever came, I'd wilt beneath his first scrutiny. My figure was built for utility, not sexuality. But every inch of me felt very sexual now. And beautiful. A woman come to life, awakened and invigorated by his long, exploratory strokes and adoring little squeezes. Syn didn't miss an iota of my reaction, taking in all my nuances before he quietly spoke again.

"But I am...your first?"

He wanted to make it a statement instead of a question. I could see that—but was damn grateful he hadn't. I needed to answer on my own. "I want you to be."

His eyes squeezed shut. His lips compressed. But he nodded, solemn and committed, bringing on the awkwardness anyway.

"Good God, Syn," I snapped. "It's my virginity, not the Holy Grail."

He cocked a brow. "Want to wager which I treasure more?"

Incredible man. Aggravating bastard. "I know, I know. You don't want to hurt me."

"Oh, I *will* hurt you."

I swallowed. Inexplicably turned on. "Then hurt me."

"*Unnnhh.*"

The eruption wasn't his choice. I pulled it from him by reaching down and cupping him...*there*.

My sigh joined his grunt. Both were sharp with amazement.

Fine. So I'd never done anything like this before. But limited experience didn't equate stunted knowledge. He was a magnificent man...everywhere. His erection pulsed beneath my fingers, stretching them apart as I watched. I gawked while exploring him more, roaming every inch of his pulsing groin. The rough texture of his cargo pants only added to how distinctly masculine he felt, even to a girl who practically lived full-time in a man's world.

I reached in farther.

Syn groaned.

Softly squeezed the swells between his thighs.

Syn swore.

Dragged my hand back up his length, savoring every hard, hot inch of the journey.

Syn held his breath. Shuddered hard.

It was heady, having this power over him. A little scary—like walking a dragon on a leash.

Until the dragon snapped the chain. And decided to breathe fire.

Syn caught my wrist. Steely grip. Clamped tight. It ordered my gaze back up to his. His face, ruthless and gorgeous, consumed my vision...made it impossible to focus on anything else, even the panorama outside the window. His temples pulsed. His lips flattened. His stare turned to blue flames...

As he jammed my hand beneath his waistband.

Held it there, forcing me to grip his heat solely through his briefs. "This what you need, astremé?"

My palm met wet warmth. Power rushed me all over again. The moisture spread along the cotton, making it cling to his engorged flesh, filling me with a primal sense of victory already.

"Yeah," I rasped, massaging him steadily. Fascination stirred into my desire. I was no stranger to male anatomy—one couldn't defeat something they didn't know—but this was an entirely new lesson. This was about Samsyn—and everything I'd so deeply craved to know about him for six years. Perhaps longer. If Destiny were a thing, I was certain it applied to us. He had to be too. Had to feel it as I cradled the essence of his body in my hand and the center of his soul in my stare. "Yeah, big guy," I emphasized. "This is exactly what I need."

A smile flickered across his face. I didn't complain when lusty urgency replaced it, matching his harsh jerks at his fly. He yanked the zipper down, flayed the panels back, and shoved his underwear free.

His naked flesh burst out.

I gasped in new wonderment.

Silken skin. Proud pillar. More moisture dripping from the tip, sliding between my fingers as I stroked him to full excitement.

"By the Creator." I used the expression to honor him, for honored is what I felt. And awed. And so, *so* aroused. "*Samsyn.*" I lifted a smile at his searching stare. "You're beautiful."

He lowered to one elbow again. His hair fanned my face as he tenderly took my lips. "And you are beyond anything my dreams could create."

"You—you've dreamed about me?"

Another smile tempted his sensual lips. "I plead the fifth."

"That only works on *my* turf, Arcadian."

"I thought everything was your turf, starlight."

"Ahhh." I managed a coy smirk. Barely. Thoughts, much less words, were nearly impossible to form with his perfect penis filling my hand. "Then you've fallen for my grand deception too."

"Is that it?" He shuddered out a breath as I added light skims of my nails to the exploration. "Very...impressive."

"Yeah, well. I'm good at that deception stuff."

"No." His retort was sudden—and snarled. "You are *not.*" Kissed me hard in emphasis. "And thank fuck for it."

Questions. About a thousand. Flying at my brain like archers' arrows in an old movie, launched at the castle stronghold all at once. With vehemence matching his, I snipped the image short. He hadn't shared his mysteries with me in six damn years; the possibility of it happening now—

especially now—was as likely as the moon turning to cheese. And selfishly speaking, his desire was much more fun than his darkness.

Oh, God. So much more.

Yeah...especially now.

He transformed again as I shifted my hold, dipping to cup the dense sack at his base. Holy *hell.* The man simply lifted a slow smile as I explored the...goods. It was as if the Creator knew, in crafting a man the size of a sequoia, he'd need a spirit to match. A warrior's drive...and a sex fiend's desires.

And a wicked, bacchanalian body to implement it with.

Especially the cock I never wanted to let go.

I told him so with a needy sigh. Showed him so by scraping back up his length, purposely tracing the thick veins, now throbbing and so damn hot. Finally, I slicked over his broad crown, shiny and taut and ready.

"I think...you're right," I told him between one pant and the next.

"About...what?"

"Deception isn't my thing." As I drove my gaze up into his, I closed my palm over the tip of his erection. "Can you tell what I'm thinking now?"

At first, he only moaned. Then growled. Then moaned again before hitching up his mouth in an expression I *had* seen before. He used the smirk on sparring partners all the time— during the moment he was done playing around and would officially start kicking their ass.

"You are thinking...that you would greatly like to be fucked."

"S-S-See?" One word, spilled in three shaky sighs, due to his suckling pressure down my neck. "I c-can't hide a th-thing from you, Cimarron."

He dipped into the valley between my breasts. Bit into the side of one erect peak and then the other. "Just the way I like it, Valen."

Cheeky? Yes. But it made me as gooey as a greeting card ad. Bantering had always been a part of us, one of many threads woven into the fabric of what we were: a tapestry that had, in so many ways, simply just *been*, from that first handclasp on the runway together. Over the years, the tapestry waited in the shadows of time, letting us light it up as we were ready. Sometimes we'd discover huge chunks of it together. Sometimes the progress was an inch-by-inch process.

Tonight qualified as a giant, freaking swath.

A beautiful, breathtaking vista.

Nothing verified that like the splendor of the man who rose back over me.

He aligned his face just inches over mine. His azure eyes impaled me. His strong blade of a nose flared. His tongue slipped out, wetting the sensual angles of his mouth...

As he fitted the crown of his cock against the cushions of my sex.

My lungs stopped. My muscles tensed.

Syn waited. Gave me a little smile. It was a unique expression from him, with a hint of teeth showing past the strained set of his lips. Unique...and sexy. Where'd he come up with that? Was that his special "deflower the virgin" look? And did I want to know how many other women on Arcadia had seen it before me?

"Sssshh, astremé."

"What?" I frowned. "I didn't say—"

"You did not have to." He brushed hair from my forehead

before kissing it. "Quiet the thoughts. Let in the feelings."

I huffed into the dent between the slabs of his chest. "I'm letting in plenty of— *ohhh!*"

A tiny throb as he slid in a little more.

So *that* was what he meant by feelings.

Then came the giddiness as he took my lips once more. And the shock as his body slid deeper into me. Stretched me. Filled me.

In places I never knew existed.

The tissues that tore. The walls that were toppled. The depths that were unlocked.

"Ohhhh...shit!"

"Brooke. Astremé. Breathe." They were commands but somehow pleas as well. The anomaly continued in his kiss, a mix of gentleness and violence that made my head spin, my body soften.

The moment it did, he slid deeper in.

I screamed into his mouth.

He took it and kept kissing me back.

"Perfect," he finally praised. "You are so fucking perfect."

He penetrated me more.

But now...did more.

New sensations began to hit. The girth of his cock stimulated my entrance in ways I'd never known...tingled through my sex as I'd never experienced...zapping the very depths of my clit. As he surged in farther, my body clenched and pulsed, compelling me to thrust upward, fully meeting every one of his rolling, pounding lunges.

I wrapped a leg around his waist. The other. Gripped his neck, needing to watch as his dark desire took over. Needing to see him succumb to it, shuddering harder against me, fucking deeper into me.

Deeper...

Yes, it still hurt—but the pain also brought waves of profound pleasure. They flooded my body, hijacked my mind. I let Samsyn see all of it too. Let him behold every drop of new awareness he gave me...the complete awe he inspired. His body took my breath away. His craving made my belly giddy. And all of his dark, prowling lust made me feel like a she-cat hunted by her mate...the only creature who could slake his hot, pounding desires.

His darkness...

Making everything so much better.

His jaw clenched to the texture of granite. He raked both hands up my thighs, curled them beneath my ass, and gripped the cheeks hard. "Let me *in*, Brooke."

I frowned. But wasn't he already—

"Oh, my *God!*"

He wasn't. But with his harder hold on my backside, he spread my thighs wider...

And then drove his shaft all the way in.

"Shit!" I screamed.

"*Shit*," Syn snarled. Held himself there, consuming my channel with his cock for long, pulsing moments. I battled to remember his coaching and breathe through the tension. Knew I needed to relax and let my body expand for him. But I didn't feel expanded. I felt...

"Tight." His rasp turned my torment into his prayer— of gratitude. "So tight. So good." It warmed through my hair as he drew back from my tunnel, hovered for a moment, and then plunged back in with a jagged growl. I could do nothing but accept it. My legs were helpless in his hold. My body was pinned beneath his. I fought to summon rage about it but couldn't. I'd wanted this. Still wanted it. Had yearned for so long to know the full force of Samsyn's lust, be the complete object of his warrior's passion, take the full brunt of passion from his burnished, perfect body. *Wishes granted.* He took me, hard and heavily. Fucked me with driving, amazing force. Nothing about his desire was negotiable, injected into my bloodstream through his consuming kisses, fused to my desire with every hard, full punch of his cock.

He was so damn beautiful.

He spread a wide smile, making me realize I'd voiced that aloud. "I am only beautiful because of what I reflect back at you." He ducked in, capturing my mouth beneath his and twisting my tongue along his. When done, he only lifted an inch away. He stayed there, consuming my personal space, letting me smell the arousal on his skin, view the desire in his eyes.

"Samsyn," I whispered. "Oh...Samsyn." Suddenly, the dreamy lilt in my voice changed. Pitched upward...into a tantalized sigh. "S-Samsyn?"

His expression changed too. There'd been a wicked method to his madness of the fresh position. As our bodies collided, his groin now stimulated my spread pussy—directly. The tender tissues responded at once, nearly crossing my eyes with arousal. My jaw dropped open—on a startled scream.

"Samsyn!"

His gaze gleamed with satisfaction. "Is *that* what you need too, my starlight?"

Underestimation of the whole freaking year. I trembled. Throbbed. Waited. *Wanted.* Was like a bird riding a scirocco gust, unsure whether I'd fly or fall, and he was the damn pressure front, controlling it all with every incredible roll of his hips. Up. Down. Higher. Lower.

Higher...

Ohhhh yes...higher.

"Don't...stop."

Why did the man answer my gasp with a chuckle? I was serious, damn it!

"I have no intention of going anywhere, astremé."

Better. He was almost forgiven for the chuckle.

He was *really* forgiven as soon as he swung one leg out in order to brace a foot to the floor. The extra traction enabled him to shuttle deeper into me...hitting more and more of my swollen, throbbing clit...all but screaming for its ultimate release...

"Samsyn!"

"Starlight." His body reflected the strain in his voice, muscles twisting against each other. He was stark and sweaty and perfect. "Fuck." His head fell. His cock swelled against my walls. "*Fuck*, this is good."

Another understatement. By miles. This wasn't "good." This was magic. Spontaneous lightning. Gravity reversed. Energy turned to connection. Two bodies as one. Two hearts beating the same.

I dropped my hand to the center of his chest, over the thunder proving my point. That brought his head back up. Our gazes twisted...and fused.

"Don't be gentle."

Twin furrows dug in between his brows. "You are so small. I do not want to hurt—"

"Damn it, Syn." I slid my other hand to his taut ass, scoring him as deeply as I could. "Hurt me!" Wet heat sprang behind my eyes. "Make me...remember you."

Another barrier in him fell. I watched the animal in him prowl right over it, crushing the last tether on his passion. Finally, a response growled from him.

"Yes."

Yes.

It echoed from deep inside, though I couldn't form any words past the shriek he tore free. Then the next. Then the moans, harsh and guttural, as he plunged his body into mine, from head to root on every thrust, claiming my passage with his ruthless force—and taking me with him. Higher...higher. Hotter...hotter. My thighs quivered and clenched. My clit bloomed and begged. My mind swirled and soared.

So close...

I knew what an orgasm was, of course. I didn't have cute toys like the other girls, but my imagination was keen and my fingers were strong. But no climax I'd ever given myself was like this, amped by the nerves up and down my tunnel, lighting me up from the inside out. With every lunge of Syn's sex, they flared brighter, *brighter*—until the circuits were blown apart.

I ignited.

Then shattered.

"Samsyn! Yes!"

He pummeled harder, bringing wave after wave of pleasure, until I wasn't conscious of the room, the moon, the windows, my mind. Everything was the pulse of my pussy, the heat of his cock...and the burst, even hotter, that erupted from him. He roared with the force of it, primal and pure in his tragedy, ecstasy, completion.

"Damn it." He panted it against my neck, continuing to pound me like a locomotive. "Damn it...take it...all of me...yes..."

I scored my nails back up, trailing them along his spine, as his strokes finally began to slow. But at the moment I thought he'd pull free, he curled his lips against my ear and directed, "Hang on, astremé."

I obeyed. Was glad I did. I was suddenly airborne, lifted from the window seat with his sex still inside me and then carried into one of the larger bedrooms. Somewhere between the two points, he kicked off his pants completely, making him naked as me when turning to sit on the bed. Without any pause, he lay completely back with me on top of him.

I didn't let go.

Neither did he.

He grabbed the comforter, folding it around us.

"Well," I murmured. "You *are* full of hidden talents."

Normally, that would've earned me a one-liner in return. I wasn't surprised when none came. Still wasn't when leaning up a little, to find myself inches above his solemn stare. With quiet strokes, he brushed my hair off my face.

"How are you?" he whispered. "Was that...good for you?"

I was *so* tempted to giggle. I'd been exposed to modern culture in very small bits over the last six years but was aware of the trite pillow talk line. Samsyn had to have been too, though nothing on his face hinted at anything besides sincerity—and concern. As if he truly worried whether he'd delivered the goods.

"Syn," I chastised. "Really?" I shifted a little as his scowl deepened. "Okay, *your* turn for honesty. Have you ever had any complaints?"

His brows jerked. "Do you really want to talk about my previous...experiences?"

Now I did laugh. "The question was rhetorical."

"And you are breathtaking."

A blush took over my face as he thumbed more hair off my sweat-dampened cheek. "And *you* call *me* the hopeless subject changer?"

"The subject never changed for me." His hands glided down my neck. Spread over my collarbones. Trailed back in, between my breasts. "Look at that. You blush all the way to your nipples."

The twin subjects of his statement became the trembling victims of his gentle pinches, hardening against the broad plane of his chest. I lifted a little, giving him better access and letting him watch exactly what that did to my skin, my breaths...my self-control.

"Does this answer your question?" I managed to sigh.

His teeth sneaked out over his lower lip as he brushed my tips with his thumbs, on his way to framing my waist in his huge, dominant grip. "And what...question would that be?"

I lifted a hand to bat his chest, but it fell to his skin instead, helpless, as he lifted me up, holding my intimate lips just at the tip of his newly pulsing penis. "The one about it being good."

He dug his hold in tighter. Stared up at me with those eyes, blue as a panther sneaking up on its prey.

"Oh, it was good."

I tugged at my own bottom lip now, raising up to brace my grip on his biceps. "Damn straight it was."

"Now it shall be better than good."

I tried to grin. "If you say so, Your Highness."

He bared his teeth. Released a hiss as he let me lower a little more. His hips jerked. His cock thrummed. "I say so."

Our gazes twined again. I paused, just for one moment, to memorize everything just as it was. The power I felt, rising up over him, his massive body flattened beneath mine. But the helplessness too, feeling the decree beneath his grip, the control of everything my sex did to his. The balance of it. The rightness of it.

The rightness of him.

I needed it all again. My blood trumpeted with it. My lungs throbbed, grasping at it. My body clenched, craving it.

"Ride me, Brooke."

I lowered a gaze, beseeching. "Show me how?"

And he did. With steady, surging strokes and mounting, magnificent passion...until we groaned together again, climaxing in white-hot need, before collapsing in each other's arms, sated, sweaty, exhausted, entangled...

Connected.

If only for a few more perfect hours.

CHAPTER SEVEN

"Did you even bother with a fucking condom?"

I'd had better wakeup calls. Ones that were a lot less confusing, for sure. Certainly ones that didn't jerk me from a dead slumber into bolting straight up, gasping at my bare-ass body, and then covering it with a comforter as unfamiliar to me as a designer ball gown. Not that the cover couldn't be Maria Von Trapp-ed into such a thing. I curled curious fingers into the mint-green satin covering my breasts, wondering what aliens had absconded with me in the middle of the night and dumped me into this strange bed.

That was when I shifted my legs.

Sore on the inside.

Sticky on the outside.

Ohhhh, hell.

Samsyn. *Samsyn.*

The moonlight...and his kisses. The shadows...and his touch. The window seat...and his passion.

And then in here...for even more.

As if summoned by my memories, the man himself growled. The sound filled the sitting room, though was distinctly different than the passionate rumble he'd branded into me last night. Razors of anger sliced it now.

"For Creator's sake. Keep your voice down!"

"Right. Sorry, *arkami.*" The snorting punctuation instantly gave Jagger away. Silently, I jerked the covers higher. Holy shit. *Jagger.* How had he gotten in? What had he seen? "My bad," he snapped, "for thinking that an entrance and egress recon, requested by *you*, would take me through an empty mansion. Should I have texted first, man? Made certain you were finished with the morning fuck before I barged in? Let Brooke do her hair, perhaps? Unhook her hand from around your dick?"

Heat drenched my face. From rage or shame, I couldn't tell. Did it matter?

Two stomps from the other room, shaking the walls as only Syn could, were oddly soothing.

"Be careful where you tread, man." His snarl, just as violent, was like another swipe of aloe on my burn.

"Because *you* were?" Jagger retorted.

"It is none of your business, Jag."

"It is *all* of my business." Another set of raging steps, faster than Syn's but just as virulent. "You specifically asked for her on the tactical team you bade me to assemble for this—the team you put *me* in charge of. It is my job to be clear about the preparedness, physical and mental, of every member of that team. *You* are not good for her readiness on either of those levels. On *any* damn level."

The whoosh of Samsyn's spin made the leaves flutter on the potted palms inside the bedroom's door. "I am your *prince!*"

"Then haul out the guillotine and chop my fucking head off." Jag's clenched emphasis was so clear, I could practically see his locked teeth through the wall. But he finished with a resigned sigh. "You *are* my prince—but you are also my friend. Right or wrong, that designation bears priority to me." There was a rustle, denoting he'd sat or leaned somewhere. "We have known each other for a long time, Syn. I know all the burdens you bear, the old *and* the new."

I swallowed heavily. Sensed Samsyn doing the same. "Yes," he finally grated. "You do."

"None of it has been easy for you. Even as second to the throne, the weight on your shoulders is immense. It is not a crime not to wish yourself burdened with the care of a regular woman as well."

Knotted stomach. Fisting hands. And I had no idea why. Every word Jag spoke was true. I'd known it all before now— but hearing it spoken was like peeling the scab on a wound. It hurt. For stupid reasons.

"Who the hell said I wanted a regular woman?"

Let the bleeding begin.

"Not *who*," Jagger clarified. "*What*." He exhaled with audible heaviness. "The heart of the girl in that bed." A stretch of uncomfortable silence. Another. I silently yearned—and dreaded—for Samsyn to say something. He didn't. "She is half in love with you, Syn. You are probably the only person who doesn't see it. Or perhaps does not want to see it?"

My breath stuck in my throat like a ball of Asuman porridge. Spread an ache through me, tight and torturous, as Samsyn's reply took forever to come.

When it did...

"Fuck."

I buried my face into the thick satin, muffling my broken sob.

"So how do you wish to handle this?"

Jagger's question, like he addressed some kind of tactical detail, jerked my self-pity to an end. My heartache turned to rage—enough of it to swing out of bed, dragging the sheet along. I jabbed it around me, covering enough to be decent. The rest of Jag's respect, I'd have to earn on my own—and damn well planned on doing so.

I would *not* be a "this" to be "handled." Nor the pathetic "girl in the bed." And no, I wasn't even the desperate thing who'd taken up fight training merely as a way of gaining Samsyn Cimarron's attention. Not anymore.

Never again.

My steps lengthened. Strengthened.

In a way, perhaps many, I had to thank Jagger for this. The epiphany might have never hit without him barging on us. But hearing the pity in his voice as he spoke of me, like I was some groupie taking up guitar just because it was what my idol played, flared a giant match inside. In the flickering shadows behind me was the desperate girl I'd once been. In the blazing light in front of me was the woman I now would be.

A woman who sure as hell didn't need Samsyn Cimarron's validation anymore. Or Jagger Foxx's, for that matter.

Easier said than done.

Especially when stepping into a sun-drenched room, dressed in nothing but a sheet, to face the warrior who'd drilled me on the training mat for the last three years—and the one who'd drilled me in the rotunda last night.

"Mr. Foxx," I intoned. "And Your Highness. Good morning."

"*Bon sabah.*" They mumbled it in unison, discomfort stamped on their faces. Made it a hell of a lot easier to disguise the wince on mine while crossing back over to the rotunda. The center glass pane was still smeared with handprints: mine and Samsyn's. Half the seat cushion flopped to the floor—practically pointing the way to my discarded clothes.

I didn't look back, despite the weight of their stares on my back, as I stooped and gathered my bra and top in one hand, panties and pants in the other. Without a word, I turned and paced back into the bedroom.

Closed the door slowly, letting its click resound through the stillness on my side—and theirs.

Sat back down on the bed.

And let a million tremors take over.

Shit. *Shit.*

So sometimes my temper overcommitted before my body could catch up. Or my heart. The heart that'd been wrenched in a thousand directions just from being in the same room again with Syn. That knew, in its deepest fibers and darkest corners, it had been just as tense for him too.

Until my memory backtracked by five more minutes. Made me cringe all over again at the words he'd spat. *Who the hell said I wanted a regular woman?*

And who the hell gave me the right to indulge one *moment's* worth of being hurt by that? Hadn't we let ourselves give in to last night because of *that* tacit agreement? That by freeing ourselves from redefining things because of sex, we could just give in to desire? That freedom was what made everything so damn amazing?

"Amazing." By voicing it, I thought to dilute its power. A match was always strongest at first flare.

Unless it had kindling to catch.

Kindling...like the way Syn's kisses had flooded my soul. Like the way his touch had launched my arousal to the stars. Like the way his body had consumed me until I forgot what existence was without it.

Just all that.

Just the fact that I loved him now more than ever.

And because of that...had to let him go.

I looked down at my hand. Forced it to uncurl from the pillow into which it had coiled. Fiercely pushed up, regaining my footing.

"Knock it off. Get your shit together, Valen."

I dropped the sheet. Picked up my panties.

Had only gotten them over my ankles—when Syn walked in.

CHAPTER EIGHT

Inside a moment, the air crackled once more. Sparked to life, breath-stealing and heart-stopping, by the attraction I could no longer hide...by the desire he couldn't cloak in return. The electricity we'd denied for six damn years...and now would be fighting for the rest of our lives. Before now, it had always been the erasable elephant in the room, explained away as "leftover energy" from the unique circumstances of our first meeting. Now, we couldn't deny what that touch had really been.

Attraction.

Desire.

Destiny.

And like idiots, we'd thrown laser beams at that star, in the form of mind-altering sex. Thinking we'd kill it. Instead, turning it supernova.

And blinding ourselves in the doing.

Blinded. Yes. It was as good an excuse as any for why I stood there with my underwear at my ankles, my heart in my throat, and my gaze unable to tear from him, shirtless and perfect, as he sucked in a long but strict breath. Let it out with equal brutality—before turning to the en suite vanity to swipe a cloth beneath the faucet.

He closed the gap between us with silent, staunch steps. "Sit," he directed, barely giving it volume.

"Samsyn—"

His head tilted, cutting me short. With a short fume, I

obeyed. My face burned again as he wiped my inner thighs, his enormous hands disguising infinite tenderness. Or maybe he'd simply had a lot of practice.

I twisted my eyes shut. *No. Don't go there.*

Too late.

"Damn it." His hand stilled. "I *did* hurt you."

I yanked the cloth from him. Hurled it across the room. Seethed out while jerking my panties up, "Don't. Damn it, Syn, don't you dare apologize for it. Not a moment of it! All right?"

Remarkably, that seemed to register. He rose high enough to park himself on the ottoman in front of the reading chaise, elbows braced to knees. "All right."

I averted my gaze. I'd never get out of here with him so close and sinewy and huge. Fortunately, my bra was nearby. "God forbid," I muttered, jerking it over my head, "that I become a burden, after all."

Yeah, I deliberately threw down the throttle on the bitterness. Not completely fair, making Syn take the brunt for words Jag had issued, but it wasn't like he'd fought Jag on them, either.

And you'd expected him to?

Fact: Samsyn Cimarron wasn't a one-woman man. Even two women. I didn't want to consider where that number ended, but his allergy to commitment was no state secret, clearly growing stronger as the years passed.

Fact: The secrets Samsyn Cimarron *did* have, he kept close and tight. Had girded with extra force by choosing the role of protecting Arcadia's security. Nobody expected a man to speak much, when blades, bullets, and his fists did most of the job already.

Fact: Facts one and two aside, Samsyn Cimarron was a

heartbeat away from the Arcadian throne. Technically, I was still American. The man wearing "the big crown" had already bucked a dozen beloved traditions by selecting an American for his bride. If anything ever happened to Evrest, Syn would never be forgiven for even having an American on the side, let alone with him in public. Like I'd even be okay with "on the side." I had zilch experience with any of this, but instinct bellowed loud and clear: a mouthy astremé with working knowledge of nunchuks and throwing knives wasn't likely to be okay with watching her man nuzzle someone else in public.

He's not your man. He won't ever be.

And *that* was the most ultimate fact of all.

It was time to face it. To accept the achy, awful *yuck* of letting him go—as a lover, perhaps even as a friend. I didn't know if I'd ever be able to look at him again and not remember those lips crushed on my mouth...those legs tangled through mine...those long fingers against my skin and inside my most intimate channel.

It hurt.

A lot.

Thank God I'd logged three years of hiding my deepest pain.

Minimizing was a great start. With terse jerks, I stuffed my breasts back into my sports bra and then layered the long-sleeved workout shirt on top. As I did, Syn finally spoke again.

"How much did you overhear?"

Why he sounded so defeated about it was beyond me. "Does it matter?" I sighed.

"Probably not."

I gazed at the top of his head, now dropped between his shoulders. Fought back the urge to kneel beside him and run my fingers through those satiny strands once more. "For the record, you held your own well in the pissing match, big guy."

"Merderim," he returned. "I think." His sarcasm made us both laugh, a welcome ease on the tension. But he was serious once more when going on. "Jagger was right...about the one thing, though."

"The one thing...what?"

"I should have stopped for a condom."

I rolled my eyes. "I already told you, Syn. I'm on the pill, and—"

"It was irresponsible," he snapped. "I was not thinking." His hands coiled into fists. "Damn it. I should have been *thinking.*"

"No. You were busy doing other things—like feeling. And making *me* feel." I let temptation take over. Slipped to the floor in front of him, wrapping a hand around one of his taut ones. "And it was all...amazing."

He wrenched his face to the side. "I was...gone. Everything was...you." His sentences were almost questions, as if he couldn't believe he uttered them. "I have never just lost all thought like that—" He stabbed his other hand into his hair. "Fuck."

I reached for that hand too. "Well, is that a bad thing?"

He still didn't look at me. "I do not know."

My grip slackened. His confusion scared me. Fury wasn't far behind. "So you *are* sorry about it."

His head jerked up. "I said nothing like that."

I lurched to my feet. "You didn't have to."

"Brooke!" His shout followed me out into the sitting room, where I was forced to return to the rotunda—avoiding any glance at the windows this time—to retrieve my boots.

Fortunately, it looked like Jagger had bought a clue and made himself scarce. "Brooke. Damn it!"

I whirled. Made a barefooted break for the stairs—until stopped by a wall of bronze muscle. I closed my eyes, refusing to look at him. Scent wasn't so easy to shut off. My lungs, heaving in and out, filled my senses with his earthy, leathery essence until I got dizzy. Uncontrollably, I swayed toward him.

I wanted him...

But you don't need him.

Empowered, I pushed back. Planted both feet. Forced my head up until I looked at him fully again.

And gulped back a sigh at his carved, swarthy jaw.

Clenched back the craving to fist his thick, dark hair.

Trembled against the pull his whole body had on mine, like the moon beckoning to the damn tide.

"Samsyn." It had twice the volume I'd anticipated. And four times the desperation. "Just let me go!"

He grabbed me by both elbows. Dipped his head, making sure every drop of fire in his gaze penetrated into mine. I took a deep breath. Let him do the same. We stared at each other, letting our hands fall and twine together, as everything filled our silence except our words. A flock of birds splashed across the lake. Morning wind rushed by the windows. Creatures in the trees chittered and scrambled and foraged, rustling branches as they went.

A pair of hearts cried out, struggling to find their way to each other.

But, once more, were lost

Blinded by the supernova.

Crushed...by the facts.

I stepped back. Samsyn yanked me back in, grinding his

forehead against mine. A rush of air left him, hot and desperate, though turned oddly cool when hitting the wet streaks down my cheeks.

He tilted his head. Let his mouth find the way to mine.

I wrenched free. He snarled. I matched it.

"Brooke." It was a raw command.

"Samsyn." It was a rasping plea.

"We cannot leave things like this."

"We *have* to leave things like this."

With that, I pushed away...

Knowing there was no other way to say it. Or do it.

CHAPTER NINE

"My lady, you are stunning!"

"Ah, indeed! Like a true princess."

"Like a true *queen*."

"Ah, indeed!"

If I weren't wearing a dress costing as much as a car, I would've puked all over the silver gems sewn into the overlay of its voluminous blue-black skirt. Orielle Preetsok and her little *bonami*, Freya Lyte, had apparently—and conveniently—forgotten every pro-Pura rant they'd gleefully exchanged over the last five days.

Funny how a royal entourage changed things—and how quickly their passions had flipped as soon as Camellia Saxon asked them to be her "local stylists" for the royal ball. As soon as Camellia started talking bullshit like local flowers, traditional hairstyles, and appropriate shoes for a party in a cave, the two women were squealing putty in her royal hands.

Lady Camellia, one.

Local bimbos, zero.

I'd indulged a silent gloat-fest on Camellia's behalf.

Eight hours later, I was *very* much done.

If either girl kissed the future queen's ass any deeper, I'd be searching for a crowbar to pry them out of her sphincter. Considering how Camellia been sewn into her seafoam-green, one-shouldered gown—literally—I was fairly sure the action wouldn't be appreciated.

At least I wasn't alone in the snark. Every few minutes, a face would appear from the adjoining bedroom. Jet-black curls. Wide doll eyes. The factors instantly gave away the spy, though Jayd Cimarron wasn't the sort to care. She was officially in hiding tonight, a staged pout in protest of Samsyn keeping her from the ball, though her fascination about Camellia's new "friends" was just as grotesque as mine. She eyed them carefully as her ladyship twirled in front of the three-way mirror, making the dress's bell skirt flare.

"Gorgeous!"

"Indeed!"

"It wouldn't be half as pretty without your help." Camellia turned from the three-way mirror in the corner of the cream and green bedroom, smiling at her two new friends. While they both already had makeup on, Orielle's in shades of burgundy and Freya's in lighter peach tones, they both still wore dressing robes, since preparing Camellia was the priority of the evening. There was no such thing as "fashionably late" for the party's honoree. "The laurel mixed with the mint leaves is perfect," Camellia went on, touching the fresh flowers woven into her intricate up-do. "And Ori, awesome call on going more delicate with the jewelry."

"Indeed!" Freya pushed it from a gritted smile, while her eyes betrayed a revenge plot on her parents for naming her something that couldn't be shortened to anything cute. "And... errrr...do you like the shoes *I* lent you, m'lady?"

I struggled not to roll my eyes. Was delighted when Jayd took care of the task for me.

"Like them?" Camellia yanked up the poof of her skirt. "Hell no, girlfriend. I *love* them. So comfy too." She lifted a foot, ensconced in one of the cream ballerina flats Freya had often called her "ugly stompers." Probably not after tonight.

"Okay, fashion fairies." Camellia pulled the two girls off the bed, into a three-way hug. "I'm officially ready for the ball and you aren't, so shoo. Go make yo'selves fleek and fly."

As they stepped back, I yearned for a camera. Orielle and Freya, openly confused. This was a first. Perhaps an only. Though I was just as baffled by Camellia's slang, I yearned to preserve the moment for posterity.

Jayd to the rescue. With surprising stealth, she whipped her phone around the corner, tapping the screen to get some non-flash shots. Suddenly, there was a stab inside my cheek. Was that my teeth, biting down to keep in a giggle?

Surprise set in—a delightful version of the stuff. Laughter hadn't been my closest pal this week. Feeling anything in general hadn't been. The circumstances that had brought the anomaly—and Samsyn and me to this mansion at all—were, thankfully, its cure as well. Throwing myself into the logistics drills for the royal visit, along with volunteering for decorating and cleaning details, had reduced me to exhausted putty every night. For a few blissful hours, I could then count on a few hours of dreamless sleep.

When I did dream, it was only of one person. And one perfect night. The moon glow across his body. The need in his eyes. The ache in his whispers. The bond of his soul to mine.

The connection I'd never thought possible.

If there was an "up" side to those damn dreams, I'd cling to nothing less than that.

Though damn it, the dreams weren't all I clung to. Because they weren't just dreams. They were memories.

And now, I *really* couldn't let go of Samsyn Cimarron.

He was here...everywhere. Worse than before. *Better* than

before. My relentless ghost. My impossible dream.

Now, more tormenting than ever—especially as Camellia motioned me over to the bed after kissy *buh-byes* to Orielle and Freya. *Damn it. The bed? Really?*

"Okay, woman." Her ladyship suddenly appeared anything but, flopping down and then patting the mattress next to her. "Come here. I'm *so* looking forward to hearing someone speak with contractions."

I laughed. Was actually grateful for it. Helped with masking my clenching nerves. Though I managed to sit, it was like lowering onto pinecones. Every inch of my skin pricked with every new detail I took in—and relived. The stitched swirls on the comforter...grating into my knees as Syn lowered my body onto his. The pristine white of the pillows, contrasting his dark, swirled hair. The tiny moan of the lake's breeze against the window...a perfect harmony for his orgasmic groans.

I cleared my throat. Even laughing to hide the pain wasn't an option anymore.

"You okay?"

I blushed. Not in a good way. "Isn't that supposed to be my line?" It was entirely too casual for dealings with the woman who'd soon be queen—or so said the cute little "etiquette expert" from the palace offices, sent ahead to ensure the "mountain folk" knew what we were doing when dealing with the royals—but talking to Camellia felt more like talking to Dillon. Well, a female Dillon. Without the moodiness. Or the overprotective brother thing.

She answered my crack with a dismissive huff. "So, you all lined up with your wig?"

I nodded. "Guess I'll find out if redheads really do have wild adventures."

"Not *too* wild."

"Agreed. Definitely."

She let a contemplative pause go by. The description was accurate. Her face crinkled into lines of deep thought. "Brooke...look...you know we've agreed to a small media presence at this foof-fest, right?"

Despite myself, I chuckled. "I'm aware of the foofy guest list, yes." And of the decision she and Evrest had made to let a handpicked selection of reporters into the ball, rather than letting rogues ransom their cell phone shots for money. Because of that, cells and smart pads would be checked at the event's entrance gate.

"Well, if you feel uncomfortable about babysitting me, that even the wig and colored contacts won't keep your identity safe—"

"I'm fine with the arrangements, Your Ladyship."

"Camellia," she rebuked. "No. Not even that. Call me *Cam*. Please. I'll only take that *Ladyship* crap when I have to."

"You're going to *have* to a lot more—especially when 'Ladyship' becomes *Your Majesty*."

"Crap." She fell backward, cutting the full plummet short with her elbows. God forbid she ruin the hairdo and the flowers *now*. "I'm never going to get used to that shit."

"You don't even hear it after a while," I assured—before tacking on a fast shrug. "Or...or so I'm told."

"By whom?"

"By who *else*?" The comment, snarky layered on affectionate, came from the other room.

Cam yelled in that direction, "Aren't you supposed to be wallowing in silence?"

A violent snort burst out. Impressive. If I hadn't known it

was Jayd, I'd have guessed Evrest, Syn, or Shiraz as the source. "If the subject's rolling around to Syn, I want in on the fun of skewering him from afar."

"Move along, girlfriend," I teased. "No Samsyn evisceration to see here."

"Fun killer."

I had no decent comeback. Apparently, neither did Cam. After a stunned silence, we burst into full laughs. The glow of Jayd's gloat was damn near visible through the walls.

"The killer says you win," I finally called.

"Of course I do."

After Camellia regained her breath, she cocked her head contemplatively. "So. You and Samsyn are good friends?"

My turn to sober up. "Um...friends?"

What the hell did she mean? Her face, now cloaked in Mother of Dragons serenity, seemed no different—which could mean nothing or everything. Had Jagger said anything to anyone? If so, had it gotten all the way to Camellia? To the whole damn island? And what *if* that were the case? What difference would it make? As far as the world at large was concerned, I was just another of Syn's "lady friends" with benefits. The only entity that said otherwise was the mass of messed-up neurons between my ears.

"Yeah." Cam pushed back up to rest on her wrists, as if shooting the shit with her gal-pals in a satin gown was an everyday occurrence. "Ev tells me you two are close buddies. Have been since the day your family got here."

"True. We were." I shut down the wistful lilt by forcing out another smile. "We *are*. He's...always been there for me." I gulped hard. Would he still be? And would he keep letting me be there for him too? The potential fallout from what we'd done, even with the hottest memories assaulting me from every corner of this room, smacked me all over again.

Cam grew noticeably quiet. Her distinctive turquoise gaze darkened like the sea beneath deep mist. "I still can't believe I'm looking at you. When Evrest told me exactly who'd be heading my security detail..." She shook her head. "Well, I didn't believe him. I watched them bury you." She bracketed the last two words in air quotes. "They covered the service on TV. It was a *really* nice service."

"Thanks. I think."

"And a week before that...the day they broke the story about Rune Kavill's attack on your home...I'll never forget it. I don't think anyone in the country will. I'd just finished interterm finals at Chapman. Every news feed in the commons—in the *country*—was carrying it. Your house—well, what was left of it—"

"Yeah." I dropped my stare to my hand—and its death grip on the coverlet. "I remember that too."

"Shit!" She bolted upright. Hauled me into a fierce hug. "Shit, shit, shit. I'm so sorry. I might've been damn near raised in the dirt, but I was also taught not to act like it. Okay, *you* can officially call me Miss Piggy."

I spurted a new laugh. Anyone who tagged Camellia Saxon as a disaster for Arcadia was simply someone who hadn't met her. The woman embodied everything that was good about the kingdom: its warmth, beauty, brilliance, and you're-with-family-now honesty. Because of that, I felt comfortable retorting, "Okay, give that one up right there, missie." I reared back, mocking out a skeptical glare. "Besides...Miss Piggy? Is she still a thing? Didn't she and Kermit ride away into the sunset and—"

"That got complicated." She twisted her lips and patted my hand. "A lot of things have in the last six years."

I returned her gesture by squeezing her hand. "Maybe you can fill me in soon."

Her grin matched the sparkle in her eyes. "I'd like that."

"Me too."

She pulled back a little, giving me that dark-lagoon scrutiny again. "So if you're okay about the wig and the contacts..."

"More than okay." The resolution of the statement opened a perfect chance to stand again. Anything to get even a step away from the bed.

"Then that means you're squirming about something else."

Hell. She wouldn't lend Arcadia just her charm. The woman had the insight of a Vulcan—without even needing the Spock squeeze. As I debated about how to respond, I wondered if the answer had started unraveling across my forehead anyway. Camellia certainly gawked like it had.

And sometimes, Jagger and his matchless timing were the best damn blessing on earth.

"Oh damn." I flashed a glance at her—*what-am-I-gonna-do-with-these-guys?*—before tapping the comm link that had chirped at my ear. "This is Badger. Go ahead."

Camellia frowned. "Badger?"

"Small, fast, and won't take any shit." It was fun to accent that with a smirk. "Hey, it wasn't my call." But I sure as hell hadn't argued with it.

"Badger, this is Robin Hood. State your twenty, over."

"Still holding at home base with Crown Jewel," I stated, using the team's code term for Camellia. "But we'll all be ready to roll in..."

"Ten minutes," Cam supplied to my expectant look.

I scowled but repeated the information to Jagger.

"Perfect." His answer was distorted by the noises behind him. The school's marching band, warming up to greet the royals' arrival with trumpet fare. Motorcycles revving. Men shouting. "We will be there for rendezvous at that time."

"Copy that." Though I still openly gaped at Camellia.

"Robin Hood out."

I didn't bother responding. Chose instead to address little Crown Jewel, now letting her stylist fuss over last-minute arrangements, including a micro-shine on the stunning tourmaline engagement ring King Evrest had put on her finger five months ago. "Ten minutes?" I charged.

Camellia looked at me via our shared reflections in the mirror. "You're ready, right? And *I'm* ready. Let's get this dog and pony on the road. The sooner my fiancé and I can sneak back here to nail each other, the better." She openly sighed. "God, I miss the palais and its...privacy."

Deciding that statement was best left untouched, I ventured, "And Orielle and Freya...?"

"Will either be ready or late." She let me have three seconds for open bemusement before laughing softly. "Come on, Brooke. You think I want to hang with those two airheads *all* night long?" She turned as the stylist moved in, wrapping a sparkling silver cape around her shoulders. "Ever heard of a thing called keeping your enemies close?"

An enlightened—and admiring—grin spread across my lips. "Hmmm."

"Hmmm...what?"

"Nothing. Except maybe that we selected your code name

prematurely, Your Ladyship."

Cam smirked. "That so? What do you suggest for a new one?"

I tapped my chin. "Buffy."

She grimaced. "*Buffy?*"

"Cute and cheerleader-y on the outside. Bad-ass bad guy killer on the inside."

"Oh." She mockingly preened. "Well in that case, Badger girl, lead on to the ball."

I took a turn at the grimace. "Guess I have to, huh?"

She snorted in commiseration. "Let's make it quick and painless. I need to take care of your king tonight, in more ways than one."

CHAPTER TEN

Entering the ball was, shockingly, kind of fun. Grand productions like this had never been my favorites, even during the days of officially being a politician's kid. The princess girl novelty of it all wore off after my tenth birthday, when Disney Channel was replaced by Nickelodeon and all I wanted to be was a normal kid hanging at the mall in a bucket hat and cut-off shorts. I'd never enjoyed any red carpet since.

Funny what a few years—and a long red wig and green contacts—could do.

When I climbed out of the town car at the LeBlanc Tower, nobody batted an eye. Not the small press corps, the jittery fans, or even the Tahreuse dignitaries, lined up to greet Camellia and Evrest with all the pomp and circumstance they could have possibly drummed up for the occasion. With my earpiece hidden beneath my "hair," I wasn't even distinguishable as a member of the local security detail. Literally, I had no name; I was just one of Cam's modern-day ladies-in-waiting, like Orielle and Freya—who bore that comprehension with a lot more pouts and huffs.

I was euphoric. Completely free to do my job, though right here in plain sight—the whole purpose of the op to begin with. Positioned nearly at Cam's side, I could protect her best without anyone raising the slightest inch of an eyebrow.

"Crown Jewel's at the red," I murmured, hoping Jagger and the team could hear me over the crowd. Though held back by barriers, they went berserk the moment Camellia disembarked from the car.

"Copy that, Badger." Jag's response was crisp and cool, as if he were merely running me through conditioning drills at the Center. "Please hold her there until our mark."

"Don't think that'll be an issue." I watched Cam charming the pants off every person in the throng, posing for pictures and signing everything from posters of the Arcadia-set movie she'd once been a crew member of, to the hokey royal couple merchandise that every shop in town was hawking now.

After thirty seconds, the comm line crackled again. "Big Wolf is in position and ready to go."

It wasn't Jag this time.

It was the voice for which I'd been steeling myself over the last six days. The voice I'd last heard in my ear, softly growling my name as early sunlight streams buffeted us from the world for a few last, miraculous minutes.

The voice pouring just as much longing and arousal into me now.

I pushed my way past clutching lungs and rubbery knees, intoning in return, "Roger that, Wildcat." Syn's radio name was the guys' nod to the bible story from which the ancient version of his name had come; I derived a completely different meaning. It was impossible to think of the man at the height of sexual temptation and not think of some dark jungle beast, on the hunt for his primal fulfillment...

I forced myself to take in the spectacle of the night instead. It was damn near impossible *not* to. The Tahreuse council had spared no funds to ensure the ball would be an event to remember. Twinkle lights spiraled the trunk of every tree. From their branches hung hundreds of golden lanterns, illuminating the entrance road in a glow that seemed almost celestial. The red carpet also covered the entrance path into the Tower, where the low stone ceiling was lined with billowing white drapes that concealed more twinkle lights.

The décor treatment served a higher purpose: to bump the "wow" factor once guests entered the main party area. Once someone stepped foot into the huge cavern itself, with its soaring walls glittering with the embedded blue gemstones, it was impossible not to gasp. The cavern's natural beauty was enhanced by colored party spotlights, glistening ice sculptures, and handcrafted local furniture with white cushions, accented by vases bursting with mountain wildflowers in every shade of blue imaginable.

"Holy mother of wow."

Camellia's exclamation made me laugh. I wasn't alone. Mayor Trieste, who'd taken advantage of the photo op to escort her from the car to this point, gave an indulgent chortle. "My citizens shall be happy to know your reaction, Lady Camellia. They have worked hard all week on the event."

"Obviously." She beamed a dazed smile. I swore Trieste grew another inch taller. Buffy had slayed another one.

But one man in the kingdom was gutted more than all the rest by her—a fact nobody disputed as soon as he entered the room. As King Evrest Cimarron strode to the middle of the white dance floor, looking every inch the dark wolf indeed, a hush fell over the room. Tonight, the king made even wolfish look distinguished, exchanging his traditional black doublet for an outfit tailored in ivory, matching the accents on Cam's gown. Like her, he'd accessorized in gold: the hook-and-eyes on his doublet, as well as the buttons up the sides of his pants, were gleams of the polished color. His thick black hair was slicked back from his face, emphasizing every prominent, handsome angle.

"Holy. Shit." Cam seized me by the wrist. "Brooke—"

"Yes?" I grabbed her back, suddenly concerned.

"Hold me up."

"Camellia? Cam? Are you feeling all right?"

"Look at him. *Look* at him!" She visibly gulped. "Would *you* be feeling all right? How the hell does he expect me to *move*, when he comes in looking like that?"

I squeezed her hand encouragingly. "I think he might feel the same way." The longer I watched Evrest, watching her with unblinking focus and a gaze that exactly matched her gown, the more sure I was about the point.

"Wh-What's he doing now? Ohhhh, no. Is he really—"

I couldn't help a tiny laugh. "Inviting you to dance? Errmm...yes, Your Ladyship, he is."

She groaned beneath her breath. "By his own damn Creator. *What* is he thinking?"

Silence. Mine. On purpose. Just for a second. "Seriously?"

"Do I look like I'm joking?"

"All right, then. Beside the fact that he looks ready to crawl out of his skin if he doesn't touch you again—"

"That part, I can deal with."

"He's claiming you. Now. Publicly. While the whole kingdom, and the world press, are watching. It's as much for them as you. He's telling them that he's not just kicking off this party; he's starting his *life*—and you're the key to that. He's telling them that you're here to stay and they'd better get used to it."

As I spoke, the edges of her mouth quirked. Before she replied, they bloomed into a wide smile. "Badger...I think I like you."

I squeezed her hand one more time before letting it drop. "Buffy...go dance with your man."

My chest warmed, watching her walk into the lights to be reunited with Evrest. The applause swelled in equal measure, an irony since the couple in the middle of the dance floor were clearly oblivious to anything but each other. With their foreheads lightly touching and their eyes completely closed, they began to sway as the band played "Why Don't We Fall in Love" with a slow, sultry twist. Few people in the room were able to rip their stares from the sight. Despite the pace of the music, the king and his fiancée didn't just shuffle back and forth like a pair of teeny-boppers. They moved against each other with their legs and hips, their arms and hands, like a poem given physicality.

Like a pair of lovers who couldn't wait to get naked with each other.

I couldn't watch them and not think of Samsyn.

And how we'd moved together like that too.

I suddenly needed air. Badly.

As if a wool blanket were thrown over the room, I sucked in a harsh breath. My wig wasn't a glam masquerade anymore. It itched and clung. My contacts burned in my eyes.

I was vaguely conscious of tapping the comm link. "Robin Hood, do you have eyes on the dance floor?"

"Affirmative," Jag answered.

"Perf. Badger's taking a recon lap on the patio."

Though I couldn't see him through the crowd, the delay of his scrutiny was tangible. "You feeling okay, B?"

"Fine," I hissed. "The dress is tight." *Lie.* The gown was damn near custom-fitted for me, but right now the million-layered skirt suffocated just like the wig. "I'll be back in five."

Once out on the terrace, I inhaled gratefully. The night flowers had started to bloom, weaving their natural perfume in with the breeze off the lake. The sky was clear except for a few frothy clouds, drifting across the moon like designer meringue atop a cream macaron.

The view demanded more than a cursory glance, but first things first: I'd promised Jag a thorough check of the area. Fortunately, with nearly everyone mesmerized by the Ev and Cam show on the dance floor, I was finished in a couple of minutes. The shadows on the far side of the terrace beckoned as an ideal spot to refile my thoughts into proper order.

Until a bunch of them moved. With a huge hulk that felt, looked, and smelled all too familiar.

From that darkness, his gaze beamed first. It was always the first thing I noticed about him. So reassuring yet strange how that hadn't changed. Even now, even after everything, my feet stopped as my heart indulged a giddy whirl, locked in the power of his brilliant blues.

I kept borrowing a page from the book of Cam, unable to move even as he did, stepping forward with his warrior-dragon surety. Yep, even with his clean-shaven jaw and his hair pulled into a gleaming knot, I could imagine him brandishing a broadsword and racing into battle. His doublet was black—as if I'd doubted *that* choice—with the shoulders and upper torso inlaid with silver threads. Those swirls guided the eye toward the medallion pinned to the middle of his chest, etched with the twined dove and hawk of the Cimarron family crest.

"Damn it, Syn." I struggled for a flippant laugh but came up short. "You scared the crap out of me."

"Just as *you* frightened *me*."

I readily embraced confusion. It trumped having to notice the rest of his luscious outfit. The tight fit of his traditional red breeches. The polished boots that hugged him up to the middle of those massive thighs. Shit, did the man have amazing legs...

"What? Why?"

"You turned white as the dance floor in there."

He'd noticed?

Don't shuck your panties, girlfriend. Of course he noticed. You're on the vital team. If you fall over, he has to worry about replacing you.

"I'm fine. It just got stuffy. The dress—"

"Looks fucking perfect."

His sandpaper voice jerked my head up. His countenance matched, turning so rough that he seemed to age a year before my eyes. His thick brows lowered over the new intensity in his eyes.

"It—it does?" And could I have sounded any more like the dip-wit teenager I'd tried so hard to make him forget?

He moved in by another step. Clenched his fists, as if preventing himself from taking a second. "You are the most beautiful woman in this whole damn place."

I nodded and added a little grin. "I think your brother might disagree."

He didn't acknowledge that. "It really looks like stars." Finally reached out, fingering one of the skirt overlays. From there, it was simple for him to drift his hand over, brushing my hand with his.

Time stopped. Heat bloomed. Inside seconds, turned to a thousand bolts of fire up my arm, through my body. Breaths stuttered in and out of my lungs. Once more, I was small yet huge, joyous but terrified, lost yet found...but oh, so very sure of the woman in me, affirmed by every inch of the man that was him. Unbreakable. Unfathomable. Unbelievable.

But for a moment, I believed.

And gave in.

"Samsyn." Wrapped my hand around his. Trailed my index finger down the length of his. Shit. This was wrong and ill-advised on *so* many levels, but he was the damn moon and I was the helpless tide. I looked up, longing for him to see what other parts of him I already touched...in my naughtiest thoughts.

"Astremé." His voice was sequoia tree bark. His gaze darkened as I curled my finger around, stroking up and down his long, thick digit. I didn't miss an inch, from the firm web at the root to the broad fingernail at the tip.

"I've...missed you."

He swallowed. "I have...missed you."

Here went nothing. Or perhaps everything. "Really?"

"Really."

"Did you...think about it?"

I didn't explain "it." The silver shards in his gaze confirmed he already knew.

"Yes," he snarled softly. "I thought about it. All of it."

My lungs refilled with air that felt made of tingles.

God, *really*? Was I thinking shit like that, let alone feeling it? *Right now?*

I cleared my throat. Forced myself to step back. "Sorry. *Shit.* Sorry."

Syn snarled softly. "Brooke—"

"Forget it." I smoothed my dress, preparing to go back inside. "I'm—it's all right. Just...forget it. We have work to do."

I indulged one last glance. Syn's face was tight, conflicted, and unspeakably gorgeous. There was a question in his eyes too—but before I could answer, the terrace was flooded with noise. Camellia led the way, towing King Evrest by the hand. They were followed by what could only be described as a small mob.

"Hey!" the little brunette exclaimed. "Jagger, you were right. We found her."

"Found wh..." My query faded as I finally focused on the faces behind Evrest and her. The *faces*—at first, as foreign to me as my own tonight—but after taking in the specific features, were as familiar to me as home.

Because they *were* home.

"Dad! Mom!" Though Veronica Valen wasn't my biological mother, she'd joyfully filled the role since I was eighteen months old. Technically, that also made her *Mom*. "Oh, my God. Look at my groovy parents!"

Dad, who'd maintained his senatorial crop over the years, sported a black shag and mustache a la Sonny Bono in the 1970s. Appropriate, since Mom had traded out her short blond curls for a sleek Cher look, a la the *Gypsies, Tramps and Thieves* era. She had spiky fake eyelashes to go along with it and red lips she was careful not to smudge on me as we hugged.

"Lady Camellia very sweetly offered to let us come join the fun," she explained.

"We couldn't turn down the chance to see our girl in action," Dad added.

"You're not supposed to *see me*, Dad. That's the point."

"Which is why you're one of the most stunning women in the room?"

Dad was one-upped on the comment by a guy who moved in from behind him. The dude finished off the comment with a saucy wag of brows that more resembled a pair of muddy caterpillars. I almost wrote him off as a creepy hanger-on, until he flashed a glimpse of crooked teeth—the teeth *I'd* made crooked, when attacking him for spilling fruit punch all over my Hannah Montana Halloween costume one year.

"Dillon?"

"Hey," he chastised as I dove in for a crushing hug. "Don't scratch the merchandise too much."

"Asshole." I punched his shoulder. "Your 'merchandise' is just fine. As a matter of fact, a few sweet *chicas* around here might be interested in logging advance payments for it." I cupped my hands and mouthed Freya's name. The woman's crush on Dil had been legendary for years.

He rolled his eyes. Probably would've tacked on a growl, if Mom didn't flip her Cher locks with diva poise and then wink at the man behind me. "Guess what, Samsyn Cimarron? We can see you back there."

Well. The man had more than one surprise entrance up his sleeve tonight. As Syn slipped around me with grace that belonged on the dance floor, my stomach swirled with more girlish butterflies. As he leaned in, scooping up Mom's hand and winking back at her, all the butterflies drowned—in the puddle now known as me.

"A pleasure to see you, as always, Madame Valen—or shall I say Madame Cher?"

"Veronica is fine, Samsyn. You know that." Even she went all girly flustered, smoothing the front of her red sheath gown. "Especially since they spared me the horror of having to wear anything with feathers, beads, or cut-outs."

"Cut-outs?" Dad did a perk-and-smirk. "You didn't say anything about the cut-outs option."

"Not an accident, sweetheart," Mom rejoined.

As everyone laughed, Dad scooted closer to her. Nuzzled her ear and muttered things none of us could hear. Probably a good thing.

"Oh, my God." Camellia gave me a soft shoulder bump. "Your parents are so cute."

"Yeah, they are." I smiled at the two of them, cuddling each other like the sun rose and set in each other's eyes, and suddenly, everything was all right in the world. "Sometimes, in a weird way, I'm kind of grateful for what happened to us. Losing so much that night...well, it made all four of us more aware of what we *did* have." When understanding softened her eyes, I went on, "Political life is rough on marriages, even outside Washington. So many of my friends had estranged parents or had to deal with scandals about cheating and lying... *Shit.*" Contentment morphed to horror. "Not that such a thing would ever happen with Evrest and you. I just—"

She cut me off with a chuckle. "Chill, girlfriend. He and I had to go through a lot to even get here." Her gaze, gone even mistier with emotion, drifted to the king. If it were possible, Evrest was an even more dashing figure out here, his brocade clothes and elegant hair contrasted by the wood flooring and rustic furniture. "We're solid—and we're going to make sure it stays that way."

As she spoke, an arm locked around my waist—attached to a hand that dug in at the right place to make me squeal. I spun toward the only person capable of knowing *that* ticklish spot. "Brother mine, in the spirit of full disclosure, I do not own this gown. If I destroy it kicking your ass, I'm going to make you pay for the repair."

"*Pssshhh.*" Dillon flourished it with a grin, uncannily

like Dad's. Though he hadn't inherited the man's genes, he'd learned the best traits. "You mean *if* you kick my ass?"

"Charmer."

"Right? Especially in this get-up." He made the eyebrow caterpillars dance again. "I haz da swaggah tonight, yeah?"

"Ew." It bounced out on a laugh. This was part of Dil's schtick, comic relief reserved for the days I came home from crazy-tough training. But right now, I couldn't tackle him to the couch to make him stop. "Time to work the room elsewhere, perv." I leaned over to murmur, just for his ears, "Freya's looking pretty awesome tonight."

He reacted as if I'd gloated over taking the last cookie in the jar. Not that the comparison had *any* validation in reality. "I'm perfectly fine right here. Where are *you* going?"

He actually looked a little sad. Guilt bit at my chest. We'd always found time to reconnect with each other, but even before the whirlwind of last week, training had eaten into more and more of my schedule. "I promise we'll get an afternoon soon, D. But right now, I'm on the clock."

He looked around, disgruntled. "I don't see a freaking time clock."

I backhanded his shoulder. Diffused his moodiness more by cocking a sassy pose, hands on hips. "Because I never clocked out."

"Ahhh," Dad chimed in. "See that, Dil? All this time, smiling nice and socializing, when she's really been protecting our king and his lady. Well done, munchkin."

"*Father.*" I glowered.

"What?"

"Can we stow 'munchkin' at home, at least for tonight?" What was with him and Dil trotting out the family only stuff at this soiree? Now, even Samsyn noticed. The knowing—and entrancing—quirk of his lips said as much. That, of course, got *Cam*'s attention. She linked an elbow with mine and tugged proudly.

"How about Jamie Bond?" she proposed. "Shaken not stirred?"

Glower. "You're not helping."

"Hmmm." Dad grinned. "That has merit. Girl with the golden gun? From Arcadia with love?"

"See what I mean?" I narrowed eyes again at Cam. "*Not* helping."

She leaned into me while murmuring her comeback. "Maybe not...but it's kept Samsyn's eyes on you nonstop." She answered my gape with a subtle wink. "Not that you needed any help."

Heat. Back to my ears, probably farther. Damn. I'd had more color in my face this last week than during three years of fight training. "I have no idea—"

"Of course you do. And now it's clear what you were squirming about earlier."

"Shit."

"*Hey.* Don't worry. It's not like the whole room knows. Just the other woman who knows what it's like to fall for a Cimarron man."

I swallowed hard. Looked to her, letting her alone see the longing pain across my face. "Sometimes, falling only gets you hurt, Ladyship."

Camellia twisted our arms tighter. Pushed closer, making sure she stamped me with her empathic smile. "And sometimes, you're already sharing the drop—and you just have to reach out to know it."

She lifted her gaze. I followed its trajectory, already knowing I'd hate myself for it.

And Samsyn too.

Yeah, you big bull. I hate you for this.

Why did he torment us both with his riveting attention... with that laser focus in his eyes? By joining it with such a taut clench to his jaw, I didn't know if he was grieving or furious? By making me feel like a drop of water in his desert *and* the Delilah who'd ruined him? I already had a thousand balls in the air tonight. A hundred strangers in the room. Another hundred corners to be suspicious of. And now, maintaining dignity in the face of "munchkin" and "Jamie Bond."

Stress bypassed my tight bodice, stabbing straight for the nerves behind my eyes. Things had gotten really complicated, really fast. Why? How? The mission had been simple: *keep Evrest and Camellia safe.* It was huge enough of a job description, despite a dozen others being tasked with the same thing, to keep me consumed for the night. Now I had Mom, Dad, and Dillon stirred into the pie, on top of gracefully wiping my drool over Samsyn...

And, in breaking news, remembering how to greet the high couple of the kingdom.

Though it'd been years since King Ardent stepped down to let Evrest deal with the day-to-day ruling of Arcadia, the king father's entrance still dictated the most solemn display of respect. His queen, Xaria, was due the same. We'd reviewed the etiquette during this week's training, but Jag only allowed the palais's etiquette coach a half hour with us, deciding—wisely—we all needed to know more about protecting the couple, not genuflecting for them.

Now, I fought to yank up those thirty minutes on my

mental hard drive. *Servers unresponsive.* Shit, shit, shit. There was a certain order of things, wasn't there? And how did I bow? And to whom?

Never had I been more grateful for Camellia's proximity. "Girls bow to Xaria first." Her whisper was clear though her lips barely moved. "But bow deeper to Ardent. Refer to either as *excellence. Majesty* is only for Evrest." And, very soon, her—though I didn't bother pointing it out again.

I joined her and the rest of the group in making the proper motions and saying the proper things. Everyone seemed to make it through the rituals just fine...

Except Samsyn.

Who didn't perform them at all.

Who'd turned into a different person from the moment his parents appeared.

At first, I assumed his tension was in line with everyone else's. Even Evrest visibly stiffened with the arrival of the king father and queen mother—though after the bows and greetings were done, he turned to pull both parents into affectionate hugs. Samsyn made no such move. Samsyn didn't budge, period. No bows. No words. No motion. He was a wall. *All* of him now, not just the figurative I enjoyed using for his torso. His knuckles gripped the hem of his doublet, now white as concrete. His face reminded me of the profiles of Mount Rushmore—in January. Granite defiance beneath stormy skies.

I wasn't the only one taking notice. While the breech earned Samsyn a pointed glare from Evrest, King Ardent chose the opposite end of the spectrum. The man was all courtesan congeniality, parting the crowd as he approached. "Samsyn, my son!" He was tall and regal in a black and white doublet over black breeches, grunting in affection as he embraced Samsyn.

His clubbed ponytail gleamed like a paintbrush down his back, making him appear more like Syn's brother than father—until he pulled away. At that point, the differences became obvious.

Ardent Cimarron was an attractive man—but knew it. He was also a powerful man—and knew that too. Most obviously, he'd used those advantages to manipulate others—and wouldn't hesitate to do so again.

And of course, as soon as I came to those conclusions, the man turned—and magnetized his gaze on me.

Why wasn't Murphy's Law a citable offense?

More to the core of the matter: why wasn't it okay to flash a huge "talk to the hand," even to one's king, when they bore down on you like a rat on a pizza slice?

"And who could *this* fresh face be?"

Sometimes, a girl really did need her dad. "Ardent, you old dog. Hands off my daughter."

As Ardent looked over, his scowl brightened to delight. "Chase! You old bonsun! And Ronnie! I barely recognized you both. But *this* gorgeous creature simply *cannot* be little Brooke..."

I envisioned little steel ropes, attaching to my smile and lifting it. "Bon *aksam*, Your Excellency." The last time I'd used the forced warble was at a senatorial picnic, when Senator Warden had gulped too many Long Island iced teas and came on to every female over fifteen. This was different. *Really* different. Senator Warden's son had been a congressman with acne scars and receding hair, not the man who fired my bloodstream simply with the force of his presence. "Yes. It's me. Excuse the crazy hair. It doubles as a great dance partner, though." My strawberry red fall wasn't as long as Mom's, but anything past my nape felt like hauling around an animal. I already couldn't wait to rip the thing off—which only added to the annoyance of Ardent's appreciative stroke of the thing.

"I imagine it does." One regal finger twirled a long strand of the fake stuff. "But I do prefer waltzing with something more...flesh and blood...do you not agree?"

"Right." I drew the vowel out, buying time for composure. The last time I'd spent any time with King Ardent, when we'd been invited to Evrest's coronation party a few years ago, he'd spared me a polite smile and handshake, nothing more. Not that I'd minded. Pomp, circumstance, and pageantry hadn't been my thing even during the princess gown days, when all I'd wanted to do was skip the receiving line and get to the cake table. "To be honest, waltzing in general isn't my jam." I gestured toward my feet. "Two left ones. Not kidding."

"Nonsense," Ardent chided. "I would stake money that you dance as if on a cloud." He swept up an arm. "Come now. Shall we?"

Shit. Really?

I gulped, hoping my true thoughts were successfully masked: that his elbow might as well have been an armed bomb. In many ways, it was. Turn down the invitation and irk the king father himself, or accept it and stumble my way across the dance floor, piling one uncomfortable situation on top of the next?

"Your Excellence, I'm so flattered. But...I'm on duty. And I really am awful."

"Not entirely true." Dillon's smooth grin didn't make his interjection less atrocious. "You knew all the steps from *High School Musical*...sort of."

I pivoted on him, filling my glare with one message only. *Shut up, or you're dead.*

"What?" He snickered. "You were so cute. 'Wildcats everywhere; raise your hands up in the air.'" He clawed at the air, making it as off-rhythm as my moves from ten years ago.

I closed my eyes, barely stifling a groan. If there was a graceful out for Ardent's ick factor moves, this wasn't it.

"Knock. It. Off." I gritted out each word. Re-schooled my lips into a tight smile, lifted back toward the king father. "Apologies, Your Excellence. Siblings love to take advantage of times like these."

"But of course." Ardent tacked on a laugh, though the sound didn't relieve me. It felt like spray butter. Same tint as the real stuff, but...not.

"My brother's color commentary aside, I *am* here for work, not play."

"Outstanding point." It wasn't the fact that Samsyn spoke for the first time in ten minutes. It was the authority he used, given his low volume and tight lips—commanding the attention of everyone present, including his father. "Miss Valen is correct. She is here as event security, not entertainment."

"Speaketh the official event guard dog." Dil earned himself my elbow in his ribs for the mutter only I could hear. Even so, he added, "Arf arf."

Before I could actually go for breaking those ribs, Samsyn covered the diameter of our makeshift kumbaya circle. Without breaking stride, he hooked a hand under my elbow, spinning me away from the ring.

"Damn it," I spat. Not him too.

"I actually require Miss Valen's input right now about some logistical matters."

Yep. Him too.

"Logistical matters?" I hissed it as he doubled our pace,

back toward the shadows from which he'd first manifested. "Could you be any more transparent—or lame?"

Too little, much too late. He didn't hear a word I said, too busy ordering Jag to slide someone into my place on the terrace. By the time he clicked the line off, we'd stepped off the terrace, through a small metal gate, and onto a path that hugged the cliff.

"Samsyn!" I barked. "Damn it; this is—"

"Quiet, Brooke."

"Seriously? You want to take another good, long look back here? Last time I checked, you left your dogs back at the palais, asshole."

"I said quiet!"

It was just vicious enough to make me bite the words back. Besides, bitchitude was possible in a number of ways. I had no trouble illustrating the point to the bull, huffing and grunting and growling through every step we took. I kept it up, despite the fact that the path was well-lighted by the moon and relatively flat, despite getting a little muddy just before Syn suddenly cut left, still dragging me behind.

We'd entered a picnic shelter of some sort. Overhead, wooden rafters dripped with bougainvillea. There were a pair of standing barbecues and a matching pair of wooden picnic tables. It was a perfect spot for such a thing. The view of the lake from here was breathtaking.

Not that Syn gave me more than a second to take notice.

Without a word—with barely a sign of warning except the way he snapped me around and then backed me up—he plowed me into one of the tables. Hiked my ass up onto it from the sheer force of how he rammed my body with his, pinning me with his crotch.

I didn't hold back the outrage in my glare.

He didn't hold back the ferocity in his.

"Syn." In my mind, it had been an outraged snarl. On my lips, it was a stupid rasp. I made up for it with my favorite standby. "What the fuck is—"

He ripped that short too. His clutch at my face, his hand digging in until I felt him shaking from it, arresting the words in the middle of my throat. "He...touched you," he growled. "Touched you as if he...knew you." He pushed in tighter, grating his clothes against mine, a decidedly intimate sound in the small space of the shelter. My body sure as hell confirmed it. The growing ridge in the center of his body was another yes.

"Knew me?"

I wasn't just being a mindless parrot—but the query was legitimate. *What* the hell was he talking about? *Where* the hell had this strange rush of caveman come from? And *why* the hell were groping each other in starlight and shadows again?

And how did I not give an inch of damn about any of those answers?

"Like I know you. Like nobody else knows you." He pressed again, looming until I had to capitulate, flattening to my back to the table. Syn lowered with me, his hand burrowing back, pushing away my wig...

As he crushed my mouth with his.

Freeing me from more than the hair.

Arousing me in more than just my sex.

Conquering me as more than just a lover.

He consumed and filled. Heated me, completed me, inspired me, instigated me...

Knew me.

He dragged away by just a few inches, looking beautiful

and bold, his features outlined in silver, his gaze glowing nearly the same shade. "Nobody knows you like I do," he commanded. "That means nobody touches you but me, Brooke Valen."

As he spoke, his opposite hand somehow—miraculously—found its way beneath my skirts. He punctuated the declaration by palming me where I was wettest and hottest...making it clear exactly how he intended to demonstrate his point.

CHAPTER ELEVEN

For once, it felt wonderful to be dressed like a princess—especially the one being roused from sleep by a magical kiss.

Corny? Yeah.

Unrealistic? Hell, yeah.

But in the perfection of right now, beneath the power of his body, consumed by the mastery of his touch?

It was complete truth.

A magic unleashed. His magic. *Our* magic.

I gave in. Let it swirl through me, overtake me, sizzle into my blood and bones and senses as I jabbed my hands up to touch him too. Anywhere I could. Everywhere I could. I unfastened his doublet, frantically twisting the hooks to reveal the sculpted bronze slabs of his chest. His dark flesh beckoned, irresistible...touchable. I grabbed at him, boldly closing my fingers around his nipple—just as two of his lunged up into my core.

"Samsyn!" It was a perfect scream.

"My starlight." It was a perfect growl. He was relentless, thrusting rougher and rougher, abrading my pouting flesh until I bucked against his hand, fucking his fingers in return. He pulled out long enough to push my panties aside, giving him better access to my soaked entrance. He worked his thumb into those folds while reinserting his longer fingers into my tunnel, working every part of my sex with long, lunging motions. "By the *Creator*...how did I get through a fucking week without this?"

I laughed softly—until opening my eyes to find him studying me, brow deeply crunched. I could almost hear his inner dialogue, trying to convince himself I wouldn't disappear. His expression stabbed tears behind my eyes. I didn't understand it, but like the enchantment of his touch, I had no will to fight it.

"You survived." I lifted a hand to his face. "Somehow, we both did."

He kissed me again. While this embrace wasn't the full-on maul of before, it jacked my arousal just as violently. Though he'd pulled a Neanderthal move to get me here, now I sensed him needing to feel the same from me—that I needed this too.

If it was need the man wanted, that was what he'd damn well get.

I moaned into his mouth while jabbing my hands into his hair. Yanked the tie free. Hurled it away. With the long, thick silk free between my fingers, I twisted in to pull him close, sucking furiously at his tongue and lips. I didn't stop there. I couldn't. My spirit's desire for him drove my body, arching it against his huge hand, my thighs quivering, my sex flooding.

"Yours. I'm yours, Samsyn." I spoke it before he could demand it, already knowing he needed it. The effect it instantly produced in him...was a look I'd never seen before. For one moment, his face flared with joy—only the next, to be overtaken by the shadows I often saw in him. But now, they didn't lurk at the back of his composure. They crowded him, possessed him, transformed him into something dark and intense...

A darkness he focused totally on me.

An intensity throbbing straight to my pussy.

"Say it again." His dictate began in his chest and curled

out his lips, twisting between us like smoke. "Say it exactly the same."

"I'm...yours." A gasp broke it apart as he rammed me deeper with his fingers.

"Nobody touches you like this but me. *Say it.*"

"Nobody...touches me...like this." I raked my hands to his shoulders, scoring the broad shelves, using the grip to keep my sanity...and hold back my climax. "Not like you. Nobody but you, Syn."

His hand worked me deeper. Spread my walls. Teased my clit. Rubbed closer and closer, lifting the hood until he pressed...

right...

there.

"Samsyn!" I pulsed and pounded. Writhed up as heat roared to the surface. Needing. Wanting. Reaching...

Then screaming as he withdrew. Moaning, so empty and bereft, but mesmerized by his straining muscles, working to free his erection. With every move he made, my dress rustled against the night, seeming deafening as an air horn. I struggled to keep my whimpers quieter. Impossible. Every time Syn flipped the layers of fabric, letting me smell him, all musky and peppery, mixed with the night flowers and my own light perfume, my mind stole more of my composure. By the time he scooted my ass higher on the table and positioned himself over me, I was an aroused, excited, mewling mess.

He stared hard, watching my reaction as he pressed on my thighs, opening my body for him. I let him see it all: my parted lips, my heated gaze, my feverish breaths. All of it sharpened as he fitted the silken head of his sex to the urgent lips of mine. I cried out, fishing through the tulle for him, but he caught my wrists and lowered them to the table, locking me down as he took my mouth in another wet, hungry connection.

When we finally parted for air, he seared me all over again. His gaze was pure blue-white fire. His face was chiseled in charcoal-dark desire. "Now tell me nobody else fucks you but me."

As if my clit needed any more reason to burn. "N-Nobody fucks me but you."

He edged in his shaft by another inch. "Nobody else gets inside you like this."

I gazed fully at him now. "Nobody else gets inside me like this." I blinked, letting him see the tears drag down my cheeks. "Inside me...everywhere."

Once more, I watched a burst of joy overtake his face.

Right before the shadows consumed again.

Worse than ever. Not just darkening him this time. Hardening him. Stripping a swath of his humanity, turning him into a creature of such lethal sensuality, my lungs worked to catch up on breath. I'd always called him my elusive dragon, but now that the dragon was really here, his violence was terrifying. His heat, nearly suffocating.

His passion...something I'd never wanted more.

He reared up a little higher. His head rose between his shoulders...the dragon preparing to incinerate its prey. From the rich curves of his lips, another low growl emanated. "Nobody fucks you but me."

"Nobody fucks me...but you."

He entered me in one ruthless drive. Impaled me to the point of delicious pain. Stretched my pussy to its limits, blowing my mind off its damn doors. "Nobody makes your body quiver like I do."

"No." I gasped it, curling my fingers around his, using him for purchase as he propelled into me. With the leverage of the grip, I was able to give back as good as he gave, meeting every thrust with the force of my own potent need. "Nobody...but you."

"And nobody makes your cunt come like me."

My mouth went dry. My body went up like kindling of the same texture. His wicked, filthy words enflamed things inside. *Everything.*

"Oh, God. *Ohhhh, God.*"

He started twisting his hips. My dress rasped with every perfect, erotic thrust. Our bodies smacked again and again and again, primal passion in a savage, stolen moment. He didn't let my stare go, binding me with his dark, determined beauty, twisting my soul with his as he cleaved me, became part of me. Just as he threw off his barriers, I pushed aside mine. Let him have me, *all* of me, as I stamped this moment to my memory forever. Made myself take in every detail of this incredible sight: his stark, impassioned face, set against the endless Tahreuse stars. Forced myself to cherish this feeling, of being connected again to the one man on earth who moved me like no other.

"Say it." Syn's clutch tightened on my wrists. His gaze zeroed in, watching every inch of my face. "Say. It."

I gritted my teeth. Balled up the air in my lungs. "Nobody... makes me..."

And then...I couldn't.

Because...I was.

A scream replaced the words. The fire became explosion. My sex clenched, vibrating around his cock, as white-hot ecstasy ripped through my body. I was mindless. Weightless.

All of me tumbled out yet sucked the world back in, knowing its light and dark, its good and bad, its angels...and its dragons.

"Coming," I finally gasped. "I'm coming, Samsyn! For you."

He gazed like the words were an incantation for immortality. Never in my life had I felt so adored, so worshiped, so desired—and even more as he suddenly stilled, letting me feel the shudders that overtook every inch of the shaft embedded inside.

"And I, astremé...for you."

His eyes closed. His lips twisted. His nostrils flared.

He poured into me.

We began to rock again, riding the tiny bursts of aftermath but not letting each other go. Though Samsyn slid his hold free from my wrists, I slipped them back up to clutch him again, holding him near, head tucked against my shoulder, heavy exhalations warming my neck. Gone was the dragon. He was back in knight mode, tracing the line of my jaw, down my neck, out over my collarbone. I could still feel his cock inside, semisoft, and was happy with that circumstance. More than happy.

I know. Stupid.

On more than a few levels.

I didn't worry about the obvious. I was still on birth control; nothing had changed over the last week...

Except that everything else had.

Everything else. The not-so-easy to deal with stuff, now parking their asses at this table like the giant elephants they were—getting ready to feast on the two of us.

One of us was going to have to start this conversation.

"Brooke."

And thank God it had been him.

I almost expelled a sigh of gratitude. The gravity in his voice confirmed he saw the elephants too. That meant I wasn't crazy. Now I wondered if we saw the same elephants.

"As a member of the Arcadian military, I am tested for many things every year."

"Oh." Wasn't the first subject I expected him to broach—but I was glad it had been. We were talking rationally. This boded well for addressing the rest of the elephants at the buffet. "Okay," I added. "Ummm..."

"I am clean. I can get you a copy of the lab results—"

"Not necessary." I cleared my throat, ending with a laugh. "In case it's not clear"—I nodded deliberately, indicating our very connected bodies—"I really do trust you, big guy."

My levity went over like a boulder plunking into the lake. "I know," he replied, voice edged in impatience, "but your respect is just as vital. I shall not have you thinking that I—" He grimaced. "Well, I am usually in the habit of carrying, and wearing, protection."

"The habit?" I punched my discomfort into the word. "You mean like racking your weights every day? Business to take care of, huh?"

My tension pushed his cock a little farther out. Though looking loathe to do so, he separated his body the rest of the way. Not that he went far. He stayed there, lodged between my legs while bracing my face between his hands. "I will not let there be lies between us—no matter how uncomfortable they are."

"Well, they're uncomfortable." I closed my eyes, battling for perspective. "And that's the stupid thing about all this."

"Stupid?" His upper lip curled with insult.

Sigh of long-suffering...if a bit exaggerated. "*Yes*, Your Highness. Stupid."

"You are *not—*"

"The hell I'm not. Or can't be. Especially when it comes to—" *You*. The restraint didn't help a damn thing. He was capable of discerning the answer for himself, and the silver glints in his eyes betrayed that he had. "Look. I meant what I said last week, when things...happened...between us at the Residence Rigale. I was ready to accept we'd only have all that for one night. Even then, I knew you were skittish about it—"

"*Brooke*." He glowered. "I do not dabble in 'skittish.'"

"Fine." I sighed again. "Whatever you were, then. Uneasy. Unwilling—"

"Oh, I was willing."

"Scared of hurting me," I finally flung. I smirked just a little. He had to let that one stick. "Your own words, big guy."

He jerked his head to the side, making his hair as much a statement as his seething mutter. "Fuck."

"And *there's* my point." When his glare tightened in confusion, I persisted, "You, having to even say that. Having to even generate the thought behind it."

"The...thought...?"

"The worry. The stress. About me." I scooped a hand against the side of his face. Pushed it back over to align his gaze with mine. "Syn, I may have been a virgin before last week, but I wasn't an innocent. I'm aware of the pressures you face and how you like...things...in your life." I took in a measured breath before clarifying, "Of how you like your women."

I expected that to bring back a little of the dragon. Maybe a lot. Instead, he unveiled more of his inner knight, rolling to his side next to me as if the picnic table were a luxurious mattress. With his head propped on a hand, he rejoined, "Is that so?"

I lightly smacked his face. "Don't be glib."

He sobered. Too fast. "How *do* I like my women?"

"Plentiful." It was practically knee-jerk, but I stuck by the conviction—noticing he didn't flinch either. "Not all at once, of course—but if that's how you jam then I'm not going to judge."

"One at a time is usually my preference, even if there *are* plentitudes."

I should've jumped his shit for the fall back to the glib, but it'd only be like offering chocolate to Willy Wonka. Moving on was the better option. "You also like them curvy. Compliant. Sweet. Simple. Big eyes and bigger boobs always help." Though that all shut him way the hell up, I tacked on the finish for my sake as much as his. "And brunette. Definitely brunette."

For a long moment, he remained silent. Finally, his taut lips released a harsh bite. "Fuck."

It weighted the air between us—but maybe right now, we needed to anchor the balloon back to earth. I'd spoken the truth, and we both knew it.

I lowered my hand. Dipped it beneath his doublet again to the warm groove in the center of his chest. "My eyes are wide open, Syn. But so is my heart. Closing one would mean disaster for the other. I'm aware of your...experience." I kicked up one side of my mouth. "Hell, I even appreciate it. But discussing it isn't necess—"

He ripped the rest of it from my lips by smashing his over them. Took my breath next as he deepened his claim. I moaned as he rolled me to fully face him. As he tangled our tongues, he twined our legs. The sound of tearing tulle was barely audible past the new tumult of my heart. I couldn't get enough of his taste, his hardness. I didn't care if I never breathed again—point proved when he finally released me, and we sucked air into heaving lungs.

Syn braced my face with his hand. Heat suffused me. And, despite the wildness of my senses, peace. Completion.

He finally spoke, with lips against mine. "It is necessary... because *you* are necessary."

His confession moving through me like a rake in gravel. No. *No.* I couldn't get used to this. Couldn't want this as badly as I already did. "Syn—"

He kissed me into silence again. "I know it is confusing. But—"

"No." I pushed back. I had to. Dipped my head and then shook it. Nothing was confusing. I knew exactly what was happening. I was falling deeper in love with him—and if I let the dive continue, I'd get the damn bends. *Danger zone. Punch the red button. Now.* "Samsyn, this—you—" I pushed out a heavy breath. "Thank you. For all of it. But—"

He growled low. "But what?"

I lifted my gaze again. Curled my fingers in against his chest. "We're not confused, big guy. We're just...conflicting." I pressed harder, cherishing the steady beat under my touch. "You know what I want from you. What I'd eventually demand. And what you cannot give me."

He dove into his surreal stillness once more. Everything except the brackets of his eyes and mouth, which visibly tautened. "What I cannot give *anyone*, Brooke." His fingers clenched against my hairline. "What I do not even *have* to give."

I raised my other hand, meshing it into his. "I know you think that. Perhaps even believe it. And I hope that one day, someone will help you learn it's just not true." My whole head suddenly felt heavy. I blinked against the pressure but felt tears spilling anyway. "I'm just sad it's not me."

"Brooke—"

A violent crackle cut him short. The ground glass grate of a comm line hail, at full volume...

Coming from the wig he'd shoved off my head, now hanging from the side of the table like a murdered animal.

"Badger!" Jag. Sounding like the pissed-off soul of that animal.

"Shit." I bolted upright, grabbing for the wig. "My comm must've come off with the hair."

"Badger! Where the fuck are you? We have a situation. Get your ass to the Tower's main entrance, stat!"

CHAPTER TWELVE

I skidded to a stop—literally—in front of Jagger. Thank God for slippery flats and polished stone floors. His thunderous expression barely faltered, changing only when he looked me over from head to toe—including the wig I'd barely pinned back on straight and the ripped section of my gown trailing behind me.

"What the hell have you been—" His voice cut short as Samsyn stepped beside me. His hair looked worse than my skirts. His doublet was lopsided, missing a hook on the bottom and an eye on the top. "Shit. You Cimarrons are determined to fucking kill me tonight."

Syn glowered. "What in Creator's name does that..." He trailed off as Jag shoved a smart pad into his grip. Dominating the screen, in huge red letters:

TRENDING NOW

#SinfulCims

Wasn't necessary to ask for a definition of the term. "SinfulCims" was given perfect clarification by the picture underneath, a shot of Evrest and Camellia in what looked like a storage room, the glittering walls indicating it was likely someplace inside LeBlanc Tower. But they sure as hell weren't fetching extra toilet paper or admiring the unique stones.

Cam's head was tossed back, Evrest's mouth against her throat. Her gown was hiked high on her thigh. It was obvious how it'd gotten there. Since Evrest's arm was still buried to the elbow beneath the green satin and harsh lust defined his face, any viewer with a little logic and a dash of imagination could determine why Lady Camellia was so "taken" with a Tahreuse broom closet.

"Damn." It conveyed my combination of frustration and admiration. Inside, I issued two shouts at Camellia.

You go, girl.

Goddamnit, Cam.

"Damn." Syn joined a grimace to his echo, pushing the pad back at Jag. "Not the image I needed, brother mine."

"Not what anyone needed," Jag retorted. "Not to the tune of three million tweets and twice as many post shares!"

Samsyn lifted a hand. "Calm down, Jagger. In ten minutes, a Kardashian will come along and make everyone forget this."

"Of course," Jag sneered. "Why did *I* not think of that? Why did I think we were working to be the country *not* eclipsed by gossip bunnies and kitten memes? The kingdom known for rich natural resources besides our king's practically bare ass?"

He looked ready to launch the smart pad at the wall. How could I blame him? Every word he'd spoken was true. Tonight was intended to be a major step for Arcadia onto the world stage, at least in the eyes of the media. This event was going to pave the way for the release of Harry Dane's movie, filmed entirely on location here and slated for a November release. Everyone would see Arcadia's stunning, sophisticated side, not just laugh it away as "the little island that could."

Now all they saw was the royal couple, bonking in a broom closet.

"You should have been here." Jagger became a different person as he turned, grinding the words into me, from the depths of his gut into the aching pit of mine. I didn't fight back. How could I? He'd given up so much to see Arcadia rise so far, way more than just the sleepless hours of this week. And what had I, the outsider entrusted with the care and safety—and, it appeared, sanity—of the kingdom's future queen, given in return? "You should have been here, damn it, *watching her!*"

A sound burst from Samsyn, short but vicious. "Calm down. Camellia is a grown woman, not a leashed puppy."

Jag's eyes bugged. "She was in a storage closet, fucking—"

"Her betrothed. Whom, I shall add, is also a man fully grown—but run so ragged the last six days, he has fallen into bed every night instead of meeting his woman's needs. Congruently, it has turned him into twelve kinds of a nasty bonsun to tolerate. Given the opportunity, I might have pushed them into the damn closet myself."

Jagger waited for half a beat before openly sneering. "Thank you for the gripping analysis. It means so much, coming from the other Cimarron who couldn't keep his dick in his breeches tonight."

I didn't know whether to punch Jag or be afraid for him. Syn didn't make the dilemma easier, looking tempted to indulge the former—intensifying my struggle with the latter— as he stomped over to bump chests with Jag.

"Tread carefully, Mr. Foxx."

"Consider the wisdom of your own advice, Prince Samsyn."

"*Stop.*" I wedged myself between them, pushing with all my might. They budged by one shuffling step apiece. "Remember the part in all this where you two are friends?"

I plunged on, wheeling on Jag first. "Regardless, he's your prince. Treat him as such, or I'll introduce your sinuses to your throat. And *you*"—I whipped toward Syn—"aren't off the hook. Neither am I. We fucked up." I stepped back, including Jag in on the rest. "I'm sorry, Jagger. I swear to you, my head's back in the game. Please give me another chance."

Jagger's nostrils tugged in. He eyed me, blatantly conflicted. Syn's presence didn't help. *Was* my head ever fully "in the game" with him around? I was willing to try—but that might not be enough. I'd followed him down that path like a rat behind the Pied Piper. Okay, he'd radioed Jagger to send a reinforcement in my absence, and where *that* person had been was a mystery, but it was a thin excuse. Samsyn Cimarron had become my illicit chocolate. One bite and I'd instantly craved another, no matter how unhealthy the choice.

I drove my nails into my palms, begging the pain to drive back my shameful tears. I refused to compound insult with injury by bawling in public.

Jag released a resigned sigh. I tied back the tears, lifting eyes of hope.

"Creator's balls," he mumbled. "I am left with few options. We are short-handed here, especially with half the former Distinct members choosing to add 'open bar' with 'town car home' and make it a *very* special night."

Samsyn rumbled like an ape that had stepped on a tack. "The Distinct were invited? Who the fuck made that decision?"

"Who the fuck do you think?"

"Evrest?" When Jag confirmed via silence, Syn slammed his head against the wall. "Noble, numb-headed fool. In love and thinks the whole world should be in love with him—including the twelve women he rejected."

"There are only six here tonight," Jag replied. "Thank the Creator. Currently, they are all soused and happy—and none of them is Chianna—so we shall bill it as a win."

I nearly crossed myself in response. Neither of them would've blinked. Chianna Smythe, once the odds-on favorite among the Distinct to win Evrest's hand, hadn't taken her jilted status gracefully. After staging a plot against Camellia that nearly had a tragic ending, the woman had escaped custody and disappeared into thin air. A popular island argument pitted those who thought her still on the island, allegedly living in the rough rainforests in the west, against theories she'd escaped the kingdom completely. As long as she wasn't here tonight, Jag was right: *win for all.*

"Grahm and Luca are watching over our drunk disco dollies," Jag explained. "And I had to dispatch Blayze early, to accompany the high couple back to the Rigale as soon as 'Sinful Cims' went viral. Queen Xaria did not take it all very well."

I tensed all over again when he canted a brow in Syn's direction. I wasn't sure what to think about the reaction. Samsyn, still turned toward the wall, barely tossed a glance over his shoulder. "Mother will be fine, Jag. You know that as well as I. She will handle it...in her way."

Jag ducked a tight nod. "Will she need additional security for that, then?"

"Not this time."

"Very well."

I frowned. Darted a look between the two of them. They spoke words I understood...but didn't. Secrets were like that. Secrets with the power to dip Syn's shoulders as if anvils had been dropped on them. To darken Jag's gaze to the shade of burnt copper. But at this moment, I had no right to push them for spillage. I had no right to push for *anything*. Not that they dwelled on shit. The next moment, Jag had his chin jerked toward me and then out the door.

"Her Ladyship, Camellia, is waiting in the town car. We felt it wise to send Evrest ahead. Creator only knows what havoc the two of them would cause if left in a space with carpeted floors and leather seats."

I tried not to laugh. "You know they'll find a way to hook up at the Rigale, don't you?"

"Badger girl, I do not give a matchstick of a damn if they use a chandelier as a fuck swing and peanut butter as lube—as long as they do it in *private*."

"Roger that." The radio formality was purposeful. I really wanted him to know my head was all-in again. As I turned to leave, I also forced myself not to glance back at Samsyn. That part gutted a little deeper.

All right...a lot deeper.

Every step seemed to pound it in. I couldn't help matching the feeling to my trip to Temptina Falls—had it been only a week ago?—after he'd arrived early at the Center and surprised me on the training mat. Flushed skin. Hammering heart. Aches in places too intimate to ignore. And stabbed through it all, like furious battlefield stitches, the knowledge that I still craved Samsyn Cimarron like a junkie on crack—and now had to face the disgusting, shivering torture of detox.

Yay, me.

CHAPTER THIRTEEN

"All right. I guess I do want to know, after all." Camellia leveled a resigned gaze through the combination of moonlight and street lamp glow gliding across the town car's back seat. "How bad is the damage? Really?"

I patted her hand. Lifted a rueful smile. "Scale of one to ten? About a nine right now."

"Shit."

"I said *right now*." I curled my fingers around hers. "Good news. The movie isn't opening for over six months. That's a lot of time to scale this back to a little blip."

"Without the whole kingdom writing me off as a slutty floozie first?"

"You and Evrest are engaged—and in love," I chided. "And, clearly, unable to keep your hands off each other." A blissful sigh escaped as I pulled off the wig and shook out my hair. "To some, that photo may even be romantic."

"If they're not a Pura." She dropped her head into her hand. "I can only imagine what new nicknames those lunatics are whipping up for me now."

"You mean all three of them?"

She tossed a glare. "That little club is growing, Brooke. You know it as well as I do."

"And will die off as soon as they run out of the good cookies." That deserved at least a quick laugh. After we indulged together, I persisted, "I'm serious. You're Buffy, remember?

You're making the world a better place, Cam. You're making *Evrest*'s world a better place. In the end, happiness gets to climb higher on the rainbow. Arcadians really like their rainbows."

A watery smile lit up her soft features. She hauled me into a crushing hug. "You're so awesome."

I grinned. "Back at you, Buffy baby."

She sobered a little. "I hope you weren't in deep shit with Jag."

"I was." I shrugged. "Probably still am. But it was due to my bad call, not yours."

Her eyes went wide. "Excuse the hell out of me? *Bad call?* You mean because Syn stepped in and did something about Ardent's letch-from-hell moves on you?"

"Crap." My turn to drop my head into a hand. "I'd hoped I was the only one who noticed."

Camellia rubbed my shoulder in comfort. "Outside observers didn't know the difference. I think Ardent was just feeling a little full of himself."

I lifted a brow. "If 'himself' is 'creepy dude hitting on the old friend's daughter,' he pounded the nail on the head."

"The excitement of the night probably got to him too. There was a lot going on. The band started playing, the press started hovering..." She rolled her eyes. "And *hovering*."

I released a breath. "Well, I'm grateful Samsyn was there."

"He's clued into you." She punctuated by tilting a knowing grin. "Nope. Edit time. He's just *into* you, period."

Her edit time...my choice time. I could return her giggle with one of my own, perpetuating the concept that something— anything—was "there" between Syn and me, or I could honor my promise to Jagger and recommit myself to reality.

What I cannot give anyone, Brooke. What I do not even

have to give.

Reality it was.

What it had to be.

I turned my gaze out the window. Beheld the passing landscape: the stark silhouettes of trees against the moon. Black and silver...so much like Syn's eyes. His darkness tangled with his light. But like the trees in my view, the darkness would always be closer, denser—even blocking out the light in places. It was all he could see, not believing the light had so much more power. That if he just believed in that force...

"So?" Cam's prompt yanked me out of the moody reverie. She grabbed one of my hands again. "Did the big guy drag you off to a dark corner and have his way with you? And if he did, I want details, girl. Every last one."

I chuffed while tugging free. "Camellia..."

"Oh, my God! He *did*, didn't he? I knew it! Ohhhh Brooke. You two are so cute together!"

"Camellia."

The car stopped. Outside, the trees and moon were replaced by the ornate archway of the Residence Rigale.

"Duty calls." I'd never been happier to spout the words— or to put on my authoritarian face. "Stay here, okay? I need to confirm Evrest's team performed the proper perimeter checks first. After that, I'll come get you."

As I'd hoped, mentioning Evrest made the woman forget all about Syn and me. Bullet dodged—for the time being. I'd be better at fielding her questions even tomorrow morning, when every step didn't brush my leg against the tear in my skirt and every breath didn't fill my senses with his scent, earthy and luxurious, mixed on his hot skin...

Focus. Perimeter check.

The lead guard from Evrest's detail, a burly soldier named Bo, answered my radio hail at once. He was accompanied by one of the guys from our local team, Blayze's younger brother, Flayre, who assured me he'd overseen the perimeter check himself. "All is secure," he stated, though ended as if tempted to tell me more.

"What?" I urged. I didn't know Flayre as well as Blayze but doubted anyone would've missed the glitch in his composure. "We don't have time for games. What's troubling you?"

"Troubling?" This seemed to be news to Bo, but the man had likely been busy attending Evrest. "Is there something you didn't report, boy?"

Flayre paled. I felt a little sorry for him. "Apologies," he muttered. "And no, not troubling, just...an observation."

"Of what?" I queried.

"The princess Jayd."

"Jayd?" The interjection came from behind me. Concern clamped Camellia's face as well as her voice. "What about her?"

My teeth clenched. "I told you to stay in the—"

"What's wrong with her?" Cam demanded.

Shockingly, Flayre fought back a smirk. "I do not wager *anything's* wrong, from what we could hear from her quarters."

I traded a horrified glance with Bo. Then Cam. "Shit!" she spat before leading the way into the mansion at a wild run. I was no more than two steps behind, with Bo and Flayre behind me.

Our steps sounded like rifle shots on the marble floors, echoing through the mansion as we raced to the level containing Cam's and Jayd's suites. I hoped beyond hope that the noise pierced through to the girl and whoever she was doing it with.

Damn. All we needed now was another Cimarron caught with their underwear in the wrong position.

We all arrived at the door to Jayd's suite, breathing hard. Didn't stop me from glaring at Camellia as she took a second to smooth her skirts. "Jayd?" She politely rapped on the door.

"Are you fucking—" Bo hissed to a stop when I jabbed a reprimanding finger. "Begging pardon, Your Ladyship, but are you insane?"

He looked mollified when I followed Cam's knock with a more severe pound. "*Jayd!* We're coming in!"

"Ready or not." Flayre's quiet sing-song was elbowed into submission by Bo.

A tense moment. Another. My ears felt physically stretched, straining to discern some sound from the suite beyond. Nothing. No rustling clothes. No movement. No frantic whispers.

I jabbed a stare at Flayre. "*This* was the chamber you heard noise in?"

Flayre, not looking so smart-assy anymore, shifted on his feet. "I... I am *fairly* certain..."

His gaze narrowed as the door creaked open.

Jayd appeared in the aperture. Fully calm. Fully dressed. Fully shitfaced.

"Cammmmm." She shoved unruly curls from her face. "Heeeyyy! Come on in. The party's right heeeere." She frowned, seeming confused, before whirling and leaving the open door behind. "But there's nuh more tunes. I had the tunes goin', damn it"

Flayre gave us a confirming nod. "The tunes" must have been the racket his team heard.

"Holy shit." Camellia hoisted a nearly empty vodka bottle

in one hand, three champagne splits in the other. On the coffee table, a jug of orange juice was half-depleted.

"At least her panties are in the right place," I murmured. Cam gave a discreet snort—just before Jayd's wail pierced the air.

"Muuusssiiic," she cried. "Jayd needs her tunes! No fancy ball for Jayd. No fun for Jayd. So she made a party here, with the tunes. Yaaayyyy Jayd. Wooooo!"

As the girl twirled across the room, Cam nodded quietly to me. "You get the water. I'll grab the aspirin."

"Affirmative."

Good thing she still watched as I said it. She never would have understood me otherwise, thanks to the explosion on the air, courtesy of Jayd restarting her "tunes." Cam's jaw dropped, mirroring my look. I'd have pegged Syn's little sister as a fan of dance favorites and happy pop, not the violent bursts that shook the windows and...

filled the air with...

smoke?

"Shit." It was equally wasted breath, shouted more from instinct than anything. My breath was fire down my throat, worsened by acrid black snakes through the room. I caught a glimpse of the terror on Cam's face before Bo tackled her to the floor. One blink, recognizing the action. A second, in relief. Safe. Okay. Camellia was safe.

And then the adrenaline kicked in.

And the horror.

And the thoughts, whizzing one after another, just like the bullets now crisscrossing before my sights.

Not music.

Explosions. *Invasion*. Ninjas.

Huh?

Ski masks. Black suits. Guns. *Very* nice guns. Searching. Determined.

I pounded on my comm piece while diving behind a sofa. "Breach! Level nine! This is Badger. We have a code-black breach on level nine!"

Fast, frantic peak out. An equally urgent scan of their careful, crouched steps, their thorough, sweeping stares. I sucked in a breath, snapping the pieces together. *They're after something.*

No.

Oh, God.

Not something.

Someone.

The Cimarrons.

"Shit!" I popped my head back up, taking in as much intel as I could. How many were there? And why wouldn't they all hold still?

A gasp of relief spilled when I spotted Flayre—until realizing *he* was leading them. Pointing the damn way for them.

Holy crap.

And that wasn't the end of the shit-fest.

Bo's voice blared through the comm line. For a second, despite everything, it was reassuring. I'd watched him get Cam out safely. But why did he still bellow through the line now? And what the hell was he saying? *Invade? Hate? Raid?*

Jayd.

"Shit!" I gasped again. *Jayd!*

I screamed her name, not expecting an answer—but receiving a strange one. I felt her voice more than heard it, my body resonating with awareness, like a radio dial hitting a specific frequency. No matter what I was ever doing or saying, every cell in my being always stopped when a Cimarron's voice vibrated the air.

I dropped low but kept my head high. She had to be nearby. What direction had she gone in? She'd been twirling across the room, complaining about the music having stopped—

I looked toward the alcove containing all the high-tech entertainment controls for the room. Shockingly, it was all as pristine as the moment we'd entered. But also the same: the totally tanked girl standing in front of the equipment, weaving to a song only she could hear, hands raised over her head, black curls bobbing...

In short, making herself a neon target for the ninjas.

Dread pounded my veins, gauzed my thoughts. My stomach rose to my throat. Not that screaming at Jayd was even an option. If those bastards knew how close they were getting to her, with every passing second...

God help us.

Just like that, time slowed once more. Every passing instant was blown bigger than life, magnified and treacherous, like an approaching tarantula. Every footfall was sludging thunder. The rifle shots were sci-fi screams of metal and fire. Moving felt like dragging an elephant through an oil slick. Somehow, I did. Crawled, shaking and frantic, to the edge of the couch I hid behind, until gaining a clear view of the archway to the entertainment alcove...

The ninjas were moving fast. They'd swept the bedroom first. Once they reemerged into the living room, they'd see Jayd—

And do what?

Were they here to capture her? Kill her?

Another three seconds, and we'd all know.
Unless I moved my elephant-in-oil ass first.

CHAPTER FOURTEEN

"Brookie! Hiiii. Hey, what're you—what the—ahhhh!"

Nothing like a few rounds from several guns, along with the sight of approaching enemy soldiers, to sober a girl up.

At least that's what I hoped. And what it seemed. Jayd, frantically panting on the floor beneath me, stared with eyes like the Northern Lights at full burst. "Wh-What is happening? Brooke?"

"Ssshhh!" Most ridiculous command ever. My pounding heart and wild nerves gave me no option. I ducked against the couch to keep from whimpering beyond that, listening as the ninjas stalked closer.

Until I saw the bright-red stain on Jayd's neck. "Oh, no." Both words stabbed through my head. "You're bleeding." Those too.

Jayd's lips trembled. "Not *me!*"

No time to process who was right. With disgusting timing, time sped up again.

Jayd's strident shriek.

The pain in my head, now delivered by shrieking banshees, set free in my nervous system.

The shadow looming over me. His sweat dripping on the back of my neck. His bellow, booming through me. "Aha! Here they are!"

More banshees. More spears of pain, tearing through my body, especially my left shoulder and arm. Pushing up on it caused my vision to double. I forced my thoughts to clear long enough for a fast prayer upward. Training and instincts were only going to take me so far.

But damn, I hoped that distance was much farther than this.

The desperation stampeded in. Annihilated everything except an instinct so old, it was trite. *Kill or be killed.* Jag had often talked to me about what to expect if I ever fought anyone for my very life, but I'd listened to his accounts like a kid hearing fairy tales. Adrenaline drowning pain? Vision clouded with rage? Every other sound in the room dropping away? Sure. And giants climbed beanstalks while wolves passed as grannies.

I owed Jag a huge apology.

As soon as I killed this asshole.

Jayd screamed again, making it impossible to think—or maybe that was due to the soldier's hand, wrenching into my hair. He hooked his other arm around my waist, using that to hurl me to the couch. I braced for the impact of the terror—for the memories to once more flood back, turning me back into that terrified girl, sucking in lungs full of dead flowers, fresh sulfur, and stark fear—but it never came. I was too pissed. Entirely too ready to look this dude in the eye and let him see exactly what I thought about him and his "friends" attacking *my* friends...

And my home.

I sucked back a breath through my teeth. Expelled it in a hiss. Jerked up my head, steeling for the blow certain to come—but not until I'd gotten a good, hard glare at this guy. Two seconds. That was all I'd get as material to analyze about him. His stance, his focus, his strength—most importantly, his weakness. There wasn't a fighter I'd met, beyond Samsyn, who didn't have a weakness.

Nothing like expecting something to go one way to ensure it didn't.

I didn't get two seconds to look at him. I got three. Then five. Then seven and even nine, as the eyes behind the ski mask turned whiter and whiter, gawking like I'd turned into a ghost. Had I? Was there a crucial step I'd missed here...that tidbit called dying?

"*Untoten*," he snarled. "*Untoten!*"

I had no idea what he was saying, nor did I care. The bonsun who'd grabbed me was now the soldier losing his shit in front of me, and I didn't need fate to toss the gift twice. Weakness discovered. Time to move. *Now.*

Though my vision still showed two of him, I lurched at the craptoid. The less fuzzy one had to be him, right? One knee to his groin and I'd buy the seconds Jayd and I needed to run for deeper cover—

I was halted short. Robbed of strength and even air by a Hulk punch between my ribs. I doubled over and dropped to my knees, gagging on waves of nausea. Somehow, I managed to battle the pain—and Jayd's next scream—to confront the giant who'd stomped to his friend's rescue.

Shit. Looked like his ski mask had been a damn good idea. Even through the thing, I could tell the bastard had broken his nose too many times. Glimpses of his skin showed pits worse than the Asuman caves. He leered at me, exposing teeth—all four of them—apparently held together by old particles of food. That had to explain his breath. As the monster used my hair to drag me back up, I prayed for relief from the *eau de dead cat* spewing with his breaths. This couldn't be right. Wasn't I supposed to be thinking of clouds and white light and the glorious times of my life, instead of wishing I could take a bath in mouthwash?

"Brooke! Oh, Creator! Brooke!" Jayd was *really* sober now. As more rifle fire thudded the air, I forced my hand up and down, motioning her to stay on the floor. Syn would never forgive me if she died. *I'd* never forgive me if she died.

Down, Jayd. Stay down!

I thought I heard myself yell it. Right before I set the stellar example—by doing it.

Okay, not me. *Really* not me. My knees, joining the pain parade with dual screams, helped drive the point. Hulkie had dropped me—right before falling to the deck himself. He hit the floor with a massive *whomp*. His unblinking eyes, bloody mouth, and bullet-punched forehead were morbid twins in my vision.

My breath returned, only it was agony too. My lips spewed wild whimpers. Somehow, I found the shut-off switch. Killing the cries didn't help the horror. I scrambled from Mr. Halitosis as far as I dared while still searching for Jayd. Where the *hell* was she? Hadn't she just been here a second ago? Fuck. *Fuck.* Had they gotten her? And who the hell had shot the giant? Had that bullet been meant for me?

I plopped onto my butt, back against the couch, fighting for every breath—

When massive arms banded me again.

I let the banshees out. Let the rubber bands fly off the tight ball. Lost my mind—and was grateful for it. If this was the end, I was sure as hell going down with a scream in my throat, a pair of crushed balls beneath my knees. One of my hands clocked the asshole's jaw. My knee jabbed his upper thigh. *Damn it.*

Not close enough. I'd just try again. I'd fight until I couldn't. Scream until I was hoarse. Struggle until they tied me up and—

"Brooke!" Jayd again. Shrill and sober as ever. *Thank God.* "*Brooke!*"

"Save...yourself." Where the hell had *that* strength come from? And did it matter? "Get out of here, Jayd! Get *out* while you can!" *Shit.* This jerk was stronger than the other hulk. And smarter. He knew every one of my evasion tactics, as if taught by Jagger himself. Maybe he *had* been.

Somebody had to lodge a complaint with the universe. Death was *not* the package I'd been promised. I wanted my clouds and angels.

"Astremé. Damn it, *please* be still."

Ohhh. So *that* was the shit up fate's sleeve.

No angels.

Only one.

And for him, I'd gladly give up the damn clouds.

My sharp sobs turned into shaky laughs. I clutched at him, needing him close. My senses collided, struggling to process how different he suddenly was. His hair was nearly gray with caked soot. The stuff was even layered on his thick lashes. Soot streaked the perfect angles of his face. He even smelled different. It went beyond the battle residue. Something deeper, more acrid. And why did he still look so eyeballs-deep in despair? Surely the insanity—or whatever the hell it'd been— was over.

"Hey...big guy?"

He smiled. Sort of. "Yes, my little warrior?"

Wow. Now that was nice. I wanted to tell him so, but turning thoughts into words felt harder by the second, and I still had important questions to ask. "Is—is everyone safe?

Cam? Evrest?"

He stared like I'd asked him how to get to the nearest wormhole but answered softly, "Yes. Everyone is fine. Please *be still*, Brooke."

"Why? Are we still under attack? Wh-What happened?" I lifted my head. *Not* slick. Pain and dizziness pushed it back down, into the pillow of his elbow.

"Damn it!" So much for gentle giant Syn. His roar tore through him and then me, terrifying in its intensity.

Shit. Because *he* was terrified?

"Bo! Where the *fuck* are the medics?"

He was answered by goobly-gook squawking. I heard the same chatter near my neck; my comm line had likely been knocked loose. I couldn't make out any words. Only knew that Bo sounded much more collected than Syn.

"Not fast enough," Syn barked. "Not fucking fast enough!"

"Syn—"

"Shut up, Jayd."

"Hey." The smoky sough was the best I could do—but watching it affect Samsyn like a dagger to the gut made *my* gut hurt. And other places. All my ribs felt crushed at once, squeezing my heart and threatening my air. "It'll be okay, big guy."

He looked ready to tell me to shut up too.

"Samsyn." I blinked hard. There were suddenly two of him now—on a regular day, not a damn bad thing—except that I lifted a hand to brush comforting fingers to his jaw and got a knife of agony down my arm instead. I writhed, letting the limb fall. Syn caught it, his grip gentle but his voice furious.

"*Damn it*, woman! Stop moving or I'll tie you down!"

My giggle felt like bubbles in my ears. "Ooooo; really?"

"Brooke—"

"You'd like that, wouldn't you? Hmmm. I'd probably like that too." My sultry smile slipped as a shiver took over. "But can we do it someplace warmer? I'm really cold all of a sudden."

Darkness began to join the chill. I flailed against it, but the current grew too strong. So strong. The black waves pulled me like a rip tide, dragging at me harder...harder...

A wave of it crashed in, too huge and mighty to fight anymore. But as blissful and quiet as the black sea was, I struggled to get back to shore—where Samsyn still bellowed like a wild, wounded animal.

"Bo! Get them here *now*. By the Creator, if you bonsuns let her die, I shall exact *your* fucking flesh as payment!"

CHAPTER FIFTEEN

Lights intruded again, all too fast. So bright. So blaring. I resisted them, along with the hands that prodded and poked and stabbed, tearing me from the sea of silence with ropes of pure pain. All of it was connected to my left upper arm. I screamed, trying to pull away, but they were damned intent on making it feel sawed-off before they actually hacked it. That had to be their plan. Nothing else could feel this horrendous.

"*Damn it!* Fucking...butchers." I dug in my heels, bucking against their captivity. In seconds, the pain in my arm shot through my body. A hundred hands swept in, subduing me again. I panted hard. Fought waves of weariness and helplessness. Felt myself losing.

Only one thought eclipsed the deluge. It spilled from my lips in a pleading whimper. "Samsyn." He'd been here, hadn't he? Bellowing and snarling and threatening at Bo and half the island. His voice, breaking my heart. His warmth, keeping me sane.

"Samsyn!"

I was so cold. So desperate to be done with this.

"Here."

Yes.

He *was* here. Commanding away the cold, infusing me with his strength...bringing the light I *wanted* to fight for. I clung to our connection, twisting it into my tendons and bones, using it to get in one breath without agony. Another.

"Don't go." I all but sobbed it, though was ashamed. Could I be any more selfish, begging him to stay when some very bad guys had just done some very bad shit? His comm line probably sounded like an awful action movie. *I* sure as hell expected reality to jump back in soon, turning this back into a figment of everyone's imagination. "But if you have to, I understand."

"They shall not move me from this spot, astremé."

"You're being sweet. And I appreciate it, but really, if you have to—"

"*Brooke.*"

"What?"

"Do you *truly* think I was going for 'sweet'?"

"Good point." There was a rustling near him, as if someone else had stepped over. He was still there, though. The rough heat of his knuckles brushed the crest of my cheek. Something pinched my arm. I winced, making him turn the soothing touch into something more directive. He hummed a soft sound. My senses glided on its velvet, soon swirled with a new sensation. Warmth. Numbness. Bliss. "Wow," I heard myself say. "Wha the hell is thaaaa?"

Syn sifted gentle fingers through my hair. "There. You can call the painkillers 'sweet.'"

"'Kay." I was fuzzy...floating. "*This* is sweet, Syn. *You* ah not." My giggle echoed in my head. I felt good enough to open my eyes. "C'mooooon, big guy. Tha was funny."

He lifted a smile, though not enough to earn me a glimpse of teeth. "Yes, astremé. That was funny."

"No. Huh-uh. Wasn't." I pouted. "Didn't earn me any tee."

"Tea?"

"No. *Teeth.*" Ow. Okay, this was officially a No Thinking zone—though I couldn't avoid the contemplation of how cute he was, cocking that ornery frown. Holy shit, the man was so jumpable.

"Teeth? Brooke...what—"

"You nevah show me your teeth, Syn. You evah stopped to think abow tha? Why no teeth?" I lifted my hand to cover his own. Just my right one, since the butcher fuckers still had my left trapped and pinned. They hadn't gotten out the saw yet, though. The limb still throbbed like a rhino on the hunt, though now it was a baby rhino instead of a bull. "You have such prettah teeth, big guy." I reached along his arm, toward his face. His eyes glittered, intense as quicksilver. His jaw clenched, though I figured the soft chuckles around the room had more to do with that than my compliment. Nevertheless, I *really* wasn't getting any teeth now.

He curled his other hand around mine. Gently lowered it back down but didn't let it go. "You need to be still now, Brooke." His long fingers curled in deeper, pushing into my palm in emphasis. "Keep looking at me—and be very still."

"Why?"

He pushed harder with the other hand, rubbing my hairline with his thumb. "They cannot run the risk of putting you out; not with a concussion still likely." A deep breath widened his nostrils. "But it has to come out, *favori*."

"Come out? Wha does?"

"The bullet."

"The *wha*?"

I didn't know who to hate more: whoever started digging into my shoulder like Hannibal Lecter with a grudge or the man helping to hold me down, invading my hell with his bronze angel's face.

Couldn't be knocked out, huh? That had to be because he

knew the pain would do it instead. And he would've been right.

★ ★ ★

My eyelids felt coated in glass and my throat the sand dune that'd created the shards. *Parched. Hurts.* The rest of my body didn't fare much better, though with every movement, my muscles confirmed the lingering fog of the painkillers.

Painkillers.

Was that it? If so...*why* was I on painkillers?

What the hell was going on?

Then the memories blared. Brief flashes at first, followed by longer stretches.

The blast. The smoke. Those men...stomping, prowling...

Searching.

For what?

Not for what. For whom.

The sweaty soldier, yelling like the kid who'd found the golden egg. Then his friend, carrying last week's dinner between his teeth, using me for punching practice. Smelly jerk-wad.

Only then...he wasn't anymore.

Somehow, the jerk-wad had morphed into Samsyn.

Samsyn...who'd held me tight and whispered I'd be okay, only to roar at the damn world like a dragon with an injured princess in his arms...

Okay, now you're just getting stupid.

It was more outrageous than thinking he'd stuck around while the medics subjected me to that torture. That he'd whispered so tenderly to me, just before the violence of their invasion...

Not memories. These had to be dreams...just like the one I was having right now. A fantasy that seemed so real, with his arms around me, his breath in my ear, his body close and big and hard. And warm. Wherever we'd landed in the dream, it was ass-freezing cold, and I was dressed in nothing but my camisole. I hunched against the chill, burrowing against the heated bricks of Syn's chest and curling in my arms to take advantage of our proximity—

Okay; attempted to.

Pain. Lots of it. Down my left tricep and wrist. Hell. The butchers had let me keep the damn thing, and now I only wanted it gone.

As soon as my moan sliced the air, Syn growled in reprimand. "*Calmay olmak*, astremé. Be still. You are not healed."

"Healed." I murmured it while letting him guide my head back down to his chest. Slowly, the scrambled eggs in my brain folded events into a cohesive omelet—though pieces were still missing. "From what?" I drowsily asked. Syn had started combing fingers through my hair, and it felt so...damn...good.

"You do not remember?" His voice was as soft as his touch, as he urged a straw to my mouth. While I sucked down blissfully cold water, he brushed the hair off my face.

"Not everything," I finally replied. A joyous moan almost followed as his fingers combed through my hair. Damn, the man had talented hands. "There was a huge blast. Lots of people...men...ninjas...everywhere. At first I thought it was a Pura stunt, but those douche bags were definitely there for something. Or someone."

"Douche bags." He echoed my slang as he often did, his tone a curious question.

"Let it slide, big guy."

Fortunately, he did. "What happened next?"

Shock. Sudden, stabbing. It turned physical, gashing through my brain, but I jerked the damn thing up anyway. "Flayre. Oh my God, Syn, it was Flayre. That was how they got in after the perimeter check. He betrayed us!"

He swallowed hard. "That much we *do* know."

"He confessed?"

"You could say that."

"Shit." Though his grim tone already clued me in, I stared into his tired eyes with the silent insistence for the spill.

"We chased him out of the mansion and up to the cliffs over the shallows. He...jumped before we could get to him."

"Fuck." I let my head drop again. "Was Blayze there?"

"No."

"Thank God." I absently stroked the seam between his pecs. "How's he doing?"

"Not well."

"No doubt."

We were silent, each lost in thought. My spirit ached for Blayze. He loved serving Arcadia and was engaged to a woman just as devoted to the kingdom. Flayre's integrity flush would stain everyone in the family for a while, especially him. There wouldn't be any security details or trusted group missions for him in the near future.

At last, Syn broke the silence with another quiet query. "Can you remember anything else, astremé?"

Soft snort. Deep frown. "I don't think so. That's where things get fuzzy."

"Ah. Of course."

"Of course?" I chuffed. "Like you know?"

He hummed out a grunt. "The rest of the room felt miles away? You noticed strange little things, like dust on a table or a mole on your enemy's arm—"

"Or their really bad breath?"

"That would fit." His lips pressed the top of my head, feeling like apology and commiseration in one. "And then, the realization that the white clouds and angels are never going to appear..."

"*Right?*" I popping up on my good elbow. "Wow. You *do* get it."

I expected him to order me back down. Instead, he let me linger for a few moments, hovering slightly over him... enraptured by another expression I'd never seen from him before. If this was becoming a pattern, I wasn't complaining— especially now. The hundred thoughts behind his bright blues had multiplied to a thousand. His lashes seemed longer as he swept that incredible gaze across my face, following the path set by his roaming fingers. "Protecting a kingdom with water as borders is not always a—how would you say it?—a *beach bash?*"

I tried out a small laugh. "That would fit." Nope. *Not* a wise move. "Whoa." Dropped my head again, as dizzy and woozy became the moment-killing wonder twins. Even with the rock of Syn's body back beneath me, the world spun, unwilling to let go. "*Damn.*"

"Ssshhh." His hand, massive and magical, moved back through my hair. He had to be on the universe's payroll, bribed to help put me back under. "You need rest now."

I snorted. "So you know about *that* now too?"

The spaces beneath my ear rumbled with dark mirth. "More than all the rest."

"Sounds like you learned that the hard way."

"As I am reminded nearly every day, astremé."

"Huh?"

"By the bullet they had to leave in my thigh."

"*What?* Seriously?"

"*Rest.*"

He didn't let me rise this time. It was wonderfully easy to let him take over, surrounding me again in the cocoon of his bulky arms. In contrast, thick softness draped me from behind: a blanket as soft as cashmere, redolent with Syn's scent. As wind, woods, and pepper filled my nostrils, surrender filled my soul. I nuzzled into the plateau of his pectoral. Another sound reverberated through his chest, sounding like a strangled hiss. It unfurled an answering sound from deep in me: a long, tired sigh.

"Rest," he murmured again. It was drenched in his typical command—but I heard the clutch of his throat at its finish.

Something to analyze later.

My eyes grew heavier. My limbs weren't far behind. Still, I forced my hand upward, stretching fingers into the comforting warmth of his nape. As always, I marveled at the feeling of the power beneath his skin, seemingly always at the ready...but always reined back for me. "You make me feel so safe."

"Because you are."

"But...Samsyn?"

"Hmmm?"

"Who are *you* safe with?"

Something told me I should've just Tasered him. The effect on his body would've been the same. The catch of his breath, more violent this time, betrayed he'd understood me very clearly. That the safety I spoke of wasn't just physical.

"I am perfectly safe on my own, Brooke."

"Bullshit."

He snorted. "I ordered you to rest."

Fume. And a very strong urge to glower. I held back, keeping my head on his chest—choosing to see him through my touch instead. Slowly, I traced fingers around the bottom of his ear, along the line of his jaw, down his neck, to the place where his heart pumped right beneath my ear.

"Someone needs to keep you safe, Samsyn." *Please let me in, Samsyn.*

"Go to sleep, Brooke."

He concluded it with a weary sigh.

But not before the beats under my fingers sped to double their rhythm.

I fell back into the dark as a smile took over my lips.

CHAPTER SIXTEEN

When I woke again, I guessed a few hours had passed at most. No gritty eyes or parched throat this time. The air was heavy with the unique hush of night, though a gentle wind blew through nearby trees.

Trees. Wind. But nothing else to clue me in about where we were. Even my surge of alertness was an interesting thing. My brain was more alert, stepping from its earlier fog, jolted in a combination of curiosity and anxiety.

I pushed up on my good arm, peering around through my mussed bangs. I wasn't home. Not in the Residence Rigale, either. This was just as old a structure, though—only fitted with more modern accessories. It was a stunning room, with double doors made of dark wood set into about twelve feet of flat stone wall. The rest of the architecture was round and also made of stone, instantly evoking the feeling of a castle turret. Custom-built into the far side of the room, in front of a wide leather couch and loveseats, was an entertainment system to drool for. The modern track lighting over that area was dimmed to half power, as were the lights set into the alcoves on either side, illuminating sleek modern sculpture pieces.

And then I gazed around the huge bed beneath me. And over me.

As Alice in Wonderland would say, things were getting curiouser and curiouser.

The bed was such an icon, I wondered if the turret had

been built around it. Posts thicker than telephone poles gave support to a canopy of red and gold damask, which pooled behind the padded leather headboard. Both sides of the bed had nightstands that swiveled out, custom-built with mini drink coolers, sound systems, and electronics chargers.

Chargers...

for things like phones.

I bolted up straighter. "Shit."

The man next to me lurched up too. Somehow, it didn't stun me at all that Syn grabbed his SIG Sauer, resting in *its* custom slot in his nightstand, and aimed it at the door. Another no-brainer: the somersault of my belly and the new focus of my stare, as every perfect muscle in his torso twisted together, fully waking my senses inside five seconds.

"Stand down, Your Highness." I forced calm into it, very aware that the weapon in his hand was deliberately made without a safety. "It's only me, big guy."

Took him only another five seconds to reholster the SIG and then twist fully back to me. "What?" he demanded. "What is it? What is wrong? Are you all right?"

"Fine." Instinctively, I lifted my left hand to cover the death grip he had on my right shoulder. Bad idea. It hurt like hell. The second I grimaced, his stress jumped by a DEFCON level. "Hey. *Hey.* I really am fine. Just kind of stupid." Big grin, and not even a forced one. "Just have to remember not to do that again."

He exhaled hard. Dropped his hand. Scrubbed it across the stubble fast becoming a beard. He looked a little tired. A lot disheveled. And too damn sexy for my now-rampaging hormones.

"All right," he mumbled. "Do *not* do that again."

As long as you don't command it in that *voice again.* Shit. Between his sleep-deprived ruggedness and his ground gravel undertone, the hormones situation was *not* faring well. And the fact that I was clad in just my camisole and panties, less than a foot away from *him* in nothing but his workout shorts, didn't help one damn bit.

For a moment, I simply let his magnificence seep in. Yes, all over again. I wondered if the sight of him, clothed or nude, would ever *not* do this to me. Though the latter was definitely a lot more fun...

"Are you feeling all right?"

He was all business now. Probably for the better. "Yeah." I kept it crisp too, though couldn't help my wandering gaze. If the man was uncomfortable about me staring, he could cover the hell up.

"Why did you cry out?"

"I saw the charger in the nightstand. It made me think of my phone. My parents—"

"Have been kept completely updated." He reached toward me again but curled his fingers back in, as if deciding better of the choice. My head applauded. My heart wanted to slap him. But things might always be like this for us now. The locked gazes, each remembering what it felt like to really be together—and then doing nothing about it.

Damn it. If only we'd met just now, instead of that night when I was so scared and starry-eyed...

"Th-Thanks," I finally mumbled. Jerked my gaze around the room again. "So...what *have* they been updated about? How long have I been here? For that matter, where *is* here?"

"A little over three days," Syn supplied to my first query. "Sshhh," he urged as I gasped. "You have needed the rest.

Everyone has."

"But Camellia—"

"Is back in Sancti, safe at the palais." He grunted in approval. "Evrest needed no convincing to cancel the rest of their tour plans. Jagger and Grahm are there, overseeing increased security in the whole complex."

"And Jayd? Is she—"

"Also safe and ordered to her quarters for the next ten years?" The grunt became a growl. "The answer to that is also yes."

The argument to his chains on Jayd would have to be tackled another time. I let out a slow breath while letting the new information sink in. "What a difference three days makes."

He cocked his head, dark hair caressing his jaw. "I know it feels like longer. But you are safe here, astremé, I promise."

"I know." I meant it. Tugged at his hand to prove it. Finished by peering once again around the room. "But where *is* here?"

"Ah." Self-deprecation quirked his lips. "The other half to Goldilocks's question."

I chuckled too. "Well, the bed's just fine. No complaints there. I'll keep you posted on the porridge."

"How about some frozen pizza and beer?"

"Hold the anchovies and we're cool." My stomach rumbled loudly. "Or maybe I'll just chew around the anchovies."

His lips twisted. "Not even Jagger is allowed here with anchovy pizza."

"Not even Jagger is..." Trailing voice. Dawning comprehension. "Wait. Is this...*your* place?" My skin tingled with little pinpricks, watching his demeanor warm with quiet pride.

"A retreat of sorts," he finally filled in. "No worries; we are still in Tahreuse—simply on the far shore of Sagique, up the mountain a bit from Noir."

"I had no idea..."

"Nobody does, except for Jag and a few of the usual guys." He shrugged, again with that new disarming touch that made me melt for him in brand-new ways. "I needed a place up here. As you know, I like coming to Tahreuse. It gives me...peace." His hesitation over the last word was unmistakable, as if the syllable had to stand for so much more. Still didn't explain the triple-time of my pulse or the nerves in my stomach. When those turned into a light laugh, he prompted, "Now what?"

My cheeks heated. "Every time you came up here, I thought you arranged for sleeping accommodations with your favorite..." I winced. "Well, you know..."

"My favorite Tahreuse town cuties?"

"Amusing way to say it."

I glared to emphasize my sarcasm—but never received the expected smirk in return. Somber Syn was back, gazing past the bed's footboard. His profile, re-torqued as if he'd grabbed the SIG again, was etched in dark intensity. "I have found it wise not to actually sleep with...people."

People.

Meaning women.

The ones he never wanted to talk about. The dozens, maybe hundreds, he'd fucked before me. The legions he'd screw after me.

Which should've made his tact a rather sweet gift. Instead, it enraged me. I'd had six damn years of "sweet." Seventy-two months of "care" and "consideration," like I was a kitten to be swaddled instead of the lioness who'd earned my place by his side, protecting Arcadia. Hadn't the bullet I'd taken in my arm proven that enough?

I released a long breath, working not to make it a huff. "But you slept with me." Granted, after we'd finished everything up in the bedroom at the Rigale, it had only been four hours at best. But it'd been sleep. The passed-out-like-the-dead kind.

No shock from *him* at that. He actually nodded slowly, as if expecting the observation. "You...are different."

I stared harder at him. He stared harder across the room.

"What the hell does that mean?"

He swallowed deeply. "I have no idea what that means, Brooke. Only...that it is."

Well, I wasn't pissed anymore. But I sure as hell wasn't eased. I couldn't decide whether he needed to be kissed, flogged, or both—or that I was even the right person to do it. The big dope gave me no hint, either. He sat there looking a hundred kinds of gorgeous—and a thousand kinds of baffled in his own right.

"Damn it, Syn." It accomplished nothing—but was better than the silence.

"Damn it, Brooke." His wasn't an ice breaker. It veered close to *being* ice, complete with the fissures hinting at a massive crack. When he scraped a hand back through his hair, the ends of his fingers trembled.

What the hell? This was all so different from the Samsyn I knew—that the whole world knew. The booming, ass-kicking dragon had retreated to a cave of confusion...

Because of...me?

Uh-uh. No way.

There was something more going on. There had to be. The damn doofus just refused to cough it up.

"You expect me to work with that?" I snapped. It whipped his head up, at least. Returned a small fire to his eyes.

"I expect you to do nothing with that."

So much for believing in the fire. "Right. Okay. Let me get this straight. That little bomb you dropped in my psychological lap? Do fucking *nothing* with it? Just...pretend it didn't happen? That *you're* not sitting there, shaking like a half-baked junkie because of it?"

"Like a half-baked—" He broke in on himself with a snarl. "You think that bringing up my past—*again*—and then talking of what happened at the Rigale—*again*—is—"

"Turning you into a sad stand-in for a crackhead." I couldn't fold my arms. Settled for cocking my head. "Yep. That's pretty much what I think."

His roar made the bed curtains tremble.

And pinned me to the pillows like a fly in honey.

Only to look back up at his looming figure, after he rolled to his knees in one powerful sweep.

Shit. The dragon was back. More dark and furious than ever.

And beautiful. And masterful. And I-need-you-to-fuck-me-now-ful.

My breath turned my chest into a bellows. He matched me heave for heave.

My lips worked against each other, battling to keep moisture in my mouth. His were still parted, exposing his continuing seethe. Well, *there* were his teeth—just not in the way I'd expected.

"Creator's *fucking* balls, Brooke." Not a roar now. Something worse. His guttural growl all but damned me. "You think I trembled because of your fixation on my past?"

Screw the honey. I shoved up on *both* elbows, defying him by straining my wound. And the pain? That shit could be a worthy ally for fury. "My *fixation*? How the *hell* is this a 'fixation'?"

"Because you throw it in my face at every turn?"

"You haven't seen throwing, mister."

He smirked with no warmth. And damn it if I didn't yearn to kiss the look right off his lips. "Threats, little one? Truly?"

"I'm not going to do this with you. I... I can't." Complete truth. Anger, ire, and arousal battled for control of my blood. I kicked free of the blankets, swinging my legs over the side of the bed. "I'm not threatening a fucking thing, Your Highness. I'm just taking care of myself by remembering the reality of all this—the reality that we won't ever be. Perhaps you should start doing the same!"

"Brooke." It was a raw—and useless—order. "Brooke—damn it—what are you doing?"

I stood. Gasped hard, fighting the dizziness. "I haven't bathed in three days. What do you think I'm doing?" The room tilted like a fun house. "Where's the bathroom?"

"Get the fuck back in bed!"

"Get the fuck out of my *life!*" I found the bathroom doorway. Clung to it as purchase, whirling around, letting him have the brunt of my pissed seethe. "No more bungee jumping for me, Syn. I'm cutting the line." *No more leaping off the bridge, reaching for you,* touching *you, only to be yanked away like a hooked fish. Falling. Bleeding.*

Lost.

The worst part? Gazing at him...and seeing just how deeply he got that.

"Brooke—"

"Leave me *alone*, Samsyn."

"*No.*"

The curtains quivered again. Before I could fully process that, he'd lurched off the bed with more seamless grace, feet hitting the floor like booms of thunder.

"Damn it, woman. You will *listen* to me!" Now, even the curtains didn't dare shake. The only element daring to defy him was the air itself, vibrating like a sword stabbed into oak. I looked up, swearing I saw that very blade, embedded down the center of the man who towered like that tree. I didn't know what to be more afraid of now: the desperation in that stance or the steel still glinting in his eyes.

I gulped hard. Stumbled backward.

He matched me step for step.

My bare feet hit the bathroom's travertine tiles. Slipped a little, in my urgency to get distance from him. I grabbed for the marble counter—and then let my ass fall to it.

"Don't come any closer!" I flung out my good hand. Syn caught it by the wrist. Dug his grip in hard. Pressed in even tighter, stepping even closer. My head fell back, trying to keep him in sight. I wasn't sure about that choice, considering the warmth of his breath and the fury in his glare, but the alternative—letting my lips smash into his thudding carotid—was out of the question.

"They shot you." The words were sparse chokes, as if he could barely speak them. "Those bonsuns...*shot* you." His jaw went taut beneath his beard. His gaze changed, showing me the horror of his memories. "I charged into that room, expecting to secure everything...and all I saw was *you*, Brooke, bleeding on the floor. I...could not think. I...could barely walk. Blood...all your blood...so much of it...and then you were so cold, and then you were just *gone—*"

"I only passed out, big guy." It was a whisper. I couldn't manage anything else. My livid rage had melted right into a lovesick puddle. How the *hell* did he do this to me? Without a backward glance, I'd plunged off the bungee bridge again.

"Facts like that are not relevant to a man who refuses to think, astremé." His head shook slowly. "And I—it was if you took my mind with you. I only wanted you back. Needed you calling me 'sweet' and teasing me about my damn teeth..."

Watery laugh. "You really do have nice teeth."

He pushed in tighter. *All* of him now. Dropped his forehead against mine. Curled our hands together and mushed them between our chests. "You were gone. I was helpless. I could do nothing...but shake like a fucking junkie."

I sucked in a ragged breath. As he let one out.

Swallowed hard. As he did.

Lifted our twined hands. Pressed a kiss to his knuckles... the same way his formed over mine. Our gazes meshed over that intimate clasp...bound in connection, in affirmation... in anguished acceptance of what this closeness was about to bring. We were as helpless to stop it as the gusting wind outside, as stars tumbling from the sky above that. That had to be the explanation for this: two stupid stars, escaping from heaven, hiding from the gods inside our souls...and making our hearts pay the miserable, beautiful price.

With a tight moan, he pushed a knuckle between my lips.

With a high sigh, I let him.

Welcomed him.

Kissed him back as he replaced that finger with his mouth. His tongue. His heat. Let him take me. Enflame me. Fulfill me.

Then matched his moan, pleading for even more...

just like a junkie getting her fix.

CHAPTER SEVENTEEN

When he finally pulled away, even more torment grooved his face. "*Brooke.*" And he shook again, like the oak with a bulldozer beneath, fighting to stay rooted in place.

My heart cracked. I grabbed the back of his neck, forcing him to look at me. "Here. I'm right here." I returned his hand to my sternum. Though every movement was a small physical agony, it was worse to watch *his* suffering: a reprise of that battle I could no more help with than understand. The only thing I could do was exactly what I'd said. Be here.

As he drew in more air, his fingers stilled on my skin. But as he let it out, he spread those strong tips...sliding them under my cami.

Up my breast.

Over my nipple.

Heated gasp. Aching groan. I gave him both as he lowered his head and tongued my bottom lip. Sighed in throaty need as he bit his way along the top one. When he shifted his touch, caressing over to the other breast, I could no longer hold in my full cry. I clawed the back of his scalp—and surged the soaked core of my body against the erect ridge of his.

Blowing wind.

Falling rain.

Doomed stars.

Inevitable. Inescapable.

If I hadn't known it before, the new surge of his tongue

vanquished the doubt. I let him in, surrendering and melting, vanquishing him in return. Stabbed my tongue harder, sucking him in, never wanting to let go, despite his conflicted groan.

"Don't stop." It was a junkie's pathetic plea. I didn't care. "God, Syn...don't stop."

That sound from his chest turned into a full rumble. "Fuck." Dissolved into a broken growl as his other hand worked between my thighs. "*Fuck*. Brooke."

I rocked into his touch. "Touch me. I need it. I need *you*."

The hand between my breasts was splayed and taut. "I can feel your heart."

"You *have* my heart. You know that, Samsyn. You *know* that."

He raised his head. His expression was primal, possessive...breathtaking. I absorbed it, letting him do the same. I smiled as he did, heady from a new realization. This was what the torment was for. This was the treasure worth the hunt, the rainbow worth the storm, the connection worth the pain. The heaven worth the hell.

He dipped his hand to the flesh beneath my panties.

"Oh!"

His eyes darkened. His lower lip vanished beneath his teeth.

As he penetrated me at once.

One finger. Two. Three.

My head fell back. So did my good arm, securing me to the counter as his fingers fucked in, over and over, spiraling my senses toward ultimate surrender. The whole time, I didn't stop staring at him. As if he'd allow it. His face was complete command, utter beauty. Determined breaths punched from his lips. Hard lines defined his jaw. Feral focus dictated every inch of his movements—including his tighter hold against my chest.

"Every beat," he grated. "Still mine."

"Yes." I nearly sobbed it. "Yours."

He twisted his lower hand. Raked his thumb through the soaked folds of my pussy. "And every throb of this sweet cunt?"

"Shit!"

"That was not an answer, astremé."

"Yes!" I blurted. "Yes, *yes*, okay? Yours. It's...all...yours. Always, Samsyn. Always."

"Yes." His echo was a seductive sibilance, trailed along my forehead as he pushed in deeper, filling me with those long, glorious fingers, drowning every other thought in my head, every other sensation in my body. "You give me so much." His dry whisper was a clutching contrast to the wet slicks of his fingers. "You gasp for me. Cry for me. Even bleed for me. My sweet Brooke. My beautiful Brooke." He pulled back, staring in full again, though the path of his gaze was aimless...lost. "You almost make me..." He gulped hard. Fucked me deeper. "Damn it. You almost make me believe."

I gazed at him harder. *Much* harder. Pounding the question my lips should've been forming—if my mouth was able to function. But the man had dropped his hugest bomb on my brain while lighting the biggest detonation to my body. One perfect swipe of his thumb, and I was a blinding, blissful blast. I screamed as the violence took over. It upended my world. Convulsed my body. Annihilated my senses.

Searing my heart.

"Samsyn!"

"Yes, astremé." It was more than just his response to my scream. It was a stamp of his surety, his possession, his seal of utter protectiveness. The control he needed, as necessary as blood in his veins and air in his lungs. And right now, I needed it too. Clutched its strength around me, to form the words I longed—*needed*—to say.

"I love you."

To my shock, his composure didn't falter.

Not instantly.

In another minute, his hands stilled. His entire body followed. His face took longer, transitioning slowly from desire to shock—to what looked like complete dread.

"Shit." I let my good hand drop. Wasn't I the ideal emotional bartender tonight? *One awesome moment killer, coming right up.*

"Brooke..."

His strangled growl made me grimace. "Forget it. Let's hit the delete key, okay? Heat of the moment. You know how it goes."

I sat up straighter. Once more, my left arm announced itself in torturous Technicolor. I should've been enjoying the freedom—there was likely a sling in my future, and I wasn't going to like that fucker one bit—but at the moment, was certain that discomfort wouldn't top this. My stomach churned. My head throbbed. And again, my heart hurt.

Please God, let there be some obliterating pain killers in my near future.

Though the man in front of me looked dead-set on keeping me from them.

"Syn. Damn it...let me up."

"Brooke—"

"*Stop.*" It was guttural and violent—and made me feel no better.

He pulled me forward. Dropped his face into my hair. "I need you to understand—"

"Understand?" I barely felt the pain while shoving against his chest. Hardly noticed the heat of my tears—at least on my skin. "Understand *what*? Damn it, Samsyn! What the *fuck* is haunting you like this?"

I didn't have to push him back any farther. He created the distance himself, stumbling back. Raked ragged fingers down his face. "*Créacu, yardim met.*"

Creator, help me.

And just like that, I was a puddle again. Sobbing as much for him as me again. Reaching for him again.

My fingers trembled too. "Let me in, Samsyn. Damn it, you have to let *someone* in."

He dropped his head. His shoulders fell. With more staggering steps, he turned from me. A long minute passed. Even the wind didn't rustle the air. Into that eerie stillness, he finally spat his reply.

"Letting someone in. Is that not simply another phrase for invasion?"

Before I could address the first fucked up thing about that statement, let alone the four thousand, nine hundred and ninety-nine behind it, the universe decided to conspire with the man. Literally.

The brief but deafening blare of a security alarm.

The *tweep-tweeps* as it was disabled.

Stomps and grunts. Swearing and shouts.

Syn spun back around. Locked a stunned stare with mine. "What the—"

He was sliced short by a bellow, filling the building from below with an authority I knew all too well. The voice that'd issued me orders on the training mat for the last three years.

"Syn!"

I slid off the counter and narrowed eyes at Samsyn. "Didn't you say Jag was in Sancti?"

"He is." He snatched a hair tie from the counter and bundled his waves into it. "He *was.*" Two seconds later, he was halfway across the bedroom. "Creator's cock. This is *not* right."

I said nothing. It'd be restating his words. The obvious both our guts had already known.

And now, the full-blown dread overtaking mine—when I detected a distinct element among the frantic voices below.

A female.

Not just any female.

"Camellia!"

I peered around for my own clothes. Finding nothing, I yanked open a drawer in the dresser, finding a pair of drawstring workout shorts. They were Samsyn-sized—giving me two strings as long as my arms to fumble with.

Not nearly the hassle of contending with his you've-grown-two-heads glare. "What the hell do you think—"

"Shut up," I flung. "And let's go."

"Damn it, woman—"

"I'm not your *woman*, Samsyn Cimarron. We just went over that part, remember?" I chucked my chin higher. "So what's it going to be? Letting me in"—I stabbed the center of his chest—"or letting me out?" Jerked my head toward the door, brows arching in triumph. The man's answer already fumed across his face.

Sure enough, Syn pivoted without tossing so much as a glance at me. Yanked open the door and stomped out, the dragon forced to stow his fire.

I didn't waste time gloating—and damn well *not* on remorse. A gut-deep instinct already told me there'd be no time for either.

CHAPTER EIGHTEEN

"Holy. Shit."

The gasp didn't emanate from Samsyn. It spurted from me—before we were even halfway down the wide stone stairwell. I was surprised even that made it free, considering the chaos spread out below.

Few other descriptors fit. I stopped as Samsyn did, fighting to accept the reality of it.

Jagger, his hair windblown and his face grimy, looked like he'd stepped in from a war zone. Grahm appeared even worse. A huge gash in his pants exposed the caked blood of a thigh wound. His hair, normally locked into a ponytail tighter than a cheerleader's, hung in a sweaty, tangled mess.

The two of them weren't even the headline shocker. That honor belonged to the *other* pair, stumbling in between them.

Cam.

And Evrest.

All four raised weary gazes at us. I locked eyes with Camellia first. As soon as her lower lip wobbled, I rushed past Syn and straight toward her. Our embrace snapped her composure. Her death grip was excruciating, but her sob was heartbreaking. I clenched back a wince and lifted my good hand to the middle of her back.

"Oh, my God." Her emotion diced it into six syllables. "I'm so happy to see you."

"And I you." I stroked her spine, pouring my energy into

giving the comfort she clearly needed. "Hey. Ssshhh. It's all right. You're here now. You're safe." I uttered the words out of pure instinct. Her grateful sigh confirmed I'd gone the right direction.

"What the hell happened?" Syn pulled the question right out of my head.

"The scumsuckers showed up in Sancti." Evrest supplied it though looked like he hardly believed it. "Breached the royal residence." That part was more vicious. I wondered why, until Camellia added on her visible shiver.

"I...was in the shower. They pulled me out...of the shower."

"Holy shit." I pressed her head against my shoulder, now realizing why her hair was so stiff. Unrinsed shampoo.

"They had her." Evrest's hands balled until his knuckles were white. "The bonsuns had their filthy hands on her. They were going to take her, and—"

"All right." Samsyn raised both hands, palms up. "Calm down."

Evrest wheeled on his brother. "*You* calm the fuck down! They *had her*, Samsyn. Naked and helpless, their knives at her throat. The only reason they didn't slash her open there was because they came looking for me. They were going to—" A brutal breath stuttered from him. He doubled over, gripping his thighs as if to tear them off. "They were waiting...to cut her open...in front of me."

Horror gashed us all into silence. Automatically, I looked to Syn—stunned to find him already staring at me. Not with the stony veneer I'd expected. Evrest's anguish had affected him. It wasn't simply brotherly compassion, though that was there too... It was something different. Something that made him shift restlessly, blink furiously—and fumble noticeably.

He averted his gaze before speaking again.

"Well, that clearly didn't happen."

"Merderim for the analysis," Evrest growled.

"Shut up," Syn muttered. He nodded toward Jagger. "Run it down for me."

Puzzlement. Why'd he pick Jag over Grahm? Despite the leg wound, Grahm was keeping his shit tighter than Jag.

My confusion was solved as soon as Jag stepped forward. Syn's demand was all he needed to snap back into it. His face was all business while responding, "It was as His Majesty stated. The cockroaches sneaked onto Evrest and Camellia's floor. It was about eight o'clock last night, and His Majesty was finishing late business with Prince Shiraz in the business offices."

"And Jayd?"

"Confined to personal quarters after seven, as per your instructions."

"Not anymore," Evrest interjected.

Jagger nodded. "King Evrest made us aware of some private...compartments...he has kept maintained beneath the palais." One discreet cough and a glance Evrest's way later, he went on, "We have relocated Jayd and Shiraz there, until your further advisement."

"Advisement?" Syn countered. "Get them the hell off the island. *That's* my advisement."

As soon as Evrest blessed that with a tight nod, Jag tapped his comm piece and relayed the order in code. "Luke and Leia are going for soufflé. I repeat, Luke and Leia are going for soufflé."

Syn caught Evrest's eye again. "The apartment in Paris?"

Evrest ticked his head again. "It is secure. Nobody thinks

anyone *really* lives beneath the Opera House anymore."

I gasped. "Are you shitting me?" I whipped a stare to Cam. "Tell me he's shitting."

Back burner, big time. Jagger was done, meaning the incident debrief continued now. "Who were the sentries on duty?" Syn asked of him.

"Hugh, Cullen, Tryst, Petyr, and myself." With the statement, Grahm officially switched with Jag. His composure faltered, though his posture stayed firm. "There is no excuse for what happened, Your Highness. As the watch team leader, I take full responsibility for what happened."

"Merderim," Samsyn replied. "I accept your apology."

"Merderim."

"And call bullshit on it."

Grahm frowned. "Highness?"

"I would have handpicked the same team. The men on that list, you included, are the elite of our elite." He folded his arms. Succumbed to a harsh grimace. I joined Grahm and Jag in reading his thoughts. Three days ago, Blayze's name would've been on that list too. "Those Pura assholes did not simply stroll through the suite's front door."

"They used the laundry chute." Jagger supplied it while opening his shoulder pack and pulling out his plus-one for every occasion these days: his smudgy smart pad. The smears disappeared as the screen woke up. Instead, an image appeared of a cream-carpeted hallway with alabaster wainscoting. The trim was interrupted by a laundry bin door, showing dents of rough use, as well as handprints and boot scuffs. But what had caused the mysterious round imprints? "Suction marks," Jag responded to our curious frowns. "They worked their way up the chute from the ground floor using high-cling cups with handholds. At the top, they simply slipped around the corner into her ladyship's bathroom."

A low snarl curled from Syn. "Impressive. To disturbing degrees."

"And expensive." I peered at the high-end equipment. "Their ropes are top shelf too. They look like Japanese silk. Strong as hell; make no noise." Deeper scowl. "Whoever these jerks are, they've got a loaded Daddy Warbucks behind them."

"Who could be from anywhere in the world." Syn straightened, blowing out a heavy breath. "There are just as many nations who want Arcadia to stay trapped in the nineteenth century as those who welcome the progress."

"Governments with this kind of flow?" Instant eye roll. Yeah, at myself. "Okay, stupid question. Of course there are."

"Not stupid," Jagger assured. "Just not correct."

"What do you mean?"

He set aside the smart pad. Lowered to an armrest of the huge leather couch, folding his arms. "The question is not who can fund the Puras. It is, who can fund them, then encourage these balls-out moves. Flayre turned traitor and then disgraced his family further by taking his own life. Now these batty *soldasks*, sneaking into the palais with the intent of taking her ladyship's life..."

Evrest looked nauseated again. And once more, Syn's face tightened with that strange mix of fear and confusion. "Where are the mealworms now?" He pivoted back toward Jag. "I trust you processed them into Censhyr? Can we go question them?"

Censhyr Prison was located in the craggy wasteland just north of Sancti. The place had been updated with only a few modern conveniences since its construction in 1860, turning life there into an ordeal that gave new meaning to the word "uncomfortable."

Not unlike the silence descending over *this* room—until Grahm broke it with his resigned step forward. Though the man looked like he'd rather have his wound bled by leeches, he kept his shoulders back and his head erect while declaring, "There were four invaders total, Your Highness. We swiftly terminated two of them. The remaining two were able to rappel over the balcony rails, into the waters below."

Syn's eyes narrowed. "Where you caught them?"

"Where they had a boat already waiting, Highness."

Agonizing silence, part two—sliced apart this time by Evrest. "The coastal patrols were already on duty, brother. They were joined by more boats within minutes. The dogs could not have hit open sea without it appearing on the scanners. There are more patrols out now, on land *and* sea, hunting for the bonsuns." He walked back over and pulled Cam against his chest. "In the meantime, Jagger felt it best to get Camellia and me out of the area."

"Jagger was correct." The words were right, but Syn's tone...wasn't. It was sparse and soft—an utterance of surrender, not a statement of command. *Shit.* What was wrong? I read him enough to know something was, though couldn't unravel the rest. "You will both be safe here," he finally added. "We shall arrange for supplies to be brought up by vendors who can be trusted."

"Supplies?" Cam's head jerked up. "What the hell are you talking about?"

"We shall apprehend those insects inside twenty-four hours," Evrest added. "As soon as they're secure in Censhyr, Camellia and I *are* returning to the palais." His jaw jutted at a defined angle, that stiffness common to all the Cimarrons.

But damn it if Syn's stubble didn't lock into the same obstinate outline. When he walked over and faced Evrest directly, I joined Cam in gasping. They could nearly be taken as twins, especially when they both were tense as bulls about to charge the ring.

"It will not be that easy, brother."

Evrest grunted. "Stop being a fishwife, Syn. Camellia and I will not be bullied into the bushes by this."

Cam pulled up straighter. "What my man said."

Grahm circled around. "My pardon, Your Majesties"— he nodded toward Cam, including her in the salutation on purpose—"but Samsyn is right. Catching those two bastards will only be cutting the head off the cockroach. The organism will live on until we yank out its guts and burn them to cinders."

Grimace. "Thanks for the visual," I mumbled.

"An accurate one." Samsyn's eyes glittered, indicating his speeding thoughts. "If this is the Pura's work—and we do not even know *that* yet—then we know they are organized now. Dangerously so."

"And if it is not them?" Jag pressed.

"Then we have an even bigger problem."

"An enemy we do not know at all."

Samsyn let his silence serve up his confirmation.

"Damn." Camellia dragged in a breath.

"Either way," Samsyn continued, "they are emboldened now. The two we killed will be hailed as martyrs." He dipped his tightened gaze at Cam. "And avenging their deaths, a priority."

"Wh-What?" She didn't bother breathing after that— until bursting with a scoffing laugh. "Oh God, Syn. Ev's right. You're such a DQ!"

Syn threw her a curious glower.

"Drama queen," I supplied for him—though followed up by twining a hand into hers. "Though this time, sweetie, the DQ is right."

She huffed at me. Evrest let out a similar sound—with resignation. "*Sevette*." He stroked a hand over her glossy chocolate waves. "Samsyn *is* right. They have radicalized this. Perhaps even turned it religious, borrowing quotes from the ancient island scrolls for justification."

Her brow furrowed. "Ancient scrolls? What the hell?"

"Seconding that." I raised my hand—not missing the nervous glances between the men around us. As motherlodes of controversy went, we'd gone for the gold. Religion *and* politics; one fell swoop. Well, no turning back now. "What the hell?" I added for good measure.

After five seconds of unnerving silence, Samsyn growled, "Mystical mumbo-jumbo from another time and place." His gaze turned scornful, blazed Evrest's way. "And not relevant to this time, let alone this conversation."

"The *relevant* thing," Jagger cut in, "is that those bonsuns will not give up until their mission is achieved."

Evrest's reply evoked a wolf's low growl. "Until Camellia or I are dead."

"Perhaps not even then." Syn scowled deeper. "Perhaps they're set on eradicating the entire Cimarron bloodline."

The words—and the possibility of their truth—hovered like ghouls in the air.

Until once more, Grahm stood taller. Looked at his prince and then his king in measured assessment. "What if...we give them that?"

The brothers blinked with the same stunned rhythm. "What are you about?" Samsyn finally charged.

Jagger, previously listening with knuckles to his chin, swept to his feet. "That is weirdly brilliant."

"*What?*" Samsyn yelled.

Jag looped a finger at Evrest and Cam. "Nobody knows we've brought His Majesty and her ladyship here. What if they *stay* here...and we announce they were killed?"

Veins stood out in Evrest's neck. "Are you completely mad?"

"Fucking lunatics may be more accurate." Samsyn stood shoulder-to-shoulder with him. "Are either of you aware of the chaos to be unleashed by 'murdering' an Arcadian king?" He ensured the air quotes got jabbed around the verb. "The homicide of *this* Arcadian king? The vacuum of stability—"

"Would be nominal," Grahm calmly rebutted.

"If his brother immediately took the throne."

Jagger delivered the gut-puncher with matching cool. My hands flew to my stomach, wondering if the pair really *had* gotten in a blow. Sure as hell felt like it. Camellia winced as if they'd gotten her too—but neither Samsyn nor Evrest moved. Their stillness bordered on eerie.

Finally, Syn snarled, "You are out of your damn minds." He side-eyed Evrest. "Some help, brother? Such as telling them the exact same thing?"

Grahm's shoulders snapped back. The same defensiveness threaded his tone. "You would ascend uncontested, Highness. Nobody would dare cause 'chaos.'"

"What the hell is that supposed to mean?"

"You lead the country's military."

"Which is why I should *not* run its government!"

Jagger squared his shoulders. "And technically, you would not be. The ass on the throne has no vote in High Council matters."

"Which is *technically* a pile of horse dung," Syn spat. "Do not play me for a fool, Jag. You live up here, but you visit Sancti enough to know the influence of the king." His lips twisted before he muttered, "Matters I know not a fucking sand grain about." He wheeled toward the room's large windows. It was still pitch dark outside. His face, reflected in the dark panes, gained a hundred new lines of stress.

Mentally, I drove nails to my feet. It was the only way to stay rooted in place instead of rushing to his side. Comfort that would only embarrass him. Assurance he didn't want.

"No," he finally growled. "*No.* This is not the solution."

Cam, kicking at the floor, let out a rough sigh. "Sorry, guys, but I still agree with Syn. How does this address the issue? Get us any closer to the big kahunas writing the checks for the Pura? Or whoever these assholes are."

Her answer came from the least likely source in the room. The man who finally snapped his deep silence to speak. "Samsyn will get closer than me," Evrest asserted.

Syn jerked a glare over his shoulder. "*Brother.* You cannot possibly think—"

"I do." Hands at his sides, shoulders leveled, Evrest had his king-in-charge mode at full force. "It is a good idea, Syn." He cocked a brow Grahm's way. "Actually, as Jag best phrased it, brilliant."

Syn stabbed a finger toward the window. "Full moon. That must be it. Your stupid dog side is taking over, right?"

Evrest chuckled. "If it means I get to sleep twenty hours tomorrow, why not?"

"As long as I get to be your lazy bitch." Camellia snuggled into his side.

"Bet your sweet ass, my little sevette."

"Get your cock out of your brain and pay attention!" Samsyn charged.

"My cock *and* my brain are in the right places, little brother. The only one not seeing this clearly is you."

"I am *not* qualified to be king!"

"Of course you are." Evrest gently let Cam go before pacing to his brother. "You have accompanied me, advised me, and protected me since the crown was placed on *my* head, Samsyn. You have seen every one of my triumphs, my mistakes, my good days, and my hell-in-a-handbasket days." A smile spread on his lips, filled with quiet emotions I could only guess at. "And you have absorbed it all with the compassion and acumen I could only ever *hope* to have."

Everyone in the room held their breath. Except Samsyn, who was busy blustering. "But your British education—"

"Yielded me nothing but a piece of paper in a frame—and things *you* already know, here"—he tapped Syn's forehead— "and here." Then the center of his chest. "Fortunately for us, the rest of the world is blinded by that piece of paper on the wall too. If we get very, very lucky, they will continue judging you by your lack of one."

I heard every word Evrest uttered but didn't match it to a meaning until Samsyn reacted. The look on his face, so vulnerable and open, gave me a window of insight—to the person most people probably saw him as. The gun at his brother's side. The brawn behind Evrest's brains. Hell, even the muscly hunk to be swooned over.

Not the charmer who'd matched wits with me over the years.

Not the man with the eyes that glistened when his brain

became a superhighway of thought.

Not the guy perfectly capable of duping a bunch of Puras with his dumb stud act—while stealing their secrets out from underneath them.

"Shit," I blurted. Dashed my stare to Evrest. "Shit. That's right." Then to Camellia. "They're right."

Syn glowered. "Fuck. Now you too?"

I let myself walk over now, pushing against the force of his resentment. "Syn...listen. This really might be our best chance of catching those wing nuts." As Evrest scooted back, making room for me, I scooped up Syn's hands in my own. "*You're* our best chance."

He said nothing for at least a minute. Silently scrutinized my face. I changed nothing about my expression, knowing I already had all of it bared to him. My belief. My hope. My love.

He dropped his head. Poured his gaze over the mesh of our fingers. I stared at him with matching intensity—and the silence that hit when he stole my breath all over again. The first rays of dawn filtered through the pines outside, kissing the top of his dark head like a blessing from the sky itself.

"All right," he finally muttered. "All right. Creator help me...I will do it."

Whooshes of breath exploded from all the men. Camellia let loose a cute squee.

After the initial celebration, Evrest sobered. Too damn fast.

Samsyn rolled his eyes. "Dare I ask what the hell is the issue now?" he growled at the king.

Evrest stared hard at the two of us. Parted his mouth to answer but clamped it shut with as much decision, teeth clacking. When Syn dropped my hands and wheeled on him, their chests slammed with an audible thud. Cam's eye roll stopped me from breaking them up. Apparently, this was typical shit for the Cimarron boys.

"Damn it, Evrest. Just be out with it."

"Remove your ugly face from mine first, soldask."

Samsyn stood down, snarling low. "Witless dog."

"PMSing putz."

"Damn douche bag."

Laughter barked the air. Mine. And, thank God, Cam's. In the wake of our strange ice breakers, Evrest held up both hands—though the angle of his head spoke more to his ultimate surrender. "All right," he muttered, "*All right.*" He folded his arms, borrowing a healthy dose of Syn's nervousness from a minute ago. "To be clear about things, I am ecstatic about the possibility of staying up here with my sevette for a few weeks. But if *you* want to get this over faster—"

"Yes," Syn butted in. "*Fuck*, yes."

"Then I would recommend one essential aid to cut your 'reign' by weeks. An...element...guaranteed to bring the—how did you say it, Brooke?"

"Wing nuts?" I offered.

"The wing nuts. Yes. A great deal of them, at least...straight to the palais receiving rooms, without even trying..."

"Barbecue bonus," I exclaimed. Waved off their perplexed frowns. "Forget it. Let's just hear what the magic wand is."

I had to admit, even I was impatient from Evrest's new pause. The man's jaw firmed, making me wonder how horrible this "aid" had to be. Satin breeches? A powdered wig? Oh God...a haircut? *No. Please, no. Not a haircut.*

"A wife."

CHAPTER NINETEEN

Now I wished he'd just meant a haircut.

With every fiber of my quaking body.

I battled the vibrations by pacing across one of the castle's spacious guest rooms—because God forbid I go back to Syn's room *now*—while waiting for Jag to return from the fishing village down the hill with something better to wear than a dirty camisole and Syn's shorts. For the time being, my attire consisted of more borrowed Samsyn-wear: a French blue dress shirt with all the tags still on it, hanging to just above my knees. *Stylin'*.

I didn't bother cuffing the shirt's sleeves. They gave my nervous fingers something to work with as I walked. Even so, I fought for the Zen clarification of each step. Worked to space them the same. Brought them down with the same pressure on the thick Turkish carpet.

Once upon a time, I'd done this once, twice, sometimes three times a day, an hour for each stint. I'd hated Jag because of it, but calm and I hadn't been the best of pals back then. I'd begged him to train me with all the aplomb of the bouncy dog from *Up*, with a matching attention span. Allowing me on a training mat with anyone would've been preregistering me for a death certificate. I'd come a long way since then—but fortunately, never forgot the pacing.

Step.

Step.

Step.

Groan.

Sink to the bed. Morose stare at the floor. Who the hell was I kidding? Back to the bouncy dog bit—only this time, it was worse. This wasn't eager stress. This was *stress* stress.

Worse.

This was what-the-hell-have-I-just-agreed-to stress.

I flopped back onto the duvet. Closed my eyes and rubbed my temples. No damn help—unless my aim was to relive the gory aftermath of Evrest's proposal, second by agonizing second.

Behind my eyelids, the scene burst to life once more.

"Wife?" Syn had repeated, as if his brother suggested returning to Sancti wearing his sliced balls as earrings. Evrest's conviction had been just as unnerving—no less so when he'd started laying out his logic. Returning to Sancti with a wife would instantly erase Syn's playboy image, making the High Council *and* the populace take him more seriously. At the same time, he'd secure the sympathy card: just as he'd found "true love," Evrest and Camellia had been "violently taken" from him. Back-door channels would be abuzz with speculation about all the upheaval the new king had been through. What *would* his political position be, especially after his brother's murder? After everything he'd been through, surely King Samsyn would desire returning to a simpler Arcadia...the security of the old ways...

It had all made complete sense.

Until Evrest's suggestion about who should be his little brother's new bride.

I was saved from recalling Syn's exact reaction to *that* by a rhythmic knock at the bedroom door. In Vermont, such a cheery greeting meant a neighbor bearing brownies or a Girl Scout selling cookies. Right now, I could only connect the sound to one person.

"Hey." Sure enough, Camellia's face appeared—followed by the rest of her. She carried a brown paper shopping bag. "Jag's back from the village. I'm playing messenger girl. Didn't know if you'd be sleeping or something."

"Sleeping?" Barking laugh. Why not take advantage of the chance? Little else validated it right now. "Sure. *You* try being told you're about to get married, that you'll be lying to a whole country about the reason why, and see how *sleepy* you feel."

Cam parked the bags on the dark wood writing desk. Rushed to the bed and yanked me into a tight hug. "I know this is all crazy."

I laughed again. Not so enthusiastically. "Understatements-R-Us, anyone?"

She tilted her head and smiled softly. "Cold feet?"

"Ehhh. Lukewarm?" I spread a hand across the bed's downy white comforter. "Look...my head gets it. The decision makes sense. Finding another woman to pull this off, even with an expedited security clearance check, would take at least a week."

"It makes sense from other angles too."

"I was listening, damn it." Apologetic glance, though I knew it wasn't necessary. Cam understood. "And I get that part too. The public will believe this. Syn and I have had a semiworking relationship for a while. And this week, we've been through a lot more than that." I prayed she didn't probe into that one. When she didn't, I promised karma payback for the favor and went on, "It'll look like we were forced to confront some dormant feelings."

Meaningful beat. Then another. "Looks like that from the inside too."

Shit. Karma had wasted no time on collecting *that* one.

I lifted a lot more than a glance this time. The woman was ready, rebutting my stare like some mystical sage, my spirit animal, and fairy godmother rolled neatly together.

"Shut up," I grumbled as she giggled. A fresh attack of nerves set in, parching me for the hundredth time in five minutes. I reached for the water on the nightstand—with my left arm. "*Shit!*"

Ugh. The sling was going to be a necessity. Gee, the wedding photos were going to be lovely...*not*.

Cam stepped over, pouring the water and then pressing it into my *right* hand. "There's a bright side here, you know. You're going to be the darling of the kingdom, then the world, with that cute little hole in your arm."

"Be careful what you're labeling 'cute' and 'little.'"

"I can see the blog headlines already," she went right on. "*The queen who saved a queen.*"

I rolled my eyes while swallowing the water. "You mean the girl so scared, she shook like a Chihuahua?"

She indulged me with another laugh. "Don't forget the best part. This will be one hell of a way to tell the world your family's still alive. Oh come *on*, Brooke." She responded to my shiver, grabbing my good hand and squeezing. "Kavill and his smarm boys won't dare take you out now. It'll defeat their purpose of being adored. In case you haven't noticed, they've had PR and recruitment problems lately."

I nodded, as much for me as her. "I've heard. Something about a bombing attempt on the World Cup games?"

"Doesn't matter now. They're fleas, and they're about to

get the blood crushed out of them." An eager grin flowed from her. "And as soon as we straighten out this bullshit with the Pura, then Ev and I return from the dead, you and Syn can get a nice, quiet annulment. Then you'll finally get to go *home*. In just a few months, you'll be watching the fall colors in Vermont and—Brooke? *Brooke?*"

I didn't blame her for turning the infomercial excitement into a cry of alarm. I would've done the same, had she done what I did. But I could no more stop the tears than understand them—

Until words tumbled, just as uncontrollable, off my lips.

"But I *am* home."

The dam in my composure, cracked before, burst open. Emotions poured out like jetsam in a flood, twisted and bizarre, defying recognition. They burst up, hot and cold at once, making even my body feel like a foreign object.

No. This wasn't a flood. It was a hurricane, picking up chunks of me and moving them into separate places...

Becoming a physical force.

I surged off the bed. Twisted free from Camellia. For a moment, dashed a gaze out to the balcony. We were on the second floor. Could I jump and survive? Did it matter if I did?

"Fuck," I rasped. Of course it mattered. *I* mattered. I didn't want to die. I really wanted to live. I just wanted to do it here, in Arcadia. Preferably in one emotional piece.

And wasn't that fate's lovely little ambush?

I'd found the land of my heart...but would never live in it with the *man* of my heart.

Which meant my week of suckage had just turned into months of suckage.

No.

I hadn't agreed to this stunt for my heart. I'd agreed to it for Arcadia.

And for Arcadia, I'd carry it through.

There'd just have to be some ground rules.

Syn and I were strong people. We'd honed our bodies for fighting and our spirits for battle. Surely we could handle a few guidelines for a sham marriage.

Or so I tried to tell myself when the door opened again— and the air was sucked from the room courtesy of the man filling the portal.

My husband-to-be.

CHAPTER TWENTY

"I think....Jagger needs me downstairs."

Camellia's claim was as sound as her hurried breath, and we all knew it—until Jag really did shout for her. That fucking man and his timing.

As Cam departed, Syn stepped farther in. By equal steps, I scooted back. "Sorry," I blurted. "Guess I'm just..."

Nervous?

It sounded just as stupid on the inside. I'd never been nervous in front of Samsyn. Correction. Never *about* him. He was shelter. Haven. Home.

Not anymore.

Not if I wanted to leave this marriage with my sanity.

His jaw clenched. I could see every formidable inch now, since he'd recently shaved. A hint of his aftershave, spicy and woodsy, tickled my nose. His hair was clean and glossy, meticulously combed and clubbed at his nape with a white satin ribbon. He already looked like the world's most perfect groom, though he still wore just a tight white T-shirt and nicely fitted blue jeans. I fingered my wet hair, still not even combed, and tucked my injured arm closer to my body.

"I...brought your medication." He lifted both hands, drawing my attention to the glass of water in one and the pair of pills in another.

"Thanks."

I downed the medicine in lieu of laughing again. We were

like a pair of kids who'd never kissed, let alone—well, every illicit thing we'd already done.

"Well." He jabbed his hands into his front pockets. "At least one of us can get through this numbed up."

That took care of the laughing thing. Now I just had to resist throwing the water in his face. "You want to be on pain killers too? I'd be extremely happy to break something for you."

His head snapped up. His eyes blazed blue lightning. "Creator's balls, Brooke. I was only—"

"Trying to be charming about stating just how shit-tastic this all is for you. I get it, Syn. I *get it*, okay? You'd rather be getting your appendix yanked, without anesthesia, than preparing for your fucking wedding. Wasn't the way *I* planned on the day going either."

"Brooke—"

"But this is for the country. *Our* country. And it's not forever. Get that into your thick skull, okay? Just show up and mumble the words. You don't have to mean them. Close your eyes, if that'll be easier. I won't mind."

"Brooke—"

"And when we get to Sancti"—I didn't dare stop until I was absolutely done, too damn scared of what he'd snarl in return—"we can make logistical arrangements for separate housing. It's a big palais. I can find someplace decent to crash. Jayd's level probably has a spare room. She and I can make it a sleepover every night. Fiddle Doodles, sugared soda, makeovers—"

I was on such a roll, there was zilch prep time for his ninja sweep, grabbing me by the waist. Or the possession of his hand at the back of my head. Or the hot sweep of his mouth, consuming as a burst of summer sun, melting me just as fast. My body was a puddle—including my good hand, wrapped around the water glass. It tipped, soaking both our stomachs, before falling to the carpet with a hard *pong*. Like I noticed. With my tongue twirled with his and my body wrapped in his arms, a tsunami could've crashed in and I wouldn't have cared.

But I needed to care.

Needed to be pushing him away, drawing an invisible *don't cross* line between us, and get down to ticking off the guidelines...

The guidelines...

Right. Those.

What were they again?

I'd remember in a second. It wouldn't hurt to wait that long. It couldn't. How could it, when it felt *so...damn...good*? His mouth, so purposeful and passionate. His body, so hard and huge. His groan, so guttural only I could hear it...

and feel it...

and know, all over again, that this man completed me as nobody else did...or ever would.

And *that* part, I refused to feel stupid for.

Back in the States, would've likely been torn apart for.

They'd tell me I had no idea what I was doing. That dedicating my heart to the man who'd also—*gasp*—taken my virginity was Chick Mistake Numero Uno. That I'd barely "discovered the world" yet. That I hadn't "shopped around" or even experienced a decent social life.

I didn't want a damn social life.

Arcadia had already given me a *life*. A purpose. An identity. A place where I belonged.

And the man I'd always be in love with.

Just one more moment.

I pleaded it to fate and rejoiced as the bitch listened for once. With his deepest dragon's growl, Syn pushed his tongue in deeper...molded our mouths yet tighter...and fitted the hardest part of his body to the moist cleft of mine. I held on to him with all my strength, every cell of my body opening to the hot fusion that was completely ours...the magic that was completely him.

Now just one moment more. Please...please...

With a jagged huff, he finally tore away. To my ecstasy, he didn't go far. But to my fear, still stared as if I were his most dreaded poison...and then its antidote.

What the hell?

And would there ever be a time when he didn't have me in this whiplash?

And would I ever want there to be?

"Astremé?"

His breath was a rickety tangle with mine. I greedily inhaled, accepting every molecule of life, heat, and desperation I could get. "Yeah?"

He dropped his forehead to mine. Kept me locked there, spreading his fingers against my scalp. "Are you...really sure about this?"

"Are you?"

He drew in a long breath. "You know I am. But you also know...my parameters."

The corners of his eyes tightened. The heat inside them again battled the frost. The captain of the ship was now helpless in the storm and had no idea what to do. I held on tight as he struggled to grab the wheel, in any way he possibly could.

"I shall stand with you today. And I will give you a ring.

And I will give you my home. And I sure as *hell* want to give you my body. But...I cannot give you my heart."

I squeezed my fingertips into his nape. "I know, Syn. And it's okay."

His tension didn't change. "You need to mean that. After what you said this morning—"

"Right after you fried every circuit on my motherboard with that orgasm?" I pushed back by a resolute step. "Like I said this morning, that's water under the bridge, big guy." I cocked my head, animated by the fresh rush of pain killers. "I can keep the shit in check if you can."

To my slight surprise and huge relief, a laugh tumbled off his sexy lips. Dysfunctional? Probably. But laughter made it easier to hide my feelings in plain sight: the ordeal I was about to sign up for, for months on end.

But after we'd dealt with the radicals and all was well in Arcadia once more, I'd be done with the crucible of Samsyn Cimarron at last. I'd say goodbye to Mom, Dad, and Dil, promising to visit them in the States from time to time, and settle in for a long, peaceful life in the Tahreuse Mountains. Maybe I'd help Jagger run the Center or open up a wing just for training young girls. Hell, maybe I'd run for Mayor of Tahreuse—but only if I could remodel the Residence Rigale. And swear never to look at the rotunda on the ninth level again.

No. I'd have to deal. Be bigger than that. Stronger. Better. Staying in Arcadia meant I'd face reminders of Samsyn every single day. Maybe that was even why I wanted to remain.

Therapy topic for a much different day.

Especially when the man of my dreams still grinned at me like a giant version of Dopey the Dwarf. Then tugged at my good hand, pulling me close to him once again, and dropped an affectionate kiss to the top of my head.

"The shit...is in check."

His formality atop my slang had never sounded more adorable. I rewarded him with a giggle, tucking my head against his chest. Syn expelled a long breath into my hair, letting it fade into a shared moment of silence. A peace not likely to be ours again for a while.

"Astremé?"

"Hmmm?"

"I am glad Evrest suggested you."

My heart rushed my ribs. My stomach rocket-jumped, joining the mess. I shooed them all away to embrace the most important thing: the glow of gratitude for this man, about to take one of the scariest jumps of his life—and trusting me to tumble along with him.

As I tightened my body to his, a set of words echoed in my head. Camellia's, from two nights ago at the Tower party.

Sometimes, you're already sharing the drop—and you just have to reach out to know it.

Was *that* the key to all this? Was I too worried about the blood and guts at the end of this plummet to even see the beauty of the view, feel the thrill of the drop? Maybe I had to accept that the roller coaster was going to derail and just embrace the ride before then.

As the sanity platoon fumed in the back of my brain, I mentally ripped up the guidelines—and let them fly away. If Samsyn could laugh in the face of his terror, so could I.

I thought.

I hoped.

"I'm...glad he did too." There. Not so hard. He'd reached out. I'd grabbed on. It felt kind of...cool. Mature. Grown-up.

Right up to the moment he dipped his head over, tilted my chin up—and then kissed me so gently, he was seriously earning the noble prince chops. He took his time, practically fondling my lips with his, dipping their soft, sweet touch over every contour of mine...until I could bear the teasing no more. With a high-pitched sigh, I opened for him. With a greedy mewl, I reached my tongue out for his. With a slow snarl, he answered.

Time stopped. If any force on earth could really make it so, I was certain we'd just found it. The air seemed to hold its breath around us. The universe halted, awed by the passion it beheld...by a connection that could only be called magic.

Long after our tongues dragged apart, Syn caressed his cheek against mine. I smiled, letting him infuse me with his scent, his touch, his heat. Our silence wasn't so complete anymore, though. In the farthest reaches of my logic, there was a tumult. The sanity platoon returned, even more pissed. *Are you fucking crazy? You ripped up the guidelines, and now this? Fine. Don't come crying to have your heart glued back together in six months. We'll still be chugging the we-told-you-so beers.*

As Syn nipped his lips around the bottom of my ear, sending tingling rain through my whole body, I skywrote a message for the whole platoon across the horizon of my mind. *F-U-C-K-O-F-F.*

Aloud, I whispered, "Holy...*shit*...Syn..."

Samsyn chuckled, though quickly dipped it to a lusty growl. "I need to go, astremé. We both must get ready. But before I do..."

I wrapped my good arm to his neck, wrapped one leg around his waist, and rasped, "Yes?"

"There is something you need to know."

"Yes?" I gave it a sleek and seductive hiss this time.

"I believe Jayd is already booked solid for sleepovers."

Mock gasp. "For *months*?"

"Well." He bit harder into my ear. Soothed the pain with languorous licks. "She *is* confined to the palais for the next decade."

"Damn." I longed to fist his hair so badly. The heat he'd incited in me, simply with his tongue and teeth...holy, ever-loving *fuck*... "Whatever shall I do now?"

He settled his mouth against my neck. "I think we can work something out...as long as you still bring the Fiddle Doodles."

I snickered. "Do you even know what Fiddle Doodles are?"

"Does it involve you dressed in this shirt and nothing else?"

"Not...exactly."

"Well then...fuck the Fiddle Doodles."

★ ★ ★

I was damn glad he liked the shirt so much. The village's general store was fully stocked with fishing equipment and spring birdwatching books but only restocked clothing items for, as they'd informed Jagger, *the major seasons*: winter and summer. He'd gotten lucky, they'd also said, finding what he did on the winter clearance shelf. As a result, I showed up to my wedding in a pair of long underwear decorated with pink flowers, some new socks, a pair of white ankle boots trimmed in silver fur, and a new sports bra underneath my groom's long blue shirt.

Thanks to Camellia, it wasn't a complete wash of an outfit. The little bouquet of wildflowers in my shaking grip was copied in a wreath atop my head, braided into little pieces of my hair, to which she'd attached a "veil" made out of a cut-up fruit net from the kitchen. Her ingenuity didn't stop there. By pinning back the shirt, she created a bustle, accented with another flower arrangement at the small of my back. With the outfit itself halfway bridal, she then attacked my asymmetrical hair and sun-starved skin. A can of hairspray from her purse helped with a few cute pin curls. The same magic bag gave up some mascara, blush, and a swipe of lip gloss.

When she was done, she took me in with teary eyes. They persisted even as she walked me to the castle's back entrance, joining Evrest in hugging me. They couldn't follow me any farther, since they were publicly dead as of an hour ago, but they could watch from the castle's covered turret, four floors up, as I descended a flower-carpeted hill toward a dark wood gazebo beneath the trees. Inside the structure was the village's spindly vicar, also retrieved during Jag's shopping spree, waiting with Jagger and Grahm...

Next to the man too damn gorgeous for his own good.

Or mine.

"Shit." It spilled out as soon as I saw him. For a second, I simply wondered if I was dreaming. Granted, none of my dreams had ever plunked him in a gazebo in the forest, but there had to be a few I didn't remember. Fantasies too damn good for the light of consciousness—and too damn hot for my upright body to handle.

Unfair, was what it all was.

Unfair that even in ordinary gear of a white button-front shirt and black suit pants, the latter donned out of "mourning" for his brother, he looked everything but ordinary—especially when the wind plastered his shirt against that massive chest.

Unfair that I harbored such wicked thoughts about that chest, only to be thwarted by his dark angel's face, set in somber lines.

Unfair that he could deepen my confusion by just standing there, so solid and magnificent and demigod-beautiful, making me forget which way was up—let alone something as silly as how to walk.

Somehow, I got it right.

Stepped closer to him.

Closer.

And soon, stood before him. Then let Grahm take my flowers so Syn could tuck his right hand beneath mine. Awkwardly—the sling made nothing easy, but at least the pain was bearable—I shifted my left hand into place, palm up against my right. Syn slid his right hand atop that.

Because of the sling, we stood close. *Really* close. I squirmed, unnerved. Fought to figure out why. Sheez, the man and I had been much "closer" than this—but suddenly, I felt thirteen again, forced to waltz with tall and perfect Paul Lincoln at the Premiere League cotillion. Only now, there was a hell of a lot more at risk than a punch-stained dress and the possibility of locking orthodontics with Paul later on.

A lot more at risk—as in a whole damn kingdom. And saving it by marrying a prince. Not just any prince. The man who stood so regally next to me. Pressed his hands tighter around mine. Even shifted an inch closer so there'd be less strain on my arm.

And ignored every syllable of my suggestion to close his eyes for this thing.

His gaze pierced down into me like blue glass, taking on a thousand facets...only miraculously, not one of them was a stand-in for a separate thought. Right now, every inch of him was *here*, present and focused and...

Overwhelming.

My breath stopped again. I barely blinked. But I couldn't stop staring as sunlight filtered through the trees, turning his gaze into light as endless as stars, as profound as the constellations. I swayed from its force. Didn't even try to fight it, knowing Syn wouldn't let me fall. He balanced me without effort, his lips spreading with the hint of a smile...perhaps even an inward gloat about what he'd just done to me.

Cocky bonsun.

I wound up a retaliating glare. Never got the chance to hurl it. The vicar began speaking. Revision: began trumpeting. The man, the size of a Hobbit, had the voice of the Jolly Green Giant. Though I joined Syn, Jag, and Grahm in repressing gawks, I was happy knowing Evrest and Cam would get to hear everything too. Not that any of it made sense. I knew everyday Arcadian, things like "how much for the tomatoes," "damn it's cold today," and "but my foot looks pretty on your neck, Jag," but only recognized every third or fourth word of the formal ceremony the little man began. Probably for the best. This was all just for show anyway: a seal and certification we could take back to Sancti, to prove we'd truly done it. Evrest had even insisted on rings. They were simple gold bands, resting on a square of red velvet in the vicar's palm—apparently, more symbolism *there* I asked *no* questions about—that were a convenient part of the guy's "upgraded" wedding service.

Aside from the Hobbit's droning, this really wasn't so bad. It was even a pretty day. In a few minutes, Syn and I could jam the rings on, and everyone could tuck into some lunch before we headed down the mount—

The vicar stopped shouting.

Samsyn slipped his hands free from mine.

Alllll righty, then. Even easier than I'd thought.

I pulled in a satisfied breath. Released it on a contented sigh. Looked back up to Syn, knowing he'd smoothly cue me on what to do next...

He looked anything but smooth. And damn...he'd ditched the gloating thing too. The only thing he appeared was... nervous. Paul Lincoln, about fifty times worse.

Ohhhh, shit.

We *weren't* done.

When the vicar started speaking again, this time in a murmur meant just for Syn and me, that truth invaded my nerves too. Made me glad that Syn circled an arm around my waist, scooting me even tighter to him...making my head tilt back as his leaned over. With our faces aligned and our breaths entwined, ancient Arcadian words again flowed around us.

And this time, Samsyn translated.

"As the sea to the moon, the brave to the sun...we enter as two and leave as one."

His rough rasp vibrated through us both.

"Wind in sails, shelter in storms, rain in deserts, always a home."

And for a moment, just one magical instant, I let myself believe he meant it.

"As tides and shore and mountains of heather..."

All of it.

"Is our bond, the Creator's gift, now and forever."

Just before I forced myself not to.

Nick of time. I was on the brink of turning things into a wet, teary mess.

But it still wasn't over.

Shit, shit, shit.

The vicar began circling us, singing softly. My gaze must have betrayed my curiosity, because Syn bent in a little more to whisper, "Settle in, astremé. He'll circle five times. Once symbolizing me, then once you..."

I did *not* want to know why he hesitated to finish. Like a dumb shit, I did the honors instead. "And the others for our kids?" When he smirked, looking cotillion nervous again, I murmured, "Guess we should be glad he's not a marathoner."

His left brow arched suggestively. "The trying part would be...fun."

I moaned. "You are such a guy."

"And you are the most beautiful thing I have ever seen."

Damn it. That shut me the hell up. Instantly joined forces with the starlight in his eyes, continuing to do so, even as the Hobbit finished the happy-joy-joy perimeter stroll and then stopped with his hand held out, beckoning us to take the rings. As I held Samsyn's and he held mine, the vicar started murmuring again. *Hell.* I had a feeling, a strong one, that tethering my tears wouldn't be so easy this time. I already made up some blame-it-on-the-pain-killers lines.

Just as softly and somberly as before, Syn spoke.

"Circle without end. Joy without finish. Love without bounds." Then, as he slipped the gold band onto my left ring finger: "And heart...with its completion."

I ordered myself to ignore the heat blooming through my hand. To push aside the electricity zinging up my arm.

To breathe away the love bursting in my chest.

Much easier said than done.

Especially because I had to say the exact same words now.

And that's all they are. Words. Just words. Just syllables you have to say, to advance the ordeal by one more step. To deepen the charade by one more layer.

But I couldn't force the mask on now. Couldn't pretend, with Syn's heart beating so close...with his face filling my vision...with his presence like the magic in every dappled drop of sun that blazed through the gazebo. Every inch of my being stretched to him. Every fear in my soul vowed courage for him.

Every ounce of my heart belonged to him.

He saw it all, imbued in every word I uttered. He stiffened as I sealed them in, putting the ring on his hand. After I slid the band home, he stared like it'd been burned there, a grimace wiggling at his lips. The expression remained as he raised his gaze to mine—and unbelievably, I smiled back. The stubborn bull probably didn't realize it, but he already honored me as his "beloved" wife. If we were going to survive this adventure, honesty had to be the secret glue. And yeah, that meant *all* the time.

For now, I concentrated on surviving the rest of the ceremony: the worst part by far. No translation needed now. The vicar's bittersweet smile—he was mourning his old king and celebrating his new one at once, after all—and animated gestures were enough to go on now.

More than enough.

It was time for Samsyn to kiss me.

The tension in his fingers, raising to lift the netting from my face, conveyed we shared the same mental boat on this one. Since the first time he'd ever kissed me, he'd never been able to just *kiss* me. The connection of our mouths was never just that.

It was the breach into our desires. The plug into our electricity. The fusion of everything we knew about each other...sought in each other...craved in each other.

Fate refused to give us a pass this time.

And damn it, even recruited Mother Nature for the task. As Syn tipped up my chin with a finger, the wind kicked strands of his hair free, brushing both our cheeks. The scent of pine and peonies swirled with his rich masculine spice, wakening the few cells in my system that didn't already want him. He was my magnet, my vortex, my inescapable addiction...and in the magical moments when our gazes met, just before ours lips did, I saw the same helpless need in his own eyes.

We were in such dangerous waters.

And jumping in deeper every time we touched.

Nothing like a morbid metaphor at just the right moment. Syn literally sucked the air from my mouth as he kissed me. I felt him shake too, battling to hold himself in check. Like my careening hormones would settle for that. The second my moan echoed into his mouth, we were both lost causes. Our tongues met. Our libidos gave in.

Vaguely, I registered the vicar's delighted gasp. Grahm's pleasant snicker.

Jag's impatient growl wasn't so easy to tune out. "You two want fucking scalpels for those tonsillectomies?"

Reluctantly—and all too quickly—we pushed apart.

Syn led the way back to the castle.

"Oh, my God." Camellia waited for us just inside the door. She embraced me and then launched at Samsyn, who grunted like a bear being attacked by a kitten. "It was beautiful, you two. So perfect!"

I couldn't help smiling—because I couldn't have agreed

more.

Evrest finished descending the stairs from the turret. Jerked his chin toward Grahm. "And look who caught the bridal bouquet."

Grahm colored as we all laughed. He shoved the spray back at me and muttered, "Should you two not be on your way now?"

"On our way?" I returned. "You mean...back to Sancti? Now?"

Syn nodded, every inch the in-control commander again. Clearly, he'd anticipated my confusion. "If we want to get to the palais before the nuptial announcement spreads, then yes."

I followed him across the building's central vestibule, still wearing a frown. "And how the hell do you propose..."

My demand faded as my surprise jumped several notches. This time, with damn good reason.

He'd pulled open the massive wooden doors leading to the front entrance—if a place as sprawling as this could really have a "main" entrance. There, on stones likely graced by stallions and carriages at some time, was horsepower of a different kind.

Sleek, shiny, black...

Gasp-worthy.

After I indulged in a couple of those, I finally squeaked, "Whoa."

"A fascinating first," Grahm remarked from the step above me, where he stood with Jagger and Evrest. "I think, Your Highness, you have rendered the Badger speechless."

"He is *Your Majesty* now, Foxx," Evrest prompted. "And his predecessor issues an approval of the choice from the grave."

"*Not* humorous," Syn snapped—though the tone didn't

touch the warmth in his gaze, lingering since our kiss. He directed that summer-sky intent back toward me. "Are you all right, astremé?"

I let myself sway in his thrall once more. I didn't know what made my knees mushier: his open concern, or the pumpkin he'd brought to the party—and turned into a Ferrari.

Not just any Ferrari. "This is a five ninety-nine SA Aperta."

"Hell," Jag muttered. "I believe *I* just fell in love with her."

"That is *really* not funny." Syn's stare iced over. I punched him before he could succumb to any more chest-thumping stupidity.

"They—they made less than a hundred of these," I stammered.

"So I was told." No more chest beating—but his posture puffed like Tarzan in a damn tree, and he curled a tiny smirk. I couldn't sock him for it this time. It felt good knowing that my pleasure gave him a little too.

He clicked a fob and the doors swung open. I stepped a little closer, instantly giddy from the smell of the clean leather interior. "Have you ever even driven it?"

"A few times. But when I come up here, it is usually for altitude training or some climbing. Not much time left over for recreational driving."

I beamed up at him. "Let's recreate away." The drive to Sancti usually took about six hours. I'd already bet we'd cut that nearly in half.

The scenery during the drive didn't suck, either. Watching Samsyn at the wheel was like observing a master equine trainer with his horse or a maestro with his orchestra. Massive power turned into pure majesty. Focusing on him helped me forget the aching goodbye to Camellia, who'd become such a fast friend, as well as the longing in my heart as we took the back roads through Tahreuse. Since we couldn't afford the time— or, most importantly, the attention—of stopping at home to tell Mom, Dad, and Dillon the "good news," we had Grahm's word that he'd inform them within the hour, and he could bring them to Sancti to "congratulate me" in person.

After we'd gotten there first.

After Syn made it clear, to *everyone* in the kingdom, that there was a new king to deal with—and to bear the wrath of.

The thought almost made me feel sorry for the two outlaws still on the loose. *Almost.* They were idiots, but they were also zealots, prepared to cut Camellia's throat while Evrest watched. Quick thinking on Jag's and Grahm's part ensured they hadn't escaped the island yet. Well, not alive. If Samsyn's team found them, they'd wish they *were* dead.

And that was more brain cells than I desired to give the subject. Right now, I refused to think about violent, foreboding Samsyn. Or closed, belligerent Samsyn. Or even reluctant King Samsyn. For the next three hours, I had sexy, behind-the-wheel Samsyn: hair free in the wind, hands sure on the controls, body relaxed and loose...his attention on nothing but the road and me. Okay, so we had to report in every thirty minutes on the comm too. It was a small price to pay for one last spurt of freedom before the circus our lives really hit the big time.

No. Not our lives.

Our *life.*

Semihysterical giggle. Like I could help it? Not for every strawberry in the fields whizzing by as we transitioned from the winding mountain roads into the agricultural valley that would be our scenery into Faisant Township.

"What is *that* about?" Syn lowered the volume on the music. We'd spent the first hour of the trip simply listening to A-Rock, the island's version of a rock 'n' roll station. The songs were surprisingly current, and it sure as hell beat our only other two choices: A-Jazz and A-Oldies. Admittedly, it was fun watching my burly husband belt out every word of the newest Foo Fighters hit.

My husband.

"We're...married."

I laughed again but didn't hold back a note of my bewilderment. He *had* asked.

"Second thoughts already, astremé?" His tone teased, but I caught the tension at the corners of his eyes, shaded beneath his aviator glasses. The hard line beneath his jaw didn't lie either. I swallowed down the thrill they both gave me. I was bound for hell, taking such delight in his discomfort.

In the end, I opted for the humorous route too. "Not if you let me call you my ol' ball and chain." Where would prying at him get me? Parts of his psyche—huge parts—were off-limits. Poking at them would only rouse the bear—and selfishly, I just wanted to enjoy the man a little more. To believe in the fantasy a while longer. Right now, we were just a pair of newlyweds on the open highway, basking in the sun and planning for a future as endless and colorful as the fields of fruit around us.

"Ball and chain." He picked his way across the words in his kid-with-a-new-food way. His face twisted as if that new dish had been lima beans. "Really? Ball and chain?"

"Another one best left alone," I quipped.

He tossed a quick glance. "I believe I want to stick with *big guy.*"

"Fair enough." I laughed again. Turned a little to see him

better, though tucked my arm in carefully. "All right. Turnabout is fair play. What do *you* get to call *me* now?"

"You don't like *astremé*?"

"I love astremé. Ditch it, and I'll have to break something."

He rumbled out a chuckle. "Ah. *There* is my girl."

My girl.

That was it. The man had to be reading my damn mind—and heart and soul—and was doing his best to test them. *Challenge accepted.* I slammed the taffy pull of my stomach to a halt and returned, "Let's just play around. Do a 'what-if.' So... if astremé wasn't already around—or some hot young thing showed up one day and claimed she was your 'little star' first—"

"*Brooke.*"

"Fine. Objection sustained. Let's just say you had to come up with something new for me. Don't be shy, big guy. What would it be?"

He was silent for at least half a minute. I actually started struggling for something to say, afraid I'd miffed him more than I'd first thought.

But then he reached over. Curled his right hand into my left, which poked out from the sling. And finally said, "I would call you my *raismette*."

"Your...what?" I'd heard him just fine. Even thought I understood the word. But ohhhh, I wasn't passing up the chance to hear him say it like he just had, with that rough rasp in his voice and that slight roll of the *r*. That single word, with that shaved granite emphasis, clenched deeper places in my body than any wanton thing he'd ever growled to me before.

"Raismette," he repeated. "It means *reason*."

Trembles. Yes, even down to the fingertips pressed against his. It was just as well that he knew, though my reaction was born of things I still didn't fully understand. "I know the word," I finally said. "But...why that?"

He shrugged. "It is my favorite of all the endearments we can choose for *wife*."

"Reason?"

"*The* reason," he emphasized.

"The reason for what?"

"For everything."

A Mack truck of emotion parked itself behind my frontal lobe. I wanted to hurl myself into his lap and out the window at the same time. My logic was stuck in the same disgusting bind, working to reconcile how a man who confessed something like *that* could still proclaim he had nothing to give a woman. And that wasn't even the real dysfunction here. The statuette for that honor had my name on it. *Ladies and gentlemen of the Academy, thank you so much for this distinction. Yes, I really am more in love with him than ever before. I've worked so hard to be this insane, so your recognition truly means the world...*

"Brooke?"

I blinked. Tried to stow the ache again. Wasn't so easy with him still practically purring at me. "Hmm?"

"Your silence is deafening."

Sorry about that, buddy. Let me get right on turning that down for you. Just don't expect it to be with the truth.

"You do not like raismette." A statement, not a question.

"I didn't say that."

But I wasn't going to confess anything else either. The goulash he'd stirred in my stomach and the anvil he'd dropped on my chest were need-to-know only. He did *not* need to know.

I went for relieving everything with another laugh. Thank God he joined in. "You know," I finally felt strong enough to remark, "if this whole thing *were* for real, we'd have some damn good stories to tell our kids."

Syn snorted. "We had them the night we met, astremé."

"Right?" This time, the laugh was more genuine. "Shit. It was your birthday. I'll bet Tryst and Cullen threw you quite a rager."

"Something like that." Our fingers had started to loosen. He retightened the clasp. "But you were the best present of the day."

"So...your friends all brought lumps of coal? I'm serious, damn it," I girl-snarled in reprisal to his dragon huff. "I was so young and silly and terrified."

He abruptly swung the car to the shoulder. Cut the engine before shifting to confront me, his hands framing my face. "Do not *ever* use those words to describe yourself again."

"*Syn*," I chastised. "I really *was—*"

"Bold and determined and brave." They weren't pretty words on his lips. They were complete command, and the firm lines of his face ordered me to obey. "And beautiful." Still a mandate, despite the ragged breath it came on. "Always...so damn beautiful."

I gulped hard. Again. *Don't feel it. Don't give in to it. Don't let it sweep you away.* But the tenderness tore in...threatening to let in the love right after it.

Countermeasures. Now.

"You know, mister," I drawled, throwing in whatever shred of sassiness I possessed, "comments like that are liable to land us in deep trouble."

His eyes flared. He bit his lower lip. "Trouble?"

It was almost a dare. Should I call him on it? It might be my only chance to actually do so. And we *were* wild and free newlyweds, were we not? What would my husband do if I really jumped into his wicked challenge?

"Mmmm hmmm." I stalled and taunted with the same naughty syllable. "Deep."

"But deep...can be good."

"Certainly can."

As we magnetized toward each other, I slid one finger down the V of his shirt. He moaned against my mouth as I slipped three buttons free, gliding into the muscled alley of his chest. He made another sound, rough and needy—and in that sweet, perfect surge, he gave me something I'd badly needed since the invasion at the Rigale.

He returned my power.

Controlling this—controlling *him*—was a mini miracle, a reconnection with so many things that those ninja bastards had taken from me. My strength. My self-belief. Even the feeling that I could do something good.

Something *so* good...

His erection swelled beneath my fingers the moment I dipped my good hand to the apex of his legs. The flesh grew hotter, warmed even more by the streaming sun through the windows, stretching the black fabric. I sighed. Syn swallowed. We sucked breaths back in together, passions growing, lust taking over.

I cupped him harder. He grunted and bucked his hips. Ohhh, I remembered this. Every incredible inch. I'd wanted it this morning after Syn had made *me* come, my channel wet and ready, my mind blown and open. But Jagger and his damn timing had taken care of that fantasy becoming reality.

Time to make up for lost time.

Now, in the perfect time. Here, in the perfect place.

I urged him back into his seat. As his head fell against the headrest, he punched a button. With a low whir, the seat slid back. I wasted no time crawling to the new space in front of him, directly between his knees. Before the whirring stopped, my fingers tore at his belt buckle.

I didn't get very far.

"Shit!" I whined, staring up like a kid denied an ice cream cone. "Help?"

Like the kid tasked with finding the chocolate sauce, his movements were fast and fierce. He barely made a sound until his cock came free, a perfect pillar of burnished beauty. As I watched, evidence of his lust brimmed from his dark-red crown, glistening in the sun. I bent my head and sucked in the milky drops, reveling in the tart taste of his desire, loving how his flesh hardened and surged beneath my mouth.

"Astremé," he grated. "Do not strain yourself..."

I chuckled, following one of his pronounced veins with the tip of my tongue. "I'm definitely not the 'strained' one here, husband."

Despite exactly what was *in* my mouth, I felt like inserting my shoe instead. Had I just gone and called him that? Nothing like kicking a guy in the figurative balls when my sole objective was bringing pleasure to the real ones.

And nothing like that same amazing guy to give a beautiful surprise in return.

"Sweet little wife..." He hissed, digging a hand into my hair. "This time, I truly must agree with you."

Emotion slammed me once more. But this time, it wasn't a truck. It was a sailboat, racing on the wind, chasing the sun— and finding it, in the gaze and the touch and the passion of the man beneath my lips and fingers. I wanted more. So much more. I showed him so. I licked him, stroked him, and squeezed him. Told him so with my eyes as I moved up...and surrounded him with my mouth. Then loved him, absorbing every thrust of his power and heat and passion...before drinking down his very life, taking him deep inside...

Where he'd be, in so many ways, forever.

Many minutes later, as his eyes returned from the back of his head and his breathing returned to normal, he slid a sultry look down at me. "Whatever am I going to do with you, woman?"

I tossed back an impish grin. "I have a few ideas if you don't."

"I have *many* ideas." He pulled on my good shoulder. "Come here..."

But as I straddled him, a hail signal blared through the car. The comm line had been programmed into the Ferrari's phone system. Jagger's voice boomed around us like Darth Vader on crack.

"Wildcat, please come in."

Correction. Darth Vader badly in need of a valium.

"*Wildcat!*"

Syn stabbed at the button, opening the comm line. "This is Wildcat." He growled as I sidled off, returning to the passenger seat. "What the fuck is the problem? This is not time for radio check."

"It is if you stop the damn car." Jag's huff turned the line to static. "Are you two all right?"

I stifled a giggle. Samsyn's mouth squirmed, battling back his own smirk. "We needed to...stretch."

Well, that did it.

I held back my full laugh only long enough for him to

mute the line. Even then, I wasn't sure about my success. Not that Jagger needed it. His retort resonated with foregone conclusions. "Stretching is not on the schedule. Get your ass back on the road, with its fucking pants *on.*"

I shrieked with new laughter. Syn wasn't so jovial. Though his sleek lips still held the hints of a sexy smile, the rest of his face was dismal. "I am sorry about this, astremé. I had hoped to return the...generosity...of your wedding gift."

I dropped my giggles into a chastising huff. Underlined it by grabbing his face and jerking him to me in a quick, hard kiss. "Haven't you figured this shit out by now, big guy? *You* were the best present of the day."

He snorted while revving the car again. "Only because the rest of it was a giant lump of coal."

I whacked his shoulder. "Shut up and drive. And sing some more Foo to me, baby."

He did just that.

Best afternoon of my life.

CHAPTER TWENTY-ONE

Nothing like a whirlwind honeymoon.

As soon as we arrived in Sancti, a whirlwind of a different kind took over. And why the hell was I being poetic? "Hurricane" was more appropriate now, begun the moment Syn guided the car to the palais's parking garage—through a throng of reporters that swarmed the car like attack bees.

"Holy crap," I blurted as soon as the gates slid shut and we handed the car off to his valet team. "Maybe the main bridge would've been easier."

"The throng *there* is certainly bigger." Syn guided me into the elevator by the waist.

"Shut the front door!"

He peered around before angling a frown back down at me. "We are nowhere near the front—" Stopping himself short when I over-smiled in apology for the slang, he bent in to push me against the lift wall. His scowl was tight, but his gaze sparkled. "Little one, we may have to come to an agreement about those colorful little expressions of yours."

Blue flames joined the mini fireworks in those eyes, now fixated on me. Like a kid enthralled with the show, I lifted my hand, fanning fingers across his cheek. "An...agreement? You mean, like a pact?"

"More like an understanding." His stare swept down, roaming across every inch of my slightly parted mouth. "Do you not think it fair that every time you trip me up with one of those, I get to...trip you up...in return?"

"Trip me up?" My echo was shredded reeds. Good thing I wouldn't be called on to sing an aria tonight—though every cell of my body sang for this man, so elegant and huge and passionate, fitting his hips between mine, ducking his mouth against my neck. "And...h-how...do you propose...doing that?"

He grabbed both my hips, notching my cleft directly against his cock.

Glided his lips along the curve of my ear...

Bit my neck...

Kissed my jaw...

The moment before he took my lips, the elevator jerked to a stop.

We broke apart, barely done straightening our clothes and composing our faces before a computer-generated version of Turkish bells announced our arrival...

Where?

My astonishment was so real, I felt it altering my face. Popping my eyes. Locking my teeth. That part was necessary to keep my jaw from plummeting. Something told me that wherever we were in the palais, *oh-my-gah* gapes wouldn't be accepted behavior.

I'd been to the complex before, of course. There'd been the big celebration for Evrest's ascension to the throne, as well as the yearly trips down the mountain for *Liberlük* in the summer and Christmas festivities in the winter. But all those times, Mom and Dad had been careful to keep us in the shadows or on the sidelines, never venturing far from the anonymity given by the throngs. Inevitably, I'd always associated the Palais Arcadia with bustle, chaos, and crowds.

There was no bustle here. Definitely no crowds. And

to borrow an apt expression from Samsyn, the silence was deafening.

No. Not complete silence. As we stepped farther down the hall—more like a magical tunnel with every inch of its walls and ceiling covered in red, gold, and silver tiles—the strains of traditional instruments bled through the thick wooden doors. Lute. Violin. Some kind of woodwind, perhaps an ocarina or recorder. A metallic melody strummed on a zither. From behind another door, the distinct taps of someone on a computer. Behind another, the cadence of quiet conversation. The décor was a fascinating mix of old and new as well. The tiles, seemingly as old as the island itself, were the backdrop to modular furniture with clean lines. Cube-style tables supported lamps that would make an antique enthusiast drool, though the pieces glowed with the clean light of LED bulbs. Beneath our feet, old carpets were newly scrubbed and spotless.

We turned left, entering a long portrait gallery. Believe it or not, I breathed a little easier. *Now* this felt like a palace. I looked up at the formal paintings, featuring Cimarrons from hundreds of years ago until now, not thinking twice about inserting Samsyn into some of those noble scenes. God, he'd look incredible decked out in fantasy-movie finery, broadsword across his back, muddy boots to his thighs, gauntlets on his thick forearms.

I'd worked that mental magic on about six paintings before noticing he wasn't peering at any of them.

His stare was fixed on me.

I laughed uneasily. "What?"

He smirked like a kid with a secret. "Nothing, wife. Nothing at all."

"Bullshit." I twisted at the clasp of our hands—but finished with a little grin. Would my chest *ever* not flip over when he used that word on me? *Wife. Wife. Wife.* Gah.

"You...like this room."

"Yes." I also liked—a whole hell of a lot—that after just a minute, he saw that.

"I am glad. I like it too." That was when he gazed up. "There is a story to each one of these paintings. Sometimes a few. Each Cimarron...what they did with their life, how they contributed to the island...the mistakes they made getting there, the lessons they learned..."

"And whom they learned them with?"

"Oh, that too. Comrades and enemies, advisors and betrayers..."

"And spouses?"

He stiffened. A pulse ticked hard in his jaw. "And others."

"Others?"

He gave me three seconds of a glance—but three seconds was all it took. One, two, three, and the full blade of his sudden rage was embedded in my gut, deep and wrenching and unforgettable.

"Royal sanction is a diamond with sharp edges. It opens every door. Unlocks every power."

"And brings anyone to your bed."

He glanced again. No fury this time. I wasn't sure how to define his look now. I only knew the way he stared, eyes cold as hail and nostrils flaring hard, sluiced deep sadness through me. Sorrow that hadn't invaded for a long, long time. Not since the moment I'd turned my gaze from the burning wreckage of my home and looked toward the sky that held my future—and beheld only darkness and loneliness.

Why did those skies dominate *his* gaze like that?

Who—*what*—had sucked the sun from his eyes?

And why wouldn't he *talk to me* about it?

Syn pivoted with military precision, giving me the last word on our exchange, as he continued up the gallery. I followed, not protesting his looser grip now, letting him keep to his thoughts for a few more steps. To be honest, I needed the respite to compose my own thoughts. I didn't have the advantage of being on familiar ground anymore. This was all his turf, and even without the trip down the magic looking glass hall, I felt a lot like poor Alice, down the rabbit's hole.

Or a lot like me, on the Sancti tarmac six years ago.

The reflection earned me a hit of courage.

You can do this. Of course you can. Because you've done it before—and you didn't have half the discipline, knowledge, or strength that you do now.

I repeated the mantra even as we passed countless portraits—including one covered in a black shroud. At my curious glance, Syn replied smoothly, "Evrest's. It will remain covered for the next month."

I didn't ask about the wide space already cleared to the left of the shroud. His tighter tension gave it away. That was where his portrait would go.

I pulled in an awed breath. Expelled it to let out a more important query. "Syn...where are we going?"

He snorted, clearly trying to summon humor—and failing. "I am surprised you do not know, astremé. They have a fun phrase for it in America, after all."

"Oh?" Keeping it light wasn't happening on my end either—especially since *he* still looked like we headed for our own execution. "Enlighten me?"

He paused for a moment, putting the words together. "*Schmoozing the in-laws?*"

I jerked my hand away. "Are you fucking kidding?"

He wasn't fucking kidding.

In the middle of my charge, a young man emerged from one of the double doors at the end of the gallery. Cream doublet. Crimson sash. Pole-up-the-butt walk. Cimarron court pages were definitely recognizable. "Your Majesty, King Samsyn," he intoned. "The high couple will see you now."

Welcome home to us.

Shit, shit, shit.

CHAPTER TWENTY-TWO

"Samsyn! *Chér-ev!*"

Syn didn't even pretend to enjoy the endearment from his father. His discomfort instantly became mine, meaning my smile was total plaster by the time Ardent strode all the way across the drawing room. Now that the setting was more private than the Le Blanc Tower's terrace, I wondered if the king father would attempt embracing his son again.

He didn't. Imagine *that*.

Their handshake evoked old memories for me. If Samsyn threw on a tie to match Ardent's, he'd be evocative of Vermont Senator Chase Valen, especially on occasions when foreign dignitaries had to be greeted. Okay, not *all* of them—just the ones who played nicey-nicey with Dad, only to fly home and order their generals to slaughter innocents, starve endangered animals, and bar girls from going to school.

I'd never understood it either. For a while, in my tweens, had even been furious with him for it. Dad would sigh and tell me that one day I'd "get the picture." *Keep your enemies closer, honey.* Here and now, I still didn't get it. But for whatever reason Samsyn forced himself to do it, I supported him. I always would. That was what wives did for their husbands.

Who the hell was I kidding?

I'd back him even without the rings on our fingers.

I'd love him even if he never gave it in return.

"Your Excellences." Syn's nods at his parents were as

formal as the greeting. The queen mother finally rose from a window seat and approached, though at a more sedate pace than her husband. The room was so huge and imposing, though the rustic color scheme and big-cushioned furniture warmed it up. "*Bon sonra*," he went on as she neared, despite the rays of early twilight glowing through the French doors overlooking the palais lawns. "I trust you are both holding up well?"

Xaria's gloss-covered lips flitted with a ghost of a smile. She was a stunning woman with bobbed dark hair, alabaster skin, and light-lavender eyes—a walking commercial for the beauty benefits of living on Arcadia. Still, there was a fragile air about her, like a bird cozy in its cage. "Well, it is certainly easier to *pretend* Evrest has died, instead of managing it as reality." She smoothed the front of her black sheath, saved from the full Morticia effect by the gown's cap sleeves. "And the press has been kind about my 'graceful control.'"

"No surprise," Syn replied. "You are...perfectly appointed." Very clearly, that was his diplomatic best. But as Xaria acknowledged her son's "compliment" with a refined nod, I already swiveled my stare around, senses heightened for a different purpose.

"Excellences," I murmured, "*désonnum* for stating the obvious, but...can we speak so openly here?" I looked at Samsyn, deducing he'd know the answer more than them. "Has this room been wired with audio scramblers? Thermal heat monitors to detect *unwelcome ears*?"

That earned me a loud laugh from Ardent, his head falling back. "Still playing Jamie Bond, eh little Brooke?"

I stiffened but forced a neutral stare. "I don't play around when it comes to the royal family's safety, Excellence."

Ardent barked with more laughter. "Well done! And you

certainly should not, since you are now one of us."

"For the time being," Xaria prompted.

"Yes." Samsyn tucked me closer to him. "But as all my teams know, appearances are only as good as what you believe. That is why I requested this immediate meeting with you both. The media will be informed that Brooke was presented to you and received your full approval as my wife and queen. We shall also publicize the wedding certificate."

"And plan a more proper celebration of the occasion?" Xaria's lips twisted and hardened, momentarily freaking me out. Damn clear who Syn got that one from.

"If you wish," Syn conceded. "After we 'mourn' Evrest and Camellia for the traditional month, as well an additional two weeks in recognition of the special circumstances." His jaw notched higher. "Those dogs shall be clear about our message. We are *not* going to easily forget their treachery."

"Hell yeah!"

My fist, pumped in support, unraveled just as quickly. Lowered to wrap around my sling. Freaking. Lovely. *Today's lesson, kids: how to make sure your new father- and mother-in-law officially think you're a cretin. It's so much easier than you think!*

I fixed my face into apologetic lines. Inched it up toward Syn.

Who already fixed a stare back at me...

Suffused with quiet pride.

And I thought the car ride had been the best part of my day?

"Beginning at once, Brooke will take her rightful place by my side," Syn went on, also in calm conviction. "Including abiding in my suite and assuming every possible duty as befits a new queen of the kingdom."

Xaria pulled in a distinct breath. The woman wasn't stupid; she'd picked up the same implication I did. As Arcadia's last functioning queen, she'd just been assigned to train the new girl. Wisely, I didn't fist-bump this one. Or even grimace as she murmured, "Of course," like a prom queen ordered to dance with the math geek.

"Well! That certainly settles things." Ardent smacked his palms together with a whomp—though it certainly wasn't the end of his celebration. With a grand sweep, he hauled me in and clutched me tightly. "Welcome to the family, little Brooke!"

Help. Though the word screamed inside, I couldn't have spurted it aloud if I tried. So this was what *Eau de Cloying* smelled like—on a sweaty man. Not the good kind of sweat either.

Gah. Was I actually analyzing the properties of my father-in-law's perspiration?

"Mmmmm. We are so happy to have such a lovely new Cimarron."

And was he actually making me listen to that creepy croon through the echo chamber of his chest as he relentlessly extended the hug?

The air spiked with a strange shot of energy. I'd have called it tension, but that was like comparing a fast jab to a Superman punch.

"Father."

Speaking of Superman blows...

And growls that threatened the very stability of my blood...

"Take your hands off my wife right now, or I shall remove them myself. And then I shall break them."

It didn't carry a sliver of ambiguity. Or humor. Or fear.

Karma saved that one through me, spidering my body, icy and sure. When Ardent didn't slacken the hold, I started running action plans. What story would we give the press about Syn breaking both his hands? Would Xaria stay quiet? The woman was an enigma—but despite her mystery, she loved her son. I saw at least that much in her proud stares at him.

Ardent let another beat go by.

Before he busted into hearty laughter again, tossing up both his arms. "And...goooooaaal! So well done, chér-ev!"

If things weren't surreal before, they sure as hell were now. It almost felt like the ninjas' break-in at the Rigale again, time moving in strange pieces of slow-motion and fast-forward, of terrifying and...

Even *more* terrifying.

Slow-motion, as Syn reached and hauled me from an erupting volcano. His face lined in terrible wrath. His eyes emitting pure dragon fire. Clearly, he hadn't yet ruled out the option of snapping Ardent's arms.

Fast forward again, as my body crashed in to his, only to be whipped nearly behind while he leaned out, brandishing a long finger at his father.

Then the terrifying part.

The seething crawl of his voice erupting from somewhere inside him I didn't recognize, raging and roiling and low.

"I am *not* your chér-ev, Ardent Cimarron. Nor will my bride be your new favorite trinket. She took a bullet to her arm, which very well could have been her *heart*, protecting your daughter. She is a hero to your country, an honor to our name, and she *will* be treated with every ounce of your fucking respect."

"*Samsyn.*"

"Silence, Mother, or I shall inform the pool *and* butler staffs that you are ill this evening."

Holy shit.

And double *whoa.*

And figurative face palm. I almost indulged the real thing too. Talk about subtext I wasn't ready for—or ready to see such blatant confirmation of, etched like tattoos across both the high couple's faces.

But it all made such perfect sense now.

Awful, heart-ripping sense.

Samsyn's face provided the hugest confirmation. So many pegs locked into place, simply by witnessing his rage with brand-new eyes. His walls against commitment. His religion of casual sex. His dedication to the warrior's code, where the dangers were defined, the enemy drawn clearly, and decisions were made from the head not the heart.

Because he didn't think he had a heart.

Because it had been broken.

By his own parents.

Your new favorite trinket. The pool and butler staffs.

Syn lowered his hand. Reached it back—for mine. When I twined our fingers, his were trembling. I squeezed tightly. *I'm here. I'm not going anywhere.*

He dragged in several more breaths before fully straightening. Though the prince was back, the dragon still prowled just beneath his civil surface.

"Are we done here, Excellences?" When Ardent and Xaria gave no answer but silence, he jerked a terse nod. "Very well, then. Brooke and I shall say good evening. It has been a long day"—a phrase barely servicing the subject, considering our predawn passion on his bathroom counter—"and we are ready for some privacy."

I managed quick nods to the queen father and mother—*awkward is in da house*—before Syn led me out, his hand again at the small of my back.

He didn't speak as we traversed down the portrait gallery and then the tiled hall. When it was time to turn back for the elevator, he pulled me in the opposite direction.

We climbed two flights of stairs before emerging onto a wide, empty terrace centered on a marble fountain with cobalt dolphins and gold-tipped sea kelp. Cypress trees were stately sentinels on two sides of the courtyard; a third side dropped into curved steps leading to a small garden with a fairy tale waterfall. All of it had views of the coast and sea.

I'd never seen anything so breathtaking—but all I could focus on was Samsyn. His pace was barely sustainable for me, though I sensed his enormous restraint. Though it torqued my own tension, I sustained from even speaking. One of us had to keep our shit together, and it sure as hell wasn't him. The air around him was stabbed with a million needles of ire. I had to keep them from multiplying. Too many, and they'd meld into yet another steel fortress around his heart.

After we skirted the fountain, heading for the palais wing on the other side, I finally dared it. "Syn—"

"Not now, Brooke."

"But—"

"I said not now!"

I halted.

He growled. Then twisted his hand free and kept on walking.

I took a step. Stopped again. The world blurred behind a salty swath. I shoved it away, swallowing hard and gritting my teeth. Pulled in a ruthless breath of the early night air, mixed with salt off the water and oil from the torches down on the beach, marking the palais's perimeter. Seagulls dipped and glided on the wind overhead, riding the currents without a care. Or did I have it wrong? Wasn't it just that they had no choice, and they needed the gusts to take flight?

But without the gulls, what would the *wind* be? Just...air. No beauty or expression or life.

They needed each other.

Needed to be pushing at each other. Tangled with each other. Living through each other.

I slumped to a padded couch. Energy sapped. Resolve drained. Heart aching.

A flightless bird.

"Pathetic." I spat it at myself, beneath my breath. Like that would slacken the brutal truth of it. *You're pathetic, Brooke Allison. Stop sulking, get off your ass, and—*

I'd been so deep in my wallow, there'd been zero awareness of Samsyn turning back around. Now suddenly here he was, planted in front of me. Feet braced. Breaths harsh. Hands fisted.

Until he plummeted too.

Straight to his knees.

Lunged his head forward, writhing it in my lap, still wordless...and seeking.

Lifted hands to my hips and yanked me closer, still trembling...and seething.

Rolled his whole torso, shoulders flexing, gripping me as if our roles had reversed and *I* were the air. *His* air. His breath. The only thing he needed.

I breathed him in too. Clutched his head, hands anchored

against his scalp, pressing our carotids beside each other. Lifeblood pounding. Breaths entangling. Heartbeats meeting.

Spirits...knowing.

We remained like that for a long time, listening to the gulls and the wind and the night and each other, before Syn twined my good arm around his neck. Guided my legs around his waist. Instinctively, I tightened those holds. As I expected, he stood, carrying me without effort. He began to walk, each step as intent as his clear blue eyes.

As soon as he stepped inside, I knew we were in his suite. The air was rich with exotic spices, seductive as burnished leather, and imbued with his masculine strength. That only made his new demeanor stand out in starker contrast, each of his movements so tender and cautious.

With slow care, he laid me across the downy white comforter on the huge sleigh bed. The fabric absorbed my weight like a cloud cushioning a pearl. He gazed down at me with the same reverent wonder. Stretched beside me with graceful purpose. Ran the back of his hand down my body with slow, silent deliberation.

When he got back up to my torso, he gently detached the sling from my arm. Unthinking sigh. It was wonderful to be free of the contraption. Good enough to try lifting that hand to his neck then his face. But without a word, Samsyn curled his fingers around it, lowering it back to my side.

"Samsyn—"

"Ssshhh." He rose over me, capturing my lips with pressure that wasn't aggressive but sure as hell wasn't shy. His mouth reached for me. Courted me. The wedding dance we hadn't had—but more. So much more. His wings sought my air. His flight craved my force. "Can we just have this, Brooke?" He tucked his forehead against my chest. "I need this, astremé. To wash it all away. Just for now..."

I pushed a thumb beneath his jaw. Made him behold the *yes* in my eyes...and feel it from my thundering heart too. I pulled him up for another kiss while hooking a leg around his waist, making him roll atop me. His weight...was perfect. He was so broad and solid and forceful, consuming my sightlines, dominating my senses.

At once, he began rocking against me. I writhed and thrusted in return, heat twisting in my core, gushing into the tunnel craving his invasion. My blood already pumped a tribal tattoo in my veins, urging me to reach for the explosion only Syn could give.

But all too soon, he rose up—though during his move, took my leggings along. He loomed over me again, twisting two fingers into the waistband of my panties before deftly sliding them off. I hissed, impatiently reaching for my own shirt buttons. He pushed my hands back, shaking his head with solemn sensuality. "Do not deny me the pleasure, woman."

Woman.

Not "little girl."

For that, I'd let him peel my damn skin off if he desired.

Feeling every inch that woman, I watched from a hooded gaze as he straightened...and then stripped naked. As every new inch of his bronze flesh was revealed, my breath hit sparkling shallows. His body had been crafted with care but hewn by battle, his long limbs nicked by scars both old and new. They extended from a V-shaped torso, shoulders that would put any football player to shame, slabs of gleaming pecs, and then an eight pack of brutal masculinity, leading to...

Oh, yeah. *That.*

Mouthwatering was trite...but as I took in the unfettered beauty of his penis, I licked my lips without thinking. The angels had surely taken weeks perfecting it. Long and virile, trailed by veins that pumped it even fuller, capped by a rosy bulb that led the way back toward me—the luckiest woman on the planet. Especially as he sidled back up on the bed, fitting his thighs between mine and caressing my pussy with that hardness while teasing my shirt buttons free.

You're so beautiful.

I yearned to say it but wanted nothing to shatter the energy between us...the flawless star of this moment, centered on a bond that only began with our physical attraction. He'd been right. Together, we could wash the rest of the world away. Right now, it was only Syn and me...and the magnificent, brilliant wonder of what our spirits and souls shared. Nothing else mattered. Not his freshly torn emotional wounds. Not the crazy story of my life, about to get crazier when the media learned the Valen family was actually still alive. And not the danger that could be waiting right outside the door, targeting *his* family.

Here, we were only the big guy and his astremé.

Just Syn and Brooke.

Man and woman.

And even better, in the husky rasps we exchanged, gazes twining into each other...

"Wife."

"Husband."

And then, not just our stares were joined.

He entered me in one stroke, cock sliding perfectly into my slick readiness. I took him eagerly, wantonly, whimpering for more before he was done withdrawing, preparing for another full thrust. Every lunge was like that too. His retreat, nearly to the point of leaving me, and then his fullness again, hitting me deep, stretching me fully. He left my bra on, not even distracting himself with my breasts. He locked his gaze on my face alone, his eyes as cutting as blue coral, his parted lips exposing his clenched teeth. He absorbed every nuance of my arousal and gave his own in return. Because of that, our climaxes climbed together, exactly in sync. Every long, deep fuck brought us closer. Higher. Hotter. Better.

When we climaxed, it was with the same acute connection. We gasped and groaned before clenching and coming, waves of completion rolling over us again and again. Syn bent in, pouring a kiss into my mouth as his cock emptied inside me, bathing my body in heat as he drenched my spirit in joy and gratitude...and love.

Yeah. That.

Always that.

Much later, after the universe decided to hand back our souls, Syn cradled me in his arms, pulled in a long breath, and released it on a rumble that already sounded like a snore. With a soft smile, I followed him into sleep. What would we have accomplished with pillow talk? For now, we'd spoken the only things that mattered.

Wife.

Husband.

We'd stress later about the rest. Probably a lot more than we wanted to.

CHAPTER TWENTY-THREE

Before I reopened my eyes, my body made me aware it was there—in all its aching glory.

I was on my back, cushioned by butter-soft sheets and pillows to match. Despite the TLC for my naked skin, my arm throbbed and my other limbs were stiff...both balanced by the delicious soreness between my thighs.

A funny memory hit, from deep in my childhood. A television commercial. Aftershave lotion? Beer? Didn't matter. *I'm a lover, not a fighter*, the actor had said, knowing smirk fully in place.

Samsyn Cimarron would never have to choose.

And damn, was I in trouble because of it.

But trouble was so much more fun when shared by two.

On that cheeky note, I sat up in bed. I was alone but hoped that'd be temporary. "Husband mine"—I reveled in the words, even if they were only a mutter to the room—"where have you gone off to?"

I received the answer faster than I'd expected.

Resulting in a frantic clutch of the sheets to my chest.

Samsyn was still near but talking to someone. After listening more closely, I guessed he was out on the terrace. Though the shades were mostly drawn across the windows, a stealthy glance inside might still give prying eyes a "deluxe view" of the new queen in her birthday-suited glory. But what had I expected? Yesterday, all of Arcadia had been told their king was dead. Today, they needed to be told that all would be okay. In essence, it was my husband's first day at work.

That's shorthand for get your ass out of bed, *girlfriend.*

I was about to go toga style with the sheet, but my gaze fell to the nightstand. Draped across it was a satin robe in light cream, accented with gold piping. The garment felt even better than the sheets, though it was a little long. I hiked part of it up in order to tiptoe to the door, cracking it open to hear what was going on.

Syn, already dressed for the day, stood with his back to me. One hand was braced on his lean hip, the other held a phone to his ear. So that was why I couldn't identify the second party in the conversation.

After confirming he was truly alone, I emerged onto the terrace. As I stepped out, Samsyn turned around.

Damn.

And *wow.*

If it were possible, he was even more bite-my-lip-worthy from the front. A fresh shirt, in dove gray this time, was complimented by a black vest with matching pinstripes. The pinstripes continued in his slacks. Everything was undoubtedly tailored to him. The ensemble formed to his physique without a millimeter of error. He hadn't conceded totally to the new king look, though. From the middle of his shins down, his pants were stuffed into a pair of well-used black cargo boots, top four eyelets empty, the extra laces whipped around and tied at the back of his legs instead of the front.

The only way he could've been sexier was naked.

As soon as our stares met again, the stern expression on his face softened. One side of his mouth kicked up. He gestured for me to sit in one of the chaises, but I shook my head and mouthed the word *shower*. I'd feel better about joining him if I was ready to face the day too. Whatever the hell it was going to bring.

I left him to finish the call, picking up enough of his Arcadian to discern it was about repairs on the water pipeline between the mountains and the central valley, and made my way back inside. I wasn't dressed to give myself a full tour of his suite yet but took a quick mental inventory of what I *could* see. At least two more big bedrooms, with a hall likely leading to more. Kitchen. Living room. Conference room. Woman.

Woman?

At that point, I simply saw red. Didn't help that her blond hair was woven with the same inimitable color, turning it a shade of envy-worthy strawberry. Her big green eyes, centered over a button nose and bow-shaped lips, peered around the living room. She didn't radiate man killer, though. Her black taffeta dress seemed from another era, its Peter Pan collar and fitted bodice cinched into a tight waist, flaring to a full skirt ending just below her knees. She carried a large patent leather purse. Add cat-eye glasses, and I'd have pegged her for getting lost on her way to auditioning for *Grease*.

But maybe that was how Samsyn liked his women.

Well, not while the bastard wore that gold band on his finger.

I yanked the robe tighter. Pointedly cleared my throat. "Miss? May I help you?"

She started like a cat with its paw on the bird. "Oh! Your Majesty." After hurrying over and curtseying low—and then lower still—she raised up with an uncomfortable smile. "I am afraid you righted the words from my mouth."

"Huh?" Wow, she was weird—but that was what I liked

best about her. "You mean, took the words right out of my mouth?"

"Ummm...yes." She smiled gratefully but swiftly schooled the look. "It sounds so much better, coming from you."

"Okaaayy." I hoped she'd pick up on my confusion. Her eyes might have been big, but they were also intelligent.

"Sweet Creator," she mumbled. "Where is my etiquette?" After smoothing her skirts and tossing her braid down her back, she poked out her hand, almost robotically. "I am Mishella, Your Majesty. I am your new *secran*."

"My new what?"

She blinked. "Secran. Errrmm...secretary? Assistant?"

Since Mishella was minding her Ps and Qs, I should've been too. Instead, a giggle spurted out. Then something worse. "Well, hell. Why didn't you just put that horse in front of the cart?"

Her face crunched. "I...did I not just—"

"I'm sorry." I took her hand, squeezing affectionately. "It's just a silly expression." I watched, a little nonplussed, as she dropped my hand to reach into her purse. Out came a legal-sized note pad, yellow pages and all, along with a gold pen. She started madly scribbling. "Mishella? What are you—"

"Making note of the 'silly expression.'" She attacked the task like...well...a lawyer in court. "The queen mother told me you had many idioms and to take meticulous notes so I could learn them."

Comprehension set in. Not the good kind. "The queen mother sent you?"

"Well, assigned me. Yes. To—"

"Assist me. Yes. I heard the first time."

While her head jerked up, the ginger brows lowered. "I

will be good at my job, Majesty. I have trained in Queen Xaria's offices for nearly a year now. I am excellent at organization, calendaring, filing, keyboard input, and even wardrobe selection."

I held up both hands. "Whoa, whoa. Untangle your panties. *Don't* write that one down." I pulled the pad from her, just to be sure. "I'm sure you're perfectly great. And I'm actually thankful you're here. Just give me a second. Or three." I fumbled on, in the face of her perplexed silence, "I just thought you'd come in here for another reason, that's all."

Her lips pursed, an expression that probably drove men crazy—not that I was certain the woman knew it. Or did she? "Another reason like what?"

More of the wide doll wonder. If her all-business-no-pleasure thing *was* an act, it was a damn good one.

"Like hooking up with Samsyn."

At least she understood that one. Her double-take was brief but blatant. After pulling out a smaller notepad from the bottomless purse—apparently, the girl believed in backup pacifiers—she pivoted to cross the room. "First, why would I commit professional suicide by 'hooking up' with anyone in the palais, let alone the son of my employer? Second, His High—errr, I mean His Majesty—has been clear about his policy on blondes for a *very* long time now, and—"

I stopped her by raising one hand higher. "Wait. *What* 'policy on blondes'?" I knew about Syn's preference for dark hair—hell, everyone did—but he didn't have a freaking policy about it...did he?

Mishella replied while turning toward the hall I'd only looked at before, kitten heels tapping on the tiles. "Prince Samsyn has refused assignations with all blonde women for years now." She stopped in front of a door as I caught up, letting me see her wistful smile. "I was a young girl when I found out, in my last year of secondary school. I cried for days. I had quite a yearning for him..."

"Like a crush?"

"Yes. A 'crush.'" Her head tilted as she considered the word. "Hmmm. Sometimes, Americans *do* have better ways of saying it."

I arched a brow. "Bet you didn't get *that* from the queen mother."

"Actually...I did."

I followed her into the room, which turned out to be a sizable office. The space appeared unused, however. No equipment on the desk or paperwork tacked to the bulletin board. The computer and printer were switched off.

"So...about Samsyn and his blondes..."

"You mean his aversion to them." She cringed as if accidentally spewing the F-word. "Errr, I mean—until you, Your Majesty."

Wasn't like the same damn thing hadn't fallen on me like a pallet of bricks. I just thanked the crap out of the universe that I had tools to control my demeanor a little better. *Ramrod spine. Tightened abs. Relaxed mouth.*

I barely managed them all.

Until you.

What the hell did that mean?

"Ummm...is this your office, then?" I took a step in, pretending the blank walls were as fascinating as the Louvre. Might as well have been. I was just as uncomfortable, considering I stood there in nothing but a satin robe. The nervousness officially worsened when Mishella blink-blinked back at me.

Gah. Not the blink-blink.

"This is not my office, Your Majesty. It is *yours*."

I really would have preferred another minute of blink-blink.

"Mine?" I laughed and prayed she'd join me. No luck. "Look, I don't really...I *can't* really...I mean, I do everything on my laptop. All my certifications are online; I do my kinesiology homework through the university's web portal; I have an email and some social media and—"

"Not anymore."

"Huh?"

"Oh, I am certain your university courses will still be fine." She said it as if the rest was totally understandable. When I only gawked back, she continued more carefully. "You are a member of the Arcadian royal family now, Your Majesty. You know what that means, correct?"

"Well...sure." *Bullshitter.*

Mishella's face tightened. Clearly, she saw through the bluff too. Great. Doe eyes had fox smarts. Just my luck. She didn't say anything, though. Simply flipped on the computer—a newer model thing with a wide screen that made my geek side tingle—and logged onto Facebook. *My* page on Facebook.

Thank God my tongue was attached, or I would've swallowed it. "Holy. Shit."

"Hmmm," Mishella countered. "That one is better than ours too."

"I have nearly a hundred thousand followers."

"Samsyn's numbers are even higher."

"Of course they are. He has a better ass."

Finally, the woman laughed. Okay, so it was a snort with

humor. Close enough. But too quickly, she looked up, earnest eyes back in place. "Can you now understand why we must consider every piece of information that is posted, tweeted, and shared?" Mishella exhorted. "If you cannot see it from the public relations viewpoint, Majesty, then look at it from the safety one. We still have no idea who murdered King Evrest and Lady Camellia. Even posting something like a rant about your hangnails could clue those animals in about getting to you and Samsyn next. They could disguise themselves as your manicurist; get back in that way."

"Shit." My belly twisted. "You're right."

"I do not want to be, Majesty." Her voice cracked. "I really do not. But those roaches are still out there, and—"

"Okay, okay." I soothed it in time to my hand on her back. "I get it." I really did. And the truth was, I should've been "getting it" more.

Ugh. I felt like a bitch-on-high for being so cavalier now. The woman was still mourning her young king and his betrothed while fearing the outlaws responsible for their "deaths." Being assigned to babysit me probably wasn't her dream job, but here she was, making the best of it despite being tagged as Syn's booty call, enduring snark about the queen mother, and having her notepad snagged from her grip. *Wonderful.* How was I going to make her day in the *next* five minutes?

This, on top of the stellar little get-together with Syn's parents yesterday, would have me setting island records in no time. *Fastest queen to become a hideous meme, coming right up.*

It was time for a change. A fast one. I'd already married Samsyn with my heart. Now I had to do it with my head. Become the queen he needed me to be. I could do that. I could do *this.*

Mishella stepped back. Dabbed the corners of her eyes while her cheeks flushed dark pink. "I...I am so sorry, Majesty."

I dipped my head, meeting her big watery gaze. "Because you're human? And you actually care about what happens to me, though you barely know me?"

Her lips wobbled upward. "You are so kind, Majesty."

I bit my cheek to hold back what I longed to retort. *If you call me "Majesty" one more time, I really will post pictures of my hangnails.* But making her call me Brooke would be as good as yanking *her* nails out and then scratching them across a blackboard.

Become the queen he needs you to be.

"Aw shucks." Going for the tease helped us both relax. "It's all good, sweetie. Besides, it's not like all of this will be for—" so much for relaxing "—uhhhh...for the palais newsletter." I forced out a grin. "Right? We can't put everything into it. We'll have to be selective."

"The...what?"

"Come on. It's a good idea." Actually, it *was.* "We can include newsy bits about what's going on around here..."

Her nose scrunched. "Such as Evrest's and Camellia's funeral?"

And this was me, being the queen Syn needed.

"After that, of course." I drew myself up higher, feigning that I'd *meant* the exchange to go in that direction, before flashing another confidence-I'm-nowhere-near-feeling smile. "So...why don't you get settled in here? I really need to grab a shower."

"Of course," Mishella said. "While you are bathing, I shall select something nice for you to wear."

"No!"

"Pardon?" Once more she looked like the kid with the coal in her stocking.

"I meant...*no problem*." I'd dodged coal, but there *were* those memories of the popped Barbie heads. If letting Mishella dress me up for a few days helped ease her transition into this new routine, I could live—*for a few days.*

Dear God, I prayed. *Only for a few days, okay?*

CHAPTER TWENTY-FOUR

An hour later, I emerged from the bathroom, turning left for the spacious dressing area Mishella had already shown me. As I padded over heated floors and breathed air with a touch of eucalyptus, I wondered if anyone would think it strange that the queen spent half her days in the royal suite's bathroom.

That was before the mirrors gave me a glimpse back into the master bedroom. And a sighting of the man in one of the big leather chairs positioned in the corner, book in hand, one ankle propped against a pinstriped leg. He'd taken off the big work boots for now, giving me an advantageous view of that foot. It was hewn into graceful angles, toes forming a perfect slant, dusted by just the right amount of dark hair along the top.

Shit.

Samsyn Cimarron even had perfect feet.

I tried to turn the observation into something witty while making my detour complete. My brain gave back zilch—especially as he looked up, gaze full of sun-on-sea blue, smile full of moon-and-stars magic. I leaned against the doorway, simply staring back. Drinking in every amazing inch of him. The pride in his shoulders, even while resting in the chair. The sheen of the reading light on the top of his head. His hand on the closed book in his lap. The gold band on it, gleaming against his burnished skin.

Mine.

I let the sight of that ring seal the thought on my mind... just for a few moments longer. Didn't feel a drop of selfishness about it either. Moments were all I had...when I could've said it forever.

"Bon sabah, wife."

If his eyes were the sunlight on the sea, his voice was the foam: smooth and gorgeous, belying strength just beneath the surface. It sent sparkling energy through every inch of me. Tilted a girlish grin to my lips.

"Bon sabah yourself, husband." I stole a glance into the living room. "Where's Mishella?"

"Off to get you some brunch. I thought you might be hungry."

"You thought right." Tickled little smile. He took such good care of me. "Thank you."

He slid the book to a circular side table, taking his very sweet time about speaking again. Well, sweet for *him*. It was agony for me, having to stand there and simply watch him, when I craved to rush over, climb into his lap, and feel his arms close around me, huge and safe and warm. After a few minutes of that, I'd open my robe, letting his luxurious clothes slide against my bare skin...

When my breath hitched, he cocked his head. Steepled his fingers. "What is going on in that brain of yours?"

I licked my lips. The truth probably wasn't a good idea, but he'd detect a lie from me in a heartbeat. He always did. "That you look too damn good to be in mourning."

He rested his chin atop his fingers. "Imagine that. I was just considering you with the same thought."

"But I'm—" I gestured at my wet hair, the bulky robe, my bare feet.

"My point exactly."

Inner swoon. Fluttering heart. And other parts...simply pulsing. I shifted my weight, praying for an ease between my legs. *Rookie move.* The squirm only gave my pussy a nice massage, tempting my clit to come out and play.

Innocuous subject matter, don't fail me now.

"What are you reading?" My eyes widened when he tilted the book up. "*Call of the Wild?* Seriously?"

"Making up for my teenage antics." He shrugged. "I missed out on many good stories."

"*You* had teenage antics?"

He chuffed. "To a degree."

I sat on the bottom corner of the bed. "When did you have to grow up?"

His gaze narrowed. His brows hunched. He actually seemed confused.

Time to take the reins.

"Samysn...when did you learn both your parents were having affairs?"

He stabbed his stare to the floor—just before bracing his feet and bolting up. I reached for his hand, already curled into a fist. I didn't care. Hung on as much as I could, battling to work my fingers beneath his—

Until his violent evasion. His brusque pivot from me. I'd expected both...but didn't know what to think about his doomed man's walk toward the terrace, slow and measured, echoing in the room like a funeral drum. The last time he'd stunned me like this had been at the Temptina Bridge, when we'd almost kissed. Had that been only ten days ago? Had I really looked at him so differently? Had *I* been so different?

Yes had never been a more appropriate answer.

Just when I thought he'd escape outside again, he stopped. Spread his long arms across the double French doors. The late-morning sun streamed in around him, imparting the effect of a newly arrived dark angel.

Or maybe a departing one.

"I was eighteen."

For a second, his calm cadence was startling. Then I remembered what always happened to my own voice when speaking of the night Rune Kavill burned down my home. Only emotional distance made the feat possible.

"That's...young," I replied quietly.

"I certainly did not think so," Syn returned. "I was a cocksure little bonsun who thought it would be more fun to sneak around at midnight with my friends than study for my secondary school finals."

I smiled a little. It was too easy to envision a Samsyn on the cusp of manhood, already starting to bulk up a little. In Vermont, he easily would've been the star quarterback, letterman's jacket on his back and prom queen on his arm. As a prince of Arcadia, he was the cut-up of the royals, saved from responsibility by the sheer luck of his birth order—and reveling in it.

"So you did," I affirmed.

"So I did." He turned from the window, scraping his hair back. "And we did what every self-respecting bunch of *gencrients* would do."

My smile lifted again. "You went for the girls."

"Persuaded them to come 'walk' with us in the gardens, yes." He returned to the chair though barely perched on the seat, bracing elbows to his knees and lacing his fingers again. "Tryst and I broke away from the others, hoping the sisters we had been courting would follow."

I grabbed the chance for some levity. "*Courting?*" I giggled. "Really?"

He shrugged. "Passing notes in class. Saving seats at breaks. Calling A-Rock and making anonymous dedications. The usual." He cocked a fresh frown. "Right?"

Contemplative hum. "Trade the walk through the garden for a loop around the mall, and you have the same thing in America. So..." I spread my hands. "Yeah. Right."

It took him a second to return to his memory. As soon as he did, his gaze doubled down on darkness. I almost told him to abort, that we could do this later, but the urgency in his posture pushed me into silence. I sensed the story like a living thing inside him, clamoring to be spoken—and I wondered if he'd even told it to anyone before. If not, he'd been hauling this burden around for nine years now. All by himself.

Whether that was the case or not, he sure as hell wasn't alone now—and even a few feet seemed too great a distance to tell him so.

I pushed off the bed and then lowered to my knees, scooting directly between his. A heavy sigh rushed from him. I separated his meshed hands, circling them with my own before pressing them over my heart...silently urging him to go on.

"We headed for a darker part of the garden," he finally grated. "A hidden grotto...behind some big stones." His whole form clenched. "But Father had beaten us there."

The rattle of his voice gave me enough information to go on. I clutched him tighter before filling in, "And he was with someone."

He didn't bother nodding. Instead he uttered, "One of the High Council members. A woman who'd been serving him for years...clearly, in a number of ways."

Envisioning the past wasn't so effortless now. My throat closed with emotion as my mind flickered with the scene. Samsyn and Tryst standing there, gaping at more of Ardent than either of them wanted to know about...

Ew.

That was more of Ardent than *I* wanted to think about.

"Did he know you were there?"

Unbelievably, Syn colored. "Indeed," he said grimly. "He knew."

Tiny flinch. I'd seen Syn's ire when he witnessed people merely trying to bend mat-training rules. His fury at the Residence Rigale's magistrate, when catching the man trying to snow me with his arrogance, was still a vivid recall. My husband's loathing of deceit and dishonor, backed by his adherence to the Arcadian warrior's code, was one of the compasses of his character. Had it been molded that way after the fateful night in the garden with his father? Wouldn't have hit me as a surprise—though I doubted it. Syn's moral code seemed sewn into his DNA, as much a part of him as the stunning color of his eyes. There were lines in his world that simply didn't get crossed—and when his own father had stepped over one of the biggest, the torment of his soul had begun. For nine years, he'd lived with a Gordian Knot in his gut. Call his father out and forever stain the Cimarron family name, not to mention the emotional blow to his siblings, or help Ardent keep the dirty laundry deep in the basement?

Though somewhere along the line, Xaria had added to that pile too.

I followed the logical line from that thought. "So when did you tell your mom? Did you go to her that night?"

"She already knew." His eyes, though fixed on me still, were distant and sad. "As soon as I saw her the next day, I just knew it. For a while, it bonded us a little. She seemed comforted that at least one person saw the truth. But then she turned no better than him, forming her little harem..."

"And you've carried both their secrets ever since."

I stated it without pity. That would have destroyed him. Nor with any sadness. That wasn't mine to share with him. I said it to him as I knew he needed it, simply as fact.

But my touch was a different story.

I could still caress his taut hands with the tenderness of my own. Could still press my lips to his knuckles, lingering their softness over his roughness. Could still hold him, comfort him, be a small piece of strength for him. I couldn't take away the pain of his parents' infidelities, but I could help him with carrying its weight. I just prayed like hell he'd let me.

The furrows across his face, persisting even now, didn't give me a lot of hope about that chance.

"Secrets." He repeated the word like asking me to pass the poison. "Are they not just another word for lies?"

I grabbed his hands tighter. Lifted them to my cheeks. Framed his face in the same way, though stroked my thumbs from the corners of his nose to the edges of his mouth, still adoring him with my touch. "I know it's not easy, big guy. As a matter of fact, it's hell. But you're not alone anymore. For as long as I'm here...let me help." I spread my fingers to his forehead, tracing the thick slashes of his eyebrows. "*Samsyn*... let me in."

The words sank into him that time—like the poison he'd just been asking for. "How do I know what is real anymore?"

"You know." I slid my hands to the center of his chest.

"You know, Syn. In here."

He dropped his hands too. Then his head. As his hands flowed over mine, our foreheads touched and held. He was silent for so long, no sound but the whooshes of his breath, but I felt all his words anyway. So many of them, alive and incredible on the air between us, consonants and vowels not mattering, a language needing no interpreter...because it was born from our hearts.

"Brooke?" It finally soughed out, a guttural whisper.

"Yeah?"

"*You* feel...real."

Throat constricting.

Heart exploding.

Love growing.

I nudged my face up at him. Breathed in as he breathed out. Sighed as he shuddered. Smiled softly as he growled lowly. "Because I am, big guy. For as long as you need me."

His chest rumbled with another low, gruff sound. He raised his fingers, splaying them to the side of my throat. Stretched them back to my nape, where he dug in to jerk my head up with a sharp tug. I gasped. Bite of fear. Wash of arousal. Then even more as he leaned over, aligning our gazes once more.

"What if I need you right now?"

I looked up, into the cut blue glass of his gaze, and silently begged him to slice me open. "What if I can't think of anything I need more?"

His stare thickened. Swept down my face until delving over my mouth...giving a heated preview of what his was about to do.

And did.

Holy. Shit.

I thought I knew every category of kiss from this man now. From tender brushes to plunging tongue invasions, he used his mouth with as much mastery as his sword. But this was something new. Something he'd never exposed me to. A conquering I'd never experienced from him. A passion not just reserved for my body. He wanted—commanded—everything now. The thoughts in my head. The desires of my heart. All the keys to my soul.

And God help me...I was helpless to refuse.

As soon as the lock fell free, releasing it all in a sensual tumble, I sighed again—though by then, Syn had already slid back in the chair, pulling me with him.

Straddling my hips around his.

Yanking the ties of my robe open.

Exposing my nude body to the blue flames of his stare.

"Creator's infinite grace," he rasped. "What a gift you are, my astremé."

I swallowed hard as his hands cupped my breasts, enticing the tips to full erection with steady tugs. "Does that mean you're ready to...unwrap me?" Coyly, I shirked the robe off my left shoulder. If the move worked its desired effect, he wouldn't want to be so careful about releasing the other arm.

It did. He wasn't.

I girl-growled as he shoved the robe's other side down and then ripped the garment completely away. I was bared to him now. Exposed...in every way I could be. Skin. Sex. Spirit. *His.*

Syn raked his hands downward, imprinting my rib cage, stomach, and abdomen with the dark-pink trails of his touch. He wasn't gentle, and I didn't want him to be. I hissed with that encouragement as he skidded lower, parting my labia, driving both thumbs up into my throbbing channel.

"Damn!" My head fell back as he thrust in deep, digging his other fingers into my mound for purchase. "Syn. That's..."

"Not enough," he snarled. "Not nearly enough."

I tucked in to kiss him while rolling my sex in time with his hands. "Not nearly," I panted—just before flipping his belt open. Beneath my fingers, his erection surged against his pants, hot and huge already.

We groaned together as his cell phone rang.

Syn swore, releasing his hands from my body in order to fumble for the device. It was resting on the table beneath his book, which had been tossed to the floor in his search. He finally tapped the green button—at the same moment I lowered his slacks zipper.

"Yes?"

He finished it with a barely stifled groan—as I freed his cock. I'd never get used to the thrill of seeing him like this. His sex embodied *him*: powerful, proud, bold, insistent. I longed to just stare at it like this. Now wasn't that time.

"Of...course. Perfect." He stumbled through his formalities as I caressed him from swollen balls to pulsing tip. "Thank you for...letting me...know. I understand. Yes. Just be certain everyone is prepared and..."

Back to the clenched groan...as I swiped a drop of his precome off the tip of his stalk. The whole shaft bobbed beneath my touch, straining with his need.

"Yes. I know." He hissed as I sucked the milk off my finger. "Right away. I am coming."

As he punched the call to an end, I quirked a saucy smirk. "Hmmm. Not yet, I hope."

Syn didn't waste time on a riposte. With his most dangerous dragon's growl, he seized me by both hips.

Positioned my drenched pussy atop his surging penis, and then plunged me back down. I cried out in a mix of pain and ecstasy. Never had he penetrated me so deep, so fast. It was terrible and incredible in the same excruciating instant.

"Minx." He riveted the word to the air while slamming me harder upon him—quelling any impression that my position put me in control of things this time. "You have made me late to the emergency High Council meeting. And you know I hate delaying discipline."

I winced as his grip tightened, increasing the pace of our thrusts. He'd leave marks on my hips—thank God. I hoped they'd be dark for days, visceral reminders of this exact moment. The quivering zings through my body. The coiled tension of his. And the pressure, squeezing hot and needy in my core, begging his cock for its ultimate explosion.

"D-Discipline?" I jibed between heavy breaths. "Nobody's keeping you here, Majesty. If you *must* go, then go..."

I squeaked as he reached around, pinching both my ass cheeks. *Shit.* There'd be marks there too.

"I am not going anywhere, wife—until you take every drop of come from my cock."

His wicked words were my empowerment. I rose up, ensuring he could better see every movement I made. Moved his hands back to my hips, surrendering even deeper to his driving, dominant pace. "As I shall willingly do, husband."

Samsyn's lips parted. His teeth gleamed, white and feral in the streams of sun pushing through the windows. Another blast of that light fell over the juncture of our bodies, making the juices on his cock gleam with every new punch into my pussy.

"Brooke!" he groaned.

"Samsyn," I rasped.

"Take me."

"Yes."

"All of me!"

"*Yes.*"

As his passion became liquid in my core, I became liquid in his arms. My orgasm shuddered through me, tightening my tunnel around his cock, pulling his strength even deeper into me. And though we rode those climaxes until they turned to soft sighs of fulfillment, I fought to keep him clutched inside—part of my body just as he was twined inside my heart, for just another perfect moment.

One more moment.

Just one more moment...please.

His phone rang again.

He spat the Arcadian expletive once more. Jabbed the red button on the phone this time but gently lifted me off his lap before he rose and headed to the bathroom to clean up. For a long second, I just remained on the chair, knees curled beneath me, wondering why I shivered despite the sun pouring in. Told myself to get the hell over it—and had almost convinced myself I could—when he reentered, looking as gorgeous and polished as before. No. Better. He looked gorgeous, polished, and supremely satisfied—that "look" certain men just *had* after they'd fucked a woman into outer space. That would certainly explain my chill.

He crossed to me, lifting my chin to linger a kiss over my lips, now deliciously tender from his attentions. "Back to reality."

His hair fell over my face. I twisted a hand into a bunch of it to keep him in place, retorting, "No, big guy. *This* is the real part. And don't you forget it."

The sensual ribbons of his lips twisted up. His gaze swept across my face, blue and vast as the cloudless sky outside. And bright with just as much hope.

"No forgetting," he murmured. "I promise."

"Good." I pressed my lips to his one more time. My heart thumped into my upstretched throat. "Then I promise too."

CHAPTER TWENTY-FIVE

Nearly eight hours later—not that I was counting—I was finally able to get warm again.

"Hey, big guy." I fought to keep it light as I damn near sprinted across the palais's biggest ballroom—impressive as hell, considering I hadn't worn high heels like this since Dad's last campaign—and jumped at Samsyn like a parched beggar at a mirage. Instead of dissolving into dust, he solidified into perfection. His arms banded around me, a protective shelter. His head rested atop mine, sure and steady. The only rickety element was his sigh, weighted as if he, too, had been holding his breath all day long.

"Well hey to you too, raismette."

Whiplash. Had he really just made it...enjoyable? My gaze, yanked up along with my face, searched the dancing blue depths of his. Holy shit...he *had*. His eyes were always astounding, a crystalline contrast against his swarthy skin, but now they were more than that. His blatant joy made them outright mesmerizing.

"Wh-What—" I finally stammered, "did you...just..."

"Raismette." He repeated it without hesitation. "Thought I would...give it a test try." He palmed the side of my face. "It sounds good, yes?"

"Yes," I whispered. Bit the inside of my lip, if only to confirm I wasn't dreaming. "Very good."

"No." His lips covered mine, though he kept his five-star

tongue dutifully leashed. "Not *very* good." With a small step back, he stared down to my toes and back. "The *very* good belongs to my beautiful wife."

I laughed, not even trying to hide the nervousness, as he gazed longer at what I'd jokingly pegged "the Brooke 2.0." The pumps, a pair of sleek mid-heels with a T-strap on top, were just the base blocks of the ensemble: a black pencil skirt and butter-soft cardigan over a silver satin shirt that tied into a floppy bow at the neck, complimented by pearl earrings and, thanks to Mishella, a French-twisty look for my hair.

It had definitely been a step from my comfort zone.

A *big* step.

Now, thanks to the man's hot and hungry dragon stare, one I officially flagged as a do-over.

Looping my hand into his only sealed the deal. The man was always warm, everywhere—forming the thousandth reason why I always yearned to be closer to him. I did just that, swinging our hands, sashaying in until our bodies were flush.

"Just thought I'd give it a test try," I teased.

Syn moaned softly. "It is breathtaking."

I fitted my lips against his neck. "Well, maybe I can think of a few more ways to...take your breath away."

"Fuck," he snarled. "Yesssss."

"After dinner with our families."

He groaned and growled at once. I winced and squeezed his hand. "Sorrrrrry." Forced a tight smile. "Didn't Mishella message Grahm about it?"

The seasoned warrior had been tagged as Syn's secran for the time being, since Grahm's thigh wound had been worse than everyone originally thought. I ached for Grahm about the sidelining but thanked God and fate and even the Creator for his service over the last two days. He'd left for Tahreuse practically right after the wedding, tasked with telling my family the crazy story behind this elaborate ruse—including the bombshell they'd finally be freed from playing dead for the world. But because of that, Samsyn had insisted they stay at the palais for the next few weeks. For the time being, security was heavily fortified throughout Sancti, more so in the palais complex. If Rune Kavill still had the resources and resolve to even come after Dad now, we'd all be much safer in the capital city.

"Of course," Samsyn finally grumbled his reply. "Mishella was very diligent. So was Grahm. I simply had other things on my mind."

"Only a million of them." I stroked the tension beneath his jaw in empathy. "Playing nice with the High Council, arranging your brother's memorial, staying on top of the hunt for those missing assholes..."

He took a turn to nuzzle *me* now. "And resisting thoughts of staying on top of my wife."

And just like that, stardust again—in my veins, through my limbs, tingling in the hand that twisted against his scalp. "Just as she's resisted thoughts of the same thing."

He let out a soft snarl while pressing his lips fully to my neck. "Oh, is *that* so?"

Soft sigh. Searing need. "That is...very so."

"Hmmm." His hands slipped lower, taunting the top of my ass. "Our radios must be in sync, raismette."

I sighed. *That man's incredible mouth.* "Sounds like we're at a go for the mission, then."

"When do we rendezvous?"

"As fast as we possibly can—"

"Fuck, yes. Copy that."

"—as soon as we're done with dinner."

His extended grunt spurred my burst of a giggle. "Sorry," I repeated. "I really am, big guy. But we have to. It's protocol."

"You want to know how much of a shit I give about protocol?"

"A big one." Stiffened spine. Not an easy feat when one's husband had just turned their body into a puddle. "It's part of the territory, Your Majesty."

After smoothing my clothes, I re-extended a hand to him. As Mishella had informed me earlier, that lovely protocol also dictated that we enter rooms together with hands clasped. There were lots of other rules about which hands went where, how we should look and *not* look at each other, and even what our pace should be, but for right now, the basics would have to do.

Annnnd...maybe not.

As soon as our palms touched, Syn hauled me back against him. Secured me there by pushing our joined hands into the small of my back. The pose was open but controlling... and aroused me in at least a dozen new ways. Wow. As in...*wow.*

"'Your Majesty,'" he repeated, gaze dropping to my lips. "So that is the way of it for now?"

I pressed my other hand to his chest. Despite the new moisture in my panties, lines had to be drawn—somehow. "*Yes*...Your Majesty."

He lowered his head. Stopped his mouth inches above mine. "Maybe I shall simply have to imagine it more...muffled."

The sensual suggestion of that last word could've made a nun horny—and dumb. I was good to go on both accounts, barely managing to stammer, "M-Muffled?"

"Mmmm hmmm." His gaze intensified. The dark beast awaited his prey. "As you scream it...and twist your thighs against my face."

I let him punctuate it with a kiss—if that was what the teasing touch of his lips could be called, giving me more breath than pressure, causing a needy mewl to curl from deep in my throat before he was done.

As he finally let me go, using both hands to steady my awkward stumbles, he took his own turn at an indulgent chuckle—and I seized the chance to get in the last word on our game plan for dinner.

"I'm ordering the kitchen to speed up dinner service."

★ ★ ★

I followed through on that promise.

Like it helped things one damn bit.

Four exhausting courses later, as Tahreuse Mountain coffee was served and dessert declared on its way, I strived to enjoy the beauty of our surroundings instead of yearning—again—to be in bed with Samsyn.

The setting really was beautiful. Out of respect to Evrest and Camellia's "memory," we dined on the candlelit terrace of the high couple's receiving room, instead of the formal royal dining room. The surroundings were as opulent but as comfortable as I remembered, though it was strange to think I'd been up here for the first time just yesterday. So much had happened since. Moving into Samsyn's suite. Getting the first of my queenly crash courses from Mishella.

A lifetime in an hourglass.

Wasn't the first time the feeling had struck lately, and

deep instincts told me it wouldn't be the last. Syn had to be feeling the same way—or maybe he was used to it. Life as a royal was definitely...full. His castle in the boonies made more sense now. Perhaps the Tahreuse digs were the only place he could let his hair down, in all senses of the word.

I logged that curiosity into my brain, along with the other thoughts and questions I'd developed during the day. It came as a shock, realizing I knew Samsyn in so many deep ways...but still knew so little *about* him.

Yesterday, having months with him had seemed like enough.

Today, it felt like a drop of water in the desert.

I couldn't wait to be alone with him again.

So much for not thinking of my husband. And bed. Oh yeah...*that*. All of it. The way the sheets molded around his torso, cutting him off just when the twin trails of muscle started to get good. The way he could pitch those sheets into a beautiful "tent" when I reached below, cupping him...*there*. The way he groaned out wicked things in Arcadian as I began stroking and—

"Do you not agree, Brooke?"

"Uh...shit. I mean *excuse me*. Yes, of...of course I agree." *Ugh.* Of all the times to phase out of the conversation, just when Xaria began talking about...

What had she been talking about?

The airport. Yes. And the flight arriving tomorrow morning, carrying Camellia's parents. They'd be grief-stricken and full of questions about the hunt for their daughter's "killers." It would be one of the toughest parts about this operation, despite knowing we could fill them in on the truth once they'd been escorted to a secure palais vehicle.

Tough—but necessary. No way could the truth be entrusted to emails, texts, or even phone calls.

"Perfect," Xaria intoned, gracefully letting my profanity slide. "So it is settled." She smiled up at Mom. "Veronica, you have my thanks for volunteering to handle the tarmac greeting with Brooke and myself."

"Agreed." I sent a heartfelt smile to Mom, wishing Xaria and her cleavage weren't separating us. The woman had fantastic boobs, but who was she trying to impress? The only explanation, that she'd expanded her "offside hobby" to include the palais banquet wait staff, was *not* worth broaching for another second. "Thank you, my awesome *maimanne*."

Mom leaned toward Xaria but checked herself before completing the move. The queen mother's formality was as hard on her as me. Mom was a hug whore—her words not mine—but Xaria had been raised to be a queen. Stories abounded about the days following her selection as one of the Distinct. Many of the remaining girls of that chosen set had simply not bothered traveling to Sancti. Ardent had selected her in less than a month.

How long had it taken him to start cheating on her?

Another question never to be raised again. Mom's comeback made that easier. "It's the least I can do, Your Majesty. It was Samsyn's kindness on the tarmac that made *our* first steps in Arcadia so much easier."

Ardent, seated on the other side of me, took ear to Mom's comment. "Syn has always possessed the drive of a fighter and the soul of a diplomat." He dipped his head toward Samsyn, though finished by raising his glass. "If anyone can fill his brother's boots, it is him." Then higher. "Long live King Samsyn."

"Long live King Samsyn." We all repeated it, adopting our best tones of respect and acclaim mixed with shock and grief—well aware that the walls really did have ears. No less than twenty palais staff members lingered within earshot, any one of them bribable by the Pura, meaning none of them could know the truth we were hiding. When Evrest and Camellia made their "miraculous return" in a few months, all of us would be just as "shocked" as the rest of the country.

The charade was going to be exhausting.

It already was.

A beautiful slice of molten chocolate cake was placed in front of me—but even as the server drizzled vanilla bean crème over it, I couldn't summon a yayza even for a bite. Brooke 2.0 suddenly felt like Restless 1.0. My clothes itched. My shoes killed. My head hurt from approaching its tenth hour of Ps, Qs, and the rest of the etiquette alphabet. The lie was taking its toll.

Luckily, the chocolate and caffeine loosened the ambiance around the table. Mom and Xaria, learning they shared a love for gardening, started talking mulch, water, and worms. Ardent did his best with me, bringing up the conditioning benefits of training in the mountains, but lost me at the carbs versus protein debate. Thank God for Dillon, who hadn't lost his ability to read me like a gypsy with tea leaves. He jumped right in, occupying the king father about the progress on the telecommunications tower in Tahreuse—exciting Ardent five times more than healthy pasta options.

I folded my napkin and pushed out my chair, hoping to sneak to Syn for a few moments of whispered dirty talk—but his phone rang. Wagering it was Jagger and his crack timing, I rose anyway. The only protesting body parts were my toes, stuffed back into the trendy pumps, but they were overruled by the bliss from the rest of me, able to finally stretch again.

Holy hell, I needed a workout. A merciless run supervised by Jag, followed by a session on the mats that would leave bruises. There'd be no chance of the latter for weeks, but I was hopeful about talking Jagger into a morning run on the beach soon.

In the meantime, if only for a few minutes, I needed some fresh air.

"Are you all right, dear? Not a bite of your dessert is gone."

Xaria's prompt tugged my gaze back down. Surprise, surprise; my exhausted-but-you'll-never-know-it smile came right back. "Of course," I murmured. "Just needing some air. I've been inside all day. I'm going to take a few minutes in the gardens."

She nodded. "But of course. Do not stay out too long, though. The night winds off the sea can be punishing on one's skin."

"Will do." There was no point in stating the obvious. The night winds in the mountains were five times worse than the breezes down here.

I caught Syn's eye long enough to point toward the door, informing him where I'd be. With any luck his call was a quick one, and I'd soon be letting his stubble "punish" my skin along with the sea air.

I'd made a good call. Pore wrecker or not, the briny blast off the Mediterranean was the perfect cleanser for my sanity, and I told it so with a sublime sigh as soon as I stepped onto the garden deck—

Invaded by a stunned grunt as soon as I attempted to walk one of the pathways to the fountain. Even packed dirt wasn't a worthy foe for my tapered heels, caked with the stuff into which they'd sunk.

"Well...shit." My mutter was carried away at once by the wind, proving to be my friend in more than one way tonight. *Go ahead*, it seemed to say. *Let me have another.* Well, if we were playing *that* way...

"High-fashion fuckers," I mumbled, yanking off the shoes. The wind rasped in agreement.

"Holy mother of fuck." Not as original but damn accurate, especially as it spilled on my orgasmic moan. After ten hours in the heels, sinking my bare feet into the cool grass qualified as a sexual experience.

"Fuck yes...fuck yes...fuuuuck yesssss..."

I broke off into a giggle. Guess I'd needed a break for my favorite slang as much as the fresh air.

I curled toes into the turf as my stare lifted to the sky. The tops of the cypresses swayed like ballerinas against the stars, making me hum a snippet of Mendelssohn as I walked. After each bar, I yanked a pin free from my hair. Soon, it filled with the breeze too. This was good. *So* good. I'd needed this reverie about, oh, nine hours ago.

"Well, look who's smiling."

I jumped.

Nearly out of my skin.

The disruption hadn't been Samsyn's. Instinct already told me that. My body always kicked into hyperawareness when he was around. Now I recognized that like everything else between us, that sensitivity had gone supersonic—especially now, in its absence.

At least I could stand down on the ready pose. My shoulders fell by two inches as I slackened my posture and freed relieved air. "Sneaking soldask! What the hell, Jag?"

"Nice to see you too."

"Aren't you supposed to be on the phone with your commander?"

"Why is that?" He approached on steps as even as his tone. He was dressed for duty, black cargo pants over a black T-shirt highlighting his lean but ripped frame. Jag had been recruited by Syn right off a Tahreuse alley, where he'd been fighting the world in one form or another since the age of twelve, when he'd decided the streets were a better gamble than alcoholic parents. That edge seemed more prominent in him tonight. Not a shock. Everyone would be more on their guard until they'd tracked and captured the two remaining men from the break-in on Evrest and Cam's quarters.

"We were at dinner," I explained. "Then Syn's phone rang with impeccable timing. Naturally, I thought it was you."

"Timing?" he echoed. "Impeccable? Me?"

"Shut up." I socked him in the shoulder.

"No. Seriously. Tell me what I supposedly interrupted. Was there something fun going on? Was Ardent 'tasting' Xaria for dessert?"

"Shut *up!*" With a laugh, I moved to punch his other shoulder—with my left arm. "Damn. *Damn!*"

Stars of agony. Grimaces, fighting it. Jag steadied me until the dizziness passed. When I nodded, able to move again, he guided me to one of the benches near the fountain. The wind kicked higher, turning some of the cascading water into a fine spray. I angled my face into them. The cold pricks of moisture felt wonderful.

"Shit." Jagger hung on to my right elbow. His other hand wrapped to my nape and rubbed gently. "Are you okay?"

"It'll pass." I hiked up my skirt, dipped my head between

my legs, and waited for the tidal wave of nausea to roll by. With my good arm, I jabbed an elbow back at him. "I blame you, dirty Foxx. You mentioned Ardent and Xaria...like *that*...and— oh God—"

"Wait." His hand stilled. "You...you know?"

"*You* know?" I pushed back my hair to get a good stare at him. "How?"

He flashed a wry smile. "Part of the job, Badger girl. Anyone who has served close to the royals knows."

"But Evrest, Shiraz, and Jayd don't." I huffed in response to his businesslike nod. "How is that even possible?"

"By Samsyn's decree, that is how."

I frowned. "I get that but don't get it. It's understandable that he won't call his parents out and publicly ruin the family honor, but why does he shoulder the secret entirely by himself? Why won't he let his own siblings help?"

He turned his head, looking up at the fountain. When the wind kicked up again, water droplets alighted in his light-copper stubble. "Who says they would believe him? And if they did, would that change anything? Is it not easier to appear as one happy, loving family if a good portion of the participants are not acting?"

I thumped backward into the bench, feeling decked in the chest. "So Syn keeps force-feeding everyone a steady diet of dysfunctional, while he barely trusts his own shadow."

"Annnnd, welcome to your new family."

"Gawd." I let my head fall back. "But I'm just here on the visitor's pass. I'm not the miracle surgeon on this one, right?"

When Jag said nothing, I lifted my head. Found his own cocked at me, a new sheen in his bronze eyes. "Do you want to be?"

Strangely, my heart pumped hard against my ribs—as a single word blared across my brain.

Busted.

"You know how I feel about him, Jag."

A lie. Jagger knew how I *used* to feel. He'd seen my girlhood crush and then my silly infatuation, given a positive spin by my dedication to fight training. Somewhere along the line, it became evident I was good at it. I understood it, honored it, and used the mental preparedness behind it to understand Samsyn better. And while it had all helped, it also hadn't been necessary. My heart, my soul, my spirit, my body... were destined to love Samsyn Cimarron. Reciprocation was unimportant—and irrelevant. It didn't, nor wouldn't, notch the compass of what I'd been brought to this island to do.

Love him. Period.

For right here, for right now, I'd do it in person—and be grateful for every touch, every kiss, every magnificent moment in which fate had given me to do it. And once we pulled off the rings and I moved back to Tahreuse, I'd do it from afar—and be grateful for all those moments too.

"Brooke..."

I held up a hand. "No. Don't say it. You never have, Jagger. Please. *Don't.*"

"I never have, because—"

"Because I've never been married to him?"

"A sham!"

His rasp was so violent, my jaw fell open for a second. I recovered by swallowing hard—and leaning away. The gleam in his eyes wasn't so friendly anymore.

What the hell was this? What was he getting at?

"He spoke those vows to you—*lied* those vows to you—as a

tactical move, Brooke. A public relations necessity—"

"A sacrifice for his country!"

I bolted to my feet. He did too. Wasted no time rushing in my wake as I spun and headed back across the grass toward my discarded shoes.

"A *sacrifice*." He caught me by my good hand, vising it inside his. "Marrying *you* should not be a fucking sacrifice." He braced his other hand to my face. His breath punched from him in harsh bursts. "A gift. That is what it should be. Brooke Allison Valen...*you* are a gift."

Insight. Me. Collision.

Dread. Regret. Carnage.

"Crap," I finally choked. "Crap, crap, crap. Jag. Ohhhh, Jag."

I shook my head, lost about how to do this. He'd been such a good friend. Had kicked my ass when I'd needed it. Had hugged me when I'd needed it. Had simply *been there* when I'd needed it. Now, was I really going to boot him in the ribs for his feelings? Feelings I'd known *nothing* about. And I thought *I'd* been good about keeping things on the down-low about *Syn*...

There had to be a kinder way. I scoured my mind and heart for it. Even prayed for it.

"Damn it, Brooke. You deserve more than what he can give!"

"Jagger." I twisted my hand free. He simply shifted his hold to my waist. "*Jagger*. I don't have a choice." I drew in a huge breath. Here went nothing. "I'm in love with him."

He circled his grip tighter. "And I'm in love w—"

"*No*. Don't say it, damn it. Don't!"

His stare turned to twin blazes. A determined tick vibrated in his jaw. "Then I shall show you instead."

I was still thrown so far from the blast of his first bomb, I didn't see the second incoming—

Until it was too late.

Until he funneled his hand into my wind-tossed hair, pulled my face up to his, and took my mouth in a hard, consuming kiss.

CHAPTER TWENTY-SIX

Shit.

Holy shit.

I should've just drop-kicked him.

Instead, short of kneeing his balls, I had to struggle against the lock of his mouth, the press of his body, the tenacity of his desire...

None of which he planned on letting up soon...

"Jagger!" I panted it inches from his mouth—the only space he allowed me. "Are you fucking insane?"

"Maybe." He muttered it like a distraction, lips barely moving. All the movement belonged to his eyes, feverish and lusty—and his hands, hot and groping. "Probably. But only because I did not tell you sooner. Because I was waiting for you to get over that ridiculous moping over *him.*"

"*Him.*" I threw it back from locked teeth. "That's right, damn it. The man I'm married to now. Your leader, Jag. Your *friend.*"

Who knew I could throw kerosene on a fire so well? He was ignited, baring teeth in a feral seethe—before slamming our mouths together again. This time, he wasn't so merciful about letting me up. He gripped my head with one hand and my ass with the other, damn near locking me in place. When I finally tore free, I panted in a mixture of fury, desperation, and a little fear.

"Jagger! Please!"

My blood was a heated roar in my head. The wind was a sudden chill against my skin. Between the two, I shouldn't have heard the sharp cracks of a single man's applause—but I did, with nauseating clarity.

Just as my senses awakened to the presence of the man wielding them.

Just before he growled, in a seethe that froze me to the core, "Damn. You are so breathtaking when you beg, astremé."

I twisted in Jag's grip—but not before catching his gloating smirk. Rage hit like a fireball. Mentally ripping up my medical orders, I coiled back and then clocked him beneath the jaw. Once more into his nose. He barely flinched from either blow, but his hold loosened. I wrenched away, letting my glare speak for me. I could barely stand looking at him, let alone wasting words. Those I saved for the man who *did* matter.

"Samsyn!"

Samsyn.

Oh God...

No.

He'd already whirled, stomps consuming the ground like a battle march.

"Samsyn!"

He flung back an arm like a muscled spear, aiming straight at me with his outstretched fingers, his message clear. *Do not come near me.*

I was very, *very* shitty about letting things go.

Especially when it came to Samsyn Cimarron.

Especially when he walked away with the pieces of my heart in one hand. And the pieces of his in the other.

Because of nothing. *Nothing!*

And he's going to believe that...how?

"Because I'm going to make him." I uttered it like a blood oath—in my mind, there was no difference—before racing across the grass, over the paths, and catching the door he'd attempted to slam in my face. The impact reverberated along my right arm, but right now, someone could've hacked the damn thing off and I wouldn't have noticed. Or cared. All that mattered was getting to Syn. Explaining this all to him with a semblance of rationality.

I'd almost thought about dragging Jag in here to help but wisely mapped out that lovely scenario in my head and determined I wanted them both alive after this. Nope; Jag wasn't going to be a fucking sliver of help.

"Samsyn." It hardly had any volume, thanks to my air-starved lungs. They didn't get any mercy from the sight of him: face twisted, body prowling, hands coiling and uncoiling, readying fists for something, *anything*, to bash in.

He found that something.

In the form of his reflection—in the master bedroom's huge floor mirror.

The whole pane shattered beneath his single blow. Glass tumbled like tears—a fitting recognition since the shards blurred in the heavy fog of mine.

He turned slowly. Glass crackled under his boots, demolished tears meeting violent ends. His head was low, his shoulders hunched...his glower stony. "You need to leave."

I squared my stance. The action drew his stare to my bare feet. For a single second, concern flashed in his eyes. That single second was my sun stream of hope.

"No," I declared. "*You* need to listen. What you saw was—"

"Don't." He stabbed that finger again. Blood smeared it now. "Don't try to tell me it was nothing, damn it!"

I inhaled. Exhaled. "Maybe I should chalk this up to the full moon tonight. In Romania, guys turn to werewolves and vampires. In Arcadia, they turn into ridiculous asses."

"Now you really need to leave."

"I am *not* your mother! Just as I know and trust that you aren't your father."

I expected what came: his contorted face, hunched shoulders, seething hiss. I hated—*hated*—tearing us both down more with this ugliness, but it was the only way we'd build back up on the right foundation: the truth. Symbolizing the point always helped too—a demonstration I gave by stomping across the six feet separating us. When I stood directly in front of him, I replanted my feet, crushing more glass with nearly the same emphasis he had.

"I love you." His widened glare gave me more courage. I jerked up my chin. Coiled a hand into the front of his shirt. "Wake up and see it, Samsyn. I'm right here, bleeding for you to prove it. There is nobody—*nobody*—in my heart...but you."

For long moments, only our breaths sounded on the air. Only the blue steel torment of his eyes filled my vision—until that color changed again. Hardened. Condemned. "I never asked to be there."

"I know." My voice broke, along with more tears. I couldn't hold back any of it from him now. I didn't even want to.

"I don't *want* to be there!"

I raised my hand to his face. Spread my fingers against the bold expanse of his jaw. "Then show me where you want to be." Stepped closer to him, fitting the angles of our bodies into each other. "Fill me where you need to."

It danced at the edge of dirty tactics. Fine; it *was* dirty tactics. But if the radio station in his brain was packed so full of baggage that it couldn't get our signal, I'd send the message where it *could* be heard. His body, swelling against the center of my stomach, conveyed the frequency had connected, loud and clear. I'd take it. Right now, I'd take him any way I could have him—and sex was one of the best ways to have him. Perhaps this was just the push to topple the baggage too. Perhaps this was what we *both* needed.

Or maybe that was a giant crock of wishful thinking.

Aside from his erection, nothing else budged.

I held my breath.

He expelled his.

Then made me wonder, with his deep and feral snarl, if the werewolf thing worked in Arcadia too. As the sound vibrated the air, I endured shivers like never before, released by a mix of desire and fear, of knowing and unknowing, of pleasure and pain...

As he dipped his head, bypassing my lips, and sank his teeth brutally into the column of my neck.

A high cry ripped from me. Another growl tore through him. He fisted my hair, positioning my head to the side in order to bite again, closer to my ear. This time, I didn't scream. My senses were too damn busy processing every new, searing sensation. He tore into me like a wild creature with its kill—meaning I really had no choice about how to respond. *Surrender.* His feast was inevitable; he'd take until he was sated. If I had any doubt of it, he clarified things pretty well inside the next moment. One grip and tear into my cardigan, and all the buttons popped free. Another into my blouse, with the same result. He shoved both garments off though slipped the long satin ribbon from the neckline of the blouse, holding on to it.

Oh, yes. Crystal clear now.

He was going to be in control. *I* was only to obey. And to feel.

And ohhhh shit, how I did.

How he guaranteed that I did.

Before we even got to the bed, he jerked my head to the other side and marked my neck with two bites equal to the first ones. He carried me to the bed—okay, it was more like hoisting me up and then tossing me there—before pausing to grab a water glass off the nightstand, pouring its contents over my feet. Once he was certain I'd gotten only a few minor cuts, he tilted his head in, now digging teeth into my right ankle.

"Ahhhhh!"

He endured my scream—more from astonishment than the bite of pain—with barely a blink. "Do *not* bleed for me again," he ordered.

"All...all right."

"You may say 'yes, husband'—and nothing more."

"Yes, husband." It whispered from me, so breathy and bare—and I hated myself for loving every syllable. It was so medieval. So subservient.

But so open...so erotic...

I wanted to serve him. Satisfy him. Be his wild animal meal.

"Now take off the rest of your clothes." He rumbled with guttural approval as I obeyed, quickly stripping off my skirt, bra, and panties. No further words, though—not even as he grabbed my knees, spread them wide, and then moved between them, letting the taut cloth at his crotch rub my spread pussy without mercy.

"Damn!" I exclaimed as he leaned over to study my face

with his assessing animal's gaze. "I... I mean, yesssss, husband!"

He showed no outward reaction to that either. Instead, rolled his hips to ensure every inch of his bulge came into contact with every fold of my arousal—including the stiff bud containing my most sensitive nerve endings. Every time he rubbed it, my skin tingled. My control thinned. My limbs trembled. Shit. *Shit.* This was...

so...

damn...

good.

At last he murmured, "Do you still want me to fill you...as I wish?"

Was he kidding? He had to be. I was visibly quivering. Whimpering like a starved kitten. I could *feel* every fresh, torturous swell of my clit. But when I didn't answer, he pulled away a little. Gave my mound a brisk, bold swat.

Dear God. He'd...*spanked* my pussy.

And heaven help me, after the initial zap of shock wore off, my whole body warmed and writhed...confirming how much I loved it.

"Y-Yes," I finally got out. "Yes, husband. Fill me up...as you wish."

"In any manner I wish?"

"Yes, husband."

He leaned back in. Rose over me once more, staring down. I stared right back...riveted. This creature above me... He was Syn but he wasn't, as if confronting his darkest fears about me had untethered something dark in him. Something wicked, wanton, illicit...something he hadn't shown me before now. Why? Had he been afraid? And if that was the case...should *I* be afraid? And if so, why didn't the idea repel me? Why did my body get wetter, hotter...

Then doubly so, when he aligned the satin tie from my blouse directly over my face...

And lowered it over my eyes.

Shit.

He was really serious that I do nothing but feel. And ohhhh, how I did.

Skin...fired to life.

Sounds...turned to wonders.

Smells...sweet mysteries.

And my sex...pulsing and hot and ready.

I was aware of so much more from Syn too. Every tug he gave the tie, looping it around my head and then cinching it in front. The shifting power of his muscles when he finished and then growled in approval of his handiwork. The erotic slide of his vest against my nipples, making them pucker and ache in arousal.

I moaned when he trailed a hand down to my pussy...

But choked it short, as he delved those long fingers even lower. Then inward, circling, pressing...

"Oh!"

...at my tightest entrance.

There was the heat of his fingers. But then the chill of lube. Where the hell had *that* come from? And why was I even wondering, when he was pretty damn insistent on working his finger up into that tiny fissure—and then replacing that digit with something else? Something thin but hard. A glass tube? Molded plastic? And once more, why did it matter? I was fighting to keep an open mind—past the unnatural breach in my backside. Thank God I'd eavesdropped on Orielle and Freya when they giggled about this kind of stuff, though I'd hardly believed my ears at the time. Men actually liked playing with that entrance?

Judging from the thick lust in Syn's new growl, the answer to that was...*yes.*

"Almost in. Now push out against it." The old Syn would've murmured it in encouragement. This one demanded it in a growl. "Open yourself, wife—and push."

"Can't," I protested. "So tight...so full."

"No 'can't,'" he retorted. "*Push.*"

I gripped the comforter. Bore down as he ordered. It seemed useless. And hard. And painful. But when I assumed the invasion had no end and the torture device would end up in my throat, Syn emitted a long grunt, coated in supreme pleasure. He gave the thing in my ass a twist. Another. Though I gave him nothing but screams in return, I couldn't deny that it began to feel...warm. And naughty. And—unbelievably— arousing.

Even when the distinct rasp of his zipper sliced the air— and I realized exactly what he planned next.

It scared me.

And clenched me.

And soaked me.

I took his cock all the way home on his first thrust.

"*Damn.*" He held himself there for a long moment, allowing us both to adjust to the tightness. When his flesh swelled against mine, I sighed. When his moan echoed through me, I joined mine to it.

"Shit," I finally rasped. "Yes, husband. *Yes.*"

He slowly drew out—only to ruthlessly plunge back in. Then again. And again. Harder each time. Deeper each time. The friction of our bodies worked the tension on the thing in my ass too, massaging places inside that vibrated in ways I'd never known. As the sweet heat of my climax built beneath my clit, it was matched by a force from deep inside, a hurricane rushing to meet a tsunami, so impossible it was mesmerizing, despite the devastation of the impact.

Devastation?

No.

This was cosmic convulsion. Cataclysm. Chaos. A rearrangement of everything I'd thought possible inside my body, erupting to a fullness I despaired of containing to my flesh, bones, and blood. Far beyond the explosion, I heard myself screaming, even begging Syn not to stop—*please, don't ever stop*—though I was certain we'd have to any second, for I'd surely be dead. By some miracle, I hung on to feel the hot bath of his seed, sealing the perfection of this passion...filling me far beyond anything I could have asked for.

I needed to tell him that. But intention connecting with words...another issue altogether. My brain hardly managed keeping the basics like breathing and feeling going.

As I fumbled through that mental fog, Syn withdrew. In the same movement, he pulled off the blindfold. He was equally gentle about removing the hard stick from my backside but also silent. Damn near businesslike. No change as he disappeared into the bathroom, returning with a damp cloth to towel off all the fluids between my legs.

No change. Wasn't that the irony of the day...maybe the century? "Change" barely approached the right word to describe the man who'd been inside me minutes ago versus the clinical automaton who swiped at me now. He still didn't speak. Refused to meet my eyes. A patient in a hospital would've been given more courtesy.

He retreated to the bathroom again. For a long time. I almost followed but clung to hoping he'd return, perhaps simply taking the time for a shower. I prayed he'd return, his knowing smirk back in place, ready to climb beneath the covers with me.

He finally walked back out. Fully dressed.

And instantly piled my fury atop my frustration. Now he'd pulled out the dirty tactics, however unknowingly—though it was damn difficult to believe the man didn't have a clue about how good he looked in workout gear. The black nylon pants and matching sleeveless shirt were perfect set pieces for the main attraction: the sculpted body I craved to explore from head to toe...with my tongue. Yes, already again. Yes, that boldly. That achingly.

"You're going out?"

"Yes." He sat in one of the reading chairs—*not* the one in which we'd screwed not more than twelve hours ago—and jerked his runners on. "I need to clear my head."

I rolled to my side—purposely not putting any clothes back on. "Wasn't that what we just started?"

He pushed a foot into his second shoe. "That...was very good." Back to the businessman, with barely a flinch. "And thank you." Was he going to shake my hand next? "But it has nothing to do with anything else."

A lump pushed into my throat. So much for hoping we could get naked in more ways than one. "Anything...you want to talk out?" No matter what, even before the insanity of these last two weeks, we'd been able to at least talk to each other.

"Thank you," he repeated. "But no."

I sat up. Then got up. There was nothing nearby to throw on, so I did the best I could about looking serious while standing in nothing but my skin. "Syn...we need to at least address the shit with Jagger—"

"I shall deal with Jagger." His tone didn't twist into mob boss territory, though its thread of quiet rage wouldn't be missed by a three-year-old. That filament wound through the air between us—a not-so-subtle test. I sensed Syn waiting for what I'd do with it.

I did nothing.

I had no other option.

The woman in me—and the friend to Jag—recoiled at the intimation. But the warrior in me gave up her grim understanding—and the acceptance of two truths. One, Jagger could handle himself, even against Syn. Two, if he got a little fucked up in the process, maybe it was for the best. The imbezak had brought this on himself—and messed up a huge chunk of my world in the process.

Because right now, Samsyn and I were right back at square one.

No.

A few squares before *that*.

He had trust issues, compounded by the ordeal of keeping them secret for so long. But I'd made a huge mistake about them. I'd mentally dropped them in a box, labeled it with his parents' names, and then begun my mission to love him so much he'd see that the box didn't have *his* name on it. *His* heart didn't have to be a prisoner of his parents' lies. The choice was solely his to trust—and love—someone.

And though I'd refused to admit it, even to myself, I'd yearned to be that someone. To be worthy of this noble prince's heart. To simply love him into loving me.

But sometimes, it wasn't that simple. Wishing on a star,

believing in your heart... It worked for damsels in towers and puppets who wanted to be real, not for a princess in love with a prince who couldn't even see the stars past his walls.

And right now, I was completely out of demolition ideas.

Leaving me to watch as he jogged away down a dark beach...alone despite the security detail flanking him. Alone, despite my body still remembering him, my heart still so full of him.

Alone, despite the tears I shed for us both.

CHAPTER TWENTY-SEVEN

Two days later, despite the perfect island morning outside the breakfast room's window, I clenched back the same damn tears. My makeup aside—Mishella had made me concede to a little mascara, blush, and lip gloss now—tears probably tasted disgusting in coffee.

While stirring hazelnut creamer into my java instead, I stole a glance at Syn through my lashes. Holy God, he was stunning. I yearned to jump him again, despite having done so this morning in bed. Okay, technically, *he'd* jumped *me*—my wrists still bore the blissful marks of just how hard and passionately—but semantics weren't important in my fantasy. I swirled my spoon dreamily, letting the scene play out. I'd find him in his office. Would let him keep his crisp black shirt and red vest in place though slide his pants down to his ankles so I could roam over his tight ass and muscled thighs...while taking him deep in my mouth. I'd let his moans vibrate through me, feeling them in every shivering nerve, as I sucked and tasted and licked his gorgeous penis, worshiping him until he...

"If you keep staring at my brother like that, I may have to charge you an access fee."

The interjection, spoken in a voice like lava and butter mixed, made me look up and then laugh. Shiraz Cimarron had a face and body one would expect on the pages of a high-fashion magazine but the demeanor of a shark straight from Wall Street. He was the poster child for dichotomy, confounding many, but I'd always admired that about him. What fun was a person if they could be figured out in minutes?

"Now there's a way to maximize some revenues for the economy," I joked back. "But it's a tax deduction for me, right?"

A feminine grumble pulled my gaze around. "Are you two already talking business?" Jayd groused. "Creator's toes. The funeral was just yesterday. Some of us are still raw."

Shiraz arched an urbane brow. "You mean the pretend funeral?"

"*Ssshhh*." She jogged her head toward the reporters in the corner—all so absorbed in tapping on their laptops, an army could've stormed the beach without their notice—and added, "Pretend or not, I hated it."

Shiraz chuffed. Muttered to me, "But she loved Paris, where gloom is everyone's middle name."

She narrowed her gaze. "Not gloom, imbezak. It is called *drama*. And *feeling*. And *passion*." She elbowed him. "They belong in that thing called a *heart*, my brother. You remember what that is, *oui*?"

"*Non*." Shiraz shrugged. "Waste of time and space. Ev and Syn are doing just fine in the mooning hearts arena."

She nudged me next. "I cannot *wait* until a woman knocks him on his backside."

Shiraz sipped his coffee. Scowled and scooped more sugar into it. "Sister, I do not get 'knocked' anywhere."

"Hmmmph. Except that damn office of yours."

"The business of the country is not accomplished by magical elves, little one." With a nod of satisfaction at his coffee, he turned from the buffet. "On that note, good day, ladies. Three days away from the office will be hell to make up."

Jayd growled. "If you die at your desk, 'Raz, I shall hate

your soul forever."

Both his brows jumped now. "And that is *not* gloomy?"

She shot a defiant pout. "Do *not* die! Nobody else is allowed to die. Got it?"

"Well, wasn't this a fun place to join the conversation?" My brother's cute, crooked grin swung into view. I tried not to notice the extra gleam across Jayd's face, but it was like ignoring a glint of sun on chrome. Forget it.

"Bon sabah, Dillon Valen." Her smile was tremulous.

"Bon sabah to you too, Jayd Cimarron." He bonked her nose with his bagel—like a doof messing with his buddy. Jayd's eyes dimmed a little. I was tempted to grab the bagel and stuff it up Dil's nose. Or other places. "You too, Shiraz."

"You as well." Shiraz's murmur was civil, though instinct said I'd have help in the bagel-ramming duties, if I requested it.

Without skipping a beat, Dil scooped up some cream cheese and capers. "Hey...errrmm...you two mind if I steal the queen for a few minutes? Private sibs stuff. You know how it goes."

"Sure!" Just like that, Jayd brightened again. I watched her mental wheels turn, already writing off his platonic behavior as preoccupation with our "private sibs stuff"—whatever the hell that meant.

As soon as we took our plates and coffee to a small table in the corner, I wasted no time seeking the clarification. "What the hell, Dil? Is everything okay?"

He stared steadily at me over the rim of his coffee mug. His eyes, possessing nearly the same ratio of gray to blue as mine, were the biggest reason people mistook us as blood siblings. This morning, I just wished they didn't look so I'm-not-missing-a-single-detail-about-things. "Hmm. Interesting."

"What's interesting?"

"That's exactly what I was going to ask *you*."

I lowered my brows. "I...don't...underst—"

"Cut the crap, B. It's me." He put his cup down. Set his forearms on the table, leaning forward. "You've been miserable since we got here. Maybe even before that. Don't feed me the line that we all just attended a funeral, either. This is deeper shit. Much deeper."

I slid my own coffee back to its saucer. "Well...shit. Is it that obvious?"

He grabbed my hand. "Slow your roll, munchkin. I'm the only one picking up the vibe."

I exhaled hard. "You usually are."

He eased up on my hand but not on his scrutiny. "So you want to spill, or will I have to tickle it out of you?"

I took another deep breath. Fought for a cheeky grin but managed only a wobble of my lips. "Nothing to spill." At least the waterworks behind the eyes were dry. They'd stay that way if Dil didn't mention Samsyn.

"Is it stuff with Samsyn?"

Fuck.

"Goddamnit." Dillon stabbed his bagel instead of spreading the cream cheese. "What's that pachyderm done to you?

"Okay, slow *your* roll." I seized his wrist, saving the bagel from mutilation. The knife clattered to his plate, forcing us to take a beat. "I love him, Dillon."

He rolled his eyes. "Last year's news?"

That spurred a little laugh. "Fine. Guilty as charged."

"But is *he* guilty too?" He went still, waiting for me to look up. The sun had angled in, frosting the tips of his dark-gold hair, beaming into his relentless gaze. "Brooke...does he love you too?"

I wanted to answer him.

And I wanted that answer to be yes.

Somehow, I even knew it was.

But the surety, once the answer to all my deepest dreams, was small consolation now. Comfort that couldn't compete with the answer I *did* give Dil.

"He doesn't trust me."

I said it with sadness, loneliness. For me...but also for Syn. I wondered if he truly trusted anyone.

Dillon's features tightened too. He gazed as if still studying me, and I couldn't figure out why. It was getting unnerving.

"Why?" he finally queried.

I took a chug of coffee. "Long story. And it doesn't matter." The liquid felt good. The day would be warm, but right now, the sea wind was chilly. "What matters is that I don't know if I ever had it. Or if I can ever do anything to earn it."

He leaned back in his chair—but he wasn't relaxed. I knew him too well to think otherwise. His shoulders were taut beneath his casual polo. When he scanned the room with his gaze, finally hitting the spot where Syn was still deep in conversation with Grahm, he slid a finger along his butter knife handle, as if wishing it were a battle dagger. "You mean like...proving yourself?"

Strangely, I laughed again. Savored a bite into a pineapple slice. "Yeah, Dil. Just like that. You have a magic ring I can toss into a fire and save the realm? Maybe an enchanted wand to defeat the guy with no nose?"

He shifted again, leaning back over the table—but kept his gaze riveted to Syn as he answered me in a tone without a note of mirth.

"What if you found the two renegade Puras for him?"

CHAPTER TWENTY-EIGHT

He almost got a face full of spat coffee.

I managed to keep the stuff down—barely—before dropping my jaw to the damn table. Then picking it back up on a soft giggle. "Holy hell, Dil. Good one. Yep, damn good one. Okay, you got me. I really thought—"

"And you thought right."

His gaze didn't flinch.

My heart didn't beat.

Still didn't, as I struggled not to stare as if he'd just nearly confessed to being allied with the crazies who'd tried to kill Camellia. "Dillon. What the fuck are you—"

"I've been Pura since last year, Brooke."

Annnd, *there* was the confession. Plunked right out like acid all over the food. Sure as hell defined the landscape of my stomach now.

"I... I don't know what to..."

Sitting here was definitely not the fill-in-the-blank for that. As the acid invaded more than my gut, I made my way out of the room. Thank God for Mishella's training about how to keep a game face, calm queen style. Trial by fire time—through every step I took toward the palais chapel. Once there, I finally dropped the façade.

I'd only been here once before—years ago, for Evrest's coronation ceremony—but the beauty of the room had left an unforgettable impression on me. The simple architecture was centered on a huge, round glass window, silver stars and golden suns representing the glory of the Creator. Frantically, I prayed for everything the place stood for—strength, serenity, the will not to slap my brother senseless—as I plunked into a pew near the front.

Dillon lowered next to me—damn him, as peaceful as the Dalai Lama about it. "It's not against the law, Brooke."

"Not against the—"

"It's become as much my country as yours!" He slammed a hand to the pew in front of us. So much for the Dalai Lama. "And I have the right to join with others to tell our leaders what we feel about its direction. To communicate our views—"

"Yes." I rose, unable to stop the acidic twitches through my muscles. "To communicate your views, Dil. Not to sneak into the king's bedroom through an air duct with the intention to capture and kill his fiancé!"

"You're right."

"This makes your movement no better than terrorism, or even anarchy. And—" I froze. "*What?*"

"I said you're right." For the first time, he fidgeted. It continued as he returned to his feet as well. He stepped back out to the aisle, starting to nervously pace. I was perversely glad to see it, which calmed me enough to listen as he went on. "I joined the Pura as a way to open up dialogue about the new direction of Arcadia. I simply felt, like many others, that things were going too fast. We have natural resources to protect, a beautiful land we don't want ruined. That's *all*." He stopped. Scrubbed a hand down his face. "At least it was...until we attracted the outside money."

Damn good excuse to let my legs give way again. "So Jagger and Syn were right. There's an external source involved."

"Who's changed a lot of shit," Dillon recounted. He began pacing again, new urgency stamping each step. "It's emboldened the handful of radicals in the movement. Made them overreact to everything...even talk of a full rebellion, if they can't succeed in wiping out the Cimarrons."

The acid turned to ice. I gripped the pew with shaking fingers. "Wiping out...as in killing?"

"Wasn't that answer made clear by what they tried four days ago?" He blew out a harsh breath. "So many of us—*most* of us—never wanted this. We still don't. But the lunatics have taken over the asylum, and now we don't know what to do...or how to control them."

I struggled to wrap my brain around all of it. Fought to comprehend the reality, so horrific that I hadn't accepted even after Evrest and Cam arrived at Syn's castle that crazy morning.

There were people on this island right now who wanted Samsyn and his family dead.

My family...dead.

"Who?" The word left me on locked teeth. I snapped my head up, drilling a demanding gaze into Dillon. "Who the fuck is it, Dil? You have to tell me. We have to figure out how to stop them."

Dillon slumped back into the pew. "I don't know." Raised a glassy gaze at me. "Few of us do. They've compartmentalized it now. Everyone knows only what they need to."

I snorted. "Of course. That's what terrorists do."

When he turned toward me, I wondered why my dread doubled. The last time I'd seen that look on his face, he'd been pulling an *F* in Calculus and didn't know how to tell Dad.

"They *have*...sent me with a message, B. For you."

Rocks. Stomach. What a delightful combination. "Shit," I muttered. Only that. It was the best I could do.

"They have the two men Samsyn is searching for. They're hiding them in the basement of a house, at the outskirts of the city—and they'll surrender both outlaws if you go and meet with them."

Screw the rocks. I was dealing with full boulders now. "*Me?* But why—" Snagged breath—released on a huge huff. "Scratch that. I know why. And do they think I'm that stupid? Mice scurry into traps, Dil, not grown women with functioning brain cells."

He held up both hands. "They just want to talk, B. really."

"And there's a nice piece of land up near Censhyr I'd love to show you."

"You honestly think they'd try anything dumb? *They* have functioning brain cells too. Whether they were behind the break-in on Evrest and Camellia's suite—"

"You mean they weren't?"

"I have no clue. And does it matter? Public perception already blames them, so fucking with the queen doesn't improve their position for being truly heard by the king and High Council." He firmed his stance, folding his arms. "That's really all they want, B—to be heard. And they trust you to help them accomplish that"—he dropped a censuring scowl—"despite your husband's fucked up views on that matter."

I smacked his shoulder for that. Syn's issues might really *be* messed up at the moment, but no one got to voice it except me.

After the clarification, I stepped back into the confusion. "I still don't get it. And now I'm *really* asking: why me?"

"Because you're perfect for the job?" he rejoined.

"*Listen*, dweeb." His countering smack stopped my snarky eye roll. "You're a reasonable sounding board, B—someone who appreciates everything Arcadia is but has seen some of America's mistakes with squandering its natural resources. You straddle both worlds."

I cocked my brows. "So do you."

"King Samsyn doesn't look at me like honey spun of gold."

He let *that* one sink in, good and deep. And hell was it good, considering how Syn's gaze alone could turn me into that dripping honey. And deep, thinking of the golden connection beneath it.

The connection. *Our* connection. I wanted it back. God, I needed it. Once upon a time, I would've given my teeth to have two days of raw sexual ecstasy with him...but the intimacy was nothing without the bond. Being his lover came nowhere near the joy of being his friend, his confidante, his partner.

If I did this—met with the Pura and secured those criminals into custody—maybe he'd see that. Surely he would know, without a doubt, how serious my loyalty was to him and Arcadia.

Not if you go and get yourself captured—or killed.

New point for the *hell no* column—until Dil's point resonated again. The Pura were pinned down like butterflies on a board. They had nowhere to pivot off their reputation as murderers. Harming another queen would elevate their brand from terrorists into monsters. And *this* queen was a trained Arcadian warrior, unafraid to turn a man's balls into mashed potatoes before stabbing out both his eyes with her fingers.

On that colorful musing, I looked back up to Dillon. What if he was right? What if, despite the rogue actions of a radical few, the Pura were just concerned citizens interested in a healthy dialogue? What if this wouldn't be good for just Syn and me? What if this was good for all of Arcadia too?

Opportunity didn't favor wusses. *Time to slide on the big-girl panties, girlfriend. To do this for the country you love and the man you love even more.*

I whooshed out a breath. Dropped a determined nod before I lost my nerve. "Fine. I'll do it—but only if they let you come with me."

Dillon damn near crushed me with a hug. "I think they'll be okay with that. Thank you, munchkin. You have no idea what this means."

As we pulled back from each other, I let him have the brunt of my wince. "You know, dork, this was easier when you were just flunking Calculus."

★ ★ ★

"Your Majesty Brooke. Merderim for coming."

"It's my pleasure. Really."

For the first time tonight, I didn't rely totally on the calm queen training. I'd felt like crap since bringing it out with the very person from whom I'd learned it, but the white lie couldn't be helped. Telling Mishella I was having dinner and a *Star Wars* binge with Dillon was better than implicating her in my slip from the palais—accomplished, ironically, by hiding myself in a load of laundry.

Still dressed in the white turtleneck and pants that'd helped with the ruse, I took a full breath for the first time in the last hour. Even meant every inch of my smile at the bearded man with the kind eyes who greeted me with a respectful bow once Dil and I had arrived at the safe house.

"I hope you understand...about having to take your phones. They will be returned as soon as we conclude."

"It was unnecessary," I returned coolly. "But if it makes you all feel better, then we understand."

The man flashed a friendly smile before leading the way toward a larger room. Instantly, we were drenched in what seemed like stadium floodlights. Close. They were stage lights, equipment commonly used in television studios. I'd been in enough campaign commercials and interviews with Dad to know that much. Not surprisingly, a professional-quality TV camera was set up on a tripod in the room's corner, pointed at a grouping of cozy furniture where three more men waited.

I took their leader's lead and smiled.

They didn't. Nor did any of them rise. Or speak.

Keep. Calm. Keep. Calm.

"As you can see," my guide said, "we have already made arrangements to record everything. This way, *nobody* will recall the meeting inaccurately."

Talk about subtext that banged a girl over the head. "I see," I finally murmured.

Time for calm queen to get her groove on again. A nervous glance from Dillon encouraged it. *Thanks a lot, brother.*

"We know you *do* see, Your Majesty. And we are humbled by the gift of your time tonight. We simply wish...to talk."

I forced my feet forward...wondering why I suddenly didn't believe him. Also puzzled why the other men seemed glued to those damn couches. And why nobody introduced themselves by name. And why their gazes were all so focused and narrowed, reminding me of the guys back at the Center when we'd group up for war games...

"Please," bade beard guy. "Come in, come in."

"I'm already in, thank you."

His angular chin notched up. "We mean you no harm, Majesty."

"Then you won't mind if I stay right here." Just steps from the door from which we'd just entered. With nothing but the small kitchen at my back. Still, the hairs on the back of my neck wouldn't relax. My gut knotted tight, just as it had the night of the royal ball...in Jayd's suite at the Residence Rigale. Just before the wall had imploded and the ninjas from hell broke in...

Shit, shit, shit.

Had any of these stony, solemn bastards been part of that raiding party? Had two of them even been part of the attack on Camellia? If so, why had I expected that pair to just be neatly tied up, ready to be surrendered?

Calm the hell down.

I drew in a careful breath. This was all simply nerves getting the jump on me. Just because the room looked like an inquisition didn't mean it *was* one. I didn't see any stretching rack or waterboarding equipment. On the other hand, all they'd laid out for snacks was a wrinkled bag of cheese crisps. Who invited someone to a party and didn't even put the cheese crisps in a bowl?

People who threw parties inside mouse traps.

Shit, shit, shit.

Why did I suddenly feel like I'd sprouted long whiskers and a tail?

And why had I listened when Dil insisted palais security couldn't know about this?

Because, at least about that, he was right.

Because you still *know that Syn's teams are loyal to Syn—*

and they'd have informed him about all this without thinking twice. Right now, you'd be joining Jayd in restricted quarters, instead of trying to make things better for Arcadia.

I hoped.

Oh dear God...I hoped.

Big-girl panties.

I was, as I'd just said, already in. Now, for better or worse, I had to face the consequences of this crazy leap...whatever they were.

Dillon hung back with me, next to the table in the dining area of the little house. I looked across the table at him, struck by the surreal feeling of all this. Even with the cheese crisps, the setup in the living room made me think of surgery prep. In here, cozy and homey reigned. The table supported a bowl of whole fruit. Beneath that was a folded copy of yesterday's paper.

But next to *that* was a pair of themed salt and pepper shakers. A dolphin and a shark.

Holy shit, I hated fitting symbolism.

"Hey, you guys." Calm queen received an infusion of peppy Brooke. Just as fake but twice the fun—or so I prayed. "All that sitting room formality gives me the heebs. Tell you what? Grab *one* light and the camera and come in here. We'll just sit around the table and talk." Which would keep Dil and me closer to the door. Which made me feel a hell of a lot better...

Until I scooted back, closer toward that door—to be stopped by a figure who stepped out from the kitchen. Graceful as a gladiator—and as huge as one. Calm as a Caesar—and as dominant as one. He'd even cut his hair into a "Roman bowl" style—but that changed nothing about the disgusting excuse for a "leader" he was.

To my dread, everything else about his face was the same. His dirty yellow gaze, filling my blood with dreading maggots. His slow, knowing smirk, turning my knees to liquid. His clicking cattle call, spurring all the men in the room to motion—except Dillon, who was paralyzed by the same horror as me.

Paralyzed by horror.

Frozen in fear.

It wasn't just a trite twist of speech.

Oh God...it wasn't.

Move. Now! You are a warrior of Arcadia, Brooke Cimarron. You know what to do. You know how to move!

Only...I didn't. I couldn't. Not when I gaped at the monster who lived in so many of my nightmares. The devil from a hell I never imagined visiting again.

"You heard our guest's request, gentlemen." Rune Kavill snapped his fingers, like a king calling for wine—except his men brought only menacing strides, determined grunts, and the smell of stale beer. "She's more comfortable at the table. So make her...and her brother...*comfortable*."

His regal drawl of the word tumbled raw panic through my senses. My lungs, heaving now, saved enough for a scream—

Silenced.

Suffocated.

Buried by the smell—*don't breathe don't breathe don't breathe*—sweet, clean, chemical—that pulled me all the way down to darkness.

CHAPTER TWENTY-NINE

"Run it again."

Samsyn flung the snarl at all dozen people in the palais conference room, including Shiraz, Jayd, and half the High Council. That was twenty-four hands. Two hundred and forty fingers—every one of them capable of tapping the big green button on the digital playback.

Yet no one heeded his command.

Perhaps because your command is stupid? Because you can push any international news feed on the laptop in front of you and see every minute of that recording, complete with callous commentary? Fucking talking heads. "Analyzing" and "interpreting" and "probing" the images of his evisceration in the name of almighty ratings.

At least he could control the delivery method of the torture.

"Damn it." He pounded a fist to the table. There had been more compliance when he *hadn't* been king. "Somebody run it again!"

He was aware of movement to his right. A shadow, small and soft, just beyond the crack now fissuring the table. He vowed to split the fucking thing down the middle if someone did not punch the play button again.

"Samsyn—"

"Shut *up*, Jayd," he snarled at the shadow.

"You are driving yourself mad!"

Madness. Fuck, if it were only that easy. If he could only succumb to that blistering darkness, holding the promise of final escape. Wooing him with sanctuary from the rage butchering his composure, the anguish ripping his guts, the helplessness turning him inside out, a carcass baking in the glare of his stupidity.

His stupidity...that had driven hers.

He had been a complete ass. Had been so strangled by his fears, begun the moment he slid the ring onto her finger, tightening every moment he was lucky enough to call her wife. The happiness had been too good to be real, but he had kept going back for more, approaching the feeling like a caveman with fire. It was strange and new, but it was good, *so* good—right until the moment he was burned. Logic had fled. Compassion was impossible. He had only wanted someone to pay for his pain, and she was the target that made sense. The one person who could take his ugliness and still love him.

Loved him...and needed to show him. Felt that she needed to prove it...by stepping into the lion's den for him.

He had fucked up. Beyond measure. And now, fate was poised to exact the highest price for it.

But if he watched the footage one more time—endured the torment all over again—maybe the Creator would think twice about that debt.

"Run. It. *Again*."

Someone—finally—moved to obey him. Everyone in the room groaned softly. He lifted his head to give weary thanks to the brave soul. Wasn't stunned to meet Jagger's determined gaze—though one of those eyes was still half-swollen beneath black and purple bruises. He did not begrudge Jag his feelings—what man could logically *not* fall in love with Brooke? He only had a problem with the bastard acting on them. They were square now. More than square. Jag was the only one who'd watched this playback with him, every damn time.

And endured the agony of her face on the screen—eyes wide and terrified, skin streaked and clammy, teeth gritted, bottom lip spliced open. Her jaw looked puffy and red, as if it would start to swell soon.

Because they had hit her. Hard. Likely because she had refused to sit before their camera like a puppet. His chest swelled, so fucking proud of her. His gut wrenched, chopped apart in horror. If he learned they had touched her in ways beyond that, they would all enjoy a meal before he killed them. Their own cocks, stuffed down their throats.

On the playback, an off-camera voice spat a direction. "Please begin, *Your Majesty.*"

Brooke sucked in a quivering breath. Her eyes moved, obviously reading a cue card. "I... I am Queen Brooke Cimarron. I am here, as the guest of the Arcadian Pura movement and their new leader—"

She sobbed. And broke his heart.

Dropped her head. And shattered his soul.

The camera wobbled, yanked upward—to focus on a face that still made everyone in the room gasp. Except Jagger, who growled. From his own lips, there was no sound—but from his nostrils, the violent huffs of wrath were strong and violent.

"Oh, look. Her Majesty is verklempt with the joy of seeing me again." Rune Kavill's sneer was stretched on a canvas of smooth. No comic book cackle as conclusion. The worm only smiled as if newly slithered from a hole in the gardens of hell. "Hello, world. You had all written me off, hadn't you? Thought I'd politely disappeared into the baseboards, to stop bothering you with my menace?" He swirled a hand up, a magician with evil up his sleeve. "Surprise, surprise. I'm not in a cute little cave anymore. I have been invited as a guest myself, of the good Pura of Arcadia, to help...let us say...*guide along* their important cause. Though I've been here for a few months now, things have certainly gotten...*interesting* on the island lately."

He punctuated that by clenching a hand to Brooke's hair. With a savoring growl, forced her head back up. Though her face twisted in pain, she jerked and spat. The shot landed across Kavill's black T-shirt. "*Don't* fucking touch me, you bowl-haired freak."

Kavill shoved her away. The sharp snap of her head and the pained press of her lips confirmed another observation: the vermin had her tied up, pretty damn tightly. "Isn't she *charming*? Can you imagine what a thrill it was to learn all the Valens didn't disappear either—and that the Cimarrons had kept them snug and safe for me all these years? What an interesting time we are *all* going to have now."

Everyone in the room tensed. The hardest part of the playback was now here.

As Kavill paused, inserting a stare for "dramatic emphasis," he was butted clear from the frame. Brooke reappeared, snarling and hissing, her face desperate and wild. She peered frantically into the camera lens...the look of someone who knew they were damned, seeking meaning before the ax fell over their neck.

"No! Don't listen to him! Syn! Don't you dare give in to this fucker. I don't care *what* he demands! Syn, I swear to God, if you love me at all—"

And then she was gone. Dropped by the plunge of a needle in her neck.

He was half-grateful for it. If she had finished the sentence, he would be bound to promises he could not keep.

If you love me at all...

She *was* his all.

His raismette.

On the screen, Kavill reappeared. "Only sleeping," he said smoothly. "But next time, we may not get the dosage so correct." He shrugged. "Oopsie."

"Fucker," Jag muttered.

Kavill signed off with an assortment of bowing and postulation and bullshit, but that part was useless. The damage had been done now. The price had once again been paid. He had been drawn, quartered, and gutted and now fought through the process of trying to jam himself back together again. There was nothing else to do until Kavill and his worms contacted them again. The footage did not lend one damn clue about where they held her. Tryst and his team had already tracked her cell phone signal—to a trash can at the palais's own main gate. Kavill hadn't missed a single opportunity to ram his victory into all their faces.

All they could do now was pray.

And he did.

On his knees in the palais chapel, he could almost smell her on the air, floral and soft. He gazed at the stained-glass stars and saw the shining lights of her eyes. He watched his fingers in the streaming sun, pretending it was the silk of her hair...

Before bowing his head and whispering words from the depths of his heart.

"Creator mine, keep her safe. Keep her whole. Keep her alive. I need her. Créacu, yardim met...I need her."

He jerked to his feet when someone burst into the chapel.

"Majesty!" The page looked like she could be Brooke's little sister, with huge bright eyes and a choppy blond haircut. But unlike Brooke, she moved like a frightened fairy, approaching him with mincing steps. "There are—errrr—there are *men* here to see you, King Samsyn." She whispered "men" as if blurting a profanity. "They—they arrived on a private jet. They were searched by the airport guards and were not armed."

He blinked. Her words made no sense. "A...private jet?" Bearing *unarmed* men?

What the *hell* was Kavill up to?

"Yes, Your Majesty," the fairy returned. "They said they needed to see you at once. Demanded to, actually. The main gate guards informed them you are not available because of the crisis, but—"

"They did *what?*" His voice throttled to a bellow. Fuck. *Fuck.* Kavill was a cocky fuck, sending emissaries straight to the palais, but he did not care. It was action. *Some* kind of action he could take, instead of sitting around with his dick in his hand and his guts on the floor. "Are they still here?" he demanded, stomping toward the visitor rotunda. "If they have been sent away, Creator help you all. Do you have any idea who the hell we are dealing with—"

He skidded short on the rotunda's marble floor. Gawked at the two men planted in front of him, flanked by a pair of palais guards who grimaced like bulldogs. He had no idea what kind of soldasks to expect from Kavill's camp, but these two were definitely not it.

The first stranger looked like one of the dolls Brooke had told him about from her childhood: neatly combed hair, chiseled face, too-perfect posture. He wore tailored business pants and an equally fitted white shirt. The second man was just as perplexing. Though he wore a plain green T-shirt and camouflage pants stuffed into combat boots, he appeared more appropriate for a rainforest loincloth and a poison-tipped spear. Regardless, they both notched their jaws higher despite his menacing glower, earning them a new degree of his respect.

"King Samsyn." The suited one spoke first. "My name is—"

"I do not want to know your name," he gritted. "Just tell me what Kavill wants and then take your leave." He nodded toward the doorway, where fairy girl had been joined by Mishella, Jagger, Grahm, and Shiraz. "Once they are gone, somebody ensure the halls are disinfected."

"We're not with Kavill." The darker man cocked his head. "We're here to help you catch that fucker."

As he eyed them with fresh bewilderment, the suited one stepped forward. "Maybe we can try again. My name is Daniel Colton—"

"Of Colton Worldwide!" Shockingly, the fairy spoke with confidence. A lot of it. "I *knew* he looked familiar. You just purchased Bortel and SpecOptical, officially expanding Colton Steel beyond just steel." She flashed a sheepish look. "I...like following the global business pages."

Colton gave her a quick smile. "Impressively so." His composure hardened. "But I've flown here because you need help—and I want to give it. That purchase she just mentioned has given me access to some very special software."

Jagger eyed him, openly skeptical. "What kind of software?"

"Programs that will help us tear apart Kavill's video footage, frame by frame, and isolate all the tactile elements of it."

"Tactile...elements?"

"Everything from lighting sources to wall paint to background noise," Colton confirmed. "In order to piece them all together, to determine exactly where that bastard is holding your bride." When disbelieving silence reigned, the man fanned both hands. "The program will work, Your Majesty. Before I ran Colton Worldwide, I was CIA—and damn good at it. I was in on the ground floor of testing for this stuff." He cocked his head, showing that he wasn't the pretty boy Syn had originally assumed. A burn scar mottled a swath of his face from forehead to jawline. "And I know a thing or two about being in deeper than you originally intended."

He found himself as wary as Jag. "Why?" he charged. "Why have you come all this way...to help me?"

Colton's head jerked the other direction. Clearly, the query puzzled him—at first. After a second, his logic clearly clicked. "Because we're on the same side, Your Majesty. Because terrorists don't get to win."

"Boo-yah." Though it was just a mutter, the man next to him dotted it with a pumped fist.

Speaking of him...

"And who the hell are you?" Grahm demanded.

The man paced forward, extending a huge hand along with his photo identification. "Captain John Franzen. United States Army, First Special Forces Group." His grip was steel, his confidence a jolt of adrenaline. As he shook hands with everyone else, they clearly felt it too. "A pleasure."

"After I do what I'm best at, he's here to do what *he's* best at."

Samsyn arched both brows. "As long as I am right in front of him."

Franzen nodded but not without flashing an eager grin. "It will be an honor to serve with you, Majesty."

Colton repeated the nod. "All right. Now that we've dispensed with cocktail hour, I need a place to plug in and log on, ASAP."

Mishella moved forward. Though she was the embodiment of courtly grace, she also was the glaring reminder of Brooke's absence. But the woman was bright. She knew that too. Wisely, she had stayed mostly out of the way, choosing to act in moments when she could be of most service to the crisis—like now. "We have a conference room down the hall. Let me know what you need, gentlemen, and it is yours."

Her hospitality was echoed by the fairy—though that was where the buy-in from the group screeched to a halt. Before Colton and Franzen could take another step, Jag and Grahm stopped them, stances as stony as their stares.

"Syn," Jagger gritted, "are you serious about this?"

Grahm's version of the argument came with his normal prelude: a calm look around, a measured inhalation. "We have always handled our own emergencies."

"We have." He reined the words to calmness but didn't spare the blaze in his eyes. "And that folly has landed us here— with my wife in the hands of a madman, likely *not* to fuck up his second chance at killing her."

He finished by moving toward his friends with an old man's shuffle. Gripped them both by the shoulders, leaning into them with the same exhausted weight. Bowed his head, letting his hair fall over his face, as words of conviction tumbled off his lips that he never thought possible.

"Trust has to start somewhere. And I am choosing to start now."

★ ★ ★

The little neighborhood was so quiet, even the swishes of the waves on the southern shore could be heard, nearly two miles away. On any map, the area still qualified as Sancti, though a hopscotch game just to the north would end in the next district over. Passméil was a land of sprawling meadows and peaceful streams, widely recognized as a zone of peace. Homes were modest, people were humble, bicycles were used more than cars, and community vegetable gardens fed all.

When Colton's "miracle software" had pointed to Passméil as Kavill's hiding place, Syn made the man recheck the data. Even now, leading his handpicked team down narrow back alleys and tree-covered jogging paths, the information was difficult to believe.

He was running on trust.

It was not comfortable at all.

As a matter of fact, with every minute that passed, it felt more like hell.

He raised his hand, curled into a fist, to signal a stop. After everyone slid soundlessly behind him, he pivoted to Franzen. And glared.

"This does not feel right. *At all.*"

"I agree." Tryst, taking up the third position, concurred in a whisper. "Why the hell would Kavill do this here?"

"My *amcle* and *tanze* live four blocks over," Jag added from the fourth spot. "Every neighbor knows each other and has for years. Why would—"

"—he not go for a ditch or a cave or a swamp?" Franzen thunked back against a tree. He had clearly fielded this question before. "It's called hiding in plain sight," the

American continued. "Nazi war criminals blended right in after World War II. They became teachers and professors and inventors; one even received NASA's highest honor. Remember the place they found Bin Laden in? Nice sprawl, peaceful neighborhood?"

Tryst grunted. "Fuck."

Jag uttered the same thing a second later.

Samsyn rendered his own feedback by turning and trudging on.

Every new step carried his painful heartbeat. Every corner they turned was accompanied by another silent prayer.

They saw nothing. They heard nothing.

Despair slithered in. Threatened to suck in his whole damn spirit.

He could not give up.

Because deep in that same spirit, he knew Brooke had not.

He held up his fist again. As everyone stopped, he hunched over the GPS tracker in his palm. Another half block, and they would be out of the area pinpointed by Colton's program. It was useless to berate Franzen again. The man had flown halfway across the globe to attempt this. It was not his fault they were nowhere closer to Kavill than before.

"Fucking needle," he growled. "Fucking haystack."

Only he could not live without this needle.

He was so bogged down in that misery, he reacted a second behind the others—as they swung rifles around, reacting to the something that burst from the bushes behind them.

"Don't shoot! God, please!"

He did not miss the cue this time. Joined the other three in a massive whoosh of relief.

But beat them all swallowing a throat full of dread.

It was Dillon Valen. Out of breath. Bloodied face. Hand, clearly broken, clawed against his stomach.

With no Brooke behind him.

"Samsyn!" The man nearly sobbed it. "Jag! Thank *fuck*."

Syn made his numb legs work. "Dillon." He grabbed the man's shoulder. Felt like shit for it when Dillon's eyes popped painfully wide. The bonsuns had dislocated his shoulder too. "What happened? Where—where is she?"

"He's still—got her." The information was ragged, gasped between bursts of agony. "She's duct taped—to a chair."

"Is she hurt?" He hated asking it. Had to ask it. Had they fucked her up as badly as her brother? What had happened to her since that first video?

"Not yet," Dillon rushed out. "But soon—I think. Kavill called you—at the palais. When they wouldn't bring you—to the phone—he went ballistic. I used—the distraction—to escape. Had to pop—my fucking shoulder—to do it." He sagged against a nearby wall. "Put the pieces together. Figured—you might be—on your way."

He leaned in, grabbing Dillon's head tenderly this time. Pressed the side of his own against it. "I owe you a debt you cannot imagine, my brother."

Dillon pulled back. "I'll owe you a bigger one if you get her out of there alive."

Franzen moved in, features sliced into hard battle lines. "How far away is the house? Can you show us?"

"Of course. Come. It's not far."

Thank the Creator, it was the truth. Within five minutes, Dillon led them to a house that could have been featured on a Passtéil postcard: front porch with a swing, backyard with a birdbath. They sneaked across that idyllic scene with steps as soft as wind and faces covered in masks, turning the tables on the pricks inside the house, avenging ninjas on the hunt.

Samsyn grimaced. If only he could elevate his mind to such lofty terms...simply charge in with the courage of that noble banner. Higher causes had been the safe focus of Samsyn the warrior. The fortification of Samsyn the fighter. The underlying code of Samsyn the commander.

They were nothing to Samsyn the man.

For the first time in his life, he charged into a battle for purely selfish gain—toward something solely for him. He hurled through windows, barreled through doors, and charged through rooms with only one sacred cup in his sights, one holy treasure to gain. It drove his dagger into two enemies who dared stand in his way. Snapped the necks of two more, in hands that looked like his but were under the control of someone else. Some*thing* else. He was a dragon, ready to incinerate... prepared to destroy. He took no pleasure in the acts. Felt no remorse. He would pay the price with his soul later, if that was what the Creator wanted. His soul was a very small price to pay for...

The treasure.

His treasure.

"Astremé."

He stopped, frozen in place like an idiot, certain he'd been wishing for this for so many hours, it was simply another dream.

But then her body trembled in its duct tape prison. The tears welled in her red-rimmed eyes. A moan spilled from her cracked lips, fighting to form his name past her filthy gag.

He tore off his mask. Rushed to her side. Battled to get out words of his own. "Brooke. My love. Raismette. It is over. All over." Fell to his knees in front of her, clawing away the dirty fabric at her mouth. She whimpered, which made him stop. "Shit. I am hurting her. I am hurting *you—*"

"Shut up, you big dork." She rasped it as Franzen appeared, putting his steadier hands to work on cutting the duct tape free. "It *all* hurts, okay?" Thankfully, her left arm was freed first. She dove that hand straight into his hair, dragging him to her for a loving, passionate kiss. "Guess that means you'll have to kiss it all better."

Franzen chuckled. "I like the way this missy thinks."

Brooke turned a curious stare on the man, clearly debating whether to slap him or thank him. Obviously she was having trouble wrapping her senses around this reality too. Before Franzen even pulled all the tape free, she jerked as if waking from a nightmare. "K-Kavill," she stammered, burrowing tighter into Samsyn. "Wh-Where's Kavill? He was just here... laughing at me..."

Franzen snorted. "Your husband put a knife in his gut."

Brooke pushed up a little. "Without me to help?" She narrowed her eyes and thrust out a pout. "*Not* fair, big guy."

"Oh, now I *really* like her," Franzen drawled.

Samsyn clutched her head to his chest, letting her listen to the violent joy of his heartbeat. "He did not say I completely finished the job, did he?"

She turned, letting him see her weak but mischievous smirk. "You really saved the best part for me?"

He tucked a kiss against her temple. "I really kept the bonsun alive so that he must stand trial and face the High Counsel for his crimes." Ran the tip of a finger down the gorgeous sweep of her cheek. "If not for that, then yes, I would have dragged him to you and let you have the final twist of the knife in his miserable innards."

She mirrored his caress, cupping the edge of his jaw as an awed smile spread across her lips. "Well, damn. You really do care."

"Beyond any limit I should openly admit, little warrior." He ducked his face, caressing the tips of her fingers with the pads of his lips. "And once you are healed, I shall prove it even more." He pulled in a defined breath, underlining how serious he really was about this. "From now on, you may have your pick of future missions, Brooke—as well as my complete trust in accomplishing them."

She turned her head so their eyes met again. Though her gaze was still painted in exhaustion, a hint of its beautiful, mischievous gleam had already returned. Thank the Creator.

"That, my husband, was *really* the right answer."

He ducked his head, taking her lips with gentle but thorough love. "My incredible wife, that is just the start."

EPILOGUE

Two weeks later, life began to feel like normal.

Too damn normal.

Making the coffee in his gut turn rogue on him in an instant.

Damn it.

He had been enjoying such a perfect morning. Tahreuse Mountain coffee. Fresh croissants and fruit. An ocean breeze filled with tropical flowers and orange blossoms. Best of all: a bird's-eye view of the photo press circus taking place down on the beach, with Evrest and Camellia at center stage. Yes. Definitely the best part. The world was going insane, for the second time this month, over the Arcadian royals—only this time, it wasn't Brooke, him, and their daring escape from the terrorists. It was King Evrest and his fiancé, back from the dead.

He couldn't be happier. Giving back the crown to Ev had been like lifting a grand piano off his back. He could return to the business of keeping the kingdom's military at the alert and ready—and trained up on the newest "miracle software," a generous gift from Colton Worldwide.

But with the ease of that burden, another worsened by the day. Sometimes, it felt, by the minute.

With Ev and Camellia back in Sancti and Brooke's doctors pleased about her physical recovery, the next event on the timeline was inevitable.

He braced himself for the moment she would bring it up.

Or maybe she simply would not. Maybe he would return to the suite at the end of one day to find her things gone and a *Dear Samsyn* note on the desk.

He pitched the rest of his coffee into a potted plant. Tore the crescent in half and hurled it to the gulls.

At least someone around here was pleased about all this.

The slider opened. His gut roiled even more as his wife emerged, stretching her arms...pressing the perfect globes of her breasts against the satin of her robe. "Mmmm," she murmured dreamily. "Good mornin'."

"It is now." He snarled it against her lips before she leaned in fully, giving him a kiss that tasted of toothpaste and sunshine. Before she could straighten, he circled an arm around her waist, yanking her back down. She squealed—for a second—and then simply relaxed against him, cuddling in with kittenish trust.

"I love it when you do this," he murmured into her hair.

"Do...what?"

"Let the fighter go. Just rest in me. Trust in me."

"Well, I do. Fully. I hope you know that, Syn."

"Enough to do it for a while longer?"

Only then did her body tense. She pushed back enough to meet his gaze straight on. "What are you talking about? What's up, big guy?"

He heard her questioning lilt but barely comprehended the words. It was so effortless to just get lost in her...to see all the facets of this incredible woman, from their first electric touch on the airport tarmac, to the ball of radiance she was in his arms now...to the brilliant mystery of what she would become, as a leader, as a lover, as a warrior, as an Arcadian...

As his.

He turned the thought into resolve. Then into action.

From beneath his chair, he withdrew a wrapped package. The wrapping paper was ornate, in the Cimarron crimson and gold, with an intricately tied bow on top. Biting his lip in order to keep his hand still, he slipped it onto her lap.

"Syn? What the hell?"

He shrugged. "Call it a belated wedding gift."

"Wedding g—" She shot him a teary glare. "But I didn't get *you* anything..."

"Oh, woman." He pushed back her robe enough to expose one beautiful thigh—still marked by the straps of the fucking swing she'd agreed to let him try last night. "The answer to *that* is very evident."

She giggled. "Horny dragon."

"Something like that." He dutifully righted the satin and then nodded at the present. "Open it."

She fingered the lavish bow. "I almost don't want to." She took a turn at the lip-biting thing, not doing *any* favors for his newly awakened cock. "Did you wrap this?"

"If I say yes, can we play with the swing again today?"

She tossed a mock glower. "If you lie, I'll know it."

She was right. Their ability to read each other had sharpened to shocking accuracy over these weeks—a good thing most times, a bad thing when all he could think of was getting her back in that swing, naked and spread and wet for him...

"It was Mishella," he admitted. "She is quite the talented multitasker."

"She's been my freaking lifesaver." She began to tug at the ribbon, scowling as the bow turned to limp strands. "I keep wondering if she'd like life in Tahreuse—or what she'd take as a bribe to like it. *Hey...*" She palmed the sudden clench of his jaw. "What's wrong?"

He sharply jerked his head. "Just open the fucking box."

The minutes went by like slow-motion as she took her time peeling back the wrapping and lifting the tissue inside the box...

To pull out another box.

A music box.

Painted with pink flowers. With a ballerina inside the lid, twirling on a delicate stand to the tinkling strains of "Für Elise."

"Syn."

She looked at the little dancer. Back up at him.

Tears erupted from her soft gray eyes. Flowed down her proud cheeks. Pooled against her silky lips. "I...I had one of these..."

"Back at home," he whispered. "I know." He pulled in a shaking breath, nearly in time with hers. Lifted a hand to her face and thumbed at the wetness on her cheeks. "I wanted you to have one like it here...hoping you would call *this* home."

"This?" Beethoven's tune continued through her tense pause, taunting him with its happiness. "You mean...*this* this? As in...here? With you?"

He swallowed hard. Searched for the words he was supposed to know...the proper, princely ways of telling her what he wanted—no, *needed*—to have with her. But her tears wrecked him. Her beauty destroyed him.

Her love had transformed him.

Fuck it.

He grabbed the back of her head. Pulled her in, kissing

her hard and deep and fully, sucking her tongue in, bruising her lips, giving her his passion...showing her the furthest reaches of his heart.

"Astremé. I cannot call this a home without you anymore. I cannot call this a *life* without you anymore." He grinded his forehead against hers, breathing her in and taking up her air in return. "I love you, Brooke. I think I have loved you since the moment I first touched you. And now, I will not let you go."

She screwed the propriety too. Honked loudly as sobs shook her little frame. "I love you too. I always have, Syn. I always will."

This time, *she* pulled on *him* for a crushing kiss. And he let her.

When they dragged apart, he pushed the hair off her face. Returned her sweet smile with a determined one of his own. "Marry me, Brooke."

She gave him a watery giggle. "Excuse me?"

"The real way," he insisted. "The real way. In the chapel, here at the palais. With a *reverante* and a choir, and you wearing a dress like meringue, and me biting my fucking nails, and—"

"Yes," she blurted, tossing back her head with it. "Yes, yes, yes!" But then she lowered her head—with a minx's gleam in her eyes. "The answer *is* yes—with one condition."

He moved the music box to the breakfast table in order to clutch her closer. "Anything, Princess Brooke."

Her lips lifted, soft and seductive. As the morning sun filtered through the palms, glistening along the tracks of her happy tears, he was hard-pressed to recall ever seeing anything more beautiful in his life. Or knowing any joy more complete.

Finally, she murmured, "We get to try the swing again."

His blood raced. His cock surged. "*That* is the condition?"

"Hmmm, yes. With a...little twist."

He arched a brow. "How...little?"

She laughed before responding, "I get to be on top. Setting the pace...playing with you...commanding you." Her laugh dissipated. Her mouth grew somber. Her eyes did too, lowering to gaze straight into him. "It means your complete trust, big guy...but it also means you'll get taken to heaven."

As he returned her gaze, he already knew his reply. It was the answer fate demanded of him six years ago, when this little star had flown out of the sky and into his life—and then ordered from him again when they'd slipped rings onto each other's fingers. It was the answer his astremé had known even before him, believing in it even when he did not—believing in *them*—and then trusting, with all the force of her amazing spirit, his heart would see it someday and also know.

And then would open.

And then would answer.

As he did now.

"I am all yours, my princess of starlight. Lead the way."

Continue The Cimarron Series with Book Three

Into Her Fantasies

Available Now
Keep reading for an excerpt!

INTO HER FANTASIES
BOOK THREE IN THE CIMARRON SERIES

CHAPTER ONE

"Here's to the adventures of Lucy and the prince!"

"*To Lucy!*"

The rally cry, fifteen voices strong, made it official. My face was surely as red as my strawberry margarita. My giant, delicious strawberry margarita. So delicious, I threw down an extra tip for Gervase, my favorite Velvet Margarita bartender.

"*Viva!* To Lucy and her *príncipe!*" he shouted, skirting the bar to sweep me into a gallant tango.

I laughed but blushed harder. *Uh-oh.* Out came the cell phone video cams, belonging to the majority of my friends and family, gathered tonight in my favorite Los Angeles bar to see me off on said "adventure" with said "principe." To be more specific: Prince Shiraz Cimarron of the Island of Arcadia, one of the world's most mysterious chunks of land, overseen by the most fascinating royal family since the Tudors. Of the whole family, Shiraz was the most intriguing—or so the western media claimed. To them, he was one hell of a fascinating subject: pretty but pragmatic, serious and secretive, an outer shell of calm hiding a cutthroat businessman on the inside...

And, at the age of twenty-five, had not had a single serious romantic relationship.

The press had indulged in *a lot* of fun with that one—and still were. A glance at the video monitor over the bar, broadcasting one of Gervase's favorite celebrity gossip shows, proved as much. The audio feed wasn't necessary to follow along, since the image montage was accompanied by headlines which blended mesmerizing and mortifying into a rare art form.

His Highness of Hotness—Hiding a Hidden Harem?

Shirtless Shiraz—but where are the Bikini Babes?

Single and Cimarron: Blessing or Curse?

Prince of Playboys...or not?

Cimarron CEO: Nasty and Naughty or Virgin in Hiding?

Sheez.

I blushed on the guy's behalf. Almost felt sorry for him.

Almost.

To be honest, it was hard to feel anything but lust when treated to a nonstop parade of Shiraz Cimarron's magnificence. Was I proud of swimming in such a shallow first impression puddle? Of course not. But it was the truth, as blatant and bold as the man's beauty itself. When confronted with both, sometimes all a woman could do was...

Stare.

God, *yes.*

The third Cimarron in line to the Arcadian throne was a work of art, plain and simple. Piercing blue eyes. Greek god lips. Strong, jutted jaw. A lean but sculpted body, likely developed from running and swimming in the constant sunshine on his island. His skin was the color of Moroccan sand, his elegant face framed by hair like midnight over that exotic land. Gazing at him was like marveling at a natural wonder; his picture should've been shuffled into the screensaver image packets between Moab cliffs and Tahitian Rainbows.

Yeah, he was that stunning.

That sinful. That unreal.

Seriously.

Unreal.

I didn't just live in LA. I'd grown up here, in the land where illusion was reality and vice versa. I'd waited in coffee lines, stood at airport security, and picked up my dry cleaning beside pasty, bad-tempered people who'd been touted to the whole world as sex on sticks. Camera angles and editing tricks could turn Broom-Hilda into a Victoria's Secret goddess—

Which meant maybe that unreal Arcadian prince was really a doughy little yokel and photo filters had done the rest.

That was it. My safety valve. The sane way to approach this little "jaunt" out to Arcadia. Recasting the stud as doughy dud meant my head could stay on straight—and focus on the bigger picture here.

The *much* bigger picture.

Like landing the contract to coordinate the hugest wedding event of the year. The Cimarron royal wedding day.

The event, a double ceremony to bind Shiraz's two older brothers to the American women with whom they'd fallen in love, would be more than the biggest coup for the wedding planning company into which I'd poured myself for the last eighteen months.

It would mean that company was officially half mine.

But for now, that company had only one president's name on the door.

Ezra Lowe.

Yeah, the same Ezra throwing me the weird once-over from down the bar. Even a couple of twice-overs.

Damn it, Ezra.

What the hell was he up to? Those glances weren't flirty, but Ez had *something* on his mind...something making him laser his baby blues right into me.

I had to get to the bottom of this.

And probably, if my bladder had any say in the matter, before I got to the bottom of my next drink.

Uggghhh.

At least Father Gravity and Mother Tequila played nice, allowing me a graceful twirl to wrap up the celebration spin with Gervase. I landed in the perfect position to sweep a saucy bow to the crowd. "And now, the principe's new wench must pee."

Everybody laughed—except Mom. She rolled eyes so closely matching my own in color, their tiny gold flecks were apparent even in the bar's dim light. "Lucina Louise. Must you be so crude?"

"Antonia Marie"—yeah, the first name, middle name hookup was our snarky subtext for affection—"must you be your daughter's damn shadow?"

"Only when I'm her designated driver." She smirked and folded her arms.

My *mother*.

Smirked at *me*.

In a damn bar.

"Okay, okay. Break it up, hussies."

Damn it. Ezra needed to be renamed the happy hour ninja. Five seconds of distraction, and the man had slipped all the way over here without detection. No way not to notice him now. His strong fingers curled over Mom's shoulders, his Charlie Hunnam scruff resting atop her poofy-styled head. Sometimes I wondered if the man's looks had gotten matched to the wrong destiny. With that lumberjack jaw and cascading Thor hair, he should've been a pussy-chasing demon with a guitar or a Harley...or both—not a bisexual Jewish wedding planner with a natural talent for crazy centerpieces, perfect photo ops, and awful phallic jokes.

Not that I had a chance to hear a single phallic funny now, thanks-no-thanks to Mom. "Who you calling hussy?" she bantered, adding a girlish giggle.

"*You*." Ezra smacked a kiss to her cheek. "Hussy."

"Gahhhh." I slashed a hand through the air. "*Stop*."

"*Pssshhh*," Mom snickered.

"I love it when we make her do that," Ez chuckled.

Pinched glower. "Excuse me. You two are already making me want to puke, and I'm only down by one Gervase special."

"Lucina Maria. Did I raise you in a barn?"

I stopped. Damn near pivoted back around, the Uber app open on my phone, to flash at her. Maybe it was time her grand mission came to an end. It had been three months since she'd married Ben, giving her more than enough time to make up for her scarcity in my teens, and it had been pedal-to-the-metal on the mommy-daughter time since then. But hanging at the bar for my Farewell-to-Fantasy-Island party, even in the name of letting me get as plowed as I wanted? It was time to land the helicopter.

I marched away to the bathroom. Thank the Good Virgin, the human helicopter didn't follow.

She let Ezra do the dirty work instead.

Even more funny? I wasn't surprised by the stunt in the

least. I was, however, torqued as hell—especially as the man pushed the door shut and then locked it.

"Are you kidding?"

He braced his ass against the portal. "We need to talk."

"No." Another adamant talk-to-the-hand. "You need to leave, and I need to pee."

He gestured at the stalls with a King Arthur sweep. "Have at it."

My bladder screamed too loud for an argument. Off to the races I went.

As I took care of business, his determined steps battled each other for echo factor. Once he confirmed we were alone, he did the butt brace thing on the lip of the vanity counter, or so I guessed from the vicinity of his sigh. "So..."

"So...what?" I countered while flushing. Getting scooched all the way back into my jacket wasn't such a slam dunk. By the time I was done, my bra strap was twisted four times over and my panties were crunched to the left of my cooch, but I was beyond caring. The better part of Gervase Special *Numero Dos* was still waiting for me out on the bar.

"So you're ready to rock this thing in Arcadia, right?"

Breath of weird relief. So this was what the looks were about.

Wait a second.

This was what the looks were about?

I stomped out of the stall on the heels of that thought, letting him see my full glare because of it. "Gee. Thanks for the vote of confidence."

Ezra plowed a hand through his hair. The move lent him more of the King Arthur vibe—though it was more the stressed-post-wars guy, not the congenial-spot-in-Camelot one. "Do you really not get it by now? *Oy gevalt*, Luce. I've got more confidence in *you* than *me* right now."

"Only because you let your passport lapse."

"That has nothing to do with it, and you know it."

Wry side-eye. "That so?"

"You think I'm making this shit up?" He scowled. "You schmooze with these royals like you belong with them, darling. We both said as much after the video conference call."

"Guess all those princess movies as a kid *did* stick."

"Whatever it was, I'm grateful." He followed my path over to the sink. "You're our best chance of landing this, Luce."

"Okay, okay." I chuckled. "Chill, sparky."

"Yeah." He whooshed out a breath. "Chill. Good suggestion."

"So what's the problem?" I examined myself while washing my hands. Noticed, with tequila-induced clarity, that my brows needed plucking, my chestnut asymmetrical bob was split end city, and the acne cream fairy seriously needed to visit my pimply princess forehead. *Lovely.* Twenty-four years old, and I still had to check for acne.

Stress for another time—especially because deciphering Ez consumed a lot of brain space right now. I stared at him as he stared at his fingers, now drumming incessantly on the counter, with abnormal focus.

Finally, he mumbled, "There's no *problem...*"

"Which was why you locked me in here and then straight-up jabbed if I was 'ready' to rock—" Hard jolt. Straight to the chest. Sudden, horrid understanding. "Shit. What the hell, Ez?"

His jaw visibly clenched. "What the hell what?"

"You're...scared." I tossed the hand towel into the bin,

using the move to face off to him. "Why are you scared?"

"I'm not scared."

"Nah. Nope. No more flying there, Superman. Out with it." I wiggled my fingers inward. "The Kryptonite. Out with it. Now."

He glared—well, tried—one last time before pacing back toward the door, fingers now laced behind his head.

Like a prisoner ready to confess.

Shit. Shit. Shit.

With his back to me, he blurted at last, "We lost the Ramone wedding."

"We—"

Shock choked the rest of it into silence. Like *that* was going to make it any less real. Or horrific. Kii Ramone's pageant of a wedding was Expectation Inc.'s crown jewel, our finest contract to date. Kii was a triple-threat star at the top of every Hollywood A List, meaning every wedding planning team in the Southland had battled for the chance to orchestrate her special day. Ezra and I labored for weeks on Expectation's proposal, appealing to the woman's Polynesian roots and sense of family, doing so on a wing and a prayer. Neither of us had a stellar point of reference on the subject of family.

But we'd left Kii's place with homemade poi and a stack of signed CDs. A realization I vigorously sank my teeth into. "But...she gave us CDs. And poi. And the verbal okay to start ordering flowers. When we won the Crystal Award for the LeHavre engagement party, *she* sent *us* flowers!"

"I know."

"Then why?" It was just a rasp from me this time as I braced both hands on the counter. "What the hell?"

Kaboom.

The stall door Ez had smacked swung hard into the bathroom wall. I was still so shocked, I barely flinched. "Who?" I finally whispered. "Who got it?"

Ezra's weighted huff said everything—and nothing. "She decided to go with a team directly out of Honolulu. She said they *really* understood the *ohana* thing."

"Family." I managed the translation despite the acid in my gut.

"Bingo," Ez muttered.

We stood together, heads bent in silent defeat, for several minutes. *Family.* There were few subjects about which both Ez and I were way out of our league, and that was one of them. Not a damn thing we could've done, nor a bullet we could've dodged.

Finally, I mumbled, "At least LTK didn't land it."

No need for translation on that one. LTK, aka Love's True Kiss, were the New York-based dynamos who'd snatched a dozen gigs from Ezra and me over the last year, including the coup of the Santelle-Court wedding. The dressed-down but uber-elegant party had landed them the covers of every major event-planning magazine, officially turning them into our cross-country rivals—though Ezra preferred the term blood-sucking enemies-on-high.

After a few more minutes, I reopened my eyes. Rubbed my temples. "Well, this is a real shit fest."

Kaboom.

Another Ezra special. Damn, those stall doors were sturdy. I almost giggled at the thought—well, that and the odd comfort inundating me. Ez was punching things—which meant he still wanted to fight. Only once had I ever seen him at less than full warrior mode. It had been when he found his real dad through an adoption connection service, and the alcoholic shithead hadn't wanted anything to do with him.

That was the trouble with planning fairy tales for a living. Life itself rarely reciprocated. Ez had learned that one the hard way. I'd been there to help him through that darkness, but I didn't want to revisit anytime soon.

Just to be sure we really weren't going there, I slid out a wry smirk. Added a slow drawl. "Feel better?"

Ez pulled in a sharp breath. "No."

"Imagine that."

"Fine," he snapped. "Go ahead. Crucify me."

"What? Why?"

"Because this is going to ruin me. Ruin *us*. You gave a year and a half of your life to me, and I squandered it for fucking nothing." He dropped his face into his hands. "So go ahead. Do it. Call me the hugest douche on the planet. Diarrhea in the cat box. Mold in the shower. Spittle on the—"

"Gah!" I held up both hands. The man and subtle had never shared the same byline, but my appetite had been murdered for at least the next two days. "Baby Jesus in a car seat," I muttered, yanking out my phone as a reminder text pinged in. Time to check in for my flight tomorrow night. "As soon as I handle this, I'm dialing the Radio Emo fan line for your ass. Isn't the 'Wallowing Pit of Dark Dedications Hour' starting about now?"

He glared. "Says the girl who probably still has Radio Emo on speed dial?"

I arched a brow. Correction: arched it and then mentally peeled it off and hurled it at him. "Below the belt."

"Calling it like I see it, Betty Stepford."

Okay, *now* he was a douche. Using the nickname I still

hated, his favorite during the six months I'd tried fitting into Ryan's vanilla mold, was salt in a yuck-deep wound. And since Ryan was ancient history as of six months ago, *douche* said it perfectly.

"I'm sorry." He shook his head. "I'm not in my right mind."

I reached up, rubbing his back. "Neither of us are, sparky. But I still love you."

He pulled me into a fierce hug. "I love you too, most un-Stepford one I know."

"Damn straight—which is why I'm going to get on that plane tomorrow, fly to the Mediterranean, and save your douchebag ass."

"You mean *our* ass?"

I jerked back. Severed the air with my gasp. "*Our*—" I stammered, succumbing to the double-take. "So the partnership's still on the table?"

"Honey bunches, you get Shiraz Cimarron to put ink on this deal, and I'll have half the *world* waiting when you get back."

I jogged my chin up like Scarlett O'Hara, donning the curtains to get her freaking plantation back. "Then consider this contract a win."

The confidence overflowed. Ezra grabbed me up into a fresh hug. "There's my girl."

I beamed a brash grin. "She was never far, baby."

He stepped away. Leaned against the counter with a relaxed pose but an all-business gaze. "So...you've done all the homework on Shiraz Cimarron?"

"You mean all the gossip web pages and photo collages you sent over?"

"Girlfriend, that part wasn't studying."

"Oh?"

"That part was *fun*."

"Yeah?" I let the smirk turn skeptical. "This isn't about having *fun* with the guy, bucky. I want his name on a contract and a deposit check, period."

His arms dropped. So did all traces of his smile. "As long as we're turning fun into the pariah here..."

Groan. "What now?"

He exhaled, now adding his big brotherly mode to the mix. *Uh-oh.* "Luce...you know to go carefully with this guy, right?"

"With who?" Incredulous—but nervous—laugh. "You mean pretty prince boy?"

"Pretty prince boy." The echo came with his careful enunciation. I never liked that shit, especially when his regard was equally somber. "That's really the angle you're taking, Miss Fava?"

Miss Fava.

Shit just got real.

And the *bigger* shit in the room knew it—which explained why he stiffened like a slap was coming. I considered it but checked myself. Ez would love easing his guilt with a little effortless penance, clarifying why he dug in on treating me like a four-year-old. That was usually the direct line to my wrath, but no way was I rewarding Ezra's exploitation of it by assuaging his guilt.

"Tell you what, Ez. Since you seem to be the new Cimarron expert on the block, why don't *you* just take over from here?"

He huffed, again all serious big brother. "Did I say that?"

And yeah, my snort was all petulant little sister. *Yuck.* "Didn't have to," I retorted. "You implied—"

"Nothing." His gaze softened while his jaw hardened. "Just

some real concern, okay? As your boss *and* friend, I want to be sure you have your eyes wide open about Shiraz Cimarron."

The weirdness in his face wasn't my eventual undoing. It was the gentle vigilance in his voice, like where a real big brother would take things, that finally melted me. "Don't worry, Ez. I'm a big girl, remember? And under the crown, or whatever the hell he wears on top of all that great hair, he *is* just a man."

He yanked away with a grimace. "Damn it, Luce. That's exactly what I'm talking about."

"Exactly what...*what*?"

A new snort. "He's a *man*, not just the title. There are... nuances to him. And you know me; I'm a big fan of nuance, but in this case..." He frowned deeper. "There's a lot of shit here I can't put together." He shook his head, letting out a motorcycle rumble of a sound. "Fuck. The man is so damn private."

"All right, untwist your panties." I smoothed both hands on the air. "Obviously, there's a lot we *do* know. Work backward from there."

"Don't you think I've tried?" His eyes developed blue shards. His jaw turned to granite. Sheez, the man *could* look hetero and intimidating when he wanted. "But all we've got is a happy royal upbringing in the Palais Arcadia, a gap year turned down in favor of four years at Aalto U in Finland, followed by a direct flight home and then straight to work as CEO of the Island of Arcadia."

"Which was three years ago," I supplied.

"Which was three years ago," he confirmed.

"And...?"

"And what?"

I took a turn at the frown. "And what else?"

"You think there's *more*?" He folded his arms. Swished his head. So much for hetero. And my patience.

"Oh, come on." My hands hitched to my hips. "Three years of nothing but work and sleep? Uh-uh. Not flying, either. The man has to have hobbies, interests." Images from Gervase's gossip show blazed again through my mind. "Shit that requires him to be shirtless. With bikini babes."

"Who are apparently just friends."

I *pssshh*ed. "Because you have court spies in Arcadia?"

"Not a one," Ez returned. "Only verified reports that those 'babes' were companions only, knowing no more or less about him than his male buddies."

"Verified reports *how*?" My eyebrows were getting a great workout today. "Is someone paying off his security detail to talk? Does he *have* a security detail? If not, are people following the man around? And who are *they*? Verified journalists or free-wheeling hacks?"

And again with the teeter-totter smirk. "Want to start talking nuances now?"

"Shit," I muttered.

"Another good way of putting it."

More of the TV headlines returned to mind—with a fresh, shocking implication. "So...nobody even knows if the guy's actually punched his V card?"

"Ding, ding, ding."

"And pretty princey himself won't confirm or deny it either?"

"Remember the part about how he likes his privacy?"

I pivoted. Faced the sink. Eyeballed the blinking red motion detector for the faucet, wondering why my pulse had suddenly upticked to match its beat. What the hell? The status of Shiraz Cimarron's virginity—or, more likely, just how far from "virginal" he'd gotten by now—was of no concern to me. *None.* That included all thoughts of how and with whom the man chose to get naked.

And now I'd gone and done it.

Just thinking of the man getting naked...

Wow.

Not. Going. There.

"Well, he can keep his privacy." My reflection scowled at Ezra's. Using the secondhand delivery system made it easier to connect with the message. Or maybe the words just felt damn good to declare. "I'm flying there to connect with his brain, not his dick, and only long enough to impress the shit out of him with our proposal."

Ez also used the mirror as his messenger, rocking out a skeptical glare. "Hope you're damn serious about that, missy— especially when that boy's fine, fierce, potentially undipped wick is right in front of you."

I did it. Went ahead and rolled my eyes. "You want to give me a *little* credit?"

"A little," he conceded. "But I've seen your libido in action, Lucina Louise—action you haven't enjoyed in a while."

I let my head drop. Batted both eyes in coy exaggeration. "I'm bringing all my favorite appliances along for the trip, darling. Extra batteries too."

He returned the grin. "Well, *ex*cellent!"

We sealed the deal like usual. Hip bump and then a hug. As soon as that was done, in our considerably clearer air, I ventured, "So aside from knowing this proposal better than my own name, what else should I do to prep for Shiraz of the Nuances?"

Though that made Ez's lips twitch, he was quick with the serious comeback. "Brutal truth?"

"Is there any other kind?"

He sucked back a big breath. "Dial back Miz Kinky Sass. Turn *on* Miss Prissy Tea Time. One thing we definitely *do* know about him? He's a straight shooter when it comes to corporate prowess. I mean, the man's daily planner probably has target goals instead of action plans, and he scores bulls-eyes on every one of them."

"Sheez."

"Bet your sweet ass, sheez."

"So what are we talking here?" I turned, meeting him eye-to-eye again. "Quick run to Costume Castle for a Mary Poppins cos play, or do I break out my nanna's Dior?"

Nanna, God rest her, had possessed impeccable fashion taste. I loved her stuff so much, she'd left a few pieces to me in her will, including a flawless black Dior, circa mid-50s, with layers of crinoline and a deep V-neck. I loved finding excuses to wear it.

"No!"

And apparently, this wouldn't be one of those times.

"This guy is your CEO nightmare on crack," Ezra went on. "Wear your pinstripe skirt suit. And nude hose. And for God's sake, secretary shoes."

I scowled. Deeply. "What the hell are secretary shoes?"

"Do you have any flats?"

"I have stilettos, wedges, platforms, boots—do boots count as flats?"

"Not *your* kind of boots."

"Then no *bueno* on the flats."

"So borrow some from your mom. And wear your hair

back. *All* the way."

I grabbed a hock of my split ends. "Hello? Layers?"

"Hello? Bobby pins? And darling, *one* earring in each ear. Pearls are best. I know you have those."

Fighting him on that one was futile. He'd been there the day Mom moved into Ben's place for good, and she'd found Nanna's wedding earrings. Ez had held us both as we'd bawled after Mom gave them to me, saying she knew Nanna would want me to have them.

I watched as the memory struck him, just as it did me—underlining the truth that bloomed, warm and full, between us.

That despite executive meetings in the ladies' room, we were a damn fine team. Despite all the ups and downs, twists and turns, dysfunctions and malfunctions of life in LA-LA Land, we'd managed to forge something rare in this strange place.

A true friendship.

Proved very clearly by my next thought.

If I looked at Ez right now, even refusing to fly to Arcadia so I could roll out Expectation's dog-and-pony for some stick-up-his-ass prince, he'd not love me an inch less. We'd hug and then begin tomorrow from ground zero. We'd find other weddings to produce—and before they came through, rent ourselves as kid party clowns if need be.

We'd find a way. We always did.

Which was why *I'd* find a way to get through this bullshit with Shiraz Cimarron. I'd do it in a stupid skirt suit and boring shoes, and I'd hit the hell out of this home run for our team and our future.

How long could the whole process take, anyway? Couple of days? Perhaps a week? I could do anything for a week, even in flats. Once Ezra had his new passport, he'd make the actual follow-up trips to Arcadia for planning the wedding, likely flying me back solely for execution on the big day itself. By then I'd have exchanged the flats for boots. Or roller skates. Or both.

One week.

An eye's blink in the whole span of my life. Barely enough for a few memories, let alone massive life landscape changes.

Yeah, I had this shit.

By this time next week, Shiraz Cimarron would be just a pretty face in my rearview—viewed through the shades I'd have to wear because of my bright, blinding future.

This story continues in
Into Her Fantasies: *Book Three in The Cimarron Series!*

ALSO BY ANGEL PAYNE

Cimarron Series:
Into His Dark
Into His Command
Into Her Fantasies

The Bolt Saga:
Bolt
Ignite
Pulse
Fuse
Surge
Light

Honor Bound:
Saved
Cuffed
Seduced
Wild
Wet
Hot
Masked
Mastered
Conquered
Ruled

Secrets of Stone Series:
(with Victoria Blue)
No Prince Charming
No More Masquerade
No Perfect Princess
No Magic Moment
No Lucky Number

**For a full list of Angel's other titles,
visit her at AngelPayne.com**

ACKNOWLEDGMENTS

An "acknowledgement" feels so small to embody this writer's humble gratitude to each and every reader who wrote after Into His Dark, supporting our little island and its royals. And yes, I said our island. My friends, Arcadia is just as much yours as mine. The magic is inside you. Believe in it. Love it. Escape to it. Be it.

For the gals (and guys!) in the Facebook, Instagram, and Twitter support-verse: Your encouragement has been amazing, and thank you!

And my writing friends, who have talked me off of so many ledges!

Victoria Blue...you are there through it all, my true bonami, and I am so, so appreciative. Thank you for your love, your humor, your constant and abiding friendship. I love you.

Jenna Jacob...your light is incredible. Thank you for the tough love when I needed it the most, and for just being YOU. I cherish you!

Audrey Carlan...a wonderful friend and soul sister. The universe knew what it was doing when it created you, and I'm so glad we've met. Thank you for absolutely everything. I really appreciate you!

Sierra Cartwright, Mari Carr, Red Phoenix: It's so awesome to share the journey with you.

Elisa: This book is magical because of you. Syn, Brooke, and I cannot be more thankful for your AMAZING help in making their story sing. Your guidance for the story and support of the characters has been precious, priceless, and magnificent. It is an honor to work with you.

Tracy: Thank you for your wisdom and incredible eye for making the words flow. I appreciate you so much!

ABOUT ANGEL PAYNE

USA Today bestselling romance author Angel Payne loves to focus on high-heat romance starring memorable alpha men and the women who love them. She has numerous book series to her credit, including the action-packed Bolt Saga and Honor Bound series, Secrets of Stone series (with Victoria Blue), the intertwined Cimarron and Temptation Court series, the Suited for Sin series, and the Lords of Sin historicals, as well as several standalone titles.

Angel is a native Southern Californian, leading to her love of being in the outdoors, where she often reads and writes. She still lives in Southern California with her soul-mate husband and beautiful daughter, to whom she is a proud cosplay/culture con mom. Her passions also include whisky tasting, shoe shopping, and travel.

Visit her at AngelPayne.com